PRAISE
THE STORMBRINGER SAGA

"Gabriella Buba writes the way the ocean moves: rhythmic and rolling, with dark currents and a powerful grace... elegantly weaves the rich tapestry of Filipino folklore into a poignant, harrowing tale of magic and rebellion and sacrifice. Every page is drenched in the pain and hope that characterized our centuries-long struggle. This is fantasy at its finest, but it's also a story about us, and about how my love for you is one with our love for the motherland."

Thea Guanzon, *New York Times*, *USA Today* and *Sunday Times* bestselling author of *The Hurricane Wars*

"A vicious examination of the struggles a colonized culture must endure to survive, bundled in a devastating storm of rage, grief, and lost love. Love, betrayal, incredible worldbuilding, and righteous female rage... hell yeah!"

Rebecca Thorne, *USA Today*, *Sunday Times* and Indie bestselling author of *Can't Spell Treason Without Tea*

"A story of secret identity and concealed powers through a magical mixed kid's double life—the narrative architecture of Filipino folklore crashing against the rise of colonial power—I'm obsessed and so glad there's more of Buba's story to come."

Maya Gittelman, *Reactor*, "Reviewer's Choice: The Best Books of 2024"

"Action, magic, romance... An unforgettable story filled with inspiration from myths across the Philippine islands. Crafted with exquisite detail that will resonate with fantasy fans—from those seeking new adventures to those like me, aching for the familiar."

K. S. Villoso, author of *The Wolf of Oren-Yaro*

DAUGHTERS OF FLOOD AND FURY

GABRIELLA BUBA

TITAN BOOKS

Daughters of Flood and Fury
Print edition ISBN: 9781803367828
E-book edition ISBN: 9781803367835

Published by Titan Books
A division of Titan Publishing Group Ltd
144 Southwark Street, London SE1 0UP
www.titanbooks.com

First edition: July 2025
10 9 8 7 6 5 4 3 2 1

A CIP catalogue record for this title is available from the British Library.

EU RP (for authorities only)
eucomply OÜ, Pärnu mnt. 139b-14, 11317 Tallinn, Estonia
hello@eucompliancepartner.com, +3375690241

Printed and bound by CPI Group (UK) Ltd, Croydon, CR0 4YY.

To all the ones who survived but healed wrong.
They broke our halos so we grew teeth.

Also by Gabriella Buba
and available from Titan Books

SAINTS OF STORM AND SORROW

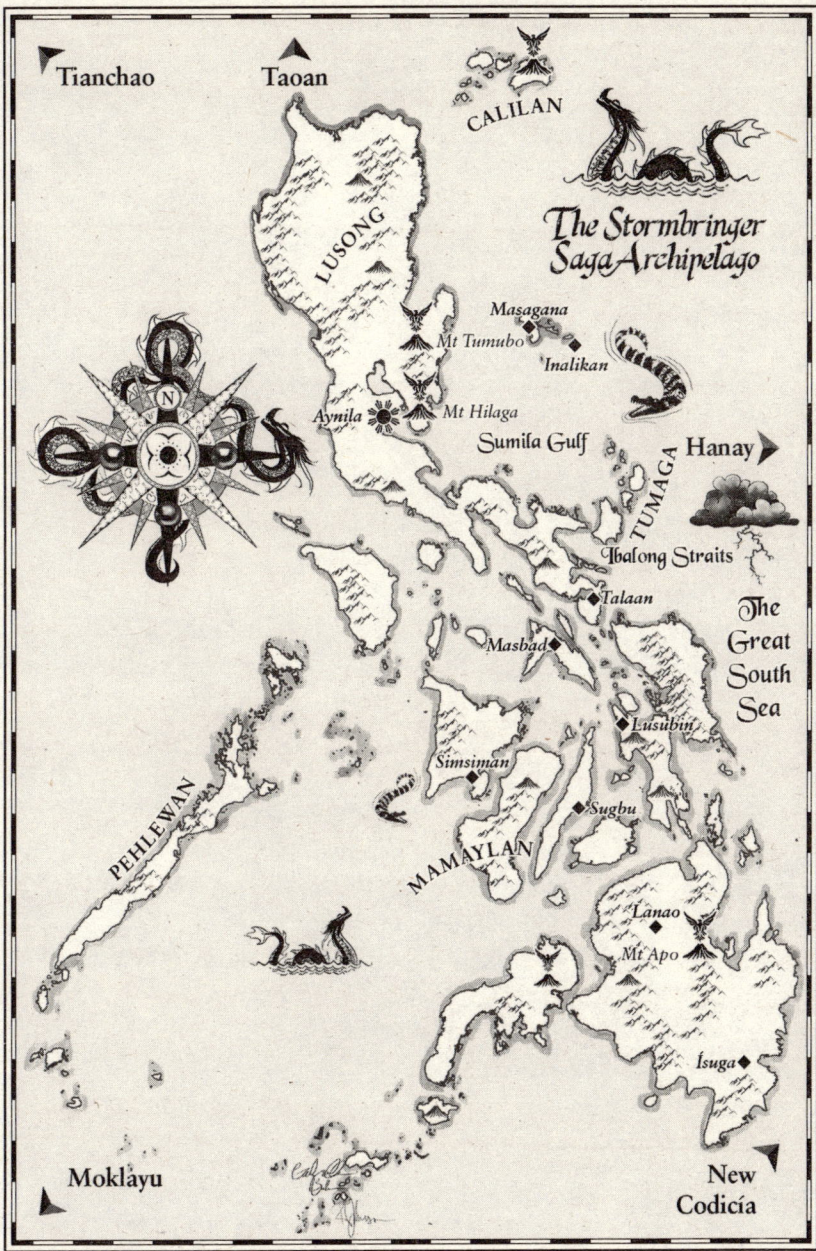

Tianchao

Taoan

CALILAN

The Stormbringer
Saga Archipelago

LUSONG

Masagana

Mt Tumubo

Inalikan

Aynila

Mt Hilaga

Sumila Gulf

Hanay

TUMAGA

Ibalong Straits

The
Great
South
Sea

Talaan

Masbad

PEHLEWAN

Simsiman

Lusubin

Sugbu

MAMAYLAN

Lanao

Mt Apo

Isuga

Moklayu

New
Codicia

PROLOGUE

LUNURIN CALILAN NG DAKILA

---◆---

FOUR AND A HALF YEARS AFTER THE FALL OF THE PALISADE IN AYNILA

The flash pan's spark glittered deadly bright as the pistol rose toward her. Lunurin's throat burned, her goddess's words ringing in her ears.

"Even you, in your battened fortress, are not greater than the typhoon. Leave in peace or be shattered. My storm will wipe the scourge of your greed from land and sea."

Alon threw himself between her and the raised weapon, her husband once more using his body as a shield.

Not again. She'd not risk losing him to Codicían treachery again.

Anitun Tabu's promise burned within her, singing lightning quickness into her blood. Lunurin moved just before the eardrum-shattering bang. She counted the space between powder flash and thunder, like lightning under an oncoming storm, as she hurled herself and Alon down. Heat and pain streaked across the back of her neck as the bullet and sound caught up, reverberating in Lunurin's lungs.

The Stormfleet delegate that Calilan had sent collapsed beside them, heart's blood staining her malong's red and yellow folds to black. Lunurin saw the moment Alon gave up trying to hold back the tide. Blood gushed across the floor, warm on Lunurin's skin. A stopped heart could be restarted, but not one that had been shot through. Not now, in the middle of a fight, and so far from the sea.

Lunurin released her grip on the lightning in her own blood. It exploded outward, Anitun Tabu's fury writ large, burning the air and stopping hearts. The Codician governor crumpled, as dead as the woman he'd shot.

The echo of divinity was still in Lunurin's voice, raising the hairs on the back of her neck with static charge. *"No peace, then."*

It had all been going so well. Diplomats from across the archipelago had gathered in a show of unity to negotiate the release of Talaan's tide-touched captives in exchange for a few of the "missionary" spies the Codicians kept smuggling into Aynila. Lunurin had been sure they were making progress with Talaan's Codician governor—until through the window, they had all seen a contingent of the Aynilan navy sailing into the bay alongside Stormfleet ships and opening fire on Talaan's shipyard.

The culmination of years of Aynila's alliance building, their efforts to prove the archipelago could negotiate peacefully with the remaining Codician territories on equal terms, shattered as cannon fire exploded around them.

Blood ran down her neck, splattering across Alon's full lips, still parted in shock or the last-ditch effort at diplomacy she'd interrupted when the governor drew his gun.

"Jeian," Alon muttered his brother's name, half-curse and half-explanation of how months of negotiations had ended in a puddle of heart's blood. His arms came around Lunurin, his power flowing over the wound, cool with salt healing. He met her burning gaze, steady as ballast. His strength was a storm surge. Divine fury roared through her, turning the clear skies overhead dark, thunderheads spiraling together like schooling mobula rays.

Despite their best efforts, today would not end in peace. But it would not end in defeat. She would not allow it. They would not falter.

Alon's determination met hers, and they both surged to their feet. "Together," Lunurin promised.

"I'll cover you."

Bamboo flasks and gourds hidden among their delegation burst open as Alon dragged every drop of saltwater in the room toward him. They moved as one, pressed back-to-back, Alon facing the soldiers leaping to the governor's defense, Lunurin the open capiz shell windows and the fire fight upon the bay.

"What are they thinking, attacking like this, in the middle of the negotiations?" one of the delegates cried.

"Get down!" Lunurin urged.

But Alon's rising wave brought all bullets to a standstill. They should never have agreed to meet so far from the sea.

Lunurin uncoiled her hair and dragged down the storm. Rain slashed through the air, shattering the surface of the sea into a white haze, hiding their ships. Let them try to pick out targets without sightlines.

She returned her attention to escaping the death trap she and Alon had led their allies into.

Lightning danced like cloth-of-gold over her hands. She coiled and struck as Codicían soldiers swarmed into the room like termites. Men in polished metal armor fell smoking, burnt flesh acrid in her nose. Rainwater sloshed across the floor, and Alon upended a pouch of salt at his hip, extending his power over the water. He sent a rolling wave across the floor and down the stairs, sweeping soldiers away before the flood.

"Out! Before they rally and we're trapped away from the sea," Alon ordered.

Alon's bodyguard Litao herded their party before him as Alon and Lunurin cleared the way.

They fought down toward the docks, tearing the last Codicían shipyard in Lusong asunder around them, exposing its soft innards to the might of Lunurin's storm.

At last, they made it to the jetty where their ship—still flying a white flag—lay half-sunk under enemy fire. Alon no longer had to struggle to salt rainwater with the whole bay at his back. He sang up massive waves that battered the docked Codicían ships to pieces, crumbling sea walls and fortifications like sand.

Lunurin curled her fingers through her streaming hair. Twisters touched down within the shipyard, shredding guard towers and flaring lightning-struck fires. She destroyed the final set of wall-mounted cannons, black powder igniting with a savage roar. Survivors fled toward the settlement beyond the fort walls before her ravaging cyclones and Alon's waves. At last, the only reverberations overhead were true thunder.

The salt-soaked decks of Aynila's and their allies' ships burned eerily, sheets of green and blue fire mirroring the bruised underside of Lunurin's storm. Caustic fumes and heat warped the air around the burning Stormfleet as the gods-blessed aboard struggled to quench the flames. Red-hot lead shot still glowed within the timbers, and Talaan's lightning-struck fortifications sent their own choking black smoke into the sky. The drought here had been long, and the fortifications caught like kindling.

Lunurin wished she could turn from the terrible sight. So much unnecessary death, and for what? What had Aynila's navy and their Stormfleet allies been thinking, putting their negotiating party and the hostages in danger? They'd gotten their own delegate killed. No doubt all Calilan would soon blame Lunurin for failing to save her—failing to save all the Stormfleet ships now perfuming the air with their smoke.

They'd been lucky to escape. No, not lucky—gods-blessed. Unlike the delegate from Calilan.

But there might still be lives to save in all this ruin.

"The hostages." Lunurin voiced her fear in a rasp, the air thick with stinging smoke.

Alon's knuckles and the cool bands of his brace brushed her nape. He lifted her drenched black curls out of his way to inspect the graze he'd hastily healed, then pressed his lips to her temple, his relief palpable. "There's still a chance. The Codicíans might not have had time to retaliate."

Lunurin's eyes burned. Their ally's blood still stained her skirts, unmoved by the drenching rain. "We were making progress. The Codicíans were going to release the tide-touched. Why—?" Her head throbbed. She still couldn't grasp how it had all gone so wrong so quickly.

"Jeian..." Alon said again in weary resignation. He pointed with his lips at a sailed guilalo headed toward the jetty.

"I will burn him to the waterline myself!" Lunurin spat.

"I won't stop you," Alon promised.

It was so unlike him that despite herself, Lunurin laughed, then coughed as the caustic air hit her throat. No matter what, through it all, she had Alon beside her. Together, they could face anything.

She caught his bad hand on the back of her neck, tracing

her fingers up his arm, brushing salt and ash from his deep brown skin. She ran her fingertips down the side of his face, pushing back the strands clinging rain-wet to his brow and cheeks, escaping the gold and pearl cuff at the nape of his neck. Black stubble stood out on his upper lip and there were dark circles under his eyes. Tense hours over the negotiating table had made his cheekbones sharper, his features hollowed. She cradled his jaw, seeking his warmth and the reassuring thrum of his pulse. They both needed a long bath and sleep— not a battle they'd faced unarmed, with no warning. What if she'd been a breath slower?

"You frightened me. What would I do if you were shot?"

Alon turned his face into her touch and kissed her palm. "You forget you bleed as well as any mortal, even with your goddess burning in your eyes."

His hot breath and faint stubble tickled her fingers. She wanted to drag him closer—

"Is this a honeymoon for you two?" There on the deck, his ship miraculously unharmed, stood Jeian Dakila, leader of Aynila's navy and Alon's eldest brother, interrupting as usual.

Jeian shared Alon's height and bearing, but he'd picked up the southern archipelago's affinity for ink. Geometric blue patterns stood out on his bare chest, ringing his arms and legs like the spotted banding of a maral leopard cat. He leaped easily to the jetty, his tide-touched wife Aizza guiding their ship smoothly into a berth.

"We never signaled any need for support." Lunurin swept a hand behind her toward the ruined fort.

"I assumed the lightning was a signal." Jeian was far too pleased with himself, and not nearly bloodied enough. Some of Aynila's ships were sinking too, but the fort had fallen, and that was all he cared about.

"Liar! I didn't call the storm until you attacked," Lunurin cried, furious that he was trying to shift the blame for this to her.

"What if the San Vincente had still been here? Or Lunurin had not been? We would have died, all of us and our allies, and for what? A garrison of a hundred soldiers?" Alon demanded.

"But she was. And now we've secured the nearest rally point for any future attack on Aynila, and ensured Lusong's gold will not finance her reconquest. With this shipyard, and the recent rebellion in Masbad, the richest regions of the archipelago have thrown off the yolk of Codician control. This is a triumph."

"They tried to kill us all," Lunurin reiterated.

"Don't fret. Aizza will have you all good as new before we're in sight of Aynila. And Alon's spies let me know the San Vincente had already left for Sugbu," Jeian assured her.

So that was why he'd attacked. Lunurin wanted to leap for his throat, snapping like a feral dog. People were dead. Alliances that had taken years to build, shattered. And this would be a personal blow to her relationship with Calilan and her family there. Their bond had remained difficult and distant, despite years, countless letters, intermediaries, and entreaties. Lunurin was beginning to believe she would never see her family in person unless she returned to Calilan herself. She'd been trying and failing to make time for the journey in between the crises raining down on their heads. Now, with more of Calilan's dead to blame on her... they might never forgive her.

She shook her head, leaving him to Alon. No one else had any chance of talking sense to Jeian. Instead, she urged several of the other members of the negotiating party who'd been injured in their desperate fight aboard Jeian's ship into Aizza's care.

"What about the priests?" Alon asked wearily. "We should leave them at the mission."

Jeian's smug expression didn't waver. "I'm afraid I no longer have them in my keeping."

Finally, Alon lost his temper. "How am I supposed to negotiate to get the tide-touched back if you keep killing off any leverage I acquire?"

Jeian spread a hand to indicate the ruined shipyard. "I hardly think we need them now. I don't know why you keep showing them mercy when it's clear all they're going to do with it is rile another assassination attempt against your wife, or our mother."

Another ship rowed up alongside the jetty. Jeian tipped his head and introduced Captain Tomás, one of the sons of Talaan's Datu, their chief.

"My father?" Soot streaked Tomás's face.

"He went to the mission to speak to the priests. Let us retrieve him together," Lunurin offered.

Tomás flinched from her. "You can't mean—the friars are holy men!"

"They won't be harmed. We've come for the tide-touched. That's all." Lunurin reassessed her bloodied appearance, trying to appear less like a madwoman bent on killing anyone and anything that stood in her way. Not everyone dealt with her as well as Alon when she had divine rage burning in her eyes.

"The witches will be locked in the munitions building. It's the only place far enough from the water. The holy fathers would not contaminate the sanctity of the church." Tomás crossed himself instinctually. It reminded Lunurin of

Catalina. It was her turn to flinch, if only from memory.

"Quickly," she ordered.

Litao gestured, sending three of his men back up toward the munitions building before flames engulfed the garrison entirely.

Tomás's voice trembled. "You'll need to take them all and go."

"And leave you without healers after this?" Alon frowned. "We'll deal with the mission, if you're worried about them."

"The friars may have riled the situation, but the drought here has been long. When the crops withered, they said it was due to our faithlessness…" His voice died in his throat as Lunurin's gaze landed on him.

"When the groundwater went to salt and poisoned the farm animals, they said it was witchcraft. A mob rounded up the suspects for them. My father couldn't stop them." He looked away, ashamed.

Along with the local healers, Talaan's garrison had snatched up Stormfleet crewmembers who'd slipped quietly into the area to determine the number of ships the Codicíans could outfit here for a direct attack on Aynila. A day or two more in either direction and this would've remained a local issue. Without the Stormfleet ships desperate to retrieve their own alongside Aynila's navy, she doubted Jeian would've been so quick to launch a surprise attack.

But Jeian was right about one thing. An attack on Aynila was coming. The Codicíans' tactics had changed this year. There'd been no more outright demands for surrender and threats of the coming Reconquista, or posturing patrols from galleons that knew better than to attack Aynila alone. Somewhere, they'd learned a dangerous subtlety. Now they sent missionaries, both Codicíans and converts, trickling into

Aynila like an insidious leak in their hull. Spies stirred unrest among Aynila's converts, and orchestrated assassination attempts on both Lunurin and the Lakan. Thanks to Alon's efforts, only once had such plans made it into—quickly thwarted—action. Still, an attack on Aynila was imminent. It was only a matter of time.

So many dead. She wasn't ready for a return to war. Lunurin had no more fury left in her. She smiled, her face stiff and aching. "I see. Aynila will welcome them, even if Talaan does not." She stepped aboard Jeian's ship, turning her face upward toward the drenching rain. It felt blissful on her blistering skin. "I will leave you the rains."

I

INEZ NG DAKILA

FIVE YEARS AFTER THE FALL OF
THE PALISADE IN AYNILA

Seawater dripped down her spine from earlier dives, making the scars on her back itch. She scanned the expectant crowd gathered on the shore and along the floating diving platform that had been built out over the oyster beds for the wet season festival.

Lunurin had finally agreed that Inez could dive last year, at seventeen. Inez had been desperate to prove it hadn't been a mistake ever since she'd come out of the water and Lunurin had refused to take the oyster she'd chosen or fashion her mutya.

The snub had stung, even when Sina filled the space of Lunurin's rejection, pulling the round pearl from the shell and announcing Inez as tide-touched. She'd crafted her mutya, a magnificent necklace of mother-of-pearl scales—and in a personal touch of craftsmanship only a firetender would think of, Sina had concealed a small balisong-style folded knife within the two scales cradling the round pearl pendant at the center.

A full year later, Inez couldn't shake the feeling that Lunurin regretted her dive. What else explained the way she'd stepped back? The way she held Inez at arm's length, even now?

If Inez could only make her see she'd been ready for the responsibility... Today she'd prove it. She knew the oyster beds better than anyone besides Lunurin. She'd prove it hadn't been a mistake to trust her, that the old gods hadn't been mistaken in her naming.

She'd already made one save after a child fell from the volcanic stone wave-breaker that was all that remained of the Codicían shipyard, preventing an accidental naming. Anitun Tabu's statue had been moored upon the stones, just below the tide line, where offerings of pounded green rice, pinipig, and sampaguita garlands had been heaped by hopeful divers.

Inez waved to the three others from the healing school now stationed along the shore with the crowd. Her friend, Bernila, caught her eye and waved back.

It was the biggest change the Lakan had made when the wet season festival was revived. No one would be named until they were old enough to understand the risk and responsibility that came with being gods-blessed, and were ready to enter training in the healing school or with the metalworking conclave.

Sina was certain that this year, all the gods-blessed would be chosen firetenders. The Amihan Moon was just a week away, all the archipelago's wild magic burning fever bright. Aynila had been preparing for months.

According to Lunurin, an Amihan Moon graced each active volcano in the archipelago just once in a generation. When the full moon, ripe with power, rested on the peak of the caldera, it became such a tempting prize that the laho would be unable to resist. She claimed to have seen the laho swallow the moon herself on Calilan as a child, and she'd taken part in the all-important rituals ensuring the hungry sea dragon spat it back out. The whole city was in a frenzy of preparations, and dignitaries from across the archipelago were expected to observe the event.

But first, the wet season namings. A shiver ran over her as Lunurin let down her hair and, together with the other katalonan, sang in the ambon. The healing school gleamed in the dappled sunlight under Lunurin's clouds, blue-tiled roofs and multiple tiers of golden stilted-bamboo buildings making a far kinder backdrop than the Palisade ever had.

Sometimes, Inez still felt the shadow of it looming. When she stood in certain parts of the central delta and the sunlight angled just so, the raised scars on her back felt less like skin and more like so many shards of shattered glass painstakingly pieced back together, fragile, barely holding back the blood. Days like that made her feel she was about to fly apart at the seams, a deep-sea creature brought into the air.

She shoved the thought away. The Palisade was gone. Even if the Codicians' threats to return were growing more and more real, Inez wasn't a helpless girl trapped within their walls. Not anymore.

As one, the katalonan cried the diver's name to the wind. "Rosa Capili!"

The past came roaring back. Rosa? From the church kitchens? It was hard to recognize her with her long dark hair unbound and uncovered. She was still small in stature, but had shed the cling of childhood's rounded features for a stubborn chin.

A fine rain fell across the water in a misty veil, glittering in the sun that peeked through the clouds. Inez tried to catch

Lunurin's eye, but failed. Why hadn't she mentioned that Rosa would dive today? Lunurin's attention was skyward, and she'd taken on that particular electric intensity she always had when Anitun Tabu was with her.

Rosa looked tense and determined, almost worried. Inez felt the shadow. The lines across her back prickled and ached, the old edges sharp, threatening to—

She did not like to dwell on her life before.

The hollow thump of running feet snapped her attention back to the water as Rosa disappeared with a splash. The pockets of shadow under the ambon played tricks across the waves, making it difficult to track her progress. Inez dropped a few rungs lower on the floating diving platform till she was up to her knees, reaching out with her other senses through the salt.

A riot of sensations rushed over her, a rogue wave breaking over her head. Inez gasped. It was overwhelming, threatening to unbalance her. A low rumble went through her bones, and she focused in on the sensation, a shield from the riot of tide and current and wave, too much sensation on her sensitive skin.

The Saliwain's passage into the sea was a dizzying rush. Aizza and Alon had diverted it carefully around the oyster beds to keep the area calm for less experienced swimmers. Inez hoped to be so trusted one day, but Alon insisted that learning big tidal workings and the directing of currents could wait until after she'd gotten a handle on healing. Given how overwhelming just the bay felt to her, she hadn't pushed for more. It was hard enough to control a single bangka over shallow water. How did Jeian's wife, Aizza, handle a whole ship at sea?

The rumble came from several large saltwater crocodiles.

They were circling the area, eyeing a pair of dugong with young calves grazing the seagrass nearby. But where was Rosa?

The deep-water thrum of crocodile hunting calls felt closer. The buwaya were anito themselves, little gods of the sea. They were growing fat on the offerings of the local fishermen and veneration as more and more Aynilans returned to the old ways of thanking sea and sky, and all the lesser spirits of the land and water too. But they shouldn't be so loud. Alon insisted she shouldn't hear them at all.

Inez tried to focus again on Rosa, on picking her quiet presence from the dozens of currents, the tide, and the noisy anito. But the bay was so alive. An overwhelming riot of feedback and sensation that pulled her in a dozen directions, making her head and her skin ache. It was too much. Alon said it should feel calming, that she only had to give into the salt and let herself be cradled, but to Inez the shallow stretches of Aynila Bay were anything but gentle.

She dropped farther into the water, up to her waist, hooking her feet in the rungs for stability. She spread her fingertips in the water, sending her awareness out across the oyster beds. *Where?*

She struggled to focus through all the noise, the way the waves crested over the surface, the way the currents shaped themselves over sharp edges and crannies, the myriad creatures that moved and swam and filtered and—

She felt the moment it went wrong, when blood colored the water and the crocodiles' attention turned, directing Inez's scattered awareness with a single-minded precision.

Salamat po, buwaya, she thanked them, and dove. Alon would say it was unwise to acknowledge them, but Lunurin would say being impolite to them was even less advisable. The sea twisted together around her body without being asked, without her direction, an almost comforting embrace that dragged her down to where Rosa had gotten her foot lodged in the razor-edged oyster reef. Inez had to resist the urge to fight against being pulled so deep so fast, her ears popping. But she couldn't panic; Rosa was doing more than enough of that for both of them. Her frantic yanking only turned the water red faster as precious breath streamed between her lips. Inez reached her just as she stopped struggling.

Balisong knife in hand, Inez broke loose the dense aggregate of shell clasped like a set of jaws around Rosa's calf and pulled her free, towing her to the surface.

The way up was harder. It was ridiculous that a tide-touched should feel uncomfortable in the water, but Inez couldn't bring herself to relax with the bay's overwhelming presence all around her, flush to her skin. It was far too much.

She found the predator-sharp attention of the crocodiles on the blood streaming into the water, a clear, unmuddied focus point. There was something about that reptilian single-mindedness that cut through the churn of the bay. She swam faster for the dive platform, reaching out for Lunurin's hand, already extended to haul them from the water.

Her back hit the bamboo planks, yanking the bay's turmoil from her with the familiar tender ache of her own flesh. Inez gladly would've stayed down, but Rosa was so still beside her.

"Inez, the water in her lungs," Alon instructed.

He couldn't be serious. A lesson, now? Inez's hands began to shake.

"Inez!" Alon had his hands full with the laceration on Rosa's leg.

No time to panic. Inez tried to push down her nerves and pressed her hands to Rosa's chest, fingertips tracing circular motions as she'd been taught. She reached for the sea where it should not be, water in lungs. Nothing. She closed her eyes, reached harder toward the bay. But her tender skin shied away from another overwhelming deluge of sensation. Instead, her mouth filled with the richness of blood in the water as the crocodiles circled closer, ever so interested. And for a moment, the spiky thoughts and painful edges of her old wounds morphed. She was not shattered glass, but the armored scales and direct bloody-minded surety of a crocodile.

Dropping with a wrenching gasp back into her own skin, she let her hands fall. "I can't, I tried!"

"Focus, Inez. You can do this." Alon's voice was steady. As if this were any other training session in the healing school. "It's not healing. Just seawater where it shouldn't be."

Inez looked to Lunurin, desperate for her to intervene. She knew how much Inez struggled with healing.

But Lunurin only pointed her attention back toward Alon with her lips. "Focus."

Inez wanted to scream. Easy for Lunurin to say. No one expected a stormcaller to heal. But everyone expected it of a tide-touched. Even the newest who came to the school could heal faster and more easily than Inez. They were quickly promoted to infirmary assistants and given more important responsibilities. Inez only failed, again and again and again, unable to feel the saltwater of blood and overwhelmed by the sea.

"Just focus on the salt," Alon coached.

But the salt was the whole bay. A roar of sounds, sensations, and lives, the tiny spec of it in Rosa's lungs impossible to differentiate.

She wanted to do this. But she could find crocodiles more

easily than a struggling swimmer. She could feel the way their scales fit together so much better than skin. Hungry. Like she was hungry, for attention, for blood, for—

She backed away from Rosa's still form, tearing her mind from the bay, away from the golden eyes in the water. *Shut up!* she wanted to scream. At Alon, at the sea, at those taunting crocodilian eyes watching her, worse even than the stares of the crowd. "Please! You know I can't."

The moment stretched slow as pine-pitch under the hot sun, before Lunurin stepped in, applying pressure on Rosa's leg and freeing Alon up to clear her lungs.

Inez had failed. She'd been so sure she was ready. No one was a better diver or a stronger swimmer. But Lunurin was right. Inez couldn't be trusted, not when it mattered.

She scrambled back, guilt pressing at the cracks in her skin, feeling fragile and furious. With herself, for failing such a basic task; with Alon, for insisting she heal under pressure; and with Lunurin, for having these impossible expectations Inez never seemed to meet. Why wasn't it enough she'd saved Rosa from drowning? Why couldn't Inez be enough?

Inez backed farther out of the way as the proper healers moved in. Aizza took over healing Rosa's leg, Lunurin helping her secure the bandage. In one smooth movement, Alon pulled and turned Rosa as she coughed up sea foam and gushes of water. So much water. Inez hadn't been able to grasp a drop.

Rosa opened her eyes, then her fisted hands. A gnarled, palm-sized shell the color of sand gleamed wetly between her fingers, more precious than gold. The dive hadn't failed after all.

Alon helped her sit up. "Can you talk? Breathe deep for me."

"Yes, Gat Alon." Her voice was hoarse from near drowning, but strong.

"Good. Then choose the katalonan you wish to name you." He indicated to her to choose between Aizza and Sina, since she'd arrived with no matriarch of her family to sponsor her dive.

Aizza was the most popular pick among divers who came alone. It was especially fortuitous to be named by a bayok katalonan, raised a boy until she'd been named tide-touched and received the Sea Lady's calling.

After a long moment inspecting the circle of women surrounding her, Rosa held the oyster out to Lunurin.

Inez winced, waiting for the inevitable rejection, hurt on Rosa's behalf. But Lunurin reached forward, her hands open in acceptance. Rosa beamed, placing the oyster in her hands.

Inez watched, stricken. Something ugly inside her convulsed. She dropped her head, the sharp ends of her mutya digging into her collarbone. She felt horribly exposed, all her desperation laid bare. She wanted to dive deep, deep, deep and never come up. She wanted the sea to swallow her whole. How could Lunurin do this? How could she accept Rosa, where she'd rejected Inez?

2

LUNURIN CALILAN NG DAKILA

Blood stained the golden bamboo of the dive platform red as gumamela blossoms, just as it had the deck of Jeian's guilalo years before. Lunurin's vision wavered briefly between past and present, between the boy Alon had been and the young woman before her now. Both half-drowned and bleeding, both so full of hope she still did not think herself capable of answering.

Anitun Tabu's gaze was a physical weight, dense as the air before a storm broke. The agony of indecision gripped her.

"By what right can you sing down the ambon if you would reject a diver's choice, my Katalonan?" asked the goddess of storms in the wind. But Lunurin, drowning in memory, still hesitated.

Alon's hand closed on her shoulder, steady, always steady. "It should be you," he murmured.

"I'm not—" She bit down, catching her frustrations and doubts between her teeth. She was not fit, not ready. No more ready than Inez was for emergency healings.

Alon's breath was warm in her ear, his confidence in her as reliable as the tides. "You are Lady Stormbringer. Who better to cry her name to the gods' ears?"

How could he be wrong?

In all the years since she had taken her place at Alon's side, since she had decided to stand for Aynila, why did she waver now, when all her goddess and Alon asked of her was a blessing?

She was a tempest. But had she not also named Alon? Her rains ended droughts as well as washed fortresses into the sea. If she could not balance between, could she truly call herself a stormcaller?

She held out her hands in acceptance, trying not to notice how Rosa's blood already painted her palms. It was not an omen. She would not let it be.

Lunurin accepted Rosa's oyster, and Sina slid a ceremonial knife into her palm. The silver and bronze hilt fit perfectly in her hand. She gave a firm twist, and the craggy shell split to reveal gleaming mother-of-pearl, like the golden full moon cradled in her hands. The weight of her goddess's expectation beat down like the noonday sun.

Let it be empty, Lunurin prayed fervently. *Goddess mine, let this one go. This is not the year to claim another daughter. Not now, not here, not Rosa. Let her go with the tides, let her tend to fire. Let it be empty. Give her peace. A life free of the decisions a gods-blessed must make. Hear me, hear me, goddess, please.*

Apprehension welled up, filling her throat as she plunged her fingers into the pale body of the oyster. Hard and slick, impossible to miss. Rosa's pearl was golden and irregularly jagged, like lightning stretching between sea and sky. It marked her as a stormcaller.

"Rosa Capili, stormcaller they will call you, and typhoons you will face." The traditional blessing felt far too heavy to lay on another. Especially now, at what felt like the cusp of the Codicíans' inevitable return, a black storm gathering on the horizon whose path not even Lunurin could shift. She tried to mirror back the elation on Rosa's face as she lifted the half-shell to her lips, eating the sacred oyster and completing the ritual. A bounty from the sea, salty as tears, sweet with regret.

Thunder boomed loud as laughter, and the sun sparkled through the rain. The goddess of storms rejoiced. All Aynila reveled in their newest gods-blessed. It was a good omen, a sign the goddess of storms blessed them still. Rosa was the first stormcaller named in Aynila in over fifty years.

But Lunurin's dread only grew. Why now? For a whole generation there had been no stormcallers in Aynila until she washed ashore from Calilan. For that delicate balance to be in flux again did not bode well. Anitun Tabu moved quickest when the need for her vengeance was at hand.

As if to amplify all her misgivings, Lunurin locked eyes with Inez. The shock and hurt in her large dark eyes seared itself into Lunurin's heart.

Alon leaned close, crushing her into a joyful embrace. She turned her face into his neck, afraid of what might be on her face. She didn't want to ruin this moment for Rosa. She resisted the urge to stay hidden there forever. Why couldn't he understand her apprehension? It was more than that she was afraid to train someone else. Even if she didn't have a goddess burning within her, training a stormcaller in Aynila would spell disaster, just as surely as the debacle in Talaan had torn holes in the careful tapestry of alliances the Lakan had been weaving together since the fall of the Palisade. Stormcallers were always trained on the barrier islands like Calilan, so that their presence did not drag typhoons in toward the main islands. This tradition had long helped maintain the storm paths around the archipelago that the Stormfleets worked so hard to maintain.

The Stormfleet was already nursing all the distrust they could want toward Aynila, without an untrained stormcaller worsening the situation. Especially now, with an Amihan Moon so near. The power and magic of the world were hurtling toward the fevered peak of Hilaga, when the full moon would rest cradled in her caldera. With all that power at the center of the archipelago, the delicate balance that the scattered Stormfleet was already struggling to hold could easily be undone, and completely by accident.

Lunurin could not afford to fail Rosa, not even once. Not when all Lunurin's greatest fears were coming to fruition. Just a few months after the debacle at Talaan, an envoy from the governor of Simsiman had arrived to demand the Lakan surrender Aynila and pay reparations for the Palisade and the shipyard in Talaan. Upon her refusal, they'd been informed that the Codicían Empire's persistent funding issues for their planned Reconquista of Aynila had been resolved by a generous donation from the illustrious de Palma family.

Her father, Mateo de Palma, Archbishop of all the Codicían holdings on the Great South Sea, was in Canazco assembling an armada of galleons, by which to retake his rightful place.

Aynila needed her allies now more than ever.

~

Lunurin tried to get Alon to pull Inez aside, wanting to relieve her after two rescues, but Inez refused to leave her post.

Thankfully the rest of the dives were uneventful, though almost one in five were chosen gods-blessed, an unusually high rate. That was to be expected on an Amihan Moon year. What wasn't was that Lakan Dalisay had claimed a handful more tide-touched than Hiraya had firetenders for her metal-workers' conclave.

Sometime between the last diver offering their family matriarch their oyster, and the Lakan announcing that the celebratory feast in honor of all those who had dived would be held in the courtyard of the healing school, Inez vanished into the crowds before Lunurin could pull her aside. Lunurin felt terrible. Inez was struggling enough to learn healing without being forced to try and fail so publicly.

She wove among the gathered festivalgoers streaming from the shore toward the healing school, trying to find Inez or any of the cohort of students she usually ran with, but with what seemed like all of Aynila spilling across onto the central delta, she couldn't get two steps without being pulled aside.

The Lakan wanted her to offer up one last blessing for Aynila and all the divers before they began serving food in the courtyard.

Biti, who was still one of the younger firetenders in Aynila, egged several newer, if older, firetenders to try coal walking under the roasting lechon. Lunurin happily shoved Sina toward that particular disaster in the making, and walked on.

"Inez!" she called out, thinking she'd caught sight of her long black braid, but it was one of the dyers who worked at Aynila Indigo, newly named as tide-touched. Her nails were stained indigo for good luck.

"Oh yes, congratulations," Lunurin said again. "You must find Casama, she'll be so pleased." Lunurin pointed the woman toward Alon's head dye mistress and tried to hurry on—but was waylaid by Aizza, worried about the size of the crowds.

"There are just so many people out for the festival. What if you brought the rain down a bit harder? It might thin the crowds."

The noise of the festivities was a lot, but things seemed orderly enough in the courtyard. "Alon has guards handling security, and I'd hate to dampen the atmosphere beyond the traditional ambon."

"But—"

Alon pulled her away from his sister-in-law. "I'll be back with you, Aizza. I need Lunurin a moment."

"We shouldn't..." Lunurin protested none too loudly as Alon whisked her out of the cheerful mayhem of the courtyard into the privacy of a kalesa, woven anahaw curtains drawn to keep out the rain.

She put her hands over her face and breathed, her head spinning from all the noise and being pulled in so many different directions. What she needed was to find Inez!

Alon's hands were cool, gathering the long curtain of her hair off her back, twisting it up in that perfectly deft and gentle way he had and securing it with her pearl hair prong. Lunurin reached for him, pulling him close, thankful he'd seen without her saying a word that she needed a breather. She drew her hands down his back, reveling in his solidity and strength, breathing in the salt breeze and fresh indigo dye of his silk barong.

"Were you able to find Inez?" Lunurin asked into his shoulder.

"Isko saw her headed home. She was up as early as you preparing the oyster beds. You both deserve to call it an early night. No one will notice," Alon promised, signaling to the driver.

Relief crested over her, and she let herself relax fully into Alon's side. They'd find Inez together, and somehow make it alright.

Things had been going well with Inez's training—or so she'd thought until a few months ago, as more and more of the tide-touched who'd dived at the same time as Inez had been promoted to junior healers in the infirmary, leaving Inez ever more desperate to prove she wasn't falling behind.

"You shouldn't have pushed her to heal Rosa. She didn't deserve to fail so publicly."

"She's ready. She needs a push."

"Alon—" Lunurin cut herself off. She'd been trying so hard not to undermine Alon's efforts. Inez had been chosen tide-touched. Her path would be different, and Lunurin wanted that for her. Alon knew better what a young tide-touched needed than she ever could. Lunurin stared out of the kalesa, which had slowed to a crawl as they began crossing the bridge over the Saliwain River. It seemed all of Aynila was out in their festival finest, some crossing, some browsing the stalls decked in flowers and brightly colored canopies that lined both sides of the bridge.

Alon squeezed her hand, tracing a fingertip over the face of her wedding ring. "I'll talk to Inez. She does so well with everything else. She's able to tune in to the sea in a way I'm envious of at times. But…"

Lunurin turned back to him as he lifted her hand in his and kissed her knuckles, then her ring. As if she hadn't worn it every day for the last five years. It was hard to imagine it'd been so long, when he still looked at her like she was the sun at the center of his universe.

She tightened her grip, using the tension of their joined hands to pull him in for a kiss, his lips so soft and full, the heat of his mouth a revelation she never tired of.

The kalesa came to a complete stop and Lunurin pulled back reluctantly, for the sake of propriety.

"But?" she prompted, smiling with quiet promise into the heated focus of Alon's gaze on her mouth.

Alon shook himself, returning to the conversation. "*But* she's been stalled with healing for months. Aizza thinks it's normal and she'll work through it in her own time. But it's been so long. I thought if I gave her a real application instead of just a class or demonstration… but you're right. An emergency wasn't the right push."

"Not everyone does better under pressure."

"You do."

Lunurin groaned. "Only you would think so." It seemed a cruel joke that she should feel surer of herself and her tie to her goddess when Codicían cannon fire mingled with the thunder than during a peaceful wet season naming festival. Would she ever feel meant for peacetime?

But that wasn't what this time was, and the goddess in her heart knew it. This had been a long dry season between hostilities, while everyone prepared for the bloody deluge that was coming. With the fall of Talaan, Lunurin had ensured the Codicíans would not ignore the embarrassment of Aynila any longer. They were coming. It was only a matter of when they would attempt the dangerous south sea crossing.

"*And we will be ready,*" Anitun Tabu promised. "*I will not let my people forget me so easily.*"

"Rosa *wants* to be a stormcaller. That will make it easier," Alon soothed.

Lunurin pressed her palms over her eyes. "That's worse.

You do understand why that's worse, right? An overeager stormcaller is twice as dangerous as a timid one."

"It will be a good thing. So many stormcallers have wanted to come to the rebuilt temple school. If things go well with Rosa, we could invite them, start repairing our ties with the Stormfleet, your family—"

Lunurin groaned aloud at the mention of her family who might, or might not, come to celebrate the Amihan Moon. Four previous meetings had been thwarted by bad timing or her family sending delegates in their place. Stormfleet politics or her mother's responsibilities to her husband and her *proper* heirs had always taken precedence over Lunurin. She refused to be hopeful after so many disappointments.

"That would be the *worst* thing we could do. My mother and tiya have all but said in their letters they think the Lakan is poaching their best and that the only proper place for a stormcaller is the barrier islands or the fleet. I know they're avoiding any meeting that isn't on Calilan to try to force my hand. If they found out I was training a stormcaller, here in Aynila… Hay nako! I'm having a hard time thinking of a worse insult I could pay them. They might just disown me entirely."

"Why would—"

Lunurin shook her head. "You don't know them like I do. Especially after Talaan—most of Calilan and the Stormfleet blame me, not Jeian, for what happened. Their dead delegate, and five ships allied to Calilan sank. They think I should've been able to work a miracle."

"We'll convince them you did everything you could in Talaan. Jeian is the one who sailed them into a death trap," Alon assured her.

She wanted to believe him. "It's more than just Talaan.

More than what my family thinks. Many of the more traditional factions don't think I should be in Aynila, that my proper place is Calilan. After all, there hasn't been a stormcaller here since the Lakan was a girl. They blame me for every ship lost in a storm headed toward Lusong, whether or not I've summoned it. They will think I'm training more young fools without a shred of control, intentionally upsetting the Stormfleet's efforts to protect the archipelago from typhoons, like a misplaced weight in their casting nets. That won't help mend the alliances Aynila needs, and soon."

Suddenly, the carriage juddered sideways. The pony balked, jerking against its traces, as the crowd surged and pushed with the force of too many bodies, desperate not to get pushed into the water. What was happening? Had another kalesa's pony bolted? Something hit the back of Lunurin's neck, and pain arched, just as it had in Talaan. She moved without thinking, ducking and turning, lightning sparking from her fingertips. But there was no pistol, just a frightened Aynilan woman clambering free of the crush.

Alon threw himself between them and pushed Lunurin's hand skyward, sending the skein of lightning up through the kalesa's canopy, away from the crowd and into the roiling clouds overhead.

Screams and another rush of bodies sent the kalesa toppling back onto both wheels as people scrambled to escape the delayed crash of the lightning's passage.

The woman fell back with a cry. She was empty-handed. There was no stink of gunpowder or the burn of the bullet across the back of Lunurin's neck. Her instincts were screaming, but this wasn't an attack. No assassins lay in wait, just frightened people.

More panic, as someone was forced over the edge of the

bridge into the water. Alon surged to his feet, seizing the churning river current before they could be sucked under, guiding them out toward the calmer water of the bay.

Litao urged his horse into the gap alongside the kalesa, opened by the crowd's mad scramble to escape her lightning. Shame threatened to choke Lunurin.

Alon grabbed her by the waist, lifting her over the side rail. "Go. Get clear. Bring more tide-touched. We have to get people off the bridge."

Lunurin didn't protest. The pure terror in the woman's face as lightning traced deadly lines in the air between them, was seared into the back of her eyelids. In a crush of innocents like this, her power was more liability than asset. She braced her feet, grabbed Litao's extended arm and swung herself across the gap. His compact black mare reared and pivoted neatly, breaking back toward the temple delta, where the crowds had not yet reached such a dangerous density.

3

ALON DAKILA

The kalesa rocked as another surge crushed people against its sides. Alon stepped up onto the driver's seat, trying to see above the press. He clenched and unclenched his bad hand, shaking out the pins and needles ache from the charge of Lunurin's lightning passing so close. He hoped Inez had not also been caught in the crush. There were just too many people. The slow wending festival gathering on the bridge had turned into a dangerous panicked tide as crowds on the Aynilan side of the river rushed toward the water and packed onto the busy bridge. A fall meant going into the water or being trampled. People were packed too tight to breathe.

He could not breathe until Lunurin was back on solid ground, clear of the crowds pushing from both directions onto the bridge. He saw her drop off the mare and begin redirecting people, off and away. Her voice carried even to him, in the loud katalonan pitch that could reach the heavens.

Litao cantered on toward the temple school complex for more help. Another surge in the crowd and a cry as more people pressed to the railing lost their footing and plummeted over the edge into the water. The wet season rains had been heavy all night. The Saliwain was running high and turbulent. With so much fresh water, it would be difficult for him alone to keep people safe if a large number went in.

Alon studied the water, tracking the swimmers, trying to determine the best place to guide them ashore. More cries rose as the crowd grew increasingly desperate. Across the dangerous mass of bodies, Alon saw his brother, Jeian, approaching the Aynilan side of the bridge. The salted indigo tattoos Aizza had given him glowed bright with power, as if he were entering battle, not causing a stampede. Alon saw a line of his warriors, recognizable by the round taming shields they'd adopted from their time sailing in the southern archipelago near Ísuga. Jeian and his men were using shield and spear to force the crowds down toward the water and onto the bridge.

Fury boiled through his veins, and Alon made a split-second decision. Lunurin would make sure the bridge was cleared. He could rely on her. Someone had to stop Jeian.

Another surge of the crowd pushed the kalesa against the railing. Alon shifted with the momentum, and dove into the water.

The turbulence where the Saliwain met the bay calmed and cradled him, the Sea Lady's mercy a balm even now. Alon took a moment to urge the currents to slow even further, to carry every beating heart to shore. His power formed an invisible net in the water, gentling the journey to the bay.

A wave deposited him, dripping and a great deal more levelheaded, on the far shore. The crowd on the other side was still pressing onto the narrow bridge, making the situation over the water more dangerous. Alon did not let his wave falter. He dragged it with him, up and across the plaza that funneled toward the bridge. It didn't have to be deep, ankle height would be enough. He held everyone's feet in place but his own.

He'd thought that after the fall of the Palisade, he'd lose the ability Aynila's drowned ghosts had to hold the living so tightly. But though those souls had passed on, Alon had been left with an ability to move and grip with the sea that went beyond what most tide-touched could achieve alone. And right now, it was a boon. But through his wave, Alon could feel Aizza's power channeled into his brother's tattoos, granting him the strength to tear free of Alon's hold.

"Jeian!" Alon raised his voice, stalking toward the battle-high glow of his brother.

Another push of seawater up into the plaza, grasping his brother about the knees. But the lines and whorls of Aizza's tattoos across his chest and arms glowed brighter yet, blue and blinding as deep water on a clear day, sending Alon's wave cascading away from Jeian's legs.

"Traitors! Spies! The lot of them!" Jeian declared.

Alon caught the runoff, pushing it up into a surge that forced Jeian's men back from the crowd a few more steps. How did he expect to tell a convert from a wet season festival goer in this mayhem, much less an actual Codician spy?

"Stand down," Alon ordered. These weren't his men, but with their captain clearly in a battle frenzy, maybe...

But no. Jeian's men were sailors. They would not be cowed by a low wave. Locking shields together, they pressed forward toward their captain.

"Jeian, what is the meaning of this?" Alon cried, desperate to talk sense into his brother.

"I won't have your peace talks now. Not after this!" Jeian snapped.

Fine. If Jeian was done talking, he'd fling his brother into the bay. Aman Sinaya could soak the battle rage out of him.

With all the grace of a tsunami dragging the tide out, Alon pulled his brother and any of his men unlucky enough to be in contact with his wave down the slope toward the Saliwain.

Except Jeian caught himself on the sturdy bamboo stilt of a building built out over the riverbank and launched himself at Alon. They went down hard, Alon's head cracking into his brother's skull with light-flashing force, before the water caught them both.

They were swept in a tangle of limbs out to the bay.

~

Alon was dripping on his inay's festival silks as she bent over him, hissing in displeasure as she tended the knot on his head. Lakan Dalisay Inanialon heaved one last put-upon sigh. She looked to Isko, Alon's foster brother and right-hand man, for a tally of the day's disaster.

"How bad?" she signed.

"Three suffocated in the crush, thirty and rising admitted to the healing halls for serious injury, and nearing seventy with minor wounds, being seen to as the healers work their way through the crowd," Isko reported. "Aizza has taken charge of the most serious cases."

His mother frowned. "Do we have enough healers?"

"No, and there's more. One of Amihan's sacred messenger birds was found dead on the center of the bridge. Sina and Hiraya have gone to offer the spark-striker's body back to Mount Hilaga."

At this final blow, she turned on Jeian. "Ay, gago! You start a riot the day of the wet season festival of all days, and now there are ill-omens!" Her hands flashed angrily.

"It was the priest's fault! Did you really expect me to sit back while he called for the death of more tide-touched?" Jeian protested. He was irritatingly hale and hearty, another boon from Aizza's tattoos, salt and indigo ink worked into his skin in dizzyingly detailed patterns that channeled the tides' strength into his muscles and Aizza's healing energies through his body.

"An Our Lady of Sorrows Saint's Day Mass was hardly a revolt. It didn't require you to crush it with soldiers." Lunurin rubbed her hands over her face, exhaustion in every line of her frame. Alon was glad to hear her say this. She hadn't been so confident when they'd first realized how Aynila's converts planned to celebrate the city's patron saint this year.

It was complicated. In the last year, since the Codicíans' worrying shift in focus to smuggled missionaries over envoys and open threats, the Lakan had decreed that any Codicíans caught in Aynila were spies and agitators, to be arrested or expelled at her discretion. After a nearly successful assassination attempt on Lunurin, not even Alon had protested the move.

A year ago, Lunurin had been ambushed by a "fishing crew gone off course" while tending the oyster beds. She'd almost been shot, before she'd drowned them all. None of the other attempts on his mother or Lunurin had made it beyond the planning stages before Alon's spies had rooted them out.

Jeian's eyes narrowed. He turned on Alon. "So you knew! You knew it was happening and you pulled your men back and let them do it. It's because of idiotic decisions like that we lost Aynila in the first place."

"I knew because my spies have been watching Father Ortiz since he started holding his 'secret' Masses two weeks ago!"

Alon shot back. "I've been trying to find out who smuggled him into Aynila and who's supported him here to close the loophole in our security. Which will be very hard to do now that you've arrested him and a handful of random converts."

"You and your spies would've watched a mob march on the healing temple and burn it to the ground a second time," Jeian accused.

"And you think arresting priests in broad daylight and hunting our own converts through the streets is a good way to convince those who are wary of us to welcome a return to the old ways? We have always worshiped many goddesses. Who are they hurting by praying to their Lady of Sorrows? You can't keep acting like this is the Aynila of thirty years ago. We cannot act with impunity. Most of Aynila has never visited a tide-touched healer. They only ever knew us as witches and rebels. They are afraid. We won't win them with force."

Jeian began to pace the room. "So, what, we do nothing? We keep waiting for the Codicíans to show up on our doorstep with their galleons and guns? We cannot afford to be lenient with Codicían sympathizers. There's no way a crowd crush harmed a spark-striker bird. It's a sign. Allowing the priest free rein was an insult to the old gods, a danger to all we've accomplished in Aynila."

"No one will say a word of ill-omens or dead spark-strikers. Not with the Amihan Moon Summit so soon. We must calm the situation," Dalisay decreed.

"How?"

"We should release the Aynilans who were arrested," Alon suggested.

"Oh, so you want to give them another chance to get a lucky shot in?" Jeian demanded.

"This wasn't another assassination attempt. I panicked

thanks to your crowd crush," Alon cut in, defending Lunurin. "Keep your focus on strengthening the navy and Aynila's defenses. You'll have real enemies to fight soon enough."

"You'd have us fall to these dissidents without the Codicians having to fire a single shot. We'll be ripe for the taking before their armada even crosses the Great South Sea. You let their priests gather a mob of supporters in the middle of the wet season festival when we most need to secure our city before the Amihan Moon! How did you all become such cowards while I was gone?"

Alon ground his teeth. "It's not cowardice to wait for the right time and place to act so there will be the least amount of collateral damage."

There was a rap on the door, and Inez peered in. Thankfully, she hadn't been caught up in the crush; she'd been waylaid by Bernila, who insisted she eat some food instead of running off and going hungry.

"Forgive the interruption." Inez inclined her head to the Lakan. "Aizza asked me to tell you that the family members of those arrested are demanding the temple release them. They don't want to bring home water witch curses."

Jeian threw up his hands in frustration. "I'm interrogating the priest."

The last thing Alon needed was Jeian getting an earful of all the latest rumors and vitriol Ortiz had been spreading. He had enough prejudices against Aynila's converts already. Alon's stomach knotted with dread. "Can you please listen—"

"Before you decide to release him, too." Jeian marched out of Dalisay's study, shouldering past Inez and ignoring Dalisay signing at him to stay.

Alon half rose to go after his brother, but Dalisay grabbed him, forcing him back down into his chair.

"Leave him," she signed. "Let him tire himself before we try to talk him down."

"He never tires," Lunurin groused. "It's infuriating."

Dalisay's brows rose. "Oh, he'll feel it soon, especially if Aizza is overseeing the most serious injuries. He's probably rushing off to nurse the low with her. You should do the same. I don't like that lump."

This mollified Alon, who lifted his inay's hand, miming mano po, though he avoided pressing her knuckles to his tender brow. "Salamat po, Inay. It's hardly a bump. I'm perfectly well."

His inay pursed her lips. "You're a terrible patient." She shook her head. "This is not the fortuitous circumstance and united front I wanted to present to all our visiting allies during the Amihan Moon Summit."

"We still have a week before the full moon. Plenty of time to talk Jeian around," Alon offered. "He'll calm when he's not battle-riled. He always does."

"I'm not worried about Jeian," Dalisay signed. "He's right you know, not about the dissidents, but about Aynila's internal divisions… and probably even about the omens. There is more we need to do to bridge the gaps. It's not just the converts, though they are a dangerous faction. I don't think you were wrong to let them celebrate their saint's day, but maybe we did need to have a presence. Lunurin, you could—"

"No!" Alon burst out, with more force than he'd intended.

Lunurin shook her head. "I'm sorry, but not if Ortiz still holds sway."

Inez flinched at the name. Lunurin went to her, sliding an arm about her shoulders.

"I don't want her exposed to their nonsense," Alon

explained, trying to keep his voice level. He'd almost lost her too many times to the Church. He'd not risk her with Aynila's converts. "The converts may still hold some fondness for Lunurin, but these missionaries have been spreading their rumors and lies too. Jeian may not be wrong that it's only a matter of time before some Aynilan convert is convinced to join a plot against you or Lunurin."

"You don't think Lunurin could win them over? Surely a saint has more sway than some unknown priest?" his inay suggested.

She might. And she probably could. Lunurin would tear down the sky if it meant a safer Aynila for those she loved. But at what cost? He refused to go back to those early terrible days, when they'd both been playing a role for the Codicían Church. Their whole lives had been cages and masks and terrible choices. He couldn't let his inay put it on Lunurin, not after everything she and Inez had been through. He wouldn't put her into their hands. Never again, hadn't he promised it?

"Leave it to me, Inay. My spies are sure to bring me something useful from all this turmoil. It might even have riled the priest's backers into a panic. I'd like to talk to the arrested Aynilans before Aizza gives them a clean bill of health."

"If you think that's best. Lunurin, I need you to go to Sina and Hiraya and find out exactly what they've seen in the flames. I want no surprises once dignitaries start arriving for the Amihan Moon. We can't let this disturbance distract us from our greater goals."

The pounding pain in Alon's bad hand eased as he relaxed, the relief of it a surprise. Had he been clenching into his brace so tightly? But he'd gladly take up any burden if it meant protecting Lunurin.

4

❖

INEZ NG DAKILA

How dare Lunurin pretend to care, after what she'd done this morning? Did she still think Inez was a child in need of comfort? Inez wanted to be seen, to be listened to and trusted. Instead, she was coddled, and always, *always* overlooked.

She twisted free from Lunurin's grip as soon as Alon's and the Lakan's attention slid away from them. It was Lunurin's turn to flinch, her hands still half extended toward Inez's shoulders. And for a brief blinding moment, Inez wanted to make Lunurin hurt, just as she'd hurt this morning. She wanted blood. She wanted—

Guilt bloomed in her belly, stronger even than the anger. Inez hissed softly, lifting a hand to where the scarring curled up over the top of her shoulder, raised lines against her fingertips. "My back…"

It was easy to blame the spitefulness of her wounded pride on the phantom pangs and itchiness of the layered scars. Pain made everyone prickly, right?

"Oh, I'm sorry, dearest," Lunurin apologized.

It wasn't the apology Inez wanted. Couldn't Lunurin see?

"How could you—" But the accusation of Rosa's naming caught halfway. It was all too tangled up with what had happened before. When Inez had been shattered. When Inez had shattered their family with her mistakes.

So much lay unsaid between the two of them. Unsaid and now, after all this time, unspeakable.

Rosa had been so much a part of their life from before, their life with Catalina. Catalina who had to be sent away, who Lunurin never spoke of. Catalina, whom Inez had taken away from Lunurin the moment she'd asked Lunurin to end her pregnancy.

Inez knew Lunurin would never say it like that. Just as Alon would never place the burning of the tide-touched village on her shoulders. Just like the sea was never *trying* to hurt her when it washed over her head in an overwhelming deluge. But they did blame Catalina.

After all, they'd done everything they could to obscure Inez's ties to her sister in the eyes of Aynila. Alon had even taken Inez into his household as a ward. As Inez ng Dakila she was under the protection of his family name, rather than still sharing Catalina's as Inez Domingo. Even if someone didn't know about Catalina and her crimes, her old name had announced her as a ward of the Church. A mestiza mistake, unrecognized by mother or father.

And Inez knew in her bones that Catalina would never have done it, would never have *broken* as she had if Inez had not gotten pregnant. Inez's pregnancy had forced Catalina to choose between her love for her family and her love of God. Inez had pushed her sister to breaking point. And when Cat had broken, she'd destroyed everything.

Late at night, and in moments like this, Inez imagined that terrible brokenness was lurking just under her own painstakingly patched-together skin, waiting for its moment to burst out, to hurt and betray and destroy everyone around her. Just like Catalina had. If she wasn't careful, it would. Couldn't the Sea Lady understand that? She was supposed to be merciful.

Why couldn't Inez find the peace Alon and all the other tide-touched did in the coming and going of Aynila's tide?

"I should know better," Lunurin continued, taking Inez's hands and squeezing. "Are the scars bothering you more lately? Have you talked to Alon about it?"

Inez dropped her gaze, unable to bear the attention she'd craved. "I will," she mumbled.

With every year, Inez saw her sister more and more in the shape of her own face, the way her hands had grown long-fingered and shapely, how Lunurin flinched when Inez raised her voice. Catalina was a haunting in Inez's bones, a bloody-minded fury that burned in her belly and turned to poison on her tongue, threatening to unmake all the work others had done putting her back together.

"I don't know why I've been so stuck, I'm trying and trying," Inez forced out. The tug of war between her hunger to be seen and the broken angry ghost inside her skin kept her always grasping then flinching from Lunurin's attention.

"I know you are," Lunurin assured her.

So why had Lunurin chosen Rosa and not her? Why was Rosa different? Why was Rosa worthy? She wanted to scream, but she was terrified she might know the answer. In the razor-edges of Cat's familiar hot-cold fury burning her own insides. In the guilt licking down her spine like lashes of the abbot's bamboo cane. One day she would shatter. The fault lines had already been laid. Inez wouldn't be like Lunurin, her goddess burning in her eyes, lightning spilling out of her skin. Instead, the ugliness inside her would leak out like an abscessed wound to poison everyone and everything around her. If the old gods had decided she was salt, she was salt in the well.

"And I'm sorry you were put on the spot to heal like that. Talk to Alon about it, and about your back. You shouldn't be putting up with discomfort. He knows about hard-to-heal scar tissue. Maybe the distraction is splitting your attention," Lunurin urged her.

Inez shook her head. She'd just given Lunurin another reason to think of her as a wounded, broken child, still in need of fixing. But before she could even try to make Lunurin understand, Inez had already lost her attention. Alon had stolen it away again.

He was rubbing at the layered scars of his braced hand, his brow furrowed. Lunurin crossed to him and placed a hand on his forearm. "Let's get you home to rest. Nothing will be decided until Jeian's cooled his head."

Alon let her thread their fingers together. "Yes, of course, you're right."

Lunurin's expression relaxed further, softening as she always did toward Alon.

Inez stepped back, but at Lunurin's gesture she followed them, wrestling with her own frustration and trying not to give into the urge to scream.

She remembered all too well the keen edges of Catalina's love, upon which everyone she loved had to cut themselves to shreds to be worthy of her affection. As angry as Inez was, as much as she wanted to scream till Alon and Lunurin finally looked, she was afraid of sharpening herself. She could feel how easy it would be, some days, to take what had been done to her—so many shattered pieces fitted carefully back into place—and turn them all outward. She could build a shell, a razor-reef of the dead bodies of what had come before, in which she would never be harmed, never be touched, except by those bleeding out on her edges.

Would their blood electrify the sea as Rosa's had? Would it feel like crocodilian armor?

This morning, over the oyster beds, Inez had sensed blood through the buwaya in a way she'd never managed when she was desperately trying to heal. That terrified her. Of course, the one time she learned anything about healing, she was doing it wrong.

While she was wrestling with this, somehow Lunurin orchestrated the conversation Inez was supposed to need. Claiming the bridge crush had left her too claustrophobic, she rode home on Litao's mount, leaving Inez alone with Alon in the back of the kalesa. Litao, perched beside the driver, shared a cigarillo, the peppery-sweet scent of tobacco drifting on the night air. Inez cast her gaze over the volcanic hills that cupped Aynila like fingers, studying the more distant dots of light sprinkled across the hills. Were they more of Amihan's spark-striker birds? Or a smoking kapre perched up in the boughs of a balete tree, like Litao was pretending to be, blowing smoke rings overhead? All Aynila's spirits, large and small, had come awake. Beings and creatures Inez had once thought only existed in Lunurin's fanciful imaginings were making their presence known, and not always quietly or peacefully.

She whispered, "Tabi tabi po," and hoped Lunurin's recent rains would prevent any spreading fires from misplaced sparks.

"What was that?" Alon asked, his attention drawn by her utterance. Irritation rose in her again at the way Lunurin had herded them, like Inez couldn't talk to Alon on her own. Like they didn't have three training sessions a week already. Like Alon wasn't just as much in the dark about the problem as she was.

But her sharp edges still ached, now with guilt, and worst of all those crocodile hunger pangs. Inez knew she had to try. If something didn't change soon, she'd start giving in to the jagged fury in her belly and the tooth-sharp whispers in the sea. They were easier than trying to do things the way she was supposed to. She'd ruin Aynila for herself. And now that she was tide-touched, where else in the world would take her in?

"About—"

"So the—" They both began at the same time. Inez snapped her mouth shut and waited.

"You did well this morning, rescuing Rosa," Alon said.

Inez heard the way he was carefully padding his coming criticism with praise, like she would crumble to dust if he was too harsh or hasty. Half of her wanted to scream that he was wrong. She wasn't fragile. Could they all stop treating her like a child? But after today, the rest of her was worried they were right.

Inez waited for the "but."

"And it was hasty of me to push you to heal. You are so attuned to the sea… if we could just figure out this block you have around healing, the rest will follow—"

"That's exactly the problem." Inez paused, reining in her frustration with difficulty. "The sea is so loud. It is the bay and *everything* in it. How am I supposed to find the focus to heal? I heard the buwaya, the way they scented Rosa's blood, the way they hungered for it. Why are they so much louder to me than anything to do with healing? I feel like there's something wrong with me."

Alon was quiet a beat too long. Inez wondered if she'd been too honest. It was impossible to read his expression in the blue shadows of the kalesa. But someone had to know, had to be able to fix this, fix her. Alon had done it before when no one else would.

"Nothing is wrong with you." He hesitated. "It's natural."

It didn't feel natural. Or... it felt all *too* natural. Like an anchor against the too-much-at-once feedback from the bay.

"I could taste Rosa's blood in the water before I could find her beating heart," Inez stressed. "That's not how you want me to feel for the salt in every Aynilan's blood."

Again, Alon was quiet just a little too long. Inez began to fear the worst.

"The buwaya aren't regular animals," he started.

"No, they're anito, I know but—"

"And you are young, training under powerful katalonan. Your attention is more potent than you know. But you are tide-touched, and we have dedicated ourselves to Aman Sinaya. We mustn't forget the sea's mercy to listen to hungry anito."

Inez's frustration bubbled higher. What she felt when the bay rubbed her skin raw and roared in her head did not feel like mercy. "But why are they so much easier to listen to than the sea?"

"As the Amihan Moon grows nearer, it gathers power like the tides. It awakens and refreshes the world, and attracts many beings of power, like the laho, who hungers for all the power the moon will bring the archipelago when she rests on the peak of Hilaga. The sea dragon will be rushing towards Aynila to try to swallow the moon, but it is not the only one. The spark-striker birds have been more active than usual, and the duwende of Hilaga's lava caves. You have seen the way Aynila has changed this year."

"I have, but—"

"They are all little spirits. We show them respect, but no more. More than that is dangerous. Just try to focus on healing and you'll be fine. It will be easier once the Amihan Moon has passed, but it's good practice to work on your focus now. You never know when you will have to heal distracted."

"How can I learn when I'm already distracted?"

"You will."

Inez ground her teeth. She wished there was someone else left among the tide-touched for whom healing and the call of the sea hadn't come easily. It was all well and good for him to talk about loud anito. But none of the other young gods-blessed were having this problem. She'd asked. Biti wasn't hearing the spark-striker birds singing in the dawn and feeding tinder to fires along Hilaga's caldera, or muttering duwende shifting stones underfoot to help an earthquake along. None of the other tide-touched had hungry crocodiles in their ears.

Alon knew what he was listening for when he healed. She didn't. She had never managed to properly heal anyone. And the harder she listened, the more she heard things that weren't beating hearts or the salt of the spirit that Alon kept trying to describe to her.

Before she could try to express this, the kalesa pulled up in front of their home. Litao gestured with the burning point of his cigarillo toward a shadowy figure just beyond the lamp-light spilling from the door and upper windows.

It was one of Alon's special messengers, no doubt bearing some additional news of today's riots and the Our Lady of Sorrows Mass.

Recognizing that her time with Alon's attention was short, she asked, "Do you think there will be more riots because the priest is being held?"

Alon reached up to give her a hand down the steps. "Things would've remained peaceful if Jeian hadn't interfered. But don't let the situation with the priest worry you. You won't ever need to see him."

Inez shivered. She hadn't known there was a real priest back in Aynila. She didn't like the idea of letting one proselytize here, even if it did keep the peace. Alon should've let Jeian kill him.

Inez flinched from the bloody thought. No. That wasn't what she wanted. It wasn't her who hated like that. If she told herself that enough, if she didn't lash out, she would avoid becoming all the things that had forced Catalina to leave Aynila.

But she wondered. Was the converts' faith as poisoned as her sister's had been? She needed to know, like prodding an old wound to see if the blood would rise, or if it was just scar pangs, the wound long healed. Perhaps it was only her ghosts lying to her, filling her with fear.

Would she know their faces? Would they know hers? Would they remember what one of their precious priests had done?

5

ALON DAKILA

Alon tried to feel sympathy for Father Ortiz, but with every word out of his mouth it was becoming harder. Frankly, Alon was impressed with Jeian's restraint if he'd said or done anything half so stupid in front of Aizza while she'd been taking care of the minor injuries he'd sustained during his arrest.

Injuries that had been significantly exacerbated by Jeian flinging the man through a wall.

"Water witch infidels, the Empire's righteous justice is coming for you and the she-witch you serve. Soon the archbishop's armada will return the faithful to the fold. By the light of your pyres, the blindness will be removed from the eyes of those you have led astray," Ortiz yelled as he wrestled free of Litao's grip and took a wild, unbalanced swing at Alon.

He could see why Aizza had asked him to tend to the situation.

Ortiz certainly had a gift for vivid imagery that the

governor's envoy had lacked in his threats. But then, the governor's envoy had survived the delivery of his message. If Ortiz kept this up he very well might not. Alon grabbed him and caught a glancing blow to the chin that clicked his teeth together. Isko, who Alon suspected had accompanied him mainly to prevent another fight with Jeian, stepped in to help get the priest back under control.

Alon worked his jaw and tried to calm himself. There would be no more pyres. He had Lunurin, and they still had time. The latest word along the Codicians' trade routes was that though the archbishop's forces in Canazco were nearly provisioned and armed, his most experienced captains had encouraged him to delay the crossing till after the worst of the wet season storms had passed.

And Lunurin's storms needed no season.

"If you won't hold still and let me heal you, I will knock you unconscious first and deal with the damage later," Alon finally declared over the curses and invectives Ortiz hurled as he thrashed.

"Witch! Worse, for you have departed from the faith, devoting yourself to deceitful spirits and teachings of demons!"

"Ortiz, will you listen to yourself?" Isko groused as he and Litao struggled to get a grip on the man.

It seemed to Alon, making rueful eye contact with Isko, that anyone still able to put up this much of a fight couldn't need that much healing. But another dead priest before the Amihan Moon would present a complication that would displease the Lakan, and he refused to give Jeian the satisfaction.

"You have lain down with witches and demons, and their uncleanliness is a mark of the beast upon your face! I'll not let you place such evils upon me," Ortiz howled, head-butting the pitcher in Alon's hand, dousing himself in saltwater and shards of ceramic.

Alon studied the blood running down his own wrist. He smiled, all teeth—an expression he'd picked up from Lunurin—and was unduly pleased to see Ortiz momentarily freeze. "I will assume you are accusing me of philandering and do not refer to the wife I took before the eyes of your god and the head of your order by such foul names. I am a patient man, more patient than my brother. But. My patience. Is not. Infinite."

Ortiz gathered himself and spat, "Demon spawn! God's wrath will surely visit itself upon you and all in this nest of evils as he did upon Sodom and Gomorrah."

Alon cocked his head. "Did your god not say he would save Sodom and Gomorrah for the sake of only ten true believers? Surely you did not return to this nest of depravity for the souls of only ten. You and I both know there are more who remain faithful than that."

Ortiz's eyes, which had been rolling in his head with religious zeal, seemed to sharpen. "And so, in the archbishop's endless wisdom, we have been sent to prepare the way for his righteous sword. Our holy mission is blessed by Santa Catalina, who faced near martyrdom yet still has returned to bring God's light back into Our Lady of Sorrows' heart. For she will surely succeed where all others have failed to return Aynila to a true and holy path."

Alon went cold and still. His spies had brought him whispers of Santa Catalina, but this was the first time he'd heard more than the name. Would he be haunted by his own good deed forever? "You'd like me to carry that tale, wouldn't you?"

Ortiz stared back, dazed, blood running down his

forehead. "All the world will know Santa Catalina's mission; she has seen it, a vision from God! And we are duty bound to carry it out."

"Who has bound you? Whose will is it? Who is sending you and so many of your brothers to die as martyrs in my city?" Alon asked. Ever since the Codicíans' efforts had shifted toward proselytization and subterfuge, he'd been trying to determine who had taught the governor of Simsiman subtlety. All the signs indicated it must be someone powerful within the Church; someone the archbishop trusted to carry out his vision before he himself made the crossing.

Now, at last, Ortiz clapped his mouth shut. Isko and Litao were able to get a good grip on him, and Alon dragged the saltwater back into his hands to finish the healing quickly.

The rumor of Catalina's involvement had to be a trap, Alon knew. Even if it were true, it was only meant to distract Lunurin. To draw her out of Aynila to where she would be vulnerable so the Codicíans could rid themselves of their one true obstacle to reconquering Aynila once and for all. They, whoever "they" were, wanted Lunurin to believe Catalina had returned. That meant whoever had taken charge of the Church's efforts to reclaim Aynila, must somehow know what Catalina had been to Lunurin. Who among the survivors of the Palisade's fall had such sway *and* such knowledge? Alon needed to find out. Whoever it was, they knew too much. They knew enough to hurt Lunurin, and Inez too.

He must talk to Lunurin, warn her, and decide what they'd tell Inez.

As he left the priest's room, he ran directly into Jeian. The blue light of Aizza's strength had faded from the banding around his arms and across his chest, but he did not look very much calmed otherwise.

60

"If you immediately undo all my efforts, I won't help Aizza the next time she asks," Alon warned.

"We need to know what he knows," Jeian insisted.

Quite suddenly, Alon didn't want Jeian to know what Ortiz had said. He didn't want anyone to know until he'd had a chance to talk to Lunurin, until they'd decided what needed to be done.

"Leave the priest to me. I knew him in the Palisade. He'll come around." Behind Jeian's back, Alon signaled to Litao to remain and guard the priest. Isko eyed him suspiciously, but kept his mouth shut.

Alon threw an arm around Jeian's shoulders. "Let the healing set, at least. We ought to check on your wife. She's working too hard."

Jeian frowned, then noticed Alon's hand, which was wrapped in a rag. Blood had begun to seep through. "Looks like you've more work for her," Jeian said and swept him along toward the main infirmary, his focus diverted.

Aizza hurried over as soon as she saw them. "Don't tell me you two were fighting again? Aman Sinaya have mercy, you're worse than twin roosters. Aren't you too old for this? Isko, how do you always stay out of it?"

Jeian's face contorted with mock hurt. "We weren't! You can blame the priest, not me."

Aizza seized Alon's hand and pointed with her lips for Jeian to fetch a fresh basin of saltwater, shooting her husband a suspicious glare.

"Isko, defend my honor," Jeian complained as he went.

"It's true," Isko provided helpfully. "The priest was slipperier than expected."

Aizza shook her head, inspecting Alon's injury. "Hala! Alon, you need to be more careful. You will lose more strength and mobility in this hand if you keep injuring it and hoping for the best. Have you been keeping up with all your stretches? These scars need frequent stretching, and nightly ointment soaks. If it tightens up more..." She plunged his hand into saltwater, still muttering.

Jeian raised his eyebrows meaningfully at him. "You should listen to her. Do you think I got so strong ignoring healer's orders?"

"You're not resting enough either," Aizza shot in his direction.

"You need rest too, Aizza." Alon pulled his hand from her grip as soon as the bleeding had stopped. "Lunurin will help me with it later."

Aizza shook the saltwater from her hands. "I can't rest. Most of the trainee healers have already exhausted themselves. They don't know how to pace themselves yet."

At Aizza's words, one of the trainees slumped over the cot of the patient she'd been tending in a dead faint.

"Jeian, carry her to the back, would you? We've extra cots set up there," Aizza instructed.

If their numbers were too thin to deal with an incident of this scale... What would become of Aynila if there were a siege?

Their students were not all newly named since the fall of the Palisade, but many of the tide-touched who had escaped the Inquisition's purges had done so by lying low, burying their abilities. The number of trained healers besides himself, Aizza, the Lakan, and Pasamba was very low. It was why he was pushing Inez so hard. She had all the makings of a truly gifted tide-touched, and Aynila needed all the healers they could lay their hands on.

"When can Pasamba relieve you?" Alon asked.

"Noon. You should've tied the priest down from the start. I don't know why the Lakan insists we tend him. Do not keep neglecting yourself!" Aizza chided him.

Determined that no one else would catch word of the Santa Catalina debacle until he'd been able to talk to Lunurin, Alon caught her arm before she could rush back to the infirmary. "Leave the priest to me. There is no reason for you to expend yourself any further. I will speak to the Lakan if she has complaints. I've placed my guard outside his door. He's too unpredictable to put our trainees in danger."

Especially Inez.

As Aizza left to check on Jeian and the overextended trainee, Isko gave him another look.

"The fewer people who catch and carry word of this new saint, the better," Alon explained. "Jeian is paranoid enough."

"When it comes to the converts, true. But you will tell…?"

"Of course, they should know first. Don't tell Sina till I've had a chance to talk to Lunurin. We need to figure out what to tell Inez."

Isko nodded. "That's probably best."

Alon went in search of his wife. He needed her, and they needed to decide what to do about these rumors.

~

He found Lunurin in their rooms, surrounded by a heaping pile of offcut oyster shells. Not the sacred silver-lip oysters that Aynilans had so recently dived for to make their mutya, but talaba, an oval eating oyster sold in baskets at the palengke. Someone had feasted.

Sina, or one of her firetenders from the jewelry workshops

in the metalworkers' conclave across the river, had delivered a toolkit. Judging by the heaps of scrap, Lunurin had been at the task all morning. In an open jewelry box by the window, where it caught the sun in a dazzle of light, Rosa's untouched silver-lip oyster shell sat cradling her lightning-shaped pearl.

Lunurin let out a shout of frustration and dropped both handsaw and half-shell to the table. "Ay lintik!"

Alon took a few steps into the room, briefly concerned she'd cut herself—but there was no blood.

"I'm going to ruin it," she lamented.

"You won't," Alon assured her.

Lunurin held up the shell she'd just discarded. Alon could see the rough shape of a hair comb, the tines neatly measured, marked, and cut to the point where the middle tooth had snapped off, ruining the whole piece.

"How long have—"

"All day! And the cook refuses to make any more kinilaw na talaba because even the guards and the dye workers won't eat any more, so now I have to start on the real one and I'm going to doom Rosa to an ugly, broken, unlucky mutya for the rest of her life."

"It can't be that bad. What if you did something simple? My inay's mutya was just a full moon pendant."

"Tide-touched tend to have necklaces with round motifs to mimic your pearl shape," Lunurin muttered. "But a storm-caller should have hair pieces. I can't explain it. It helps with attunement, with balance. So much of our power is bound up in our hair. I need to do this right!"

Her expression creased with frustration. Alon felt her fear of failure tugging at his blood like the moonrise. Everything in him wanted to fix this. And especially after his altercation with the priest he needed to hold her tight and know she was right beside him. He knelt beside her and cradled her hands in his. "Easy, easy, love. If you ask Sina for help, no one will ever tell Rosa."

"But I would know. And it wouldn't be right. If I was just going to hand it off to someone else, I should have done so before all Aynila. Did you see how Inez looked at me? She's so angry, and I don't blame her." Lunurin's face was red now, her black curls frizzing free from her bun as static crackles of electricity from around the room raced toward her. "She wanted me to name *her* and I was too much of a coward. I should have stayed a coward."

She reached for him, her frustration spilling over.

Alon opened his arms, letting her dissipate all the heat and electricity into the deep salt well of his spirit. He was lifted by her power in turn, a give and take perfected over the years, soothing as a balm. "Easy, easy. I'm sure Inez understands."

She buried her face in his shoulder, her arms locking around him as she squeezed, grounding him as much as herself. At last, she relaxed her tense hold as she let out an inarticulate groan of frustration.

She still sounded so upset, Alon couldn't help but ask, "Is this really about Rosa?"

"Yes!" Lunurin wailed. "No! I'm not sure after the twentieth damn broken comb. I just can't see myself training anyone, much less Rosa. She's so much a part of the past and every mistake I ever made back then, with Inez, with Catalina... how much I failed to see before it was too late."

"You didn't—"

"I did! If I hadn't failed Catalina, Inez would still have her sister."

The way her voice twisted on Catalina's name, grief and fury, the pain still so fresh after all these years. It reminded

Alon of how much Lunurin had loved her.

Were it not for that final betrayal, Inez might still have her sister—and Lunurin might still have her Cat.

His lungs ached at the ugly, foolish thought. Catalina's betrayal could not be undone. Lunurin's misgivings about the past had nothing to do with their marriage and everything to do with Inez.

He clutched his wife even tighter. Wishing desperately this was a wound he could heal as easily as a broken bone. But hearts were different.

"I have to find a way to get past it. None of it is Rosa's fault. Her future as a stormcaller is the last thing I want to risk ruining with the Stormfleet delegates about to arrive. So many are still apprehensive after Talaan, especially my family—" Lunurin broke off, rubbing angrily at her face, like she could claw the frustrations out of her skin.

How much of it was the reminder of the past tearing at them, and how much of her anxiety was about her arriving family and the Stormfleet? Sometimes, Alon thought Lunurin might prefer the cut-and-dry antagonism of her father raising an armada to kill them over the back-and-forth dance of entreaty with Calilan and her mother's family.

The terrible weight of it all bowed her shoulders. She was Lady Stormbringer, and she would stand for them all, come what may. He thought of the priest, the terrible seed of knowledge he wanted Alon to plant in her mind. The Codicians' unknown spymaster trying to twist Lunurin back into their Lady of Sorrows, their Santa María.

She was his wife. Alon would not help anyone hurt her. He'd silence Ortiz and this rumor. He would keep his family safe. They needed no more anguish.

Ortiz might be lying. He might be telling a terrible truth.

It didn't matter. Alon was the only one who could protect Lunurin. It was all she'd ever asked of him: safe harbor.

Alon pressed his lips to her knuckles, lifted her hands from the delicate skin of her eyes. He kissed her calloused palms, red and smarting in new spots from the hours spent grasping saw and shell. "Talaan wasn't your fault. We'll prove that to our allies."

"We lost so many. We were lucky there wasn't a galleon still stationed there. If there had been, even together... we couldn't have done it. We were lucky, so lucky. I feel like I should have been able to do more. There's no way we can turn aside the Codicían armada alone." Lunurin's voice caught. This admission cost her. To the Lakan and their allies, she was the invulnerable Lady Stormbringer. It was only in his arms she could afford to be afraid.

"Not alone. But we will not be alone, unarmed and unprepared as we were then. The Amihan Moon will help us consolidate our alliances, we have been preparing for nothing else for months."

"How can you sound so sure, especially after the bridge crush? Whether they're convert or returned to the old ways, everyone in Aynila has found a way to mark it as a bad omen, and the dead spark-striker is not even common knowledge." Lunurin's dark eyes searched his for reassurance.

He pressed his brow to hers, holding her gaze. "The mistake in Talaan was mine, not yours. I should never have let my brother out of my sight. I made the same mistake yesterday. We still have time to prepare, to gather allies. The Great South Sea is a long and dangerous crossing, even for an armada. It does not all rest on you alone."

Lunurin drew two fingers down his chest, tracing the embroidered waves spilling down the front of his barong. "You can't take the blame for Talaan either. I just wish this"—she swept her hand toward the mess of broken shell—"could've waited till a better time, when I could afford to focus."

"What if you asked for help? You don't have to pass Rosa's mutya off to Sina, but she might provide guidance, or one of her craftspeople? If you shape the shell, they could do the inlay work on a comb of tortoiseshell or horn," Alon suggested.

Lunurin dropped her forehead to his shoulder. "That's a much better idea. I wish I'd thought of that before I broke twenty practice combs."

"It was good practice. And everyone ate well."

Lunurin snorted a huff of laughter. Her breath was so warm through the thin material of his barong. "What would Inez and I do without you? We'd worry ourselves into knots and catastrophes."

"And probably kill someone. Who knows though, it might solve some of the catastrophes," Alon agreed, relieved to see her smiling, though the back of his neck prickled thinking of how this secret would affect Inez too. But Lunurin had as good as begged him not to let her get caught up in the past.

Alon's resolve hardened. He wouldn't do it, at least not right now with so much still unconfirmed. He would not let the Codicíans inject Catalina into the tangled net they found themselves in. It would be too cruel.

He would keep Lunurin wrapped up safe in his arms as long as he could, as long as he breathed. Aman Sinaya grant him the strength to stand beside her. All the power of a summer storm coiled under her warm brown skin, and she deigned to rest in his arms. Alon rested his head atop hers. The scent of her hair, sesame oil and jasmine, filled his senses as their breaths and heartbeats fell into sync.

At least he could ease today's frustration and give Lunurin

a place to vent her fears. He wouldn't let the past rear its ugly head and poison what he and Lunurin had built together, not yet. Not with so much at stake and nothing to be gained.

He pressed his lips to the nape of her neck. Lunurin lifted her head, her dark eyes catching his with heated intention, and he was drowning. He kissed her. Her fingers threaded into the hair at his nape, pulling him closer. Her touch was electric, and he was water before her.

With a sweep of her arm, she cleared her worktable. Broken shell scattered in all directions. The saw bounced off the floor with a clatter and they both jumped, glancing toward the shut door, to see if anyone would come to investigate. But the distant doings of the house continued undisturbed.

Lunurin's face creased into a laugh. "They're avoiding my tantrums, I fear."

Alon kissed the wrinkles above her pert nose. "Good… if anyone comes to check on us, I might do something drastic."

"Promise?" Lunurin teased.

Alon grinned. He lifted Lunurin onto the edge of the desk and went down on his knees. He gazed up at her, taking in the plump fullness of her kissed lips, how they parted enticingly, her panting breasts under the sky blue and semi-translucent piña-silk of her blouse. She was magnificent. He went under it, nuzzling against the soft skin of her belly, feeling her abs tense and twitch, up into the valley of her breasts before he found the sensitive peaks, leaving them pebbled and tight under his tongue.

He loved the way she wrapped around him, dragging him in, her whispered encouragements tickling in his ear.

"Yes, yes, yes—" The rest was lost in a sigh of pure satisfaction as he closed his mouth over her breast, doing some nibbling of his own. He bent lower, the complicated lotus flower knot of her tapis skirt blooming open at a tug. Alon filled the space between her thighs, seeking her heat, delving in the way that made her buck up into him, such that he had to pin her hips to protect his nose.

No teasing, no time. Soon enough they'd be needed; all of Aynila demanded their attention these days. But let him taste the salt and musk of her now, warm and so very present. Everything he needed. Her hands locked into his hair, ornaments and ties falling loose under her demanding fingers, tracing encouragements up and down the back of his neck so delicately compared to the way her strong calves hooked over his shoulders, bunching and flexing as she arched and pointed her toes. Her quiet panting made her belly flutter delightfully under his hand.

When she was hot and wet and tugging with familiar desperation at his hair, he followed her pull up, sealing his mouth over hers, and sliding home, drinking down her moans like the sweetest coconut wine.

She was so much and all around him, the only sea he wanted to dive into and never come up for air.

He'd learned not to squander such moments. Not when time was so very short.

6

INEZ NG DAKILA

She shouldn't be doing this. Alon had spies specifically for tasks like this. But after Rosa's naming, the priest, the converts, and the threat of the Codicíans' planned return with an armada... Inez could feel the past, an old poison welling up again. She needed to see it for herself. She needed to see it up close and know if she, too, would break like her sister had, like everyone around her seemed to be waiting for. Why else did they treat her so carefully? They could see her shatter points too.

She had to know.

It'd been easy enough to convince her friend Bernila to tell anyone who asked after her that Casama had asked for help with a few of the dyers who'd newly been named tide-touched. Besides, with so many injured in the crowd crush, there would be no lessons. And Inez was useless for anything but menial labor about the infirmary, changing bedding and hauling buckets of saltwater. She couldn't deal with the repeat humiliation of being useless in an emergency.

It was easy to make the decision to slip away. Alon could chide her later.

On her way to the only Christian shrine she knew of, she passed through a busy palengke market, weaving with the crowd and avoiding laden carts towed by horned carabao. As she went, she bought ripe purple mangosteens for breakfast. One thing led to another, and the stall owner had soon talked her into okoy fritters: tiny river shrimp in a crisp rice batter with shreds of green papaya and bean sprouts for crunch. The oil from the okoy clung to her fingers, making it hard to squeeze one of the mangosteens open between her palms. As she passed under a particularly large balete tree, where people left offerings in the crevices of the twisted trunk for protection and good luck, Inez paused. But she saw no Christian iconography among the jasmine garlands, betel nut packets, and rooster feathers. These were offerings to the anito of the forest.

Inez tucked a white segment of the ripe purple mangosteen into the tangled, pocketed trunk and murmured, "Tabi tabi po."

She waited politely for any response, but the balete and any anito that might call its branches home made no response. The rustling of leaves overhead only sent a scattering of sunlight across the shadowy space beneath the tangled roots, dancing across her face like a kiss of butterfly wings.

Why couldn't the bay be so polite?

Inez walked on.

Alon was right. Aynila had come alive with many gods. Maybe that was why the bay pulled her attention in so many different directions and left her feeling so scattered.

She was close now to the place where the Codicíans had first found local Aynilans worshiping the statue of Anitun

Tabu, which they'd renamed Santa María, Our Lady of Sorrows. On a beach not far from the port, a small shrine and a cross had been erected to mark the location of the "miracle" of Santa María turning to wood and salt.

How Cat had craved such recognition for her piety and devotion, eager to prove her worthiness by her acts of faith. She'd been furious with how little Lunurin prized her role embodying Santa María in the pageantry of her Saint's Day Festival. If Catalina had been named after Santa María and granted the Church's blessing to embody her, Inez expected she would've spent weeks before in fasting and silent prayer to purge the base sin of humanity from herself like the ascetic saints she so venerated.

Cat had considered Lunurin's lack of veneration for her patron saint a great failing. She'd known everything about her own patron saint, who was lesser known but locally venerated in Codicía, Santa Catalina de Palma. Her life had been marked by service to laborers and farmers, and a great devotion to the Church, which was rewarded when she was visited by visions of devils and angels and went into ecstasy for the last years of her life. Lunurin came from a long line of saints.

Catalina had insisted it was divine proof she'd chosen the right path. Inez thought their mother had named her so in hopes of increasing the chances that Abbess Magdalena de Palma would take them in. Inez had been named after Santa Inés, the patroness of bodily purity and chastity, to prove she was meant for the convent. Of course, when her namesake was forced into a brothel, her body was sanctified by God so that all who saw it were blinded. Inez had spent many hours in prayer for such protection from roving eyes and hands.

Inez had always wondered why Catalina craved sainthood so, when all the women saints Inez knew of were doomed to terrible tragedy. But Cat had not been alone in her veneration. Judging by how well-tended the shrine to Santa María looked, it had not been forgotten by the faithful of Aynila.

Inez picked her way across the sand beneath the nipa palms, unaccountably nervous. She scanned the shore, alert for the long dark bodies of slumbering crocodiles. She spotted a tangle of sunning scaly limbs near the mangroves at the far side of the beach, but tore her gaze away, keeping her attention on the shrine. Surely if she paid them no attention, they would ignore her too?

The palm eaves over the little alcove had been changed recently. Below the cross someone had erected a number of small saints' statues. Inez recognized Santo Niño with Santa María and Josep beside him. Nearly a full nativity. The partly open interior of the shrine had been swept since the latest storms. A few pools of wax indicated where candles had burned down. Inez placed her last mangosteen on the ledge and cleaned a wilted spike of fire orchids away.

She stood quietly a moment and wondered if she ought to try to pray. What had she come here for, again? It had felt so important last night, with Catalina's ghost breathing down her back, her scars rubbed raw by the bay.

What made the saints of the Codicíans' god different from all the many anito and idols of the islands? Seafaring folk, merchants, and sailors came and went, bringing their stories and gods. If she prayed to these saints and left offerings, would they awaken with the power of the Amihan Moon? Would they rumble like the crocodiles, or shiver in the leaves like the balete? Or, transplanted so far from their native soils without their priests to tend them, would they remain as blind and dumb as they had when she'd prayed to them in their church?

Anger bloomed, swift as the cut of a knife. These were worse than dead gods. They were cruel. Kinder gods would not have demanded her sister betray them all to prove her faithfulness. And no saint had ever heeded Inez's desperate prayers as a girl.

Inez pulled herself away from the razor-edged thought. It wasn't true that no one had heard her. It had been Lunurin, wielding lightning at her fingertips, who listened, who lifted the pain away. Alon and the Lakan who had granted her the sea's mercy. Aman Sinaya hadn't closed her ears to Inez's pleas.

What she'd needed then was healing. And the sea had provided. So why couldn't she offer others the same? Why didn't the sea sing of mercy to her ears, no matter how hard she listened. Couldn't Aman Sinaya see how hard she was trying?

These little gods were deaf and dumb. To prove it to herself, she murmured her way through an Ave María. Silence. Nothing. Only the nagging feeling Catalina would be disappointed in her for not saying at least ten, with how long it had been since she'd attended confession. They sat on her tongue, waiting for her to finish her penance.

Penance for what? She'd always wanted to ask. They should be asking penance of her, begging on their knees, and it would never be enough.

She lingered a moment longer, stretching out her senses, determined to prove these silent statues and their terrible cross held no more power over her.

All there was here was the breeze playing through the palms overhead, and the lapping of waves on the beach.

"Who do you listen for?" came a low hiss from the tangled

bodies sunning beside the mangroves at the far edge of the beach.

So clear and direct. Clearer even than they'd been in the bay with Rosa.

Inez did not need to turn her head to know that reptilian golden eyes gleamed from under arching roots. *Not good*.

"Not for you po," she muttered under her breath. She should get out of here before her listening caught the attention of any more anito. This was exactly the opposite of what Alon had advised, wasn't it? She shouldn't be here, chasing the ghost of her sister's betrayal.

But before she could turn to leave, another figure cast their shadow over the altar.

Inez shuffled to the side. She kept her head bowed, mumbling her way through her Ave Marías, and watching from under her lashes.

It was a woman, older than Inez, her hair covered by a blue veil that mostly shielded her face. But her skin seemed a touch paler than most native to the archipelago, more golden than the rich brown hue most achieved after the long, hot dry season. Inez hated when Jeian's disdain for mestizos like her was vindicated.

The woman set a spray of white dama de noche on the altar, crossed herself, and stepped back to stand beside Inez. The sweet smell suffused the small space quickly.

Inez continued her Ave Marías, wracking her brain for the best way to make her exit before she was recognized. Why hadn't she thought of wearing a veil or salakót hat to conceal her own face? If the woman was devout, she must have attended Mass in the Palisade.

A snatch of the other woman's prayers caught her ear. "—blessed Santa Catalina—God our Father—holy love—"

Inez nearly reached out and seized her. Luckily, old habit carried her lips into the Glory Be without pause. But no matter how she strained to hear, she caught no more details besides a stray "grace" and "faithfulness." The rush of the incoming tide was too close and too loud. Why did this woman pray to Santa Catalina? She wasn't a popular saint here in Aynila, not like Santa María and Santo Niño. Inez had never heard anyone talk much about her, except her sister and Abbess Magdalena.

She ignored a rustle of scale on sand that seemed far closer now.

"Why pray to silent saints, when we can hear you so well, little sister?" asked a big female crocodile with a throat rumble that Inez felt through her feet. It took everything in her not to bolt away from the water.

At last, the other woman completed her prayers with an amen.

"Who is Santa Catalina patron of?" Inez asked.

The other woman studied her. Inez was glad she'd had the presence of mind to tuck her mutya necklace beneath the collar of her shirt. The top of the strand might even appear like a rosary tucked close to her heart.

"She is the patroness of martyrs and all who are persecuted for their faith."

So, she did not mean Catalina's namesake, the patron saint of farmers and fieldworkers. Who was this patroness of martyrs?

"We could use her guiding hand these days," Inez agreed.

"I hope you weren't caught up in the attack at the Our Lady of Sorrows Mass?"

"Umm… no. I tend to pray alone these days," Inez said.

"If you would prefer not to pray alone, there is a group

of us who meet for vespers. You could learn more of Santa Catalina…"

Inez found her head pulled up on a string, just as the other woman had no doubt intended. "Oh, I have so missed… vespers." Her lies were beginning to sound thin even to her own ears, but apparently not to this evangelist.

"We have a new location since the attack. This week it will be on Wednesday in a warehouse along the river. Count four docks up from the old Palisade bridge. Tell them Our Lady of the Rosary sent you."

Inez inclined her head graciously. "I hope I will see you there. I'm so glad we were lucky enough to cross paths."

"There's no luck, when it comes to faith." The woman crossed herself and left the shelter of the shrine.

Inez shouldn't go. There was no need. She should just tell Lunurin and Alon.

She looked back at the little shrine, the serene-faced saints, the dark wood of the cross. They held no power, nothing but old wounds. She'd proved it. She was stronger than that now. But Santa Catalina… Phantom pain rippled across her back. Her mind spun. What if they weren't just fanatics whispering to dead gods?

What if her sister really had returned?

7

LUNURIN CALILAN NG DAKILA

Alon encouraged Lunurin to spend some time on Hilaga, where she'd have full access to Sina's forge and workroom. Lunurin took a bangka across the Saliwain River to the metalworkers' conclave. She needed to make real progress so she could focus on the upcoming Amihan Moon.

While they labored over Rosa's mutya, she and Sina finally had time to talk. Lunurin had been so busy with the Lakan preparing for the arriving delegates, she had not had much time to spend with her friend. The firetender was preparing for one of the most momentous occasions for Amihan's chosen in a lifetime. The very air in the enclave seemed to hum with all the preparation and excitement.

"I'm not pulling you away, am I?" Lunurin asked. "You can pawn me off on someone else."

Sina shook her head. "Nonsense. Shaping your first mutya is a big responsibility. And my mother is tending the sacred flame tonight. She'll not let anyone else near the peak until she's seen signs that Hilaga has accepted back the dead spark-striker."

But Lunurin could read the stress in the set of Sina's broad shoulders. Ceremonial soot from offering Amihan's messenger bird back still stained her fingers and smudged her face where she kept rubbing at the old scar bisecting her brow.

"So Hilaga is unsettled," Lunurin surmised.

"Yes, but not in the way she should be. We expect rumblings and so, this is a year given to fire. It's just…" Sina grimaced, gesturing like she could pull the right words out of the air, making the forge and every oil lamp in the room flare.

"That good, huh?"

"So, take yesterday's pearl dives. There should have been only firetenders named. Or at least, many more firetenders than any other gods-blessed. Not that Rosa and all the new tide-touched aren't a blessing, of course!" Sina added hastily.

"Could it just be that with so many tide-touched lost to the Inquisition, we're still finding our balance? By numbers, there are still more firetenders." Lunurin tried to reassure Sina. But she and Inez had been guarding the oyster beds all week for fear of a spate of accidental namings. She'd thought it odd that Inez had only had to make one save.

The Lakan had been thrilled her ruling that only adults would be allowed to dive had held, but children named far too young were what you expected in an Amihan Moon year. That was how it'd gone when Lunurin witnessed an Amihan Moon as a young child in Calilan.

"Maybe, but something about the balance of magic feels off. All the oldest firetenders agree. I suppose, with you in Aynila, we'd not get droughts and fires. But it's not what we expect. Meanwhile, the sea and wet season storms are set to be so strong this year… My mother fears it will grant the laho more power."

Lunurin's skin prickled. The massive sea dragon was terrifying, even without the boost the pooling of the archipelago's magic would grant it during the Amihan Moon. Though it hungered, it must never actually be allowed to eat the moon. It was the responsibility of Hilaga's firetenders and all the people of Aynila to ensure that didn't happen.

"Is there anything we can do?" Lunurin asked.

Sina grinned wickedly. "You'd make Jeian's whole month if you convince Alon to let us deal with that Lusitan slave ship anchored beyond the port. We could burn it to the waterline as an offering to Amihan."

Lunurin winced. The Lakan's policy of barring slave ships from entering the port but not denying their resupply had been yet another point of contention between the brothers.

"We have enough enemies with only the Codicians. We don't need every foreign empire determined to wipe us out. I like it no more than you, but they'll be resupplied and gone any day now. I don't think even you want all those deaths on our heads," Lunurin replied.

Sina lifted one shoulder. "You asked. Anyway, we don't know it *wouldn't* work."

They labored on the mutya late into the night, till their eyes started to play tricks in the lamplight and Isko chided them for working too hard. "Don't think I won't tell Alon you worked through the night."

He came over to the workbench, studying the fruit of their efforts. Lunurin held a handful of mother-of-pearl raindrops cut from the offcut edges of the shell, which she was carefully drilling holes into.

Sina turned her head absentmindedly and kissed his

frowning mouth as she twisted gold wire into a many-toothed comb. "You're no better. How are you only now coming home? Don't tell me Alon and Jeian are still at each other's throats."

Isko hesitated. "The Lakan still has me hovering as though they are. But no, it's just been busy. Come to bed when you finish." He wiped the smudged soot from his wife's brow and left them to it.

~

It took most of the night, and half the next day, plus Sina's expertise and deft hand with gold wire wrapping, but Rosa's mutya was finally finished. Lunurin wished she could've taken more time, but it would be cruel to make Rosa wait for her mutya any longer than necessary.

As Lunurin put the finishing touches onto the final twist of wire that would hold the mother-of-pearl to the comb, Sina said, "See, it's beautiful. I don't know why you were so scared to make Inez's."

Lunurin grimaced and glared at her. She didn't need the reminder of how much she'd failed Inez. By tradition, it should have been her presenting Inez to dive; her who accepted the oyster and named Inez to the old gods.

Sina winced. "Sorry, that was supposed to come out more supportive."

"I don't think Inez will ever forgive me," Lunurin lamented. "I wish Alon and I weren't pulled in a dozen directions right now. I worry we're failing her."

"She'll find her way. It isn't all on you. You both have a much bigger family now, and Aizza is supervising her training closely. Even the Lakan is always ready to make time for her.

It's hard for every gods-blessed the first few years. Look at Biti, she's burned down her second forge. At least it's the wet season now, so the flames aren't likely to spread too quickly."

Lunurin sighed. "I wish everything didn't feel so fragile. I don't want any more omens!"

"That, I understand." Sina leaned close, showing Lunurin how to cinch the wires even tighter. "We can weld the joins, for extra security."

"*No need,*" the goddess of storms whispered, warm and pleased as a summer storm.

"Lintik, come to me," Lunurin whispered, conjuring a single seed of lightning to her fingertip before she sent it zapping down to weld the twist together into a singular whole.

Sina picked it up, turning Lunurin's handiwork back and forth in her hands. "Oh, I will have to remember that trick. It has a different quality to the way a firetender would accomplish it."

"You're sure it's ready?" Lunurin asked, staring at their creation.

They had wired a mother-of-pearl thunderhead to a gold wire comb of Sina's making. The lines of wire detailing the swirls on the face of the "cloud" brought it all together. There was a gold filigree setting for the lightning pearl, and sparkling chains of sunlight trailing every raindrop.

Sina drew a fingertip over their handiwork. "Clouds are not symmetrical. Now get yourself home before Alon sends a search party to find you. You have a mutya to bestow on your new student."

~

Lunurin repeated this mantra to herself—*clouds are not symmetrical*—as Rosa opened the lacquered jewelry box holding her mutya. The cook had laid a generous merienda spread, from chewy palitaw rice cakes coated in shredded coconut and sesame to fluffy white siopao buns stuffed with pork. But Lunurin was too anxious to take a bite. She sipped coconut water, relishing the coolness in the face of the relentless heat and humidity of the early wet season.

Rosa hadn't said a word. Lunurin hid a wince. *Goddess mine defend me, she hates it.* Lunurin should have boxed up the oyster, the pearl, Rosa, and shipped all three off to Calilan as soon as she'd been named. What better gesture of goodwill could there be?

What had she been thinking, trying to make someone's mutya?

"It's traditional," Lunurin started, "for a stormcaller's mutya to be a hair ornament, but if you would prefer a pendant…"

Rosa looked up, her dark eyes glistening with a hint of tears. "It's beautiful, but I've no idea how to wear it."

Lunurin smiled in relief. "That, at least, I can teach you."

She wished she had any other wisdom or guidance she could offer.

She went around the low table to kneel behind Rosa. "May I?"

Rosa nodded, and Lunurin gathered the younger woman's hair in her hands. Long, straight, and inky black, she would not have as much trouble as Lunurin did keeping it bound.

"Braided buns are most secure for my hair, but as you've no curls, let me show you a knotted style my tiya preferred."

Lunurin had come prepared, with a bottle of sesame hair oil, a horn comb, and a dozen indigo-dyed hair ribbons. First, she oiled Rosa's long hair, which reached down to her waist. Lunurin wondered how quickly it would grow once she'd taken up her mutya and the mantle of a stormcaller. Then, she gathered the hair onto the top of her head in a simple but secure knot.

"At night I keep mine braided. Now that you've taken up your mutya, you must never let it down until your teachers tell you. An untrained stormcaller can do a great deal of damage, even during the wet season."

"Teachers?" Rosa asked. "There are others in the temple school who can teach a stormcaller?"

Lunurin winced. She had not yet broached the fact that she couldn't train Rosa.

She secured the knotted bun in place with a few ribbons. "There. You can just take the loop of hair from the center, catch it on a tine of your mutya, and press it in along the front edge to secure it all with just your comb. At first though, it's easier to have extra ties, so nothing comes loose."

Rosa held the box out to her. "Would you?"

Lunurin was taken aback once again by the trust in Rosa's open expression. Would she shatter it when she told Rosa she'd have to be sent away from her home for training?

Lunurin lifted the comb carefully from the box. It felt different now than when she'd been making it. Since being bestowed upon Rosa it had changed, no longer simply one sacred oyster among many. This was Rosa's mutya; through it she had been chosen by Anitun Tabu, and it would forever bind her to the goddess of storms.

As she tucked the comb into Rosa's hair, she felt a dozen curious winds sweep in through the windows, twining like friendly street cats around the pair of them.

Rosa stretched out her hands, weaving them into the

breezes and tugging. They coiled tighter and faster, a visible cyclone grabbing and yanking sheets of banana leaf from the table along with the ribbons, shreds of coconut—

Lunurin dragged down a loop of her own hair, tangling the tail of the cyclone into her tresses and binding it back up with an experienced counter twist. The spinning breezes fell apart and lost direction. She swept them back out of the windows into the clear afternoon sky.

"And that is why it's very important that you don't train in Aynila." Lunurin did not dare release the seed of the cyclone Rosa had unwittingly called into being. Fed into the open air, where it could drag a dozen high-altitude currents into its orbit, they'd have a tornado ripping apart the indigo huts, or worse, a waterspout tearing down the bustling Saliwain River.

Isko would have a fit. He'd already banned Inez from training at home after a certain dye vat tidal event.

Rosa wrung her hands together. "I'm sorry, I didn't know—"

Lunurin laid her hand over Rosa's. "I know. It's my fault. I should've given you your mutya somewhere you'd have more space. Next time, we'll try the lava flats, or out on the bay."

Rosa grimaced. "I just wanted to say hello back. I've never felt the wind like that."

"Breezes are friendly. The problem is they're very... suggestible. Even the most refreshing breeze doesn't need much convincing that it would rather remove a roof." Lunurin twirled her fingertips upward in demonstration.

"Oh."

"It's why stormcallers do not train on the main islands of the archipelago. Between training mishaps and how much typhoons are drawn to us, it's easiest to deflect our mistakes if we are already on the barrier islands," Lunurin explained.

Rosa's expression shifted. "But you stay in Aynila."

"I trained on Calilan."

Rosa balked. "I can't train on Calilan."

"Maybe not Calilan, but any of the Stormfleet delegates coming to the Amihan Moon Summit will be far better equipped to train a young stormcaller—"

"No—I am Aynilan. I belong here, especially now."

"Especially now, you should be anywhere but here. Rosa, it will take years before you've trained enough to not cause more harm than good with your abilities. I will do my best during this summit to find you proper teachers. There's no reason your brother can't go with you, if he wishes. You won't have to go alone."

Rosa's expression furrowed. "We can't leave. You're supposed to train me."

Did Alon feel this inadequate with Inez?

Lunurin sighed. "I'm sorry. This wasn't how I intended to tell you. But it will be for the best, I promise. I am not someone you should emulate."

"You're wrong!" That stubborn chin wobbled dangerously, and Lunurin felt the accusation anyone less in awe of her would've hurled. Rosa turned and fled, bruised as a thunderhead threatening rain. It was all Lunurin could do to keep her distress from yanking all the breezes back into the room and lifting the nipa palm roofing straight off the upper story.

As Rosa's stormfront rolled out, Inez rushed in, turbulent as a frothing wave. Lunurin braced herself. Had something gone wrong at the healing halls? Surely, Alon wouldn't have pushed her to heal so soon, and right after the crush?

"Inez?" Lunurin called out, before she ran off to her room.

Obviously talking to Alon about her concerns hadn't gone as well as Lunurin had hoped.

Inez hesitated at the top of the stairs, her back to Lunurin. The light silk of her top had melded to her skin with the humidity and her exertion. Her scars stood out darkly across the expanse of her back. Alon and the Lakan had done their best to heal them down as smoothly as possible, but the deep purple-reddish coloration refused to fade, despite the years. Lunurin felt another spasm of sympathy.

"How were things at the healing halls?" she broached, hoping Inez might turn to face her.

Inez sounded upset. "Fine."

"I've got your favorite, palitaw…" Lunurin wheedled. Cook had pulled out the kabayo, a coconut grating stool specifically for the fresh coconut threads coating the rice cake.

Inez let out a huge sigh and came into the sitting area, dropping down long-limbed and dramatic on the cushions. "It's about Catalina."

Lunurin froze.

There were a lot of things she was prepared to face, including a sixty-gun galleon under full sail. But it seemed impossible to talk to Inez about Catalina without dragging up all her trauma and guilt from the last terrible days of the Palisade. They just ended up screaming at each other. Lunurin was so tired of fighting about Cat. It felt too much like fighting *with* Cat.

"What about her?" Lunurin asked carefully.

Inez's expression darkened, and she exploded. "Why won't you even say her name when we're alone? What are you so afraid of? Why can't we talk about my sister?"

Lunurin's heart twisted painfully. So many had died because she'd refused to see that Cat would never change.

"Where is this coming from? Is it because of the priest? You don't have to go to the healing halls until the Lakan has decided what to do with him."

"No." Inez flopped back on the cushions, looking away. "I didn't go to the healing halls today."

"What? Why? Inez, I know yesterday was difficult, but you know they need all the trained hands they can get in the infirmary right now."

Inez snorted derisively, throwing her hands up over her head for inspection. "Mine are hardly trained."

Lunurin moved to sit beside her, trying to catch her eye. "But you know what the healers need and when to make them rest. You're doing valuable work and getting important experience just assisting."

"What's the point if I won't ever be able to heal?" Inez demanded, pushing herself up on her hands to face Lunurin at last.

Lunurin reached out and squeezed her arm reassuringly. "I know it's hard, Inez, but you can't ignore what your power is meant for. If you don't find ways to channel it, it's far more likely to hurt you and others."

"How am I supposed to do that with all this noise? I've been trying and trying, and I'm so tired of failing! I'm getting worse at shaping the sea than I was in the beginning! Everything is wrong and I want to stop. I want to stop, and you of all people should understand," Inez wailed.

Lunurin tried to soothe her, but Inez pulled out of her hold. "You're not failing, you're learning. I know you'll figure this out. You have good teachers. You can trust them. You need to learn this."

"You are such a hypocrite. You suppressed your power for years!" Inez spat.

"And you saw how it hurt me. Hurt everyone around me. I was destroying pieces of myself. Inez, look at me." Lunurin's throat ached like she had a hailstone stuck there. "You want to talk about your sister? I suppressed and hid my power from her because I was afraid of frightening her. Look how much more I hurt her than if I'd been honest from the beginning. You might still have her if I weren't so stubborn. Don't repeat my mistakes."

Inez dropped her gaze, anger in every line of her frame. "That's not what I mean."

"Then what do you mean?"

"I heard—" Inez stopped. "I don't know. People were saying things about her."

"What kind of things?" Lunurin asked, worried suddenly that the riots and the priest's arrest might have brought Catalina's betrayal of the tide-touched village back into people's minds. Inez didn't need that legacy attached to her. Lunurin wouldn't let that crime rest on her shoulders. "Who's saying it? Was Jeian muttering his usual nonsense again?"

"No, I heard... I thought..." Inez shook her head. "Never mind."

Lunurin took a deep breath and a step back from the pain of old betrayals. "I understand if the situation with the priest has been upsetting. I know it's unsettled me. But you can't let this convince you to stop learning to heal entirely. Everything will settle back to normal once the Amihan Moon has passed."

Inez swiped a hand across her eyes. Her teardrops slashed across the room violently, cutting shallow divots into the bamboo walls. "You aren't listening!"

"You need a break. I understand that. We'll let Alon know you'd like to train with Casama in the dyeing huts until after the Amihan Moon has passed. How about that?"

Inez rubbed furiously at the patch of scarring that curled over her shoulder, then pushed to her feet. "You never listen. I'm no good at anything a tide-touched should be. Even the bay feels wrong. Trying harder is just making the crocodiles' voices louder."

Lunurin reached out, but Inez twitched her hand out of reach and strode away. Lunurin pressed her fist to her forehead, wishing momentarily she could split open her skull and grate everything smooth on the kabayo that had produced the fine threads of coconut now strewn about the room. If she couldn't handle two young women, that did not bode well for her success with their Stormfleet allies and her family. What had the Lakan been thinking, asking her of all people to be a diplomat?

8

◆━◆

INEZ NG DAKILA

Inez hadn't been planning to attend the vespers. But after her blowup at Lunurin, she knew she needed more than a half-mumbled prayer she might have overheard. Lunurin wanted details. Inez would get details.

It couldn't be coincidence, and it wasn't just Jeian's distrust of converts spreading like Lunurin seemed to think. Inez had to know what people were saying about her sister. Bernila had told her no one was allowed anywhere near the priest except Alon, not even other healers, so these converts were her best bet.

There was something hauntingly familiar about sneaking through the streets of Aynila after dark. Following the bank of the Saliwain, listening to the rush of the water, not knowing where she was being led. The fear and pain, and the anger—she jerked away from the sense-memory in the water.

Tonight, she wasn't tide-touched. She was a faithful convert, just like everyone else. She'd worn an unusually high-necked dark blouse that completely covered her scars, and a dark veil for further anonymity. Yet even the modesty of the attire brought back memories of the convent and her old life. As a comforting counterpoint, the balisong pendant of her mutya weighed against her breastbone, a reminder of her identity now.

At first, she'd scoffed at the idea of vespers with a bunch of secretive converts in a warehouse. What would vespers be without the solemn tolling of the church bell calling the faithful, the choir hymns, the hundred or more gathered together in prayer? The high vaulted ceiling of the cathedral, the glitter of stolen mother-of-pearl. But tonight, the past was alive, and not just in the cadence of the hymn. There was no escaping it.

Before she could think better of it, she knocked on a door marked with a wooden rosary wrapped around the handle, offering the cryptic message that Our Lady of the Rosary had directed her here.

She was allowed in. The dark interior of the warehouse was warm and hazy with collected bodies and the smoke of lit candles, like a sea of distant stars. She'd missed the introduction. There seemed to be around twenty or thirty gathered, but it was hard to get a gauge of all those present before the candle-laden makeshift altar.

Sina would call this a fire hazard. Inez studied the shadowy corners of the warehouse, piled high with sacks and boxes. Was it food? Cloth? Something more flammable?

The group moved into a psalm reading, and Inez shuffled deeper into the room.

"Save me, O God,
for the waters have come up to my neck."

Inez shivered, thinking of how the sea had risen in the

Palisade; how people climbed and climbed and could not escape.

"I sink in deep mire,
where there is no foothold;
I have come into deep waters,
and the flood sweeps over me."

Alon, with the aid of Aynila's tide-touched ghosts, had brought the flood, dragged it higher and higher, in vengeance for the massacre of the tide-touched village on the slopes of Mount Hilaga. Inez wished she had been tide-touched then. She'd have helped, gladly.

"I am weary with my crying;
my throat is parched...
More in number than the hairs of my head
are those who hate me without cause..."

It wasn't hard to guess how the converts felt about the tide-touched... and would feel about Inez, if they realized who she was. Still, there was something as comforting as it was heartbreaking about the cadence of psalm. Inez slipped into the flow and pattern of it with an ease that frightened her. It was far simpler than diving into the bay.

As she listened and made response through the prayers and psalms, she eased toward the altar. She didn't recognize the man leading the prayer group; she'd never seen him attend a Mass in the Palisade. He did not look mestizo, like her and the woman who'd directed her here.

Whispered conversations flowed around her in the dark, like water on a pebbled shore.

"I hear they're holding Father Ortiz in the water witch's temple."

"They should be ashamed."

"They say Archbishop de Palma will soon return to reclaim his seat in Aynila. Soon enough, our trials will be over."

"It won't be soon enough if they have Father Ortiz now."

"I won't even set foot on the central delta since they raised that abomination before God."

"Wasn't Lord Alon baptized? Could we petition him for the father's release?"

"That was before he married a witch."

"Brother Arcilla say she's Our Lady of Sorrows in truth. If only she could see the evils the water witches have brought to our city, she might listen."

"They are literalist fools. She brought the storm. I was there in the church, I saw it. Brother Arcilla would not suggest it if he'd been here then."

"If Santa Catalina believes she can be saved, I believe she'll listen to reason."

Inez tried to move toward the source of that last murmured hope, and the one who knew the prayer leader's name. *Arcilla.* She would remember it.

Arcilla seemed to have realized the room's attention was drifting from the readings. He cleared his throat. "On that note, let's say a special prayer to Our Lady of the Rosary, Santa Catalina, to intercede on behalf of Father Ortiz."

Inez edged closer to the front, straining to catch every word of their plea to Santa Catalina.

"Santa Catalina, we faithful dutifully prepare the way for you. We beg you to intercede on behalf of a faithful man of God, Father Ortiz, who, following the missionary's path, has fallen into hardship. We beg that you will bring the light of God back into Our Lady of Sorrows' heart, that she will smile upon us once more. That she will return Aynila to a true and holy path. May your coming be swift and true."

"Amen," Inez chorused, her head swimming. The room felt too close and hot, the flickering candlelight far too bright. She'd wound too deeply into the crowd. Could they see her face? Recognize her? Her heart beat fast in her throat, making it hard to breathe.

But there was no way to move, to get out into the fresh night air, without drawing a dangerous amount of attention to herself.

Arcilla stepped down from the makeshift altar into the gathered worshipers. "Brothers and sisters, who else needs intercession? What prayer requests can we raise together?"

A woman lifted her hand and stepped closer to the altar, into the light. "Might I request Saint Augustine's prayer for the sick?"

The woman was pregnant. Horror dawned as Inez realized how ill she was. Her request was labored with her shortness of breath, her cheeks flushed with far more than the heat of the room. Her face and hands were visibly swollen with pooling fluid.

"In the absence of Father Ortiz, let us lay hands together upon our dear sister and pray with her for the safe delivery of her child," Brother Arcilla intoned.

The crowd moved. Inez found herself being swept along, pressed close against the pregnant woman. She tried to push herself back, to create some space between them, but the woman misunderstood, taking her hand and pressing it over her distended belly. She was warm—no, hot, burning with fever. Inez flinched and tried to pull away, but the press of the crowd was inescapable. Hands reached around her, touched her back and shoulders. Her scars ached. Bile rose in her throat.

And through the waters of the woman's womb, far more like the ocean than the blood Alon was always trying to get her to sense, Inez felt how very wrong things had gone and were about to go. This woman didn't need prayers. She needed a tide-touched healer, and soon.

Inez was such a poor example of one, she couldn't even tell what was wrong, only that what should have been a safe, nourishing sea for the fetus was contaminated, and so hot. The fetus was struggling like a drowner, gasping, gasping.

Inez tore her hand away from the woman's belly. Desperation clawed up her back, old scars burning anew. It was faith like this, like Catalina's, that insisted every ailment could be prayed away. It was faith like this that killed, that led to betrayal and death, and so much pain. It was this faith that had poisoned her sister.

The heat of the room was so close. Sweat broke out all over her body. This woman was letting herself and her child die because she believed in prayer. Because her faith had taught her to fear tide-touched healers more than she feared the sickness burning within her. And the port was so near. Inez wished that she were the kind of tide-touched who could use the salt of her patient's blood, or a stray tear, to work a quick and subtle healing.

But all she had was desperation. Even trying to reach for the bay was too overwhelming, so she ended up tuning in to reptilian whispers in the dark.

As the prayer ended and the pressure of the crowd eased, Inez leaned close. "You are sick beyond prayers. Beyond even one of the Tianchaowen herb-healers. Have you seen anyone for the fever—"

The woman pushed Inez away. "And let godless heathens put their poisons in me? Get away. Prayer is the path to healing. My faith will be rewarded."

"I'm trying to help you!" Inez snapped, suddenly angry beyond reason at everyone in this smoky warehouse. "You're burning up; you're dying!"

"Who are you?"

More hands grabbed Inez, pulling the veil from her head. Inez tried to yank herself free, but there were so many hands in the dark. Inez's skin crawled. This was so much worse than the bay.

"A spy? A non-believer?"

"Who told you where we were meeting?"

"Who sent you?"

Dozens of voices overlapping, shouting, hands pulling at Inez's arms, her clothes. Fear seized her by the throat, choking tight. Desperation churned in her belly, ugly, angry, and vicious. Inez reached for her mutya and her power, unsure if she could fight her way out of this crush with just a knife. In all her many lessons with Sina on the use of her balisong knife, and with Lunurin in self-defense, there'd never been more than two other sparring partners.

In this mob, she could hardly move, much less fight. She twisted, felt the material of one sleeve give and tear as a man tried to wrestle her arms behind her back. It gave her enough movement to reach, her perspiration-damp fingertips making contact with the temple of one of her attackers. The blackness roiling in her belly flowed through her like deep water. In that desperate, furious, hateful moment, Inez managed something she'd never once achieved in the halls of healing. The man dropped, unconscious in an instant, his awareness snatched into her sweating palm.

Inez watched him crumple as if sinking through water, slowly, slowly, stunned at the power at the tips of her fingers.

But she wasn't out of danger yet. Others lunged at her, hurling invectives. She flung her power out through the salt pooling on her palms and wherever sweat-slicked hands grabbed her. How dare they touch her? How dare they grasp and scream? One touch and she could silence them, dragging them down into the deep waters of her soul. She'd thought she lacked a healer's salt well, but no. The waters of her fear went deep.

Hands went slack and fell away, their vile words silenced. Her skin stopped crawling. Would that she could've made men stop touching her as easily as this long ago.

Bodies crashed insensate to the packed dirt floor. Two, three, five—

Feeling their numbers dwindling, the crowd scrambled back, screaming in fear. "Witch! Devil!"

Several people Inez hadn't even touched dropped to their knees praying to God, to their holy Santa Catalina for protection against witch-workings.

Inez didn't hesitate. She didn't have time. She had to get out. Out of this press of bodies, out of the smoky warehouse. She needed to get to the water. She had to find somewhere to pour out this terrifying deep-water drowning.

She reached for the port but shied at the way the bay roared in her head. It was not what she needed. The quietest space was once more under armored crocodile scales. *"Caught in a feeding frenzy, little sister?"*

She stumbled out into the night—sweat pouring from her skin, blood and crocodile whispers pounding in her ears—directly into the arms of Alon's spies.

9

ALON DAKILA

Alon peered over Lunurin's shoulder. She had a map of the archipelago spread across her desk. Atop it, she was charting everything they knew about the shattered Stormfleet splinters on translucent rice paper sheets. From the regions the smaller fleets patrolled to the holes in their net, ship type and number, the names of captains and particularly skilled or influential katalonan, supply ports and allegiances, all marked in indigo ink.

Invitees to the summit had been circled, the particular challenges they faced noted. Pirates plagued the Sumila Gulf; continued clashes with the Codician strongholds in Simsiman, Mamaylan, and Sugbu; general difficulties with resupply and safe dry season harbors, caused by Codician control of the archipelago's central islands. If her family had once more picked others from the Stormfleet to represent them, Lunurin would be able to speak to their concerns.

The calm of the evening and the scratch of bamboo nibs was shattered when the downstairs door of the bahay na bato slammed open, feet pounding up the stairs.

Litao called up, "Gat Alon, Dayang Lunurin, it's Inez!"

Inez stumbled in, her eyes terror-wide, one sleeve hanging from her shoulder by threads. Her hair had come loose, falling in ragged hanks across her shoulders. She looked younger than she was, a child again, frightened and in need of help.

Lunurin gathered Inez in her arms. "What happened?"

Alon grabbed the shawl Lunurin had abandoned, draping it around Inez's shoulders.

The room grew crowded as others followed her in: Litao; Isko, roused from his study; and one of his spies. Alon had a terrible suspicion. *Sea Lady have mercy.*

"Gat Alon, she was discovered at the convert prayer meeting. She knocked ten people unconscious. We await your orders," his spy reported.

"She was *where*?" Lunurin yelped.

Alon, checking Inez for injury, found nothing beyond her panic and minor bruises and scrapes. But power and terror were roaring through her like a flood, and she wasn't making any sense, hyperventilating, her words barely sensible.

"I was—converts—and Catalina—praying, and pregnant—"

"What about Cat?" The way Lunurin's voice caught on her old lover's nickname, left him winded.

Alon locked eyes with Isko. They both knew exactly what Inez had heard.

"Did you…?" Isko signed.

"No. Don't," Alon signed back firmly, ignoring his deepening frown. Now wasn't the time. They needed calm to have that difficult discussion.

Right now, his own fear had him by the throat. If Catalina really had returned, how far would Lunurin go to lay her misgivings about the past to rest? He couldn't lose her. Aynila could not afford to spare their Lady Stormbringer, not now. Catalina was one good deed that would never stop haunting him. He never should have sent her into Codician hands.

"Breathe with me, Inez, try to breathe," Lunurin coaxed.

Inez gulped for air, like a diver preparing for a deep plunge, but with none of the control. He held out his hands. Inez latched on, her grip damp with perspiration, and the flood pushed into him, washing over his head and driving him under. It was more than just the force of water—it was something grabbing him by the feet and dragging him down.

Lunurin seized him by the shoulders, pulling him up while Inez unwittingly tried to drown them both. As he struggled against the torrent, he finally recognized what it was swamping Inez and shattering her focus. It was power, concentrated by the Amihan Moon. Luckily Lunurin knew well how to weather a deluge of divine power. Through him, she soaked it up, drawing off the violent deluge while Alon reached to retrieve Inez.

Only years of experience, and Lunurin feeding wet season winds and seeds of lightning into his blood, allowed him to stay afloat and haul Inez up from the depths. They held on until Inez poured out all the magic and terror making her eyes wheel and her body gasp spasmodically for air. Had Inez's struggles over the last months been the Amihan Moon's influence the whole time?

Finally, Inez breathed from her belly, and the tale spooled out. "There's a woman, she's pregnant and she's so sick, burning up. I tried to convince her to see a healer instead of more useless prayers, but the crowd turned on me and I panicked. I panicked and I don't know what I did."

"So you put *that* in other people?" Alon asked, hoping desperately to be wrong. He turned to his spy for confirmation. "Ten?"

A nod.

"And did that include the woman?"

"I—I don't know." Inez fisted her hands and tucked them under her arms. "I panicked. I think I used healer's sleep. You'll be able to fix it, right?"

Alon pressed a hand over his eyes, horrified. Ten people, and she'd still almost managed to pull him *and* Lunurin under. "Yes, we'll try, but do you have any idea what you could've done to those people? You know how dangerous it is to hold someone under without experience and saltwater. You know the healer's mandate!"

"I didn't know what I was doing! I was afraid. They were so angry." Inez turned away from him, pressing into Lunurin's side instead.

"I trained you better than that!"

"I was alone! What was I supposed to do?"

Alon felt a pang of guilt. Inez had been so afraid. Could he blame her?

But she should never have been there. She wasn't a child who didn't know better.

"I have people to deal with this. You should never have walked into danger like that. You know the converts hate and fear the tide-touched just as much as the Codicians ever did."

"Inez is not a healer, yet," Lunurin hissed. "How dare you judge her for defending herself?"

"She is tide-touched. She can hurt people with her power. Is that what you want her to learn?" Alon retorted.

"I didn't mean—" Inez tried to get a word in, but Lunurin stepped in front of her, protective as a mother cloud leopard and just as dangerous. But Inez couldn't hide behind Lunurin forever. She needed to take responsibility.

"Not every tide-touched will be as much a peacemaker as you. Do you think Aizza worries about the people Jeian hurts with her strength flowing through his tattoos?" Lunurin challenged.

Sea Lady have mercy, but he wished Kawit were here. It was his council Alon needed. He had no idea how to teach a tide-touched who didn't—or shouldn't—heal.

Inez needed training and guidance, but toward what? If he set her to sea on a ship, would she learn to focus, or founder? And who could he entrust her to? Jeian's captains would never take a convent-raised tide-touched. He was failing her. He'd never felt anything like what Inez had just done. How could he teach her to control it?

"That's different. And you know I don't approve of Jeian's antics," Alon shot back. "Inez wouldn't have had to hurt anyone if she hadn't wandered into danger! Alone, without telling anyone what she was doing or where she would be—"

"Please, I just—" Inez tried again.

But now Lunurin was angry. There was a flash of lightning overhead, followed by a low, ominous roll of thunder. "It's your responsibility to make sure she can defend herself. You and I both know what's coming! She is tide-touched, and every Codicían on every galleon will want her as dead as either of us."

This accusation caught Alon where it hurt. It wasn't that he didn't want to teach Inez larger workings, the manipulation of the sea and waves. But when it came to open water, even in a bangka within the bay, Inez couldn't seem to trust the cradling of the tides. Alon had thought that focusing on healing might help her tap into the gentler aspects of being tide-touched, before she had to wrestle a storm surge or keep killer waves from smashing a ship to driftwood. She had to find a way to be at peace with the rhythms of the sea.

"I'm trying to train her properly."

"*Properly* won't matter if we're all dead!"

"Then help me, Lunurin! Why won't you try to train someone?" Alon asked.

"You know why."

"You're so afraid, but what if what Aynila needs is more gods-blessed like you? What becomes of Aynila, of all of us, if something happens to you?" Alon demanded.

10

LUNURIN CALILAN NG DAKILA

Maybe it was the shouting, or Alon with true fear in his voice. More likely it was that Lunurin and Catalina used to fight *just* like this.

Inez flung herself at Lunurin's middle and burst strategically into tears. She'd employed this method to defuse so many fights, but never since leaving the convent. A hard lump formed in Lunurin's throat, the memory of Cat softening to her sister's need sharp and bright. It had worked—until it hadn't. Lunurin hated that Cat hadn't been able to let go of the Church for Inez, if not for Lunurin.

Alon's words hung in the air between them.

They weren't even arguing about Inez anymore. They shouldn't be arguing like this in front of her... and half the household...

Someone had to deal with the disaster Inez had stumbled into.

"You're being unreasonable." The leaden weight of Lunurin's voice could have becalmed a fleet at full sail. "We can quarrel later. Tonight, we need to fix this."

What was Alon so afraid of? Was this all about whatever the Amihan Moon was doing to tide-touched magic? She'd never felt anything like what Inez had unleashed on them. Only fear could explain how unreasonable he was being.

"She—"

"No. A woman is sick, in need of a healer's aid. Inez cared, and I know you care," Lunurin cut him off, determined they'd say nothing to further upset Inez. "One sick woman and ten under healer's sleep. A whole prayer meeting saw Inez strike them down. We need an excuse to ferry everyone to the healing school, and to help those who need it."

"You want me to arrest an entire prayer meeting? When we're still dealing with the aftermath of Jeian's arrests and the crowd crush?" Alon balked.

"We won't arrest anyone," Lunurin insisted. "Inez has a fever. We need to trace the sickness. We'll quarantine those exposed, for the safety of Aynila."

"A fever. You want me to fabricate an outbreak?" Alon said the words slowly, voice rising at the end, aghast. "After the week we've had?"

Lunurin raised her eyebrows. "Shall we let them run wild through the streets with tales of the water witch who cursed them instead? That will improve morale."

"Please, I didn't mean..." Inez whispered, her voice cracking.

Lunurin laid a gentle hand on Inez's head. "I understand, I do. You know you can always come to us. You kept yourself safe, that's what matters. But to fix it we'll have to deal with the consequences." She lifted her head to meet Alon's dark, unreadable gaze. "Won't we?"

She could see Alon's desire for peace in Aynila warring

with his common sense, but finally he bowed to her will. "Yes, of course."

Lunurin pointed with her lips. "Isko, we need to draft fever notices to post around the warehouse district. Litao, on Gat Alon's orders, have all the converts transferred to the temple's quarantine. Inez and I will go on ahead to warn the healers. Alon—"

"Yes, I'll see that my people handle it, and we'll try to find the woman Inez noticed."

The defeat in his voice tugged at Lunurin's heart, but she plowed on. "Inez needs a fever first."

She would not hesitate. Not while Inez was in danger. She wouldn't have converts saying that Inez's accidental weaponization of healer's sleep proved all their fears and mistrust of tide-touched was justified. Not this week. Not with Ortiz returned to Aynila. She wouldn't let anyone hurt Inez like that—not even Inez herself.

"We need to move quickly."

Alon again extended his hands to Inez. "Come, let me show you how to raise a fever to show the intake healers."

Inez's expression scrunched with guilt. "Are you sure? After what I just…"

"That proves you can do this." Alon's voice was harder than Lunurin would've liked, but she let it slide, crossing to help Isko.

"You'll have to concentrate, the effect will dissipate otherwise."

Lunurin tuned out Alon's continued instructions. That was tide-touched business. She dipped the face of her wedding ring into a tray of indigo ink to stamp the outbreak warnings with the shining sun of Aynila's seal, putting the weight of the Lakan's house behind the order.

By the time they'd finished, Inez was sunk into a chair, her head lolling forward on her chest. Her face was red, sweat curling the baby hairs at her temples, her eyes half-lidded in concentration that could easily pass for illness. Satisfied, Alon went with his guards.

Not wanting to break Inez's concentration, Lunurin spoke soft and low. "You're doing great. I'm just going to carry you and get us both to the healing halls."

Lunurin slid one arm beneath Inez's bent legs, one behind her back, and lifted her with a grunt of effort. Inez had hit her growth spurt late. She was now much taller than Catalina had ever been. How much of that height came from breaking the rituals of fasting and deprivation the convent had so encouraged? They'd all grown up so used to being in want.

Lunurin swept Inez downstairs, minding her ankles and head around the stair banisters. They needed to get to the healing halls before Alon arrived.

~

Inez burned in Lunurin's hold, hotter even than a firetender, her torn blouse now drenched through with sweat.

Stepping at last into the golden lamplight of the infirmary, Lunurin called out, "Where's Aizza, I need help! Inez came home with a fever. Alon sent me ahead—he fears it's catching."

The intake healer, who had been half-dozing on an empty cot, bolted to her feet as if she'd seen a ghost. "What did Gat Alon say? Breakbone? Ague? Quickly, through here, let me examine her. Bernila! Run for Dayang Aizza," she called to a student healer working the night shift with her.

Bernila was a friend of Inez's and protested being sent away. "But—"

"Now, please!"

Lunurin followed the intake healer through to the quarantine section of the temple. "Alon dosed her before we left, fever reducer and a sleep aid."

"She is burning!" the healer exclaimed, pressing her cheek to Inez's brow.

"Her fever is already coming down, don't expend your energy. There are more coming, more serious cases," Lunurin warned.

"More!" the healer's voice rose precipitously. "How many more?"

"I think ten or so showing symptoms. Another twenty with close exposure." Lunurin was sorry to ruin this woman's night, but if it meant protecting Inez...

"Sea Lady have mercy, we're too short right now. We let most go home to rest now that the worst of the crush injuries are stable. I need to talk to Aizza," she exclaimed, rushing off.

Lunurin didn't think Inez's act would hold up to serious scrutiny from Aizza or any of the more experienced healers, but it had done its work. And just in time as Alon's guards carried in the first victims, all too still, barely breathing.

Alon and the recently roused Aizza bent to the serious cases, expressions drawn in concentration. Lunurin directed the guards, having them secure the converts who remained civil, if furious, into quarantine.

For the ones still wailing hysterically about water witch curses, Lunurin instructed the healers to dose them with calming herbs, and—in the worst cases—send them to sleep as well.

"Just fevered ramblings," she assured Bernila, restraining the patient as she thrashed and fought.

Bernila frowned. "I see Aynila's not all that different from Talaan."

Bernila had been rescued from the fort in Talaan. When they'd broken the lock from the munitions' building, she'd thrown herself upon them, armed with a powder barrel stave studded with nails. Anything to avoid a death by burning. Lunurin hadn't been surprised by how well she and Inez got along.

"Only the converts," Lunurin hedged.

"Converts can be dangerous," Bernila murmured when her patient finally went limp. Lunurin helped straighten knotted limbs so that she lay comfortably. "Christianity has a way of catching worse than wet season fevers."

Lunurin wished Bernila had convinced Inez of this before she'd decided to sneak into a convert prayer meeting. Nothing Lunurin or Alon said was getting through lately.

There was a shout as Litao and a guard carried in another unconscious woman. She was drenched in sweat, her belly big with child. This must be the woman Inez had been so worried for.

Lunurin cast a critical eye over Bernila. Her eyes were sunken, her lips dry and cracked. She was overextended. Lunurin held her back. "It can't be you, not tonight. You're too tired."

She debated pouring her strength into Bernila, but did not. After the fall of the Palisade, they'd discovered few gods-blessed could handle the power Lunurin could move in a crisis. There were often ill effects. Alon had compared it to drinking lightning; Sina to walking over fresh lava. As exhausted as she was, Bernila might try something foolish with such a lift.

Bernila frowned. "Who else? Let me at least examine her." Drawing saltwater between brown hands, chapped from so many long hours of soaking in saltwater, Bernila placed them over the woman's brow, then her belly.

Her dark eyes snapped open. "You're right, her infection has progressed dangerously. Get Gat Alon. He's the most rested of the experienced healers."

Lunurin went from the main hall toward the more specialized healing buildings. Built on stilts over a concrete-lined ship berth that was once part of the Palisade, it had been converted into sheltered pools for when very serious cases needed direct, but sheltered, access to the sea. Alon had ordered all the converts Inez knocked out brought here. She hoped they still had the energy for such a complex case.

She found the temple's most experienced healers kneeling in the sea, circled around a patient, synced in rhythmic tidal breathing. Alon, Aizza, and Pasamba each took a deep final breath, diving deeply after the patient, though only their hands were underwater.

Alon had roused Inez, and she was at work as well, drying the patient just pulled from the pool. Lunurin helped while she waited for Alon's attention, checking over the too-still forms awaiting their turn.

"They know?" Lunurin lay a hand to Inez's neck, checking she had no lingering effects from her charade.

Inez nodded without a word, tugging up the neck of her borrowed healer's robe self-consciously.

Lunurin had expected Alon would need Aizza's experience and knowledge of the true problem. It was the rest of the city that must never learn Inez had "attacked" a prayer meeting.

The healers' dive was long. Lunurin counted with a pearl diver's intuition. They were tide-touched and had better breath control than she did, but even she began to worry at how long all three remained down.

Just when she was about to intervene before all three passed out, Alon's hands squeezed convulsively. At the signal, they surfaced together, gasping for air.

Pasamba swore roundly, pressing a hand to her diaphragm. "Aman Sinaya bless us, Gat Alon, you warned us it was deep but this… She really pulled them so far down unaided?"

Inez ducked her head, avoiding both Pasamba's gaze and Lunurin's outstretched hand.

"The rest aren't nearly so deep. We can do it." Alon glossed over the main inquiry.

Pasamba shook her head. "We might need the Lakan. They've been under so long, and so deeply. It will be delicate work. Dangerous if we bring them up too quickly."

"Yes," Aizza agreed. "We've been stretched too thin, tending so many from the crush. Pasamba and I are liable to make mistakes. We'll tell the trainees it's heatstroke, but we're keeping them for observation. And we'll keep them quarantined until we're less exhausted."

"I can help with the exhaustion, at least," Lunurin offered. "Bernila diagnosed a pregnant woman with a dangerous infection, she needs support."

Alon tried to get out of the water, but had to sit on the edge as gravity and lightheadedness from his dive caught him.

"You've been working hard tonight too. You aren't fresh enough to tackle such a delicate case," Aizza warned.

"You're right," Alon admitted, stretched so thin his hands shook.

Lunurin reached for him. He clutched her hands convulsively tight, his weight collapsing onto her. She caught a breeze circling through the temple complex, using it to stir the still waters of his power to white-crested foam. She poured all the strength she dared into his frame, wary of overtaxing even Alon after the way she'd had to pull him up from the mire of magic Inez had unleashed.

Too soon, it was done. Alon lifted his head, strong enough to face yet another emergency. When would there finally be time to rest?

Alon kissed her knuckles and rose, steady and sure.

She looked to Aizza and Pasamba, wanting to do more. "I have done the same for Inez and Sina. They handle it well. Maybe I could offer you a lift?"

Pasamba shook her head. "Inez is used to you, and the Lakan's family has always been better able to handle power. I'd rather be tired than out of commission."

"Let's not test it tonight. But maybe—" Alon cut himself off.

Lunurin wished she couldn't read his peacekeeping silences so well. He'd only meant they shouldn't take risks when all hands were so needed. His tone was mild, but with their earlier fight still unresolved between them, it was impossible not to think he meant Rosa and how he'd begged her to think of Aynila's future. Could Rosa be trained to help their healers without overwhelming them?

They shared a long look, then Alon went to aid Bernila.

Lunurin turned to Inez, still head down and tending to her victims. "Go help Alon. You should see this through to the end."

Inez all but snatched herself away, going after Alon without a word. Lunurin sighed. Nothing she said was right these days.

II

ALON DAKILA

The moonset lay golden as narra blossoms floating on the indigo darkness of the bay as mother and child were delivered safely at last. Alon laid the infant, wailing her indignance and resilience, on her mother's breast.

Through the muddy layers of exhaustion that fever could inflict on even the most experienced healer, Alon realized that somehow, Lunurin's ploy had been a success. She and Inez had labored on beside him, bringing whatever he needed and breathing strength into him when he flagged. With shaking hands, he rewrapped the large egg of Bool salt he'd insisted the temple acquire. Lunurin caught the weight before he dropped it, strong even when he was drawn to breaking.

More and more often, he felt he was at his limit, drawing from a dry well and barely staying ahead of a hundred incipient disasters. Yet his mother and brother and all Aynila just kept asking for more. Only Lunurin, his perfect storm, was always there to refill his reserves. No matter what they faced, she was beside him, pouring out her great strength with a generosity he did not deserve.

He *had* to tell her about Catalina. But even his tongue was weighted with exhaustion.

"You know, Kawit always insisted that Bool salt made fever less draining," he said instead. His throat went tight, and a wave of grief bowed his head.

Lunurin steadied his hands. "Tito Kawit always knew best."

The grief was a sharp, lingering ache; he wanted to share it with no one but her. They'd leaned so much on Kawit through the terrible years of his mother's exile and the earliest days of their marriage. Sometimes he'd hear a thump on the stairs, that familiar heavy tread of his tito's laho-wounded stiff leg and cane and he'd expect to see Kawit coming up to the kitchen to tinker with a new salt or ply everyone with food.

Alon made a mental note to record the finding on Bool. "I still haven't found anyone to take on his studies of salt types. It would be a terrible shame if—"

"You will," Lunurin assured him. "We won't let his knowledge be lost. Codicían greed has taken too much from us already."

She gave his hands another squeeze, strength flowing into him like the moon lifting the tide. Would that he could stay just like this, with her, and face no more emergencies tonight.

So of course, just as he'd forced himself to push the grief back down, going to return the rare salt, the Lakan arrived.

Alon handed his burden off to Inez and moved to intercept his inay as she swept down on Lunurin with the unerring accuracy of a diving kite. At her heels, Jeian observed the disarray of the infirmary with raised eyebrows.

The Lakan clapped her hands sharply, grim as a towering tidal wave. "What is the meaning of this?"

The dozens of trainee healers called in to help jumped to their feet and bowed deeply. Dalisay swept her hand out, encompassing the chaos of the healing hall. Stressed to over-flowing, woven nipa mats had been laid out on the floor to accommodate the influx as word of the fever spread from the port inland.

"And you're somehow the root of it all?" The Lakan's sharp, furious hand sign was clear as a shout. Inez sank back behind Lunurin, her face red with shame.

"I never meant! I didn't—" Inez's shaky hand sign was half obscured behind Lunurin.

Alon interceded on Inez's behalf. He collected his inay and guided her to the privacy of her study within the halls. She allowed it, but pointed with her lips at Inez, signing, "Come along."

He hoped their half-true cover story would go over as well with the Lakan as it had with Aizza and Pasamba.

Once they were all closed in the study, Alon began, "Things became... complicated when Inez got swept up in an operation my spies carried out to contain some dangerous elements among the convert groups. But despite the complications, the operation was a success."

His inay's eyebrows spiked toward her hairline. "A fever from the docks is a success?"

"We've quarantined a particularly evangelical prayer group whose leadership is believed to have smuggled the priest into Aynila."

"And how was Inez swept up in this?" Jeian eyed Inez with barely veiled suspicion.

Lunurin stepped between them as Inez shrank into

herself. Jeian did not make any secret of his mistrust of mestizos. Alon gritted his teeth in frustration. His brother had done the exact opposite of mellowing with age, and had absorbed none of Aizza's good humor.

Alon tried to get ahead of the fight, with minimal belief he'd succeed. He was just so tired. "She wasn't where she was expected to be, and my people were a bit overzealous. She's safe now, that's what matters." As a last-ditch effort, he held an arm out between Jeian and Lunurin, unsure who to stare down to prevent an altercation. Lunurin's hair was slipping loose, and rains had started to drum down overhead. This did not seem to deter Jeian.

"What matters is the fever," the Lakan signed, dragging their attention back. "The Amihan Moon is only a week away. Diplomats will be arriving any day. Must I tell them our harbor is closed for quarantine?"

"When things went south, I needed good reason to place certain elements into quarantine. I couldn't have word spreading of a water witch cursing converts," Alon explained.

His inay studied his expression. "No. That would only make things worse with tensions so high after the crush. So the fever was entirely fabricated?"

"Yes, it's healer's sleep, very deep, but there's no lasting damage based on Aizza's assessment. She suggests we tell people it was merely heatstroke and we are being cautious. The collapsed worshipers caused a panic, my people had to get Inez out… one thing led to another and here we are."

His inay pressed a hand to Inez's brow, frowning in concentration as she confirmed the claims herself. Even Inez's ears were burning red.

"Glad to see some real results from all your spies and machinations for once. What was your student doing running with converts?" Jeian prodded.

"I wasn't—" Inez began, but the Lakan hushed her, instructing her to open her mouth so she could examine her tongue. Alon hoped later, when his brother wasn't looking for a fight, he could get his inay's read on Inez's magic. A month ago, she had struggled to gather enough power to use healer's sleep on one cooperative volunteer.

The Lakan stepped back from Inez, signing, "You're over-extended, and you'll feel it tomorrow, even with the boost from the Amihan Moon. You're on night duty till the last of our 'fever' patients are discharged."

Inez nodded, gaze downcast. "Yes po."

"I need to examine the others. The effects shouldn't have lingered so long after she broke her concentration. What have we really gained from this?" the Lakan asked.

Alon answered. "We're closing up the security holes that allowed a Codicían priest to slip into Aynila. The prayer group's ringleader, Arcilla, isn't Aynilan, he's a convert from Simsiman. He'll have likely been smuggled in just like Ortiz, but six months earlier."

"Why didn't we already know about this if he's been here six months already? Why are your spies letting Simsiman get so comfortable plotting against us?" Jeian challenged.

Jeian had no patience for subtlety. Alon couldn't help but think that in Simsiman's defense, he may very well have started this himself. After all, where had he sent Catalina but to Simsiman, the largest of the remaining Codicían strong-holds in the archipelago. That must be where the Codicíans' spymaster was located. Someone had to be whispering in the governor's ear. Paired with reports on this group's prayers to Santa Catalina... someone in Simsiman knew Lunurin's weak points too well. Had Catalina herself given them away?

"At least Alon's machinations don't sweep half the city into the crush. He's thoughtful like that," Lunurin snapped.

She'd stand by him through anything, flood or fury. Alon's guilt choked him. She trusted and supported him so whole-heartedly. Yet he was keeping such a terrible secret from her. He had to tell her. There was no way she wouldn't find out now that the healing halls were crawling with converts—she should hear it from him. Only not now. Not in front of his brother who needed no more reasons to distrust mestizos. He just couldn't do it, not now.

Jeian raised a brow, not to be outdone. "If Alon's so thoughtful, explain how Inez got swept up with a bunch of converts? You have to admit it's suspicious. She has the pedigree for treason, after all."

Inez looked ready to cry for real this time.

Alon pushed his brother back a step, before Lunurin tore into him with her teeth. "Drop it. I won't protect you if my wife decides to kill you. No one has suffered at the hands of the Church like Inez has, and I'll not have you disparaging her. Especially here in the halls of healing where she's been working so hard."

The Lakan hissed sharply, heading off the fight. "Jeian, Alon. Not now."

Alon found himself mimicking Jeian, nodding meekly before their mother's ire, but Inez had finally had enough. She turned on her heel and fled the study.

Lunurin went to follow, but the Lakan snapped her fingers again. "Let her go. I need you here, and Inez needs some time to herself. How quickly can you draft notices to say what triggered the fever quarantine was only heatstroke?"

12

❦

INEZ NG DAKILA

Shame and fury swirled, burning her insides as the steam of the compounding room stung her eyes and nose. The huge pots of simmering ginger tea were obviously to blame for her watering eyes. The tea was a catch all to treat nausea, arthritic aches, and all manner of mild illness, as more patients arrived fearing fever. But Inez stayed put. The fumes had driven everyone else far away.

She grabbed a ladle and hunkered down, hoping to be left alone till morning. Luckily, even tonight there was a lull in the hours before dawn. It was before the night fishermen returned with their catch, and not yet time for sailors to get under way. Aynila slumbered.

Inez wished she could join them. Instead, she sweated in her steamy sanctuary.

Away from all the eyes and without the distraction of labor, the night finally caught up with her. Alon and Lunurin would be busy with the Lakan now for weeks. They hadn't had the time or patience for her apologies or explanations, much less questions, about the terrifying dry land drownings she'd caused—except when Alon had yelled that she should've known better, of course.

Her frustration built with every waft of hot, spicy steam that came off the pots, making her eyes water and her nose run.

Eyes burning, she mopped her face with the sleeve of her borrowed robe.

"Inez, are you alright?"

Inez gave her nose one more savage wipe. "I'm fine."

She turned. Bernila was in the doorway, bearing a tray of empty clay cups.

"Why are you still here? There's no way they're still letting you heal."

Bernila waved this off. "How could I miss out on all this excitement?"

Inez wrinkled her nose.

"I'm kidding. I didn't want to leave the infirmary short. At least till the morning crew shows up." She set down the tray and gave Inez a hug.

Inez squeezed her back, hard, hooking her chin over her shoulder. "I'm in it this time."

Bernila huffed a laugh. She stepped back to empty her tray. "You really are."

"Are you working any other nights this week?" Inez asked. "I'm on nights till the last fever-scare patient is discharged."

Bernila winced as she arranged clean cups on her tray. "But that could be weeks!"

Inez groaned and dropped her face back into her hands. "What was I thinking?"

Bernila blew out a long breath. "I didn't say it, you did."

Inez's hackles rose. She glared at her friend. "Look, I didn't mean—"

"To attend a prayer meeting full of hateful, paranoid converts?" Bernila asked.

Inez clenched her fists till the ladle handle creaked, reining in the urge to scream. Bernila *had* been betrayed to the Codicíans by converts.

"You of all people should know how dangerous they are," Bernila added, as she carried her tray over toward Inez's simmering pots.

Inez's teeth clicked together. Unsaid but loud were all Bernila's thoughts—about her, about her sister and every "hateful paranoid" convert like her—and Inez had had *enough*. She could not deal with this tonight—not even from Bernila.

Bernila held out her hand for the ladle. "What exactly did you think you'd find—"

Inez swung the ladle toward her. Bernila jumped back, sending cups cascading to the floor, where they shattered.

"*You* mind the pot! The steam is too much. I need air," Inez spat.

She stalked out into the courtyard, veering away from the illuminated infirmary hall toward the quiet wing where serious cases were checked into private rooms.

Just when blessed solitude had descended once more, she saw the guard and realized she'd come too far. No one was supposed to be back here. It was off-limits until the priest was dealt with. She recognized the guard, Tibay, posted outside the room.

Bernila's words circled and darted around her head like angry mosquitos. What *had* she been trying to find?

Alon and Lunurin had no time for half-heard prayers and new saints. But if anyone would know the truth of Santa Catalina, it was Father Ortiz.

If Catalina was being used by the Codicíans... someone had to find the truth before her sister betrayed them all over again. Inez couldn't let Catalina ruin everything Aynila had rebuilt.

If she had Ortiz's word to corroborate what she'd heard, surely then Alon and Lunurin would listen. They'd understand why she'd gone to the convert meeting. Everyone would.

She quickened her pace, fumbling for an excuse. "Tibay! Aizza's wrestling with a belligerent patient in the main infirmary. She sent me to get you for help."

Tibay was young, and knew her. He didn't question her nearly as much as he should have. Litao would have his hide—later. He nodded smartly and jogged off. The sound of his footsteps faded, leaving Inez alone facing an innocuous-looking door, behind which was a Codicían priest. *A Codicían spy*, she reminded herself.

These rooms were not prison cells—they'd merely fit a bar diagonally into the inner frame of the sliding mechanism. Inez removed it before she could second-guess herself. She needed answers. If she could knock out ten furious converts, she could deal with one priest.

The bamboo door slid open a crack. She peered inside. The priest looked so small curled on the cot against the wall. He'd never been a big-boned or muscular sort, and he couldn't be more than five years her senior. It was hard to reconcile such a broken little man with the fear and helplessness she remembered so vividly from Father DeSoto's office. How had these men held such power over her and Aynila for so long?

Her back itched with memory. The weight of the cloth had been so very heavy.

Inez forced herself to go on. She had to find out what this priest knew about Santa Catalina, and about her sister.

Alon just wouldn't listen to her. He was still too upset that she'd finally used her healing, but done it so wrong. He wouldn't even help her understand what she'd done. As if she should just know instinctually what was wrong and how to not do it. No one was listening, not even her friends. She wanted to scream.

If Father DeSoto had taught Inez anything, it was this: everyone believed a priest. If she could get Ortiz to admit what he knew about Catalina, Alon would listen. Even Lunurin would have to pay attention.

She shoved the door open fully, casting the light of the hall across the priest's face. He flinched awake with a start. Inez recognized the look. The heart-pounding, sharp-ache-in-the-chest startle, the bitterness of bile and fear at the back of the throat. She felt no pity.

"You!" Ortiz spat.

"Me," she acknowledged, proud of how steady her voice sounded as she entered and shut the door behind her.

The room felt much smaller from the inside, walls and darkness pressing close. But Inez couldn't fail. She needed to get out of him what Alon and his spies had failed to discover.

"Lay Brother Arcilla sent me." She spoke the lie into tense silence.

"He sent *you*?" His intonation had changed, but not for the better. Ortiz raked his gaze over her healer's robe of indigo and white, her gleaming mother-of-pearl necklace. Did he see another tide-touched interrogator, or the schoolgirl ward of the Church he remembered? Inez needed a third option.

"Who else could get this close? Known converts aren't welcome in the temple," she lied easily. That, she'd learned from Lunurin. It was one thing she was convinced even a tide-touched should know.

Skepticism was writ large across his face. "You are the one who's to help me get aboard the Lusitan ship?"

Inez couldn't hesitate, not if it meant gaining his trust. "Yes. They'd planned to petition Lady Stormbringer and Lord Alon for your release, but I warned them such a plan was sure to fail. I'm to help instead, before an example is made of you."

"An example? Is it true the new Lakan is putting Christian heads on pikes?"

Inez knew she had him. Fear had overcome his good sense. "She still has the governor's head," she lied. "Shrunken now. A talisman of their victory. I should hate to see you join such company."

She waited while Ortiz studied her. With her slight frame, a face he knew and who'd once been so devout, she was easy to underestimate.

"Why are you helping me?" he asked.

"I want to find my sister." This was true, in a way. "I have to find Catalina."

"In that, we can help each other." Ortiz smiled at her, the way men did when they were pleased to have something to hold over you.

Inez flicked open her balisong knife and cut him free of his bindings, wanting to encourage his feeling of superiority. "She was supposed to join a convent in Canazco. Has she really returned?"

"Santa Catalina has returned to the archipelago. She was granted a vision of Aynila's return to the light of God—"

"I don't need more saint's prayers. I'm trying to find my sister. When did she come back? Where is she now?"

"If you want the truth behind the saint, that will have to wait until we're out of Aynila," Ortiz responded smugly.

"Tell me now. Otherwise, why should I risk myself to help you?" Inez retorted—but then a sound from the hallway sent her skittering deeper into the room.

"No time," the priest hissed.

Inez refused to get caught here and now without having gained *any* new information about Catalina. "If I get you out of the temple, then we talk."

13

INEZ NG DAKILA

Sneaking a priest off the central delta felt counterintuitive. For so long, only priests had been able to carelessly flout the Palisade's strict laws. But without the Palisade walls and rotations of soldiers, if she could get him to the water, they'd be clear. Aboard a bangka on the bay, she'd have all the leverage she needed to learn everything he knew about Catalina.

But tonight was not a normal night. With most of Aynila rising early to avoid the heat and intense humidity of the early wet season, word of the fever had spread quickly, sending all those with the slightest symptoms hurrying to the healing halls to be examined. Even amid all the strangers coming in and out of the infirmary, the priest stuck out like a baphomet moth, strikingly black and stark white, looking far too much like a spirit of the Palisade's dead returned.

She forced him to change out of the black cassock and dug out another healer's robe of almost the right size, standing guard while he struggled into the unfamiliar garb.

Inez's back prickled all over horribly, warning her to never turn her back on a priest, but she kept her eyes glued to the door, trying to figure out the best way out of the temple complex. Why must the infirmary be so busy tonight?

Right. That was her fault too.

A flicker of lamplight fell across the doorway, and she lunged to shove the priest farther into the depths of the storage room. She pressed them both as deeply as she could behind a large crate. The space was narrow, tight for one, an impossible squeeze for two. Inez hoped the darkness would be enough to hide them.

"Don't move," she ordered.

Bernila entered, no doubt in search of more ginger for the infusion pots. A globo-style coconut oil lantern swinging in her hand cast light and shadow wildly around the room, dazzling Inez's vision.

Inez didn't move, didn't even breathe. Bernila would find what she needed soon enough.

"Get rid of her, or you'll never find out what became of your sister." Hot stinking breath slid down the back of Inez's neck, far too close. The skin-crawling sensation on her back exploded into an army of live ants trying to bite through.

Inez cursed herself. She should know better. Priests loved their empty threats. What had she been thinking, giving this one such leverage over her?

Bernila's head bobbed up. "Inez? Is that you? Why are you—"

Shut up with all the questions! Inez wanted to shout. Why must Bernila have so many questions?

She shuffled backward, ignoring how her back pressed into the sweaty bulk of Ortiz. Ignoring how his breath came fast and panicked down the back of her neck. Ignoring how much she wanted to rip off her own skin.

She ought to slit his throat here and now and face the consequences. Lunurin, at least, would understand.

Then again—after tonight, maybe not. Jeian wasn't the only one with doubts, just the only one to voice them. And she'd caused so much trouble for the Lakan.

She had to do this. She had to find out what he knew about Catalina. That wouldn't happen if they were discovered now.

"Buwisit ka! Just leave me alone!"

"Have you been crying? Inez, I'm sorry I upset you. I'm just worried." Bernila took her words as an invitation, the light of her lamp creeping closer.

Inez could just imagine how it would reflect off the whiteness of Ortiz's face crushed beside hers, his sweat glistening.

The sweet scent of burning coconut oil filled the storeroom. Inez imagined dashing the firetender-molded glass lantern to the floor and watching the flames spread. At least then she'd have a different problem to deal with, and in the confusion and panic, who could say how the priest got out or exactly what had happened? Desperation rose up in her like the tide.

Bernila gasped, and Inez made a split-second decision. The closed heft of her balisong knife settled into her palm, weighting her fist.

She lunged forward. She was taller, and Bernila was off guard, hardly expecting an attack. Sina's lessons with her balisong knife and Lunurin's with staff and kali sticks might not have been much use against a mob, but against Bernila?

Inez swung hard for her temple, hoping to drop her quickly and silently. Bernila ducked, pulling from the saltwater at her hip—but she was exhausted, and it merely splashed into Inez's face, dripping harmlessly.

She closed the distance before Bernila could recover or pull the water back into her hands for another attempt. She brought both hands together and down onto the top of Bernila's head, cutting off her cry for help with a sharp click of teeth and the blooming scent of blood. Had she bitten her tongue?

Inez couldn't worry about that now. She twisted one of Bernila's arms behind her, bending close. "The priest, he knows something about my sister. I'm taking him to the Lusitan slavers. Tell Lunurin I'm sorry."

Then, she pressed her sweaty palms to Bernila's brow and let the terrifying darkness in her belly roar through her, pulling her friend down.

She went limp, and Inez lowered her gently to the floor. She doused the oil lamp and pulled Bernila deeper into the storage room where it might be some time before she was discovered. She hoped that having been less frightened would mean Bernila was easier to wake, but she pushed the worry away. She'd get the best care here.

Inez tucked her balisong knife away, hooking it into an interior tie of the robe at her waist. "Now we go, quickly. Before we run into anyone else."

Ortiz went without any further barbs about Catalina. Inez didn't know if this pleased her, or if she was missing an opportunity to gain information.

Once out of the temple complex, Inez hurried Ortiz down toward the oyster beds. The nearness of the bay dragged at her awareness, scraping across her already raw skin like the surf pounding a sandbar. The nearly full moon cast a blue-white light that gleamed off the water, contrasting with the dark hulks of vessels at anchor. Even accounting for its size, the Lusitan slave ship anchored beyond the mouth of the harbor stood out for the way the light caught in the drape of its white sails. Did they think themselves immune to wet season winds as well as irate stormcallers?

The bangka was still tied to the diving platform built for the wet season festivities. Through gaps in the bamboo, Inez eyed the reptilian bodies resting below.

"Hello, little sister, shall we hunt together?" came a low crocodilian rumble, audible above the rush of the surf.

Ortiz froze halfway down the pier.

Inez found her awareness slipping among the buwaya. She wanted to borrow their armor and single-minded focus. Especially now, when she couldn't let anything distract her from getting the answers she needed. Not even the bay, so loud from the nearness of the Amihan Moon, its hidden currents belying the peaceful scene in the moonlight.

Her vision sharpened, till every bamboo slat of the pier was visible in stark relief. The raw-skinned sensation of her back dulled, armored hide a welcome barrier against the nearness of the incoming tide.

"In." Inez gave Ortiz a shove when he hesitated again, nearly pushing him over the edge onto the canoe.

As well he should. It was unwise to get into a bangka with a tide-touched you didn't trust. Crocodile-sharp, Inez was pleased to see fear revived in the Codicían's eyes. Too long had she lived in terror of men like him. Let him have a taste of it. She hoped he choked.

She hopped into the rocking boat, ignoring the priest's scrambling and bleating. With the double outriggers, it would take far more than that to capsize them.

As soon as she stepped into the bottom of the boat, puddles of saltwater lapping over her toes, the rocking ceased, the bangka suddenly as steady under her as if it were atop deep-set bamboo pylons. Was this only crocodilian focus? Why could Inez never do things the way a tide-touched was supposed to? When she'd first struggled with healing, Aizza had suggested she might be more of a fit for the sea. But lately, her utter failure to work *with* the tides had put an end to those hopes.

Besides, it would mean joining Aynila's navy, and Jeian wouldn't have her, even if she could convince Aizza she'd be useful. She was still mestiza, forever suspicious due to her upbringing in the Church, and Jeian would never let her or anyone else forget it.

She was doomed to be tainted by what her sister had done, forever.

Inez needed to know if it had been worth it. Had Cat gotten what she wanted by sacrificing Inez and the hidden tide-touched village to the Inquisition's wrath? If she had, wouldn't she be happily ensconced in a convent in Canazco, at peace with her eternal vows and the foreign god she'd chosen? Why had she come back?

Inez couldn't help but fear it was for something terrible.

She had to find out. She had to stop Catalina from ruining everything all over again. Maybe then she'd finally be able to shake off the terrible legacy of what her sister had done, and what had been done to her.

Ortiz crossed himself and began muttering a prayer under his breath. Inez grinned, threw off the tie-lines, and sent them hurtling into the center of the bay with a twist of her oar like the lash of a crocodile's tail. Now she would get the answers she'd gone searching for in that convert meeting.

Ortiz's voice pitched higher in fear.

Inez dropped the oars, bringing the bangka to a stop and letting it spin idly far enough offshore that Ortiz couldn't hope to swim back, and plenty distant from any of the other ships and the bulk of the Lusitan slaver in the distance that no one would be drawn to investigate.

Out here, she was the one in control.

She pointed with her lips, then again with the end of her oar when Ortiz was either too night-blind or too stupid to pay heed. "See? The Lusitan ship hasn't set sail. Now tell me everything you know about my sister."

"Is now the time? Come on, we will lose the tide if you keep delaying. There will be time enough to talk of Santa Catalina once we're safely onboard," Ortiz bluffed.

"I've no intention of following you aboard a Lusitan slave ship," Inez scoffed.

Ortiz cocked his head, his pale eyes catching the light as flat and cold as glass. "Do you think you can remain in Aynila after freeing me? After attacking that woman? I doubt even your Lady Stormbringer will be able to protect you for that."

Inez shook her head. She'd never intended to free him, just to corner him in her little bangka in the center of the bay and get her answers. But now Bernila was unconscious. And Tibay knew it was her who'd lured him away from his post…

Inez realized, suddenly, how bad this all looked. Could Lunurin overrule Jeian's suspicions of her right now?

Dread and that familiar desperation broke through the crocodile focus that had gotten her out on the water. Inez crushed it down. Yes, that terrifying, head-spinning power had saved her in the prayer meeting. But she could've killed people. She'd nearly hurt Alon and Lunurin both, trying to bleed off the incomprehensible torrent of magic and madness.

Her back prickled painfully. Ortiz was right, damn him.

"She's returned to the islands? You promise?" Inez asked, her voice a great deal less steady than she might have wished.

Even if she took him back right now; even if she killed him and returned with his drowned body... would they forgive her for freeing him in the first place? For hurting people, hunting a ghost and a rumor when there were real enemies facing the archipelago? The embarrassment she'd bring the Lakan... she was Inez ng Dakila now, claimed and protected by Alon and Lunurin. How could she shame them like this?

She couldn't return to Aynila now. She had to continue, find her sister, and stop whatever it was the priests would try to use Catalina for. She had to make sure Cat couldn't be used against them again. She couldn't go back until she made sure.

The moonlight fell harshly across Ortiz's features, glimmering uncomfortably on his white teeth. "You have my word. I'll even take you to her once I've concluded my business with the Lusitans."

"Alright," Inez agreed, and dipped her oars into the water. Her every attempt to grasp at the currents around the little hull slipped off as they cried out in overlapping voices for her attention.

She didn't trust her scattered focus to make sense of it, not with the Amihan Moon's frightening power. She rowed them the rest of the way by the strength of her back toward the hulking black shadow of the Lusitan slave ship.

As they drew nearer, the stench of the tumbeiro—as the Lusitan sailors sometimes called the ships—hit Inez in a damp, festering miasma of human suffering. Beasts brought to market for slaughter were not kept in such filth and cruelty. Inez stared up at the sails, white as burial shrouds, and wondered if she was making a terrible mistake.

But on the other side of this trial, there was her sister. If she could find Catalina and get her out from under the Church's thumb before she betrayed them all again... Inez was sure she'd be able to untangle the knot of everything that was wrong and broken inside her.

She had to believe she could save her sister from herself. If she could pry Catalina from the Church she clung to, send her somewhere she couldn't be used against Aynila again, then she could avoid the fate of becoming her. Of betraying everyone she loved like Cat had.

The shadow of the ship fell over Inez, and she shivered. She had lived too long in the black shadows of monstrosities like this. It felt so wrong to be walking into the teeth of another of her own volition. What was she thinking, a tide-touched who struggled to call on the bay, who was clumsy in a bangka, getting aboard this floating tomb?

The sounds of the sea, of creaking wood and rigging, were broken by a call of alarm from the lookout on deck. Lanterns were lifted high over the side, casting light on the water. Inez tried not to notice how many interested reptilian eyes caught the light like gold coins before their long scaly bodies sank under the waves—as if to remind her it wasn't too late to pitch the priest into the water and rely on a feeding frenzy to solve all her problems.

She listened hard as Ortiz stood and began negotiating his way aboard the ship. Lusitan was different enough from Codicían that she had to pay close attention to parse the words, especially as her ear for the language was years rusty with disuse.

She smelled burning sulfur matches, and knew there were matchlocks trained on her. She followed Ortiz's directives to pull the bangka alongside the ship only after a rope was thrown down into the water. The priest looped it around his waist and was pulled aboard.

Inez more than half expected to be abandoned, or even

fired upon. She tensed, prepared to dive overboard and dare the rough embrace of the bay.

But that would mean returning to Aynila, to Lunurin and Alon, a failure. An apparent traitor, just like her sister, and she couldn't, *wouldn't*, face that. Not after they had done everything they could to protect her from Catalina's legacy.

She stood up in the circle of weak lamplight spilling over the side of the ship. "Please, I need to find my sister, Catalina. You have to take me with you!"

The looped rope dropped down into the bottom of the boat with a thud that vibrated through the small hull of her bangka, dull and heavy and final.

"Come aboard!" Ortiz called down.

Inez bent and picked up the rope, securing the loop under her arms. She stared back at her city straddling the delta, lamplight warm in capiz windows.

Was she really leaving Aynila like this, with nothing but borrowed healer's robes and her mutya?

But what had Catalina left with? Borrowed clothes, Lunurin's gifted rosary. Everything they'd owned had been swept away with the Palisade.

The first yank took her up, dragging her away from the safety of her bangka. The second dropped her down into the bay. The water closed over her head in an instant: the sand and reef-edged scrape of the in-flowing river and the out-rushing tide, tangling currents and mingling salinities closed around her on all sides, an agony. Against every instinct, she screamed, precious air streaming away as useless bubbles, her vision turning black.

I4

ALON DAKILA

Alon and Lunurin were at the Lakan's palace doing damage control when word of the priest's escape reached them over breakfast.

While Lunurin and the Lakan worked to close the security loopholes the priest's escape had revealed to ensure the security and safety of the diplomats, who were due to begin arriving the next day, Alon headed for the healing halls to find out all he could before Jeian ran roughshod over everyone involved. He hoped Inez had gone home to sleep. This was the last bit of chaos she needed to be caught up in.

He was too late to keep his guard, Tibay, out of it. Tibay was young and single and often picked up night shifts from other guards. He'd already been interrogated and arrested by Jeian for dereliction of duty before Alon made it to the temple. He left the healing halls under Litao's watchful eye, and headed for the port where his brother had headquartered Aynila's navy.

"I'm not sure you can get ahead of this one," Isko griped,

never liking to be hurried for anything short of a fire.

"We don't need Jeian kicking off another riot. I'm already hearing the fever must be something unnatural for it to affect a tide-touched. I've been trying to keep Inez's name out of it, but Jeian has no such qualms. Next time he opens his mouth, I might just let Lunurin go for his throat."

Isko rubbed the furrow between his hawkish brows. "You haven't told her, have you?"

Alon's throat went tight with guilt.

"You'll have more to worry about than Jeian if you don't come clean soon," Isko warned.

"We haven't had a moment alone since the prayer meeting debacle." Alon tried to defend himself.

"If you're afraid of her reaction, it's only going to be worse delaying."

Alon looked away, refusing to engage, or think too closely about how very right Isko was. "I *will* tell her. There just hasn't been a good time and—"

"Some of the converts are bound to talk."

"They can't. Aizza thinks they're confused from the 'heat-stroke.'" It was the only good news that had come out of the temple since word of the priest's escape.

"Hmm, yes, 'heatstroke'… and that story is still holding up?"

"With the people it needs to." The Lakan was content to continue spreading the word that Inez's victims had suffered some strange mix of heatstroke and religious ecstasy, rather than a botched healer's sleep or a catching fever. "Not a word otherwise. Inez is in enough trouble."

Luckily, those revived so far all claimed to have no memory of the events leading up to waking in the infirmary. But how much of that was reluctance to betray their network of converts and Codicían spies, and how much was Inez's influence, was unclear.

Alon grimaced. It was going to be hard to convince Jeian that now was not the time for further escalation after Alon had so flagrantly contributed to their current crisis. If the healing halls hadn't been so overrun, making it impossible to track who'd come in and out, it was unlikely the priest would've escaped.

He'd intended to demand Tibay's release as soon as they arrived at the navy's headquarters. Instead, before he could say a word, his brother snagged him around the neck and dragged him around a corner, pushing him flat against the wall. Isko ducked out of range of their scuffle with the adroitness he'd always shown in their youth.

"Please don't make me tell the Lakan we're back to roughhousing," he complained, but he didn't interfere.

Alon tried briefly to wrestle free, but—by dint of ten years' seniority and his time at sea—Jeian was significantly broader. When it came to brute strength, his kuya could still wrestle him into a headlock.

"Salt take it," Alon protested, throwing one more rebellious jab of his elbow into Jeian's annoyingly solid gut.

Jeian didn't even have the decency to grunt, just got hold of his bad hand and twisted it behind him. Alon shot a look at Isko, trying to get an assist, but as always Isko refused to be drawn into a physical altercation. Perhaps he was letting Alon suffer for ignoring his advice.

Jeian snapped his fingertips together in front of Alon's nose, commanding, "Quiet! Listen!" in trader hand sign.

Alon subsided at last. By some trick of acoustics and the hollow bamboo poles that made up the walls of the building, conversation from the room on the other side was quite clear and distinct. And he was listening to a familiar voice with a heavy Codicían accent. "You know the last time I crossed a Dakila, I lost these fingers?"

Alon could imagine his spy Pedro de Isla's pantomime, right hand spread for dramatic effect, index and middle fingers missing at the knuckle. The gasps were audible.

"Bitten clean off. By what? Oh, you don't want to know. But I tell you what, I'm not keeping quiet this time."

Someone began praying rather loudly, and Pedro scoffed. "Faith can't save fingers. But I hear information will. One of you must know something that'll get the Lakan's sons off your back."

And secrets began to spill. Who knew someone, who'd been working on a plan to smuggle the priest out of Aynila. The merchant captain who was known to be willing to ferry converts from Aynila to Simsiman, for a price.

Alon and his brothers listened intently, until talk drifted to useless, panicked trivialities—someone who knew someone still keeping a Santo Niño statue and the like. At this point Jeian's men came and dragged Pedro out of the room in another brazen display of force.

They hauled him down the hall, past Alon, Jeian, and Isko, who followed until Pedro was released into Jeian's office, where he grinned broadly and took a bow.

Jeian closed the door to his office. "See? I can gather information too."

"When you arrest my spies in your scoop of every convert and mestizo in Aynila?" Alon asked archly.

"You can't use crew barracks as a makeshift prison," Isko added. "It's not a long-term solution."

"I can, since your plan of keeping prisoners in the temple turned out to be completely ineffective. Converts can just waltz in and out whenever they please," Jeian shot back.

"How many times have you run that trick?"

"Oh, seven or so times since my men arrested Pedro being smuggled into Aynila with last night's catch."

"I didn't tell you about the hole in our harbor security so you could arrest *my* spies," Alon protested. "And all these arrests aren't helping the situation. We can't have rioting in the streets as ambassadors are arriving for the Amihan Moon. You're charging ahead, just like you did in Talaan, and hoping someone else will pick up the pieces once you've smashed through the front door," Alon accused.

Jeian scoffed. "We'll end up worse off than Talaan if we do nothing. It's the Christians that are riling people against the Lakan and all the tide-touched."

"Then help me fix it!" Alon cried. He spread his hands. They couldn't afford to be at loggerheads. "Yes, they fear us. Yes, the fever scare has made things worse, but we can't arrest, interrogate, and torture our way into Aynila's good graces. You *know* that."

"I didn't start the outbreak. That's on you and your house."

Alon gritted his teeth, furious on Inez's behalf.

Isko raised a hand, asking for silence, and Alon subsided. Isko wouldn't raise his voice to be heard over the Lakan's blood sons, just as he wouldn't join their squabbles, but it had always made him, the middle "brother," the best mediator.

"Maybe the fever scare can be an unexpected boon."

"How?" both Alon and Jeian demanded.

"Word of fever is spreading faster than the heatstroke story. Don't wait for Aynila to come to the healing school. We should be sending healers into Aynila to calm any lingering fears. Do not let the converts say they were abandoned and afraid. It will only divide the city further between those who trust the tide-touched enough to seek out the healing halls and those who don't," Isko suggested.

"Not alone," Jeian insisted. "We need guards to ensure the safety of our healers."

Alon shook his head slowly. "Not guards... or at least, let's not say they're guards. We'll send herb-healers with the tide-touched trainees. All they need to bring is herb bundles to boil in water. It will harm none, but assuage many fears."

"Precisely," Isko agreed, clearly pleased they'd seen the logic of his plan and stopped snapping at each other's throats. "Let Aynila see how hard its healers are working to make sure there is no danger. Give them choices in who examines any suspicious symptoms—herb-healers or tide-touched. If we can use the fever scare to show people this, maybe we can begin to bridge Aynila's divisions before they tear us apart."

"My lords," Pedro interrupted. "I have important news. I was lying under a fisherman's haul, getting covered in fish slime to bring it to you, Lord Alon."

Jeian frowned. "You said nothing of news."

"You arrested me, Lord Jeian. Your brother pays me. Well, I might add."

Alon controlled his expression with effort. He didn't want to be in a headlock again. He and his brother needed to stop working at cross purposes to protect Aynila. If that meant letting his brother in on some information...

He signaled for Pedro to go on. He trusted he paid the spy well enough for discretion when it came to truly sensitive matters. "Why are you back so soon? Why not send a message the usual way?"

"This could not be trusted to a messenger. The Codician armada is no longer waylaid in Canazco waiting for favorable weather for the crossing. They were sighted resupplying in

GABRIELLA BUBA

Hanay. We've been misled. The worst of the Great South Sea crossing is behind them. Our timeline has grown very short indeed, my lords."

At Pedro's words, Alon saw their hopes for a long summer to solidify Aynila's alliances and prepare their defenses fall to ash, like a nipa palm roof in a lightning strike. His endless efforts to stay ahead of the disasters were for nothing. He'd missed this. He'd failed Lunurin. They didn't have five to six months to prepare while the great wallowing war galleons made the slow and difficult crossing. They had no time and no allies. There was only Lunurin.

As a sailor, Jeian understood their position in even more intimate detail than Alon. His expression had turned grim and stern in a way that made him look eerily like their father. A pang of terrible grief caught Alon amid his shock and dismay. His remembrances were usually angrier, so tied to the loss of Kawit and most of the hidden tide-touched village his father and Catalina had betrayed.

"A month?" Alon asked, desperately willing Jeian to propose a longer interval before their doom.

"Two weeks. Three, if all the gods smile upon us, and the wet season winds are weak this year."

When had wet season winds ever been weak since Lunurin came to Aynila?

"I need to speak to my wife. She's with the Lakan. When you've wrapped things up here, join us. Please release my guard, Tibay, as well. Isko, go to the healing school. Apprise Aizza, see what you can do about finding her a few real herb-healers to pair with our students."

Not waiting for Jeian to argue, Alon strode out, Pedro at his heels. He needed Lunurin. How had all his spies missed this?

144

15

LUNURIN CALILAN NG DAKILA

"The armada could reach Aynila in two weeks, perhaps three if the crossing from Hanay is difficult."

Lunurin absorbed the news like a blow. Alon looked no better delivering it. He crossed to her, and she threaded their fingers together, needing his nearness as a ballast against her mounting dread.

Catching the armada mid-crossing in one terrible deadly typhoon had been their best chance of shattering the Codícian attack before it reached their door. Lunurin never again wanted to be cornered, forced to unspool the terrible power of her goddess in the heart of Aynila. A stormcaller's rages were meant for open water, not the vulnerable city they all called home.

But a siege was one of the few scenarios where Lunurin would feel justified in calling down such a calamity, as long as they had enough open sea for her and the rest of the Stormfleet to untie the spooling knot of killer winds and roiling waves before it wiped the face of the archipelago clean of life, as surely as it would feed everything and everyone beneath it to the depths of the sea.

The Lakan bowed her head in thought. "And now we must ask our allies to fight and die with us, knowing our best chance for victory is already lost?"

Lunurin's heart sank. With the debacle of slain diplomats and sunken Stormfleet ships still so fresh on everyone's mind, now they would not be mending fences but asking for ships and men?

"You are very sure? How much can we trust the word of a Codícían who has betrayed his own countrymen for gold?" the Lakan signed.

Alon opened his mouth, but it was Lunurin who answered. "Let me confirm it. Hanay is not Canazco. I have spun up storms farther out upon the Great South Sea."

"It's dangerous," Alon protested. "Scouring the seas on the wind is not the same as seeding a storm. Like a healer following a soul too close to the realm of the dead, you could become unanchored from your body. It's not a working you should perform alone. What about Rosa—"

"No. You'd never lean on Inez like that. Don't ask me to involve her when I'm likely to hurt us both." Lunurin did not like to think about how badly she might hurt Rosa, pushing herself beyond her limits.

"You may not have experience of joint workings with another stormcaller, but I've seen you, Alon, and Sina do together more than any of you could've done alone. A tide-touched anchor might be exactly what you need to ride the winds as far as you must," the Lakan advised.

"Whatever comes, we will face it together," Alon agreed, squeezing her hand.

Lunurin squeezed back. "We can try. Together."

For the attempt, Lunurin chose one of the upper balconies of the Lakan's palace. It was a good vantage point where she could grasp for the high-altitude air currents.

As soon as she closed the sliding doors behind them, Alon pulled her into his arms. "You don't have to do this. I've already sent all the necessary messages. In a matter of days, we will have confirmation of the fleet's position from other sources."

Lunurin leaned back into him, supported like she were floating in calm waters. Would that she could stay like this forever. "You know I have to try. Anything I can do to delay them, perhaps even drive them back to Hanay for repairs or to wait out the worst of the wet season gives us time to gather allies and defend Aynila. It's time for my storms to be out over deep water, not destroying everything we have rebuilt here."

Alon kissed her brow. "Confirmation is all my mother asks. I need you to return to me."

Lunurin walked to the rail and stared out over the triple delta of Aynila, separated by the branching Saliwain River. From the plaza at the foot of the steps that led up to the Lakan's palace, the city spread down to the port. It was hard to pick out the scars of the fire that had raced inland from the Codicían bombardment. There was the rebuilt central delta with the tide-touched temple complex, more and more businesses and homes being built up around it and covering over the scars of the Palisade. Across on verdant Mount Hilaga, she could see the metalworkers' conclave. She did not want to share responsibility for the city's destruction a second time.

"Will you let down my hair?" she asked.

Alon joined her, loosening the deep indigo silk scarf she'd

tied hastily this morning. Lunurin pulled her mutya down, and Alon freed the ties that held her hair in its twisted bun.

Once more, she leaned back into his touch as her hair fell loose around her shoulders and down past her knees. His gentle fingertips chased shivers across her scalp.

"Are you ready?" Alon had gathered up her hair in one hand, his tide-touched power helping to keep her tethered in the now instead of being drawn up into the winds that swirled down to pull at her hair and attention.

Lunurin turned toward him, clasping her hands and her mutya around his. It was an intimacy she'd once never imagined, which now came as easily as breathing. Her lightning pearl-topped hair prong and comb, his mother-of-pearl brace of rings on his bad hand.

"Now I am."

Alon pulled their clasped hands to his chest, lifting the second half of his mutya into their grip. It had once been a false rosary of carved sampaguita beads, hung with a pearl-set crucifix—until he'd shattered it for the funeral rites of Aynila's murdered tide-touched. Under Sina's skillful hand, it had been remade in an image fit for the rebuilding of Aynila. She had extended the remaining strand of sampaguita buds, interspersing them with golden tambourine beads etched with the names of the dead whom Alon had consigned to the waves. Lastly, she'd modified the cross into a fully bloomed sampaguita, the round pearl cradled at its center.

In their clasped grip, the rumble of distant thunder met the roar of in-rushing surf, their spirits mingling even more closely than usual. Lunurin felt anchored, secure in the steady depths of his strength. Alon would not let her be swept away by the wind and rain, lightning and hail, the roiling storm of her goddess.

He released her hair, and the wind caught it up. Lunurin let her head fall back, turning her face up toward the sky, grounding herself through the clasp of Alon's hands, his mutya, and the deep well of his spirit.

It wasn't just the wind; regional storms across Lusong reoriented themselves to her. She had to work quickly—the last thing she wanted was to hurry the armada's progress toward Aynila.

"Anitun Tabu, Goddess of Storms, vengeance comes at your hand! Will you grant me your strength, your far-seeing eye?" Lunurin sang out her prayer, her voice strong and carrying on the rising wind.

It twisted around them both, dragging free even Alon's sleek dark hair from its low tail.

"*Ask and it is yours, Daughter mine,*" her goddess promised, catching Lunurin up in her arms. "*Let us see how far the winds may carry us.*"

It was as easy as raindrops on her face and as gentle as a sea breeze. Lunurin let herself be swept up and away from her body without hesitation. Alon would hold her safe.

She and her goddess scoured the sea for the approaching armada. It might have been hours. It might have been days. In the arms of her goddess, such human concerns were far from her. There were only the wet season winds, high and cold and perfectly free. They followed the curling edges of budding storm systems spread across the sea, leaping cloud to cloud as easily as river stones upon a crossing. But the farther she flung herself from the archipelago and the seat of Anitun Tabu's power, the harder it became. She was spread thin as mist, stretched upon the endless northeast wind, a fading specter of herself. Even the single bright thread of her and Alon's tangled mutya grew faint.

When at last she caught a glimpse of the armada, distant white sails just breaking the far eastern horizon, she knew she was too weak to do what Aynila needed. Not if she also wanted to return to her own body.

Still, she tried to push herself further, leaning into the raging fury of her goddess on the wind, still straining toward her enemies. *"These are the ones who came and killed, who massacred my beloved's children, who wrapped me in rosaries and erased my true name, leaving my people only sorrow. Will you not help me?"*

"Yes. Yes. Yes." One final great typhoon. Were they not bound to her bones for a reason?

Her people had suffered enough. For years, Lunurin had closed her eyes and ears to Anitun Tabu's pleas, ignoring her vows. She would not let her hesitation be the reason more were lost and the yolk of oppression returned to Aynila. This was what she had been born for. Why else did they call her Stormbringer?

"No."

It was whisper-soft in the roar of the freezing high-altitude winds. Yet Alon's pull was an undeniable tether. He would not let her spend her great strength on one final storm. He would not let her chase divine fury beyond the point of no return. Not while he still breathed.

Wrapped in the arms of her goddess, nothing mattered but the destruction of her enemies. Lunurin considered the gleaming mother-of-pearl tie that spooled out behind her, fine and gossamer as a spiderweb. Lightning was a searing spear in her hand. If she cut herself free, she would have just long enough to twist together her typhoon. Would it be long enough to see her enemies shattered upon the water before the raging winds shredded her untethered spirit?

"*Not like this. Not alone.*" Alon's plea carried across hundreds of miles through their mutya and pierced the clear, shining surety of Lunurin's fury. Hadn't she promised Alon she wouldn't use up her life in pointless vengeance? That she would stand beside him? How could she leave him like this?

She let herself be pulled across the vast gulf of the sea back toward her body, into Alon's waiting arms.

"I'm sorry," Lunurin rasped, as his tears of relief mingled with the rain falling on her upturned face.

She reached for him, brushing the wetness from his cheeks. Her fingers trembled with exhaustion as divinity drained away, and she sank into his steady strength.

Alon crushed her to him. Her skin crackled at each point of contact as the storm of her mind shrank back into her skin. She gasped, and he kissed her.

"Promise me, promise me." He breathed the words into her.

She'd put so much fear in him.

"I'm not leaving you. I promise, I promise," she vowed, clutching him tighter.

They might have stayed there forever, wrapped in each other's arms, their hot skin cooled by the falling rain—but cannon fire from the port interrupted their reverie. They both swung toward the balcony, panic sluggish in Lunurin's veins through her exhaustion. Was it an attack?

No unfamiliar ships approached the port. Even the Lusitan slaver had decided not to overstay their cold welcome, having sailed on sometime before the dawn.

It looked like Jeian's flagship had fired upon and sunk a merchantparao that had just weighed anchor to leave the port.

Alon covered his face for a beat too long. When he

dropped his hands, all his vulnerability and fear for her had been covered by a closed, stern severity. Lunurin recognized his public face in crisis; she'd not seen it as often since he no longer had to carry out his father's will in the Palisade. She half expected him to turn and leave her without a word.

But he paused. He turned and kissed her deeply. "I love you. Please rest soon. Convey my apologies to the Lakan."

"What shall I tell her?" Lunurin stared, aghast, as smoke rose over the harbor, hoping desperately that none of the invited diplomats had arrived early.

"That we learned this morning there was a certain merchant captain implicated in smuggling converts out of Aynila. It would seem Jeian saw fit to act swiftly, in case they were harboring Ortiz." And with that, Alon set off to do what damage control he could.

Lunurin rushed to convey the news to the Lakan and the council before panic spread. Aynila was at war with itself, and a Codicían armada—financed and led by her own father—would be upon them in a matter of weeks. If they tore themselves apart, they wouldn't need to worry about the armada.

16

❖

INEZ NG DAKILA

Inez woke to black, but not true night—a stinking, terrible darkness. She was belowdecks on a slave ship. And she'd rowed herself across the bay and asked to be brought aboard.

Her lungs burned with the fetid air and the recalled terror of her near-drowning in the bay. She shuddered. What a poor excuse for tide-touched she was. The bay alone had hurt, and now they would be out over open water, farther out to sea than Inez had ever been in her life. What had she been thinking?

She realized the pain hadn't stopped. The comforting weight of her mutya necklace was gone, its absence a raw wound on her soul. She instinctively tried to press her hands to the place it should be, searching—had it broken off? Been taken? But she quickly discovered her hands were shackled and tethered to a wooden beam, to which her feet were also tied. She could barely shift at all, on account of the bodies of the other captives packed in around her.

Inez strained, desperately trying to grasp her mutya, to wrench free, her breath coming faster and faster, sweat breaking out over her body as she yanked at her bindings.

Voices cried out in Tianchaowen, and the bodies on either side pressed close, pinning her in place. She nearly screamed.

"Stop. Stop. Stop." Someone grabbed the chain, dragging her hands down to her waist.

This, at least, she did understand.

The speaker held her arms down and the slack returned to their bindings, letting those on either side of her pull away and stop crushing her.

Time passed strangely in the near blackness of the hold, the pitch of the sea and all the myriad discomforts of thirst, hunger, and her bound, prone position. There were women, not shackled like Inez and the men, but they remained huddled on the opposite side of the hold. At some point, the Lusitans must at least open the hold to offer water, right? Their cargo wouldn't have lasted long without it.

Inez took her time with a more careful self-assessment, not dragging on her chains and upsetting the captives on either side of her. They'd not relieved her of her balisong knife and pearl of her mutya—it remained hooked securely within the folds of her robe from her fight with Bernila. But no matter how she twisted and contorted, she couldn't get it into her hands or communicate with the women free in the hold to get their help.

Thirst throbbed in time with her spirit, raw and aching from her near-drowning in the bay and the absence of half her mutya. She tried to keep her attention away from the sea, afraid of being overwhelmed again. But it was impossible to ignore the waves slapping against the hull, and a rumbling hum that grew louder, resounding through the hold like the body of a drum. It was crocodile singing, she realized. She'd been followed, their myriad scaled bodies swimming alongside the ship even now.

At last, a blinding light appeared overhead as a deck hatch was thrown open. A Lusitan sailor appeared, his dark shape blotting out the blinding sunlight. Inez was unshackled from the beam and dragged up onto the deck.

She struggled ineffectually against the manhandling, blinded by the beating sunlight, her eyes burning. She gasped greedily at air that wasn't so rank with ammonia it burned her lungs.

Even Ortiz recoiled from her, wrinkling his nose at the concentrated odor that had soaked into Inez's pores and now wafted up from the black pit at her feet. Somehow, Inez felt more trapped than ever between the black horrors of the hold at her feet and the sneering priest before her.

Once, she might've believed the stories that Aman Sinaya wouldn't let one of her tide-touched children drown, but with the memory of the bay rushing into her lungs… She didn't dare cast herself into the arms of the sea with nothing but endless deep blue water in all directions. The waxing Amihan Moon hanging ghostly on the horizon tugged at her, but she was paralyzed.

"Are you sure this one is a water witch, Father? Never seen one half-drowned. Many ordinary girls have necklaces." The captain pointed at her like a dog, the gleaming mother-of-pearl scales of her mutya glinting about his wrist.

Something deep within Inez split open, sharp as crocodile teeth. Hate boiled through her. How many times had greedy old men just like him taken anything that was hers and hers alone? She could practically hear DeSoto's voice chastising her for vanity, crushing her sweet-scented sampaguita

155

rosaries, having her painstakingly pick out the neat rows of white flowers and leaves she'd embroidered into the hems of her plain white postulant's habits. Hours spent saying her Ave Marías, kneeling on scattered rice as punishment for braiding ribbons into her hair. He'd broken her down little by little, until everything about her was curated to his will. And now they would take her mutya?

She lunged for it, hating how it lay on his skin, hating him and the priest who'd thought they could declaw her so easily. A furious desperation rose in her from so deep it ached. The pearl of her balisong, hidden away in her sleeve, keened against her skin at the separation from the rest of her mutya.

But she was only a bound girl, a tide-touched who was afraid of the sea. The sailors shoved her to her knees, their barking laughter ringing in her ears. The captain held her mutya up to the light, mocking her.

Ortiz shook his head. "We spent a generation laboring to drag that city into God's light, and you backward monkeys have fallen to superstition and witchery in only a few seasons?"

Inez bared her teeth at him, her fury blacker and more crushing than the deepest dive. "Thirty years stealing and raping, you mean."

He clicked his tongue. "Do you really think your sister will welcome you back like this?"

"Shut up."

But Ortiz spoke over her, warming to his sermon. "A feral jungle witch of a girl? Holy Father bless my work, what will it take to make you presentable now? More than a miracle. Not that you were ever much good as a postulant, either..."

Another priest who thought he could mold her, remake

her in his own image. Take the pieces of her and rearrange them to his liking. Never again. She'd rather die.

"Shut up!" Inez wished she could fill his lungs with saltwater, drown out every word he'd ever thought to voice.

"Everyone knew exactly why you were DeSoto's favorite," he continued.

The crushing fist of Inez's fury was a staggering weight that she did not know how to release. But then, the shape of the wave calling came to rest deep in her throat, at the back of her tongue, unfamiliar but not unpleasant. It pooled, heavy with salt and everything she needed.

The hum of crocodile singing tripped off her tongue easier than any prayer the temple had taught.

She croaked a command. The sea below gathered her in, anchoring her in her skin, in her power as she had never been before. She drew on the salt tides that cradled the slaver like a maggot in a kapre's palm. "Tahimik! Let the sound of the surf drown out your voice."

The sailors holding her arms fell away from her, crying out as the deck pitched, throwing everyone off their feet but Inez. As the deck rose and fell, she balanced lightly as foam on the crest of a wave. She twisted, dragging a hand free of her bindings to sweep out an arm, making the deck buck. Below, the crushing pressure of the sea hungered just as she did, and she would feed it every life that fled before her on the deck.

Ortiz cried out to his God as he slid. She wished never to hear his voice ever again. "Shut. Up. Shut. UP!" she roared, stalking across the rolling deck toward him, white-faced and scrambling on his belly for purchase like a sand shrimp stranded at low tide.

He was still praying to his God, his mouth forming

familiar pleas, pleas Inez herself had made. For mercy, for intercession, for justice. Too bad his god had never heard mestiza girls. Not like the deep water heard her now.

She had prayed to those same deaf, dead, and maddened saints, begging them to preserve her chastity, for them to return her to the purity and virginity for which the women of the Church were so prized, while a man like Ortiz ruined her.

"SHUT UP!" she screamed.

Salt spray drifted across the deck as the waves rose up, encircling the ship. Inez gathered it to her hand and sent it slinging outward, sharp as shattered glass. It cut lines across Ortiz's face, and finally he stopped praying to scream.

One more step, and the sea mimicked her stalking movement, rising and crashing down in a tremendous wave that flooded the deck, picking up Ortiz and several others to sweep them overboard.

Inez snapped her fists shut, fingers locking together tight as teeth, sinking them all, determined that no one would fight their way free from the grasp of the sea. "Malunod ka!"

Fed to the waves. Down and down into the crushing deep where there would be no sound, no breath, not even light.

At last, it was quiet but for the sated roar of the waves. The sound was so similar to crocodile singing, Inez wondered that she hadn't recognized the melody before.

Then, the trailing rope looped around her wrist pulled tight. Another caught her around the neck. She tried to cry out, to wash herself into the sea where she'd be free of these maggots. Forget logic, forget the distance to land, she was tide-touched, a daughter of the sea. Better to dive deep than be taken.

The captain was quicker and cleverer than Ortiz. The rope at her neck yanked tight. Inez was dragged across the deck, her borrowed robe tearing on rough planks as blackness danced before her eyes. She fought the lack of oxygen, fought to remain conscious, to send them all down into the sea's grip, but without air she couldn't sing the wave calling that the crocodiles had taught her tongue.

She reached with everything she had for saltwater. She had to break free; she needed a wave! But she could only sense as far as the foot of saltwater she'd sent cascading into the hull, the hundreds of terrified hearts shackled in the dark, thrashing against the rising waters, like fish on a barbed harpoon.

Inez choked, tearing her attention from the terror she'd caused. Her hold on the sea and the salt singing in her blood faltered.

Once more, darkness closed over her head.

It was quicker this time, a blink—like a large wave catching and dashing her against the reefs, spotty disorienting blackness—before she struggled back to the surface.

But sailors could move quickly across a pitching deck. Inez came to, tied to the great iron links of the anchor.

"Stop the waves now, witch! Or we'll cast you into the sea."

The rasping laugh that scraped out of her throat startled Inez. "Do it!" she demanded. "Send me down into the salt. Do you think I'll go down alone? You and your ship will join me. We will all rest at the bottom of the sea together."

At her words, the captain pointed to the dark hatch in the center of the deck.

"You wouldn't, not with so many aboard. I know you witch-types. Your navy would've driven us from Aynila, but witches are soft. You value the lives of chattel."

Inez hesitated, her predatory focus falling away. In her

hesitation, Aman Sinaya remembered her love for her people. The sharp-toothed wrath Inez had called up ebbed back into the wide blue bowl of the sea like it had never been.

She glared at the captain and spat, her fury impotent as the sailors dragged struggling captives out of the cargo hold, roping them by the neck to the anchor chain alongside Inez, to ensure she didn't forget.

Women and young girls wept and cried out, the sunlight beating into their eyes after weeks below decks. Unspeakable pain, and Inez could do nothing. She might survive sending the ship down, but she'd never be able to parse the hundreds of lives aboard and separate the innocent from the guilty before the sea swallowed them up like raindrops upon the waves.

She paused her ineffectual struggle against her own bonds to watch, darkly satisfied, as the slavers let down their shore-boats to search the water for their fallen compatriots and Ortiz, swept overboard.

The surface of the sea was still and calm as glass. Inez willed it so. All the better to prove Ortiz had been fed to the depths. Irretrievable. Silent forever.

Just like she'd wanted—

Reality broke through the buwaya-madness that had overtaken her. Without Ortiz, how would she ever find her sister?

A different kind of desperation came over her, and Inez reached out. Had she really just drowned her very best chance at finding Catalina? She struggled to recall the struggling sensation of lives within the hold, but she felt no beating hearts in the waters surrounding the slave ship. She dove down, nothing—*no*, not nothing. Saltwater crocodiles cruised the depths, bellies full. They did not waste the sea's bounty.

"You sing beautifully, little crocodile. Thank you for the meal."

Without the insulating protection of her own fury, Inez flinched. What had she been thinking, feeding the power of the Amihan Moon to hungry crocodiles, making an offering of her enemies to anito that knew none of Aman Sinaya's mercy? She'd even sung their songs to the sea, and the sea had listened.

As if they would not crush the life from her as easily as priests and slavers. She was as much a fool as Alon thought her.

She retreated back into her own skin with a snap like a pearl diver's tie-line breaking.

17

LUNURIN CALILAN NG DAKILA

With the grim confirmation she'd needed from Lunurin, the Lakan had called together the council of Aynila's matriarchs to discuss how they would rethink the upcoming Amihan Moon Summit in light of the armada's crossing.

Lunurin held her composure together with her teeth. Beyond her fears, beyond the council of matriarchs deliberating in the Lakan's study, Anitun Tabu thundered at the edges of her exhaustion, furious that they had not been able to rain down destruction upon the approaching armada. But at this time of year, with the wet season's prevailing winds, who was to say her storm would not merely usher their doom across the sea faster?

When she wasn't wrapped up in Anitun Tabu's embrace and the beautiful, clear straight line to the destruction of her enemies, Lunurin knew these things. She knew, even if her goddess did not, that a storm could not solve *every* problem. She'd watched for years as Father DeSoto and Governor López's shipbuilders developed galleons designed to withstand the worst storms and the greatest waves that tropical seas could brew, that all the gods-blessed as one could twist together. Even should she summon a typhoon strong enough to strip every bit of greenery from the archipelago and lay their cities low, the battened-down galleons would merely shut their hatches, lay their grounding chains, and kill and kill and kill. Her power wasn't enough. They needed allies.

Lunurin knew this, but she'd thought she had months to mend her ties to Calilan and the Stormfleet, to convince them to stand with her for Aynila. She'd never imagined herself here, having wrung out all her strength without even delaying their doom and unsure if her own family would even bother to attend in person, much less any of the other Stormfleet factions.

Sina's warm hand closed around her shaking ones, pressing warmth into her blood. "Should I send for Alon?" Sina asked softly.

"He has enough crises to manage. Please don't remind him his wife is another," Lunurin said, taking a step closer to lean into the warmth of Sina's power.

Sina chuckled and pressed their cheeks together. "I'm beginning to believe that crises enjoy flocking together like spark-striker birds. There is never only one. And if you think there is, you aren't looking hard enough."

Lunurin snorted, converting her laughter into a cough as the Lakan and Sina's mother, Hiraya, glanced in her direction. "I hope Hilaga can spare you both."

She clutched Sina tighter for a moment. Lunurin still occasionally missed those early days of her marriage when Alon's cousin had lived with them.

With Sina's borrowed energy, she was at last able to focus

beyond the grey haze of her own exhaustion on the Lakan's council.

"We can't spare any more firetenders from preparations for the Amihan Moon. We've already placed as many as we could to work on Aynila's fortifications. If we offer more for the Stormfleet's use…" Hiraya shook her head. "It would cut us off at the knees, especially now."

"Then what do you propose I offer our allies? I am about to ask them to put their lives on the line for our city," Dalisay countered.

"Tide-touched," Lunurin spoke up. Faces lined with many years of wisdom and now a great deal of stress turned to her. "It has always been a point of contention that Aynila draws away any tide-touched with real power to the healing school. In my youth amongst the Stormfleet, it was an expected loss of our best and brightest to the main islands. Why would they return to life on the fleets once they had established themselves in Aynila, or anywhere in the central isles during their training?"

"Surely you see I am in even less a position to give up my tide-touched than I am my firetenders." Dalisay's hands flashed her dismissal of the suggestion.

"Not now, not in wartime. But what if we changed how we trained at the healing school? We could ask our healers to spend a few months, or a wet season, aboard a Stormfleet ship before their graduation. There will be those, like Aizza, who much prefer a shipboard life to that in Aynila, but would never know it if not for the opportunity. Let us be clear we are training up our tide-touched not only for Aynila's benefit, but for the gain of all. At the very least, a rotation of young healers aboard the fleet will improve relations with our allies across the archipelago."

"It will disrupt their training so much..." This objection came from Casama. The old dye mistress was one of the Lakan's dearest confidantes, and no small number of her most skilled dye workers were students on apprenticeship from the healing school.

"There will be no training to disrupt unless we can convince our allies to stand with us. I am prepared to be generous now in the hopes we have a tomorrow to regret our commitments," Lunurin countered.

A knock at the door disturbed the deliberations as a servant entered.

The Lakan frowned. "No interruptions when my council is meeting," she signed sharply.

But Isko pushed past the servant into the room, looking worse somehow than he had that terrible day when the abbot and his bully squad had raided Aynila Indigo. On his heels came Bernila, smears of blood dried down her front, a knot coming up vividly at her hairline.

Lunurin's heart sank into her belly.

"Isko, we are in closed council," the Lakan signed almost resignedly. "Let us at least pretend we observe proprieties before our allies are here scrutinizing our every move."

"You know I would not break with protocol if it weren't of grave importance. Forgive me," Isko signed back, as he bowed in apology to the assembled matriarchs and katalonan for his breach of decorum. "I mean no disrespect, but I must speak to Lunurin in private. It's about Inez."

The Lakan huffed a soundless sigh, signing, "It can wait. I have need of Lunurin's council."

"We believe she was taken when the priest escaped," Isko said.

Lunurin's heart clenched tight with fear. Her sudden intake

of breath rattled the capiz windows as the air in the room quivered with her. All her plans and worries were dust and ash in the face of Inez, alone, in terrible danger.

She bolted to her feet. But Sina was at her side, her arm around Lunurin's back as hot as metal under the beating summer sun, the only thing stopping her from seizing Bernila and demanding she tell her everything. Lunurin longed for the cool depths of Alon's comfort.

Sina bowed to the assembled matriarchs. "We will return swiftly and report on what must be done about the priest's escape. Until then, do excuse us."

Lunurin focused on breathing, on controlling her emotions. Had they not just decided that she must ensure a calm wet season, with weak northeastern winds? The fine drizzle on the tiled roof had already become a pounding downpour.

"What do you mean, *taken*?" Lunurin demanded as the door to the council closed. "Taken where? By whom?"

Isko winced. "Not exactly taken. Taken is a… generous description."

"She helped the priest escape," Bernila said. "They fled Aynila aboard the Lusitan slave ship."

Bernila couldn't mean—surely she didn't—she was confused—Lunurin's justifications tripped over themselves.

Isko's expression was so very grave. "I fear it must be true. Tibay confirmed that it was Inez who pulled him away from his guard post, but we're keeping that detail quiet for now."

"And Bernila?" Lunurin managed to choke out.

"She was discovered unconscious in the back storerooms of the healing halls, just before noon. Aizza was able to wake her but…"

Lunurin turned to Bernila.

Bernila chewed nervously on her lower lip. "Inez attacked

me. When I found her helping Father Ortiz escape."

"Why?" Lunurin wailed, struggling to modulate her voice lower.

Bernila flinched, her hands fisting tightly. "She said she had to do it, that Ortiz knew something about her sister. The Lusitan slavers were involved somehow. She said she was sorry. I tried to stop her, but—"

Lunurin pressed her hand over her mouth, half-sick with fear.

"You did well to tell us, Bernila," Sina soothed.

It should be Lunurin saying those words, but all she could think was that she must somehow catch up to that ship. Every moment she delayed, Inez got farther away. All that came out of her mouth was, "I have to go after Inez."

This held far too many parallels to that terrible day when the abbot's soldiers had ransacked Aynila Indigo hunting for the "witch" saboteurs who had destroyed the Puente de Hilaga just weeks before its completion. It had been Rosa then, rushing to find her with news that Inez was in deathly peril, having faced the abbot's wrath and been caned within an inch of her life.

Lunurin turned, caught Bernila's hands in her own. "Thank you."

And she left. Sina would give her regrets to the Lakan, and Isko would ensure that Alon was apprised of the situation. She could trust them.

She was already evaluating which of Alon's ships and which captains were in Aynila. Whose ship was fastest? Or should she select the best-armed? They had already lost so much time. The Lusitan ship would have almost a full day's head start. Who could ensure they had every bit of speed that her winds and tide-touched currents could conjure?

Could one of Aynila's navy karakoas be spared? Surely in service of capturing Ortiz, Alon could convince Jeian it was worth it.

~

The kalesa driver she hailed nearly killed them both and several pedestrians at the speed Lunurin demanded she be taken to the port. She paid her thanks in gold for his haste and rushed to Aynila Indigo's warehouses, where she would be most likely to find captains whose crews were still engaged in delivery or loading and therefore not spread out through the port drinking and carousing on shore leave. She needed a ship prepared to set sail before the tide turned. They had already lost so much time. Inez was in terrible danger.

Lunurin wished suddenly that she had agreed to Jeian's plan to sink the slaver the moment it had the audacity to lay anchor outside Aynila Bay. If she had, then none of this would've happened. Inez would be here. She never would've been tricked or coerced or stolen away by another priest. Alon ought to have let his brother beat the man to death.

If the slavers had never been in the bay, if the priest had never been in the healing school—

Lunurin had let too many shadows of the Palisade fall over Inez. She should have been more watchful. She should have seen that something was terribly wrong, that Inez was frightened—and like Catalina, Inez had a way of letting fear drive her to extremes. Lunurin knew all of this. But she had let herself be distracted by her duties, by leadership and diplomacy and the needs of Aynila over the needs of her family. What had she been thinking?

"You there, are you loading or unloading?" she called out

to a captain overseeing the work of the long shoreman.

She needed a ship whose hold was empty. Cargo would only be dead weight.

"Lunurin!"

Alon had come after her. He always would. She could feel the tether between their souls, no longer gossamer as spiderweb, stretched thin by distance and power, but hundreds of silk threads woven into a tapestry of promises and trust.

Lunurin turned aside from the captain, trying to figure out how she could possibly make him understand why she had to do this. The closed, stern expression Alon still wore told her she had become yet another crisis he must weather.

So much had been on his shoulders these last months. They'd both been pulled in a hundred different directions when they should have been paying attention to Inez. But Alon had always been able to bear his duty over his love. He wouldn't understand that she could not put Aynila first. Not when Inez was in danger.

Guilt was a brick of wet mud in her belly. She almost wished he would tell her she was being unreasonable, a fool. He should call her selfish, for she was. Inez consumed her every thought. Even this moment of stillness set her teeth on edge.

"What is it?" she snapped, readying herself to rebuff even him. She almost wanted to fight. It would make the pain of parting easier. Nothing came before Inez's safety. Nothing. Inez was more her family than any of her blood relations, her sister in all the ways that mattered.

Alon did not speak, did not offer up a single cause for her to lash out at him as she wanted to—as she had to, if she meant to leave. He grasped her hands in his, pulling her aside from the rush and bustle of the warehouse.

She turned her face away. She refused to be swayed by the disappointment, or worse, that would be in his eyes. "Alon. I have to go. Every moment I delay, Inez is taken further away from us and into greater danger."

"Don't." Just the one word, soft as rain on her face.

"I know you must think me selfish and foolish, but she's in terrible danger. I can't do nothing. I promised I'd never abandon her. I have to go." Had that promise been to Inez or to Cat? Did it matter? She'd failed.

She made the mistake of meeting his eyes. Alon's face was stern and set, focused on seeing them all through the crisis. Lunurin pulled her hands free of his—and his expression cracked with a soft, wounded sound swallowed back behind his teeth.

Alon folded to his knees and curled his arms around her waist. He buried his face in her midriff. "Don't go. I cannot do this without you. It's too much. I can't see us through the Amihan Moon and gathering our allies. I cannot hope to protect Aynila without you. Please don't go. Don't leave me alone."

His words were hot against her skin through the fine material of her blouse. She laid her hands atop his head. "Alon, I…"

He looked up at her, desperation a naked wound on his face, his dark eyes pleading. "I will send my very best after Inez. We will get her back. She is your sworn sister, as much as Isko is my brother. She's my student. We will get her back. But…" He clutched her with a tightness that conveyed more than need, a vulnerability greater even than when she'd nearly given herself over to her goddess's vengeance. What was he so afraid of?

"Aynila." Lunurin breathed it and felt the weight of

responsibility, a whole city of lives on her shoulders. It would not survive without her.

"I won't survive without you," Alon said, as if he'd read the fear from her very blood. What was blood but saltwater to one blessed by Aman Sinaya?

Lunurin leaned into him, torn between her promises. She had vowed to always put her little family from the convent first, to love and protect Inez as her own sister. That warred with another promise, written on her heart in lightning: the vow she had made to her goddess long ago, as a girl of twelve on the shores of Calilan, and again and again since. A vow to stand for her people, to exact vengeance for all their dead.

Distantly, in the winds dancing around Hilaga's peak, her goddess spoke. *Are you prepared to cast it all aside for one gone astray? One ship lost at sea? Did you not promise me your heart if I would grant you the blood of your enemies? And have we not tasted it?*

The words rasped out of her. "I promised…"

She'd promised Alon too, many things, so many over the years, through all the storms he had weathered without hesitation. Never hating her when she faltered.

"I know, I know she isn't a little girl anymore, but how can I let her go down this dangerous path alone? When I know what became of Catalina? I could've acted. I could've made Catalina and Inez leave before it was too late and I failed, I failed them both! How can I fail Inez again?"

"This isn't the same. And none of it is your fault. We can still fix this. I've already convinced Jeian to tell Aynila that the merchant ship he fired on was smuggling the priest out of the city. That Ortiz is dead. No one else ever needs to know Inez was involved. We will protect her, and we will get her back."

"I..." Her fear for Inez was a choking tightness in her chest. It was so hard to think through, as hard as it was to see reason when she was wrapped up in her goddess's vengeance. But she must try. For Alon, for Aynila. Once again, Alon was willing to lie to protect her and her family. To help her move heaven and earth till reality suited their purposes, and all he asked was that she not abandon him.

Inez was not a little girl anymore. And as much as it pained Lunurin, she was not exactly a hostage in this situation. She had lured Tibay from his post, attacked Bernila, and gone with Ortiz all the way across the bay to board a Lusitan slave ship. She was tide-touched. No one could coerce tide-touched over open water.

Inez had knowingly and repeatedly put herself in danger. The prayer meeting, then the priest... Lunurin had no idea what Inez thought she was chasing but even Lunurin couldn't paint her as the helpless victim in this situation.

"I need you," Alon begged.

Lunurin's heart twisted, torn between her vows and every protective instinct she'd ever harbored for Inez; caught between promises made, both human and divine. For a heart-stopping instant she feared they would tear her apart.

It was so much. But if today had taught her anything, it was that she and Alon could not save Aynila alone. They must gain allies in the upcoming summit, or there would be no Aynila to bring Inez home to.

Alon needed her.

"I know." Lunurin bent and pressed her brow to his, seeking comfort in the deep well of his soul when all her own spirit wanted was to fly free on distant winds, to scour the seas again for her lost sister. "You're right. I can't leave you and Sina to gather allies for Aynila alone. I will not leave you to face my father's armada without me."

"Do you mean it? You'll stay?" The disbelief in Alon's voice cut at her, but he had every right to it. He knew her, knew her so very well. He knew the storm of her mind, even when she herself could not fathom which way the churning winds would carry her. And he knew it went against everything in her to put her family aside for the greater good. She was not a born leader like him, able to weigh the needs of many, to choose peace and diplomacy over bloody-minded vengeance.

"Yes, for you, for Aynila. It isn't just me and my family against the world. I am your wife, a Dayang of Aynila, a katalonan. I have responsibilities here." Admitting it tore asunder a small, secret piece of Lunurin's heart where all her vows to Catalina and her old life in the convent lived. Despite how it had ended—*because* of how it had ended, in betrayal and death... those promises mattered.

But she was not Inez. She could not go chasing the ghosts of the past, when so many thousands of lives now hung in the balance of her choices.

18

•••

INEZ NG DAKILA

Inez struggled for breath against the rope tying her to the anchor chain, which stretched across the deck and over the bow. Each swell and pitch of the ship on the waves pressed her weight against the rope cinched tight around her throat. Inez stood on her tiptoes, trying to get purchase on the deck, fighting against her instinct to reach out to the cradling gulf of salt below. She worried that any further signs of unnatural interference would frighten the sailors into casting her and the others tied beside her into the sea. And she expected the crocodiles trailing them would be as happy to feast on her as her offerings.

As the long hot afternoon wore on, her focus narrowed, each breath caught in the lull between swells. She wondered what would happen when she tired and was no longer able to remain poised on her tiptoes, balancing her weight against the ship's lists and rolls and keeping the pressure off her throat. Would she slowly suffocate, too weak to stand?

She took no heed of anything beyond her fight for air,

till the rhythm of the ship's movement shifted and men clambered up the ratlines. Rigging was drawn taut. Every sail unfurled to catch the light wet season wind and speed their passage south.

Inez tried to scan the horizon, but she was facing the wrong way. Were they trying to outrun a brewing storm?

The slavers were still scrambling. Men ran to and fro across the deck, the captain shouting orders, until the mad dash resolved itself into boxes of munitions and powder packed down the gullets of the deck cannons.

Then, something went wrong. Before black snouts could be rolled forward to protrude from the gunports like wild boars, there was a wave of heat. It rolled across the water, up over the ship in a shimmering wall of super-heated air—like Sina about to blow a forge to smithereens.

Inez jerked the chain, trying to get the attention of the woman tied beside her, as she held her breath, screwing her eyes shut. Heat blasted her face. Screams rose as the unwary breathed in, singeing nose hairs to dust, scalding lungs. The world exploded as black powder ignited and cannons fired, shrapnel exploding outward well before anyone aboard was prepared.

Inez stared at the destruction of the deck in amazement. She'd not even seen the enemy ship, nor heard an opening salvo.

The captain, his left side torn to tatters of skin and bone, staggered across the deck toward her. He seized her with his remaining hand, the second half of her mutya making electrifying contact with her skin. "You! Witch, get us out of range before these pirates tear us to shreds."

With the nearness of her mutya, Inez sent her awareness down and out across the surface of the water till she encountered another hull, a great crescent-shaped karakoa, shallow-drafted, but built for speed in a way foreign ships never were.

The karakoa seemed to radiate heat, like the beating rays of the sun.

"I can't like this," Inez rasped, yanking at her bonds.

The captain loosed one of her hands.

"Do something!" he ordered, shaking her shoulder.

Inez smiled. "No." With her freed hand she dragged him closer and twisted, ignoring how it cut off her ability to breathe, spots flashing before her eyes. She closed her teeth around her mutya on the captain's wrist, and no small amount of skin. He tore free, howling. Her mutya stayed between her teeth.

She didn't dare open her mouth to scream as the anchor spooled free, dragging her across the deck and down toward the waves.

With a jarring crash, the anchor chain caught on something damaged in the blast and stopped, leaving Inez dangling just above the water.

Above her, the screams and struggles of her fellow captives assured her she hadn't gotten everyone killed yet. She thanked the sea for small mercies.

Inez twisted, wrapping her legs around the anchor chain. She found a foothold and managed to lever her weight off her neck and still-tied arm while she strained to reach her balisong knife. Flicking the other half of her mutya open, she began to saw at the tarred ropes holding her to the anchor.

She started at her neck. Wary of cutting herself, it was slow going. Her whole body ached with the strain of holding her weight as she swung above the waves. She stared across at the approaching karakoa. She didn't recognize the feathered pennants streaming above the arrayed fins of the roaring laho carved into the prow. They snapped in the backdraft like flames, red and black with gleaming copper insignia. Perhaps the Lusitan captain had been right—these were pirates, preying on the rich cargoes of foreign trade ships. A dangerous endeavor, and one for which a great many city states of the archipelago would disavow them.

Their rowers strained at the oars, the chanting of their helmsman keeping time. Even the heat shimmering over the water thrummed with each cut of the oars in the waves.

It reminded Inez of Sina urging her forge fire awake after banking the coals through the night, her hands twisting patterns in the smoke, her voice a husky croon of greeting. Yet the firetender aboard this ship was so much more powerful. She'd never seen Sina control fire beyond a range of a hundred feet—but the pirates had flashed the slaver's powder long before they'd come in range of its guns.

The distance between them closed, far faster than rowing or even the light winds filling the crab-claw sails should have made possible. The karakoa glowed like molten bronze, its great laho-shaped prow cutting through the water like it were the great beast in truth, salt spray turning to steam in the hot air. The rope at her throat finally gave and Inez sucked in greedy lungfuls of air, hacking at the remaining tie at her wrist.

And then Inez saw her, alone near the rear of the raised platform above the rowers. Her black hair lifted on the heated winds she drew around herself like silks, her hands long-fingered and elegant. Inez wondered at her power. Her ringed fingers flashed in the sun as she shaped heat to do her bidding, so very far from the volcano she served. She was incandescent, like staring into Hilaga's magma chamber. It almost seemed as if she had swallowed the sun, the great golden torque about her neck reflecting its light more brightly than any mirror, directing the super-heated air as she sought through the slave ship for any remaining flammable materials.

Caught up in the rising heat, Inez once more hummed the reptilian prayer for a wave. The longer this chase went on, the more likely it was the captain would think to cut the anchor free, losing the weight of Inez and the poor souls tied beside her. Who knew how much of their cargo the Lusitans were prepared to cast overboard?

The call to the salt was a song older even than the tide-touched, and with it she dragged up a rush of water and currents, forcing the fleeing slave ship broadside into the path of the firetender's fury.

Another explosion rocked the ship. Inez smiled, clenching her mutya necklace tight in her teeth as the slave ship listed wildly. Slavers slid across the decks into the sea. The weight of the anchor dragged Inez down toward the water.

She took a deep breath, like Lunurin had trained her to for pearl diving. No matter what happened, she couldn't scream, not like she had in the bay. It was still a shock. The anchor dragged her down faster than any dive, faster than the currents had ever taken her. She went down and down, struggling to break free. How long did she have before even she would not be able to swim for the surface? Her chest ached with pressure. Her ears popped.

Finally hitting the end of the chain, her downward hurtle halted. All around was dim blueness, as deep and dark as an indigo dye vat, but so still and calm. The great pressing weight of the salt and its deep chill was an unexpected balm on all the parts of her that felt overexposed and raw.

She could've closed her eyes and stayed curled here in the crushing deep forever.

Then, she registered the struggling bodies farther up the

chain, jerking and fighting for their lives, precious bubbles streaming toward the surface. All around, under the shadow of the ship, circling crocodiles considered the easy meal that had been dropped down to them. One darted forward. It would only take one drop of blood to start the feeding frenzy.

"*NO!*" This time, Inez did not lose precious air in the command, instead croaking from her throat and clicking her tongue.

The great black bodies veered away from the anchor chain with its tied, struggling bait, diving down toward her.

She braced for the pain. For tearing, rolling, blood. A huge black snout struck her arm, biting down just inches from her hand, catching the trailing ropes. Its death roll jerked Inez wildly, and the last shreds of rope binding her wrist gave at last. She was torn free into the depths of the sea. With the last of her strength, Inez closed her fingers on scaly hide.

～

Inez hacked seawater onto an unfamiliar deck. A burning hot hand thumped her back, a dozen overlapping voices drowning out her thoughts.

"What?" Inez asked.

"Oh good!" the back thumper exclaimed, pausing in her attempt to hammer Inez through the deck. "So, you really can't drown a tide-touched. Though I'm still not sure I understand how they kept you aboard a slave ship."

She extended a fire-scarred hand. Inez tried not to stare. They were not like the Lakan's burns—smooth, pale swaths of scar that broke up the deep brown of her skin where oil-fed flames had licked up her legs. These were dark, rippling burns in an angry red that wrapped around her arms and across her palms. What could burn a firetender so deeply?

The other gods-blessed spoke Pangilog, from the inland rice kingdom around Mount Tumubo in central Lusong. It had taken Inez a moment to place her accent; it was like bending her ears around a bamboo pole to make sense of the familiar-sounding words in their unfamiliar order, but Aynila had always been a diverse trade hub, and it was not uncommon to hear Pangilog in the markets and port.

"I've never had a crocodile let me take anything from its mouth, but I'll not question the will of the sea when a tide-touched is in the water." The firetender reached into the folds of her salampé sash and held Inez's mutya out toward her, cupped carefully in her scarred palm.

Inez half expected to feel that same violated, soul-raw fury, seeing her mutya in another's hands as she had when the Lusitan captain had taken it. Instead, she felt only blissful warmth, easing the deep-water cold from her bones.

"Thank you po." She appended the respectful address belatedly, her fingers closing around her mutya and grasping it to herself, desperately thankful it had not been lost in the chaos. She cast her gaze toward the buwaya in the water. Golden eyes gleamed bright, one tooth now missing from its sharp smile. Inez included the anito in her thanks.

"The others—" Inez began, worried that the buwaya would not have minded the fine distinction between slaver and slave once there was blood in the water, even if they had for some reason decided she was one of them, a little crocodile.

"Were there more than three tied to the anchor with you?" the firetender asked.

"No." Inez did not let herself sink, exhausted and relieved, back down to the deck yet. "But we must offer the buwaya something. How many slavers died in the blast?"

The firetender's bright focus was a palpable heat that Inez did not shrink from. They locked gazes, the woman tugging her mutya earring thoughtfully. Inez didn't dare look away first.

"I'll pay my debts to the sea as a tide-touched believes best," she said at last.

She signaled to her crew, several climbing aboard the slaver to see it done.

Respect, at least, Inez had read in her gaze. It was a place to bargain from. She'd stepped from a slave ship onto a pirate's; she wouldn't forget it. "And what do pirates intend for a cargo of slaves?"

The firetender grinned. "I'm Captain Umali Suba—and you may call us pirates, but the Tianchaowen have decided they have use for the enemies of their enemies. In their latest dispute with the Lusitans, they have declared that any ship bearing Tianchaowen slaves is a pillager and a pirate with a bounty on their head. So we are not pirates, but privateers."

"And they'd pay it even to wokou?" Inez used the derogatory term Tianchaowen merchants reserved for pirates.

This sent a cackle up from the nearby crew, who were engaged in tossing explosion-mangled bodies into the sea.

"Bold words. What may I call you?" Umali asked.

"Inez..." She hesitated, not wanting to reveal her ties to Aynila. Who did not know Lakan Dalisay Dakila? "Domingo," she said instead. Unlike in Aynila, her old name carried no connotations of betrayal here.

Umali did not bat an eye at the Codicían name—but then, she only had to look at Inez to know she was mestiza. "Well, Inez. Their officials have had enough of the slave ship stink along their coasts. And since the Lusitans will not cease raiding their coastal cities for captives, they are offering one thousand silver tael for a slaver's pennant and manifest, more when captives are returned to Tianchaowen ports. Masagana will pay the bounty. We'll put the Tianchaowen captives ashore there."

Inez recognized the name of the Tianchaowen trade hub a few days sail beyond Aynila, on one of Lusong's outlying islands to the east.

"And me?"

"And you? Well, if you don't plan to swim off with your crocodiles, where else would we take a lost tide-touched but to Aynila's famed healing school, rebuilt at last?"

Inez shook her head, not daring to search the water for the buwaya that had saved her. "No, Masagana is fine."

Without the priest, she had no proof of her wild quest to find her sister. And after what she had done in Aynila, there was no going back, not without anything more than rumors to show for it. Jeian would paint her as a traitor, a broken tide-touched full of crocodile guile. Inez couldn't convince herself he would be entirely wrong.

The captain's expression furrowed with confusion, but she inclined her head and turned away to the business of freeing the ship's human cargo and repairing the berth enough to limp it into port.

Inez's thoughts leaped ahead. She might have just killed her best lead on Catalina, but there was a church in Masagana. Father DeSoto had designed it himself. He'd often dictated letters to her for the brothers assigned to the satellite parish regarding the upkeep and preservation of the church against the difficult environment of the islands. There might still be faithful there who would know more about Santa Catalina. After all, local saints were their own kind of little gods to the faithful of the archipelago.

19

ALON DAKILA

If Pedro could bring Catalina through the aftermath of the Palisade's destruction alive, surely he could slip Inez free from the trap she'd leaped into.

So Alon was generous as he paid his spy an advance and secured a berth on the fastest trade ship in Aynila Indigo's fleet. Nothing moved Pedro like gold. The longer Inez was missing, the less likely it was he could convince Lunurin to leave this hunt to others.

He had almost lost her twice in the span of only a few hours. He hadn't been prepared to face the depths of his own terror at how easily she could be taken from him. Her soul snatched away by her goddess on the wind, or by her own will as she chased after Inez.

And so, at last Alon was forced to admit the secret he'd been keeping from his wife. Only not *to* his wife. The words kept sticking in his throat when he tried.

"The Codicíans are spreading some rumor about a Santa Catalina having returned to the archipelago. Inez is likely

183

chasing that rumor," Alon informed his spy.

Pedro winced. "Then I should tell you now, since you've clearly not had time to read the reports: she's not the only one who's returned. Abbess Magdalena de Palma made the crossing from Canazco last year. I spoke to a navigator in Sugbu who'd taken her as far as Talaan. It's likely she went on to Simsiman, but I've no proof of it."

Alon cursed. This as good as confirmed the rumors were a lure set for Lunurin. "So she's coordinating the Codicíans' missionary ring." He'd known that the spies the Codicíans had been sending knew too much of Aynila, too much about Lunurin, and there were few Codicíans who paid such close attention to the native powers of the archipelago. It made the abbess a dangerous and important asset, enabling her brother, Archbishop de Palma, to outmaneuver the power-hungry former abbot, Rodrigo.

"If she's joined the convent in Simsiman, she's not keeping vows of silence like the other sisters," Pedro agreed. "But try as I might, I could not find any proof that Sister Catalina accompanied her on the crossing from Canazco. And I doubt even I can slip unnoticed into Simsiman, given the current tensions."

"Hopefully it will not come to that. Whether Catalina is in Simsiman or has remained in Canazco, her name alone is enough. I need you to find Inez and bring her back to Aynila before anything happens to her."

Pedro bowed deeply and departed for the ship, leaving with the setting sun.

~

The first day of the planned Amihan Moon Summit had arrived. From his vantage point in the plaza, Alon studied the port critically for any remaining threads of their narrative that were out of place. The wreck from his brother's attack yesterday morning had been hauled into one of the ship repair berths. Luckily, the ship had not been Aynilan, but from Sugbu. At least no Aynilan lives had been lost in this debacle-turned-cover-up.

Already, berths were filling along the docks, newly built up and down the port to accommodate their guests. He could see a ship sailing under Aynila's golden sun pennant bearing Lunurin out to greet the first contingent of the Stormfleet. Their ships had just begun to enter the arms of the bay, their mixed pennants streaming in the breeze. Most numerous among them was that of Calilan, Lunurin's home island, which had once been the training ground for the whole Stormfleet, from Lusong down to Ísuga. Alon hoped desperately that this time, his wife's family had come in person.

At the thought of her family, his guilt ate at him. He had to tell her about Catalina. With Inez gone and especially now that he had proof of the abbess's presence. He had to tell her now that she had agreed to stay.

It had kept him awake all through the night, tossing and turning while Lunurin slept the sleep of one pushed to their very limits beside him. She'd been so still and quiet that at times, he'd reached out just to feel the beat of her heart and trace the rush of blood through her veins, to remind himself that he'd not lost her yet.

But—once again—this was the worst possible moment to come clean. Inez aboard a slave ship was bad enough. He feared that proof of Magdalena's involvement would only give Lunurin more reason to believe it must be her who went after Inez.

Alon ground a knuckle into his furrowed brow and

cursed the mercy of the sea. Would that he had but a drop of Lunurin's vision for simple solutions, even when they required bloodshed, and he would not be in this tangled predicament.

He could not dwell on it now. The Lakan's servants had summoned him to the healing halls. Then, he would have to join his brother down in the port to greet yet more delegates. The true test was only just beginning.

His inay's study in the halls was beautifully appointed, indigo silk cushions softening dark polished wood. Dalisay was not yet dressed to receive their many noble visitors, who would be flocking to the Lakan's palace this evening for the feast. Casama and her teams of seamstresses had been laboring over her indigo and gold robes for weeks.

Alon presented the report her council had requested, outlining and—against his better instincts—defending Jeian's reasoning for sinking the trade ship. The timing of the ship's visits to Aynila and the issues they'd faced with the missionary spies, Codicían assassination attempts, and lately these subversive prayer meetings, couldn't be coincidence.

His inay reviewed the document. "Good. This will reassure many."

"There's more. Jeian says he didn't intend to fire on the parao, and I believe him," Alon added.

Dalisay raised a brow in inquiry.

"He wanted to take the captain prisoner and root out every spy he'd smuggled into Aynila. That, I believe. He tells me one of his gunners, a firetender, tried to overheat any metal aboard the fleeing merchant vessel, thinking to force them to throw the anchor overboard before the ship caught fire, and instead blew a store of powder in the belly. He claims he's never been able to flash black powder at greater than a cannon length before."

She frowned. "Bad luck? Amihan Moon power surges? Fires this close to the summit are to be expected."

"Either way, we should send him to Hiraya. There's been too much bad luck with the Amihan Moon so close. I don't like that experienced gods-blessed are being affected now."

"Yes, we want him away from powder stores. Let no one say we did not secure our city before the summit." Alon winced, and Dalisay smiled. "Unity and security can coexist. We will forge that balance. You'll be happy to know the deluge of outbreak patients is much abated since you and your brothers arranged to send healers into the city. I'm proud of you all. Look what you can accomplish when you work together."

Reminded of the other revelations from his spy network that he wasn't sharing with the family, Alon could not quite gather himself to make the correct response. How was he going to come clean to Lunurin now?

His inay went on, signing, "We will build upon it during the summit. It was a mistake to divide Aynila on the day of the wet season festival. We must bring our city together, not create more reasons to despise each other. During the eclipse festivities, I will see that we honor all Aynila's gods and saints alike. We will make it clear that all, no matter their gods, are welcome, so long as they do not work with our enemies."

She showed some modifications she'd made to the planned festivities and rituals and how it would affect the mapped layout of plaza security.

"Yes, of course," Alon managed.

"Anak ko, what is it?" she asked, dark eyes searching his face. "I'll not keep you too long. Your brother is not waiting. He just swept Aizza off to rest before the feast tonight."

It had been decided that the Lakan would not show favoritism between the arriving delegations by receiving any individual party before the welcome feast tonight, leaving her sons and Aynila's katalonan to fulfill the role instead. After the day and night he'd had, Alon couldn't imagine he looked in top form to greet delegates.

And though Lunurin had promised him she would stay, that she would not let him face the oncoming disaster alone, Alon feared that if she'd known the truth—the full truth he was keeping from her—she never would've made such a promise.

He had to tell someone. Not Isko, who could afford to put Sina before all else. He was not bound by duty to Aynila the way Alon was and always had been. Not his spy, who would never question his secrets.

"I've learned something," Alon began—and the whole sordid tale spooled out, about Abbess Magdalena and the rumors of Santa Catalina. How he had silenced those prayers—or thought he had, until Inez caught wind of them.

How he was afraid, so very afraid that the moment he told Lunurin, he would lose her. She would race to save Inez, and in the process they would both fall into the cage together. Even if she stayed, stood beside her vow to defend Aynila, it would put Jeian at her throat. His brother needed no reminding that the Codician half of Lunurin's family were no mere bystanders to Aynila's destruction, but its chief masterminds.

All night, Alon had chased his worries in circles, till his fear was a tangled, choking wrack of kelp he couldn't escape.

"—I just wanted to protect her," Alon swore. "But now..." Dalisay's cool hand came up to cradle his face, and Alon fisted shaking hands. "I don't know how to tell her after everything that's happened," he admitted. He bowed his head, awaiting his inay's judgment. She pulled him close, pressing her cheek to his before releasing him.

"For Aynila? Or for your wife?" the Lakan signed.

Alon let out a long breath. "Both. It's always both."

"Then let me remind you, my son: what is best for Aynila may not be what is best for your wife. You must never forget that. Especially not if you will one day be Lakan after me."

Her words struck him in the chest.

She signed, "I would not like you to repeat the mistakes I made in love and family. The way I 'protected' your father and you, keeping you separate from my doings with the old temple."

"This is different—" Alon protested.

Dalisay cut a hand through the air between them, "Tell me this, are you protecting her? Or patronizing her? Inez is your student, but her sister. Lunurin deserves the truth. What is it you're so afraid of, really?"

Something in Alon cracked, the lie he'd been repeating and repeating, trying to make true, crumbled before his inay, his fears laid bare.

"That she'll leave me. It's the way she is about her family. With Inez in danger and all her lingering guilt over Catalina weighing the scale… I'm afraid she would not stay for me alone. I don't know what I will do if I have to learn the answer. I can't face it."

Even now, after everything Catalina had done, and all the years that had passed, Alon feared he would be second to her. Always.

It didn't matter to his heart all the reasons why Lunurin might feel duty bound to protect Inez and Catalina from being swept into a power play for Aynila once again. It hurt. It hurt to always come after her other family. Would he come after her family from Calilan too?

Worst of all, if Inez came to harm because of this selfish, desperate fear, Lunurin would never forgive him. He'd never forgive himself.

20

❧

LUNURIN CALILAN NG DAKILA

The air was electric as if there were a storm overhead, coiled to strike. The nearness of the Amihan Moon now sang in the veins of every gods-blessed across the archipelago. Many had gathered here in Aynila for its coming—mere days away, judging by the fullness of the waxing moon that had hung like a golden coin in the sky last night.

The waters of Aynila Bay were like a planted rice field, filled with myriad ships. There were great karakoa long enough to bear seventy warriors; square-sailed vinta with magnificent stripes of white and indigo; big-bellied katig trade vessels; and red-sailed Tianchaowen junks. Pennants of every color flapped in the unceasing breeze, declaring envoys from across the archipelago and the inland rice kingdoms of Lusong.

Ships were anchored, in some places so densely that a sea-footed sailor might run from deck to outrigger across half the bay without ever touching the water.

Gathered in their finest silks aboard red-sailed junks were

Tianchaowen dignitaries from the vassal states of Panay. Lunurin saw arms and backs intricately tattooed in the dizzying patterns popular in the central islands around Sugbu and southern Ísuga. The brown chests of their warriors were festooned in hammered gold. The mesmerizing t'nalak abaca textiles in black, white, and red from southern Lanao draped their master weavers, accentuated by matching hair combs trailing long-beaded tassels, interspersed with mother-of-pearl. The great Datus of Paragoya wore large headdresses adorned with glossy kalaw hornbill feathers. Mutya in styles she had never seen glinted like moonlight on open water, brass girdles studded with pearls and scales; mother-of-pearl set into jade bangles; intricate carvings worn as pendants alongside agimat of jade, bronze, and gold.

And joining them now, the Stormfleet ships with their sleek silhouettes made for chasing into the teeth of a storm. Lunurin would greet them with Sina and Rosa and guide them into the crowded harbor.

Lunurin marveled. There hadn't been such a gathering in decades. She let her power swell outward, her breezes dancing among the ships as if weaving through a bamboo forest. Different languages and dialects tickled her ears as her breezes filled the sail of their balangay. Isko steadied Sina as Lunurin's exuberance sent their ship across the surface of the bay like a shot, expertly threading the crowded waters. Rosa cried out in glee, her hand trailing through the winds in their wake, fingertips greeting newly spawned breezes.

A mist of rain filled the air briefly with rainbows as Anitun Tabu herself blessed them with an ambon. *"Be woven together, a tapestry of many threads, a sail stretched taut but unbroken before the coming storm."*

Lunurin threw her head back and laughed, joyous with

her goddess. The blessing sparkled through her blood like the glittering mist. She met Rosa's yearning gaze. She wished it could be Inez she was introducing to her family.

Lunurin pushed the painful thought away, before her worry for Inez overcame her. Anyways, her family wasn't with the fleet now, no matter what her inay's letters had alleged. Especially not during the wet season. They couldn't be spared from Calilan. Her tiya's strong steady presence on Calilan, north of Lusong, was the lynchpin in a complex network of stormcallers spread across the barrier islands guiding the majority of typhoons safely around the archipelago.

But Rosa was here, and still so hopeful. What better place to let her get a taste of her power than in the wake of their goddess's blessing? With everything happening, Lunurin had been neglecting her responsibility to Rosa.

Lunurin joined her, showing her how to pluck sound from the breezes, bringing her snatches of a hundred different conversations. Swirling rainbows caught in the mist, the blessing of their goddess dancing over the waves.

"For this, I'd weather any storm," Lunurin admitted.

Aynila was alive once more with magic, and she was here to revel in it. It made all her personal fears seem small and far away. With allies such as these and Anitun Tabu's blessing, how could they fail? Anitun Tabu had all but declared it. If they stood together, weaving their strengths into one, they would not be shattered and splintered. They would never again be forced into hiding.

Then, the wind in her sail died. Their balangay came to a juddering stop that sent Isko and Sina stumbling once more.

Isko glared. "Hay nako! Can you warn us?"

"That wasn't us." Lunurin released Rosa's hands, reaching for the winds she had set to filling their sails.

From among the Stormfleet ships, a single large paraw slid forward on its own nest of breezes. On the deck, Lunurin beheld her family for the first time in fifteen years. Her mother, Talim, Datu of Calilan. Her Tiya Halili, the commander of Calilan's Stormfleet, and her wife, Kalaba, who had crafted the dugong bone amulet that had allowed Lunurin to seek respite from her goddess's terrible vengeance as a child. Lastly, her mother's husband, Ragasa, who had been the loudest proponent of returning her to the sea when her power first went awry on Calilan.

Shock arched through her like lightning, followed closely by joy and an agony of longing. She stared harder, half sure her eyes were tricking her. Had they finally, actually come?

The next shock was how the years had weathered and changed them all. Would they recognize her? Her Tiya Halili's prized hair, intricately knotted and bound, was white as fresh coconut at the crown, shifting to grey and then the night black of Lunurin's memory. Her inay's face bore lines of worry and stress like the frozen ripples of cooled lava rock. Her Tiya Kalaba's strong swimmer's shoulders had rounded, making her seem smaller now than in memory.

The consternation on all three faces was as clear as the wind stolen from her sails. Lunurin quickly twisted her hair back up, jamming her mutya through the heavy bun to secure it.

This was not going to be the happy reunion she'd hardly dared hope for.

Lunurin caught up a single thread of the breeze streaming across the bay, and with the care and control she had trained so hard for under her Tiya Halili, she guided their craft alongside.

She bowed deeply. "Mabuhay po kayo," she greeted, full

of formal respect, signing her desire to come aboard and deliver the Lakan's message of welcome.

Tiya Halili spoke over her, her worry amplified by the wind she used to send her words across, the familiar scent of Calilan's beach breezes mingling with the flowering katmon trees pricking tears to Lunurin's eyes. "Ay! Careful! What if you capsize someone? You don't know the cut of their sails or how their winds are shaped."

"Forgive me, no one was in any danger," Lunurin began, trying to reassure her tiya she was well in control. She flicked her fingers, bringing the outriggers of their ships parallel to ease boarding, disentangling herself from the rapturous joy of her goddess before her embarrassment and welling shame soured the fine weather of Anitun Tabu's blessing.

She ignored the overloud concern on Isko's and Sina's faces, signaling behind her back that it was fine. Sina signed back, asking why her family was afraid of rainbows. Rosa covered a snort of laughter with her hand. Lunurin shook her head minutely, stepping aboard the Stormfleet ship. Tiya Halili and her inay stepped forward to greet her, their partners a few respectful steps behind.

Lunurin approached hesitantly, relieved when her inay offered her hand. She bowed, offering mano po. It frightened her how thin and worn her inay's hand felt in hers as she pressed it to her brow. Her memory of them was forge-calloused and strong. But the steady heat of her was the same, comforting as a hearth.

"Kaawaan ka ng Amihan." Talim offered the traditional firetender's blessing, then pulled her up, embracing her.

Halili tugged her face down to her level, pressing her cheek to Lunurin's. "Too long, how you have grown!"

The scent of her tiya's hair oil, coconut infused with

ylang-ylang, filled her nose. She held them tightly, stooped at the knees to their height, trying not to mind them both patting her bun, checking her hair was secure.

"I began to doubt I'd ever hold my firstborn again," her inay whispered.

Tiya Kalaba stepped close too, squeezing Lunurin's hands and rubbing their noses together.

Then, before they had even released her from their embrace, the scolding began. "Are you very sure this will hold?" Talim fiddled with her mutya, slicking her frizzing curls down with the heat of her hands.

"Walang hiya! You should not show such intemperance," Halili added. "You are not thinking of all the other storm-callers who might be caught up and endangered by you. This is just how you lost so many in Talaan."

"I will never understand you," Talim muttered, still fixing her hair, so close the warmth of her was rosy on Lunurin's cheeks.

It was too true. Her inay had never understood her. She was hearth and home; Lunurin was the wild sea-born storm she'd handed off to her sister the very first time Lunurin had frightened her with her power. Her inay had set Lunurin aside long ago, investing her time and attention in her husband and their children instead.

It still stung. Lunurin stepped back from their arms, even when most of her wanted to fall to her knees, clinging, and never let go. She tried to catch Tiya Kalaba's eye. She had always been the most forgiving and calmest of her family, as was fitting for the tide-touched wife of a stormcaller. This reunion could use the steadying ballast of a tide-touched voice. Lunurin wished that Alon could've accompanied her, but, after the merchant sinking, she understood why he must glue himself to Jeian's side. They could not afford another incident with so many dignitaries as witness.

But Kalaba was no help, keeping her head bowed, and Halili was not at all appeased. "Storm take it, you never listen. If you capsize us here and now, you'll leave the Codicíans no work at all!"

"Tiya, Inay..." Back upon a Stormfleet deck, the scolding brought back a childhood of constantly being found wanting. She had always been too much: too reckless, too dangerous. She'd heard it all. She was a liability to Calilan, a danger to the Stormfleet, an ill-omen to her people best sent far away.

"And you're training another?" Halili's skepticism was loud.

Lunurin tried to divert attention from her myriad failings to something more positive. "Tiya Halili, this is Rosa Capili. She was newly named a stormcaller at Aynila's wet season festival last week."

But Halili hadn't finished, barely even glancing at Rosa. "Your wind control is so slipshod, you summon an ambon and drag even your volcano's highest air currents into propelling a little balangay?"

At this Sina flared, unable to keep silent. "And why should she not? In Aynila, we do not defend our domains so jealously. A stormcaller may call upon Hilaga's air currents as surely as her winds may feed my fires. Do you begrudge us Anitun Tabu's blessing?"

Talim addressed this, one firetender to another. "It shows a frightening lack of control. The ambon should never be called lightly, and never alone. Such a risk!"

"She was not alone. We together are two of Aynila's katalonan," Sina protested. Lunurin wouldn't have dared.

Her inay narrowed her eyes, Ragasa murmuring in her ear—all doom and fear, no doubt. Would that he could have remained in Calilan. Why must she split her inay's attention with him even now?

Talim sniffed. "You are young to be a katalonan of so great a mount as Hilaga. I see now why all the signs insisted we travel for this Amihan Moon. None of you have any idea of the gravity of the situation. Haven't you noticed? We have seen it even in our flames on Calilan. They gutter, too weak for a year of fire. But I see Aynila feels no need for moderation."

Lunurin knew she should stop Sina... but all the air had seized in her lungs. Her family had not come for her at all, but because of the signs her inay had read on Calilan and their fears about the Amihan Moon. That was why they'd finally come instead of sending a delegate or insisting again Lunurin must come to Calilan.

Sina flared at the insult. "My family has tended Hilaga for eight generations. We know what she needs. Our fires burn as strong as ever."

"And no one doubts that," Isko cut in, as skillful talking down firetender tempers as negotiating a business deal. His tone was so firm and logical, it was impossible to yell over him.

Lunurin struggled to get her breathing under control before anyone noticed her reaction. She hated how vividly it still hurt to be found wanting by her family. What had they come expecting? After the fall of the Palisade and all that had happened since. And now, as her power swelled and her goddess danced for joy in the winds... Did they think they'd find a girl still hiding from her own strength?

But she wouldn't undo Isko's effort to smooth things

over because of her disappointment. Aynila needed allies. With only weeks before the arrival of the Codícian armada, they did not have the luxury of a long wet season to court the shattered splinters of the Stormfleet. She must make her peace with her family and win over her Tiya Halili, who still controlled the largest portion of the fleet.

She bowed deeply. If she could just prove that she was no longer a liability, but an asset, that their doubt of her abilities was misplaced... She'd make them see Talaan had not been her fault.

"As Isko says, this is a reunion, and we are all now family. Please, Inay—Datu Talim, let me extend Lakan Dalisay Inanialon's warm welcome of you and Calilan's fleet to Aynila." Lunurin fell back onto diplomacy.

She could make herself innocuous with the right words, as she once had in the convent, when nothing she did would ever please the sisters or the abbot. When nothing could make her worthy of her father's acknowledgment. Just as nothing she did now would make her mother proud of her.

But Talim was glaring at Sina. She shook her head, sniffing. "Family! Don't remind me."

This final insult to her marriage smarted sharp as a stove burn. Lunurin flinched.

Ragasa added, "Do not think our coming means we bless this fool's endeavor Dalisay is pursuing."

It was her stepfather's sneer that set her off. She would not bear his derision. Too many had been lost for Aynila's freedom. It was the Lakan's labor of utmost devotion that had rebuilt so much. She would not suffer it. Not anymore.

Her fury was distant thunder. As the sky overhead darkened a kiss of static danced over her skin, her hair frizzing free in a halo. Her tiya cried out, trying to wrestle the budding storm from Lunurin's control. Talim tried to seize Lunurin's hair again. Lunurin caught her hand and held her fast, staring down into her eyes. Fear for her, or of her?

There was more divine fury in her voice than there should have been. *"Will you embrace blessings offered or close your ears and hearts?"*

She wasn't a girl of fifteen who could be shamed and scolded. Not even by her inay and her best intentions.

"Lunurin! Stop this now," Talim pleaded as lightning flashed overhead.

Lunurin only tightened her grip on her inay's arm, and with it her hold on the storm, trapping the Stormfleet beneath the low-pressure pocket.

In the roll of thunder that followed, Anitun Tabu boomed, *"We will not be made tame and small, for I am no gentle goddess. We are a reckoning. We are the Storm. We are vengeance. And none shall forget it."*

Lunurin would not be carried away by her goddess's fury as she had been in Talaan, and almost had been again over the Great South Sea. This was simply about respect. She released her inay and stepped back, drawing herself up to her full height. "As honored guests of Aynila on such an important occasion, you will address my Lakan by her titles or not at all. I am Dayang Lunurin Calilan ng Dakila, and they call me Stormbringer. It is by my efforts your fleet finds welcome and allies in Aynila instead of Codícian cannon fire."

She let Tiya Halili grasp at her storm to no avail, meeting the shock and dismay in her inay's expression without blinking. And she ignored Ragasa, sweating and blustering without ever managing to offer an apology for his unprovoked rudeness.

She crossed to Kalaba, lifting her tiya's knuckles to her

brow. "Mano po, Tiya, you are invited to the Lakan's feast tonight. I pray the rest of your party will be more amenable to the Lakan's hospitality then."

Kalaba patted her cheek. "You've learned to balance the storm within you." She winked. "And I see you've found the peace of Aman Sinaya's blessing too."

Lunurin squeezed her hand, grateful for her words of approval, and bowed one last time before she and her party crossed back to their balangay.

When she was balanced on the outrigger, she wet her hands and ruthlessly smoothed her unruly hair back into place. She allowed the thunderhead to unspool into a clear sunny day, as if it had never been, giving their ship a light push toward shore.

Isko blew out a long breath. "I see you were not exaggerating the situation after Talaan."

Lunurin winced. "I know, I know. I've squandered our one chance at goodwill for a temper tantrum."

Sina wrinkled her nose. "I don't think Calilan came with much goodwill for you to squander. It's good Alon couldn't join us. If he'd heard them speak of the Lakan so... And to you!"

Lunurin tried to swallow down a horrible feeling that she'd do more good searching for Inez than dithering at diplomacy while her family assumed the worst of her.

21

INEZ DOMINGO

Inez had never seen the shrine in Masagana before, but she'd stained her fingers dark with ink annotating the blueprints of their wide stone walls for DeSoto.

At first, she had wanted to work as a teaching assistant to Father DeSoto. His buildings and bridges were far more interesting than Sister Philippa's endless sermons on propriety and catechisms.

She should've chosen boredom and scoldings.

She'd transcribed the instructions for the modified lime mortar patches on the westmost corner, where cracks kept opening in the coral boulder walls. The church had been one of the first designs DeSoto was responsible for when he crossed from New Codicía. Modeled on the squat, square adobe buildings of his youth in Canazco, it was ill-suited to the way the archipelago shifted and rippled with the fitful sleep of Amihan's children.

Standing in the shadow of its great crumbling stone walls, a fresh new roof of anahaw palm softening the hulking square corners of the church, a shiver of disgust skated down Inez's back. She briefly wished she could drag in a great wave to finish grinding the walls to dust, just as Alon and the tide-touched ghosts had brought down the Palisade. Would that she never had to be reminded of that man's existence ever again.

She forced herself to take one step forward, then another. Inez crossed herself out of habit as she stepped through the church doors, letting her eyes adjust to the dim interior.

She clenched her hand into a fist before double-checking the cloth pouch looped at her wrist, which Umali had given her to hold her broken mutya necklace.

She need not have worried. These church walls housed no faithful brothers, with their pious prayers and lecherous hearts.

"Oh." Her indrawn breath echoed through the sanctuary. Several locals turned to look at her. Inez stared at the mix of mother-of-pearl mutya and rosary prayer beads, worn by some at the same time. She ducked her head and shuffled into a pew at the back, and the small congregation turned back to their observance of Friday prayers.

She'd been prepared for the life-sized statue of San Josep clutching a carpenter's square in one hand, modeled after DeSoto's own preferred drafting tool, a little hubris of his writ large. He had been very proud of the central detail of his first church.

But San Josep was not alone upon the altar. To his left was a serene-faced Buddha with cones of incense and calamansi offerings. To the right, a wooden anito statue of Anitun Tabu. In the central aisle, a bronze effigy of Amihan hovered, its wings spread over a nest filled with burning bamboo splits. And in the west wing of the church, below a window overlooking the port, Aman Sinaya's shrine cradled a perfect miniature sailed paraw in her vast blue hands, like a child in its mother's arms.

When the gathered... converts didn't seem the right word anymore... rose to pray, Inez's feet carried her straight to Aman Sinaya's vast blue palms, where offering plates of huge oyster shells were filled with glittering white salt.

She lifted a fingertip to the beautiful mother-of-pearl inlay of waves along the hull of the ship, wondering at the workmanship.

All around her, prayers were made to saint and anito alike in a lowland dialect that was intelligible to her, but with a unique intonation quite different from Aynilan.

Masagana had not torn down their church; instead, they had reclaimed it for themselves and their community of beliefs. One of the many knotted aches that Inez had grown accustomed to living with seemed to dissolve. Perhaps there was a place for mestizas like her, raised in the Church but given to the sea, if Aman Sinaya's hands could cradle a ship beside San Josep rocking Santo Niño.

She offered her thanks to Aman Sinaya, placing on her altar a crocodile tooth she'd found lodged in one of the scraps of rope dangling from her wrist after Umali hauled her from the water.

What had come tearing out of her, clawed and hungry, aboard the slaver? She half disbelieved that the gentle lady, Aman Sinaya, had such black depths within her as Inez did; that her mercies held space for crocodiles and vicious tide-touched.

But when Inez voiced a crocodile song, Aman Sinaya had answered. Why now? Was it only the Amihan Moon sending her magic wild and wayward? Would she always have ears for crocodile whispers?

Inez walked on, studying the many shrines and statues

on the altar. There were more saints she hadn't seen in the eastern atrium accompanying San Josep and Santo Niño—Santa María, San Francisco, and San Isidro.

At the conclusion of the small service, Inez approached several of those wearing crosses and rosaries, asking after the Codicíans who'd served this church.

Unlike Aynila, where the tension between those who welcomed a return to the old ways and the converts was at a boiling point, with secrecy and distrust multiplying in every direction, Masagana seemed to have found a comfortable compromise. The group were happy to talk.

"Oh, it's been a long time… they left after the earthquake, it was just this time of year too," the prayer leader told her.

"Was it four… no, five years ago?" another woman chimed in. "The roof caved in on poor Father Salcedo, and the two younger priests who served with him set sail for Aynila, planning to return with funds and support for the rebuilding. But they never did."

"We ended up patching the roof with anahaw thatch so the interior wouldn't be ruined, and it's held up wonderfully," the prayer leader agreed.

Inez wondered if the priests had been lost in the Palisade, or never made it to Aynila at all. Her heart fell. If there had been no priests here in so long, how could they know anything about Catalina? "It's been so long since you've had anyone ordained to hold services…"

"Oh no, there are many priests and missionaries who visit on their way to Aynila, and sometimes those making the crossing from Canazco to Simsiman and Sugbu get blown off course and resupply here."

"Have you heard of Santa Catalina?" she asked. "They say she's a local saint, like Aynila's Lady of Sorrows."

Brows furrowed in thought. "Oh yes, I think so. Guardian of martyrs, right? That young priest, didn't he say she'd returned to the archipelago?"

"What have you heard?"

"Where is Marifina, didn't she…"

Several more women were waved over, and stories began to spill. "My brother is a sailor on a Codicían merchant vessel. He says in Masbad, he got to see the prayer book that saved her life."

"She's in Masbad now?"

"Well, her prayer book is. They say it was a miracle, how it floated above the floodwaters and by clinging to it, she was saved."

"I heard she was providing aid during the drought in Talaan before the shipyard there fell."

"I heard she had a vision of Aynila's return to God's holy light in Mamaylan. They say Santa María appeared to her in the clouds."

"No, no, that was in Sugbu. In Mamaylan, they have a cloth soaked in the holy water that poured from the spear wound that appeared on her side, just like our savior. I have cousins in Mamaylan, they'd tell me if they had a real live saint."

"I think you're confused. I heard she'd seen the vision in Aynila."

"Before or after she left for Canazco?" Inez tried to get a word in edgewise, as overwhelmed by the deluge of information as she often felt in shallow water. But no one knew for sure, and the way information came into Masbad—from sailors, missionaries, and visiting family—meant it was hard to pin down the exact timeline of Santa Catalina's miraculous acts.

For an instant, the mocking face of Ortiz loomed large

in her memory. What had she been thinking, killing her one good lead before she got the information she needed?

She hadn't been thinking. She'd felt herself breaking and she'd wanted the whole world to sunder with her.

She'd never be able to chase down so many rumors of sainthood!

Head spinning, Inez went back out into the sunlight, perching on the edge of the wide stone foundation. What now? She might be a poor excuse for a tide-touched, but even she would not be able to slip unnoticed into any of the major Codícian fortresses like Mamaylan or Sugbu. She would be put to the pyre long before she found anyone who had actually met her sister and wasn't just sharing the latest tsismis and traders' talk.

What options did she have, then?

She picked at the fraying edge of the orange sarong she'd traded in exchange for speeding the drying of a salt-harvester's beds on her way up from the port. It was the one lesson of Alon's that hadn't been a struggle. They'd both been so hopeful then. She'd ruined Aynila for herself just as quickly as her sister had. Why couldn't she have figured out how to croak waves into doing her bidding sooner? Even if she were strange, if she could've turned a slave ship, even Jeian would've let her join Aynila's navy.

Gravel crunched and a shadow touched her feet on the step. Inez looked up.

The firetender captain, Umali, was studying the iron filigree of the church gates. Her presence in the world was like a beacon-flame upon the shore, her finery glinting in the sunlight. She didn't just burn; she shone. "Did you not find what you were looking for, my tide-touched friend?" she asked.

"I found exactly what I was looking for, but it won't help me in the slightest."

"No priests, at least. I'll never understand the sway they have. A single priest in a port will sour the whole city on gods-blessed. You're tide-touched, I'm sure you know."

"I know," Inez acknowledged miserably.

Umali tugged at the teardrop pearl of her mutya hanging from her right ear, the tilt of her head making the leaping flames of her mother-of-pearl ear cuff seem to leap and quiver in an unseen wind. "I'm told you've already found work with the local salt-harvester."

Inez shrugged one shoulder. Casama would've consigned the sun-faded orange-to-yellow annatto-dyed cloth to her rag pile, but it was better than what she'd had from the healing school after her misadventure. "I needed to trade for something, or they'd have thought me a charity case when I entered the church."

"You've too much pride to be a salt-harvester on a barrier island," Umali declared. "You'd do better on a ship."

"Is that an invitation?" Inez asked. Maybe there *was* a way to run down at least some of the rumors of her sister's miracles.

"Masagana is small, but the Tianchaowen trading hub here was grateful for our service, and generous. I've never taken such a large ship so quickly before. Usually, more captives are thrown overboard. I owe you a crewman's portion of the bounty, at least." Umali patted a pouch hanging from the intricate bronze belt cinching the folds of her patterned copper tapis skirt. It clinked merrily.

"I may be useless to you after the Amihan Moon. I've never even been to sea before. Next month, I could be dead weight," Inez warned. The last thing she needed was a new person disappointed by what a poor excuse for a tide-touched she was.

Umali waved this off. "You don't need to be tide-touched to sail."

True, but Inez doubted Umali would've sought her out.

"I'm no healer either."

Umali grinned. "I wouldn't want a healer anyway. They've no stomach for a pirate's life, far too merciful. A healer wouldn't have insisted I feed slavers to her crocodiles."

Despite herself, an answering grin pulled at Inez's lips.

Umali offered her a hand up from the steps. Inez again noted the large burn scar that bisected her palm. The dark rippling surface curved all the way across and between her fingers, then up her arm, disappearing under the folds of the sash she wore from one shoulder to the opposite hip. Inez couldn't imagine what had caused such an injury to a firetender.

Save for the men's putong kerchief about her brow, rather rakishly keeping her long black hair back in its top knot, Umali dressed head to toe like a Pangilog katalonan from the slopes of Mount Tumubo. What had driven such a powerful firetender from her volcano? Not many firetenders took to a life at sea. Sina and most of Aynila's metalworkers hated to be out over deep water, even more so when they couldn't see Hilaga's peak.

Inez grasped the offered hand. Umali's grip was so hot, Inez almost wanted to hang on tighter as her belly clenched, a strangely pleasant shiver rippling up her arm.

"Glad to have you aboard." Umali steered her away from the church, toward the port and the wide stretch of the sea. "Let's see if we can find some jeweler's wire. I can help repair your mutya before we set sail."

22

LUNURIN CALILAN NG DAKILA

Before their boat had docked, Lunurin leaped from the deck. What had the Lakan been thinking, sending her and Sina to welcome Calilan? Between her temper and Sina's spiky pride, they'd been doomed from the start. No, her family would never see her as anything more than a dangerous, imprudent child they were glad to be rid of.

Had her tantrum done anything but prove them right for placing the blame for all their dead in Talaan on her head? Lunurin's eyes were hot but she refused to give in to tears, studying the Stormfleet contingent they'd left behind. So many silver and silver-lined pennants. So many captains allied with Calilan, even if they did not consider themselves under Halili's command. Were there any captains present not already allied with her family?

She'd expected those captains to arrive first. Her invitations hadn't been as well received as she'd hoped.

What if they all felt, as her inay did, that Aynila and her firetenders were ill-prepared for the coming Amihan Moon.

Had they come only for that, with no interest in an alliance?

How was she supposed to rally support from the Stormfleet if they had all taken her family's misgivings as truth? Calilan feared her. She had to tell the Lakan, make her understand that Lunurin was the last person she should want as an intermediary with the Stormfleet.

Aynila needed the strength of their ships, and they'd so little time left to gain it. Once again, Lunurin wrestled with the feeling that Aynila would be better off if she'd gone after Inez. What kind of wife could not even bring the support of her family to her husband's side? Alon had once said that their marriage represented a diplomatic tie to Calilan he would not see erased. But now, when Aynila needed to call upon those ties, her family had only derision and scolding for their long-awaited reunion.

It was nothing new. What had any of those she called family ever brought her husband but grief?

She found the Lakan in her study in the healing halls, ensuring the fever outbreak fears were fully laid to rest.

"Back already?" she signed.

"I lost my temper! I may as well have threatened to sink the Stormfleet. It's a disaster," Lunurin signed.

"So soon?" Dalisay inquired mildly, not at all as outraged as she ought to be.

"You saw the weather from here. My family took it badly. They are afraid of me. I am the wrong person to gain Stormfleet allies for Aynila."

Dalisay brushed aside Lunurin's panicked torrent. "I disagree."

"How can you say that?" Lunurin signed back, fearing her voice would rise in a wail of frustration.

"You are our Lady Stormbringer. You will convince the

Stormfleet captains that Talaan was your success. That your goddess is with you, as I see her burning in you now. Your presence alone is proof that the old gods smile upon Aynila and our efforts."

"What if it's not enough? I know you and Hiraya have been worried. It should be a year of fire, and I've turned it all to rain and wind. The Amihan Moon is coming so close after the start of the wet season. What if—" Lunurin cut herself off, unable to fully voice the fear that she might be the cause of everything. She'd been on the bridge when the crush started, and she'd made it worse by panicking. What if her lightning had knocked that spark-striker out of the sky? What if—

"I am not the right person to balance this," she finished instead.

The Lakan took her by the arm, steering her out into the main infirmary hall. "Let me help you refind your balance, anak ko."

My child. Lunurin wanted to protest that what the Lakan wanted was impossible, but she went. Her own mother had not claimed her so warmly, had never tried to see her as Dalisay always had.

The Lakan brought her to the young mother Inez had saved, praying quietly while her newborn slept, thumbing through a rosary of shell and polished coconut. Lunurin felt suddenly that Inez was, *must* be, nearby. Here in the infirmary, as she usually was, and should be now.

"Offer Aynila's frightened and sick your blessing," the Lakan instructed.

"She will not want Anitun Tabu's blessing," Lunurin signed back, irrationally angry at this woman for the fact Inez was gone from her.

The mother looked up from her prayers and smiled. "Santa María! You were missed on Our Lady of Sorrows' Saint's Day. It just wasn't the same without you. Would you pray with me?"

Lunurin had half expected to be attacked as viciously as Inez had been in that prayer meeting. She pushed through her worry, offering a quick prayer for the continued health of child and mother.

The Lakan tugged her onward. "Heavy rains may smother fire, but lightning may also spark the first flame, and a strong wind awakens long-banked coals. We will find our own way."

To the converts she was Santa María, Our Lady of Sorrows. They offered mano po, and she made the sign of the cross over bowed heads. To others, she was Lady Stormbringer, and they begged her for Anitun Tabu's blessing of their mutya. This Lunurin gave, twisting threads of breeze around petitioner's fingers as they extended their mutya. Lunurin let her winds carry their names anew to Anitun Tabu's ear.

Their faith in both sides of the goddess that Aynila had come to know buoyed her up like rising wind over volcanic updrafts.

"You see," the Lakan signed, "Aynila is blended now. It will never again be the Aynila that existed before the Codicíans came. We've changed too much, but this city still loves you and remembers all you have given for it. Our differences will not tear us apart, but make us stronger. We will make our allies see that."

"I believe in Aynila, but my family can be as stubborn as I am."

"Give them time to adjust. It is a hard thing for a mother

DAUGHTERS OF FLOOD AND FURY

to see her own child full-grown without her guidance. You cannot imagine the guilt I carry for all that my sons were forced to face alone during my exile. This reunion has been a long time coming, but let your family see you as Aynila does, and they'll understand."

Lunurin bowed to the Lakan's wisdom, hoping desperately she was right.

23

INEZ DOMINGO

In place of the simple S-hook catch that had secured Inez's mutya, Umali had welded shut three strong twists of silver wire. Her handiwork rested against Inez's skin with a lingering warmth that kept drawing her hand to her nape.

It didn't mean anything. Umali wanted the silver of more easy prizes, and Inez needed a ship to chase the truth of her sister.

The pattern of buwaya back ridges artfully worked into the twists of the new triple-stacked clasp was incidental.

As they left Masagana's hook-shaped port, still trailing their crocodile escort, Inez wondered if all this was really just the humming nearness of the Amihan Moon's power. Part of her hoped so, that her magic would go back to normal.

Only… what if normal meant useless? What if she lost her crocodile whispers, but didn't ever figure out healing and all the rest the way a tide-touched should?

When Masagana had dropped away on the horizon, Umali waved her over to the helmsman's covered seat at the rear of the ship. Large oars were affixed there, which could be levered up out of the waves when they passed over reefs or sandbars and when the ship was carried ashore.

"Here, have a feel for how my *Agawin* flies," Umali offered.

What a fitting name for a laho-prowed karakoa, ever hungering to snatch the moon from the sky. But Inez hesitated. They might be pirates who appreciated *dangerous to our enemies*, but *dangerous to our ship with no land in sight* seemed a good way to ruin her welcome. "I've never guided anything larger than a two-person bangka, and badly. You don't want me to capsize us on our first run out."

Umali snorted and twisted her fingers. Inez studied the dexterity in her burned hand. It seemed her fingers and palm had not lost much mobility at all, but the way she held her wrist, where the burn wrapped almost entirely around like a wide bangle... or shackle. Inez wondered if the ointments and massages that Alon had taught her for the scarring on her back would help.

The rising heat Umali was sending into the crab-claw sail wavered and died. "I'm sure it will not be so dramatic as that. But here, try alone, so our abilities don't blend badly."

Umali shifted from the oar cradle and pointed with her lips, indicating Inez should take her place.

Indecision froze Inez in place. She couldn't afford to ruin this.

Umali leaned closer, her hands sketching out the *Agawin*'s double outriggers spread like wings to each side of them. "You forget: we build for tide-touched. You won't capsize us so easily as those big-bellied, deep-keeled foreign ships."

"We aren't even in sight of land if you're wrong," Inez protested. "I'm not terrified like I was then."

"Were you terrified? Or angry?" Umali asked.

"Does it matter?"

"You seemed angry to me." Umali's gaze was a challenge. "Come, show me why crocodiles are following you to sea. If it's only going to last for the next few days, you might as well see how far you can push it."

The heat of Umali's power expanded against Inez's senses, lifting her as she had during the attack on the slaver, making her face flush and her heart beat fast. It was a rush. It was an offer.

"It's on your head if we sink," Inez said.

"I want to see you try."

She seemed to mean it.

Shaking her head, Inez slid into the seat. The small space was warm with the heat Umali radiated like a furnace, but Inez wouldn't blink first. And nestled into the firetender's rising heat, Inez couldn't feel a single prickle or itch of her scars, like baking the ache away on the lava flats at noon.

She wrapped her hands around the oars, avoiding where Umali's more experienced grip kept the karakoa to its course. The dark wood had been worn smooth by countless hands.

She closed her eyes. Unlike during so many previous lessons with Alon and Aizza and even the Lakan, she didn't try to close herself off from the "distraction" of the overloud sea and crocodile whispers. She didn't try to ignore her own agitation and anger. She was furious at being stranded far from home, and even more angry that her exile was her own fault, that she might never find the truth of her sister she'd left seeking. She channeled her awareness of the sea through her escort of crocodiles, who rumbled a lazy greeting. The buwaya were perfectly at ease in deep water, so far from home. They gauged the roughness of the waves, its salinity, and the movements of any nearby prey by the sea washing over their sensitive snouts into their toothy mouths. By the feel of the salt—not unlike a tide-touched.

The drop-off here was far more sudden than the vast shallow spread of Aynila Bay; these barrier islands were very close to the shelf that gave way to the depths of the Great South Sea, skimming along the border of the Sumila Gulf.

What could it mean that it was so much easier to harness the sea drafting off a firetender's heat, except that she was stealing from the glut of the Amihan Moon's power?

But she didn't have time to worry about whether she'd lose this too, and have it twist awry in her hands. She had a ship to capsize.

First, she memorized how the buwaya saw the *Agawin*, how the shallow hull skimmed over the waves. The rhythmic slap of the water, steady as the deep thump of a crocodile mating call. How the position of the oars cut the water, the curling currents of their wake spinning off behind them. She jumped when Umali shifted her grip to cover Inez's hands, showing her how pulling the oars changed their tack in the water. Inez let the shape of the hull and their draft through the sea fill her mind. A crocodile song weighed, familiar and salted, on the back of her tongue, curled behind her teeth.

"Ready?" Umali asked, her hold loosening, fingertips sliding down the backs of Inez's hands.

"Are you?" Inez asked.

Gripping the oars tight, she let her request to the sea vibrate from her throat and trip off her tongue. Half-croak, half-roar, now that she wasn't too furious to think, she tasted the harshness and strangeness of the sounds that came out of her, deeper and louder than seemed possible.

The way Umali's gaze whipped to her, Inez knew it wasn't

the musical prayer for the attention of the sea that she'd expected. Before Inez could regret trying, the force of the deep-water currents here caught them up with a bone-jarring rush. Inez was thrown back into the seat with a shout of glee. She almost faltered, expecting a scolding for her lack of control, for putting the ship in danger.

But Umali's voice was hot in her ear. "I knew you were angry. I like how you roar."

Inez shook her head incredulously.

"How fast can you take her?" Umali asked.

Umali had said to push it. Inez made a demand, loud, and without hesitation, the *Agawin* leaped forward, her prow cresting through the waves like a flying ray, as if her dragon-headed prow might really take flight and swallow the moon. Inez leaned into the oars, sending the ship cutting back and forth across the surface of the sea like a lashing crocodile's tail. It might be stolen and temporary, but it felt so good.

Umali's grip slipped from her hands as she punched a drift of hot air into their sails, flinging them forward faster. The whole hull vibrated with pure, glorious speed.

The captain threw her head back and laughed, tears streaming from her eyes at the whipping of the wind. Inez's chest went tight at the sight, an equally strange and foreign flutter in her throat that tasted nothing like crocodile sea songs.

24

ALON DAKILA

With his inay's words still so heavy on his mind, and spot thunderheads swirling over the bay, Alon feared he'd been wrong to leave Lunurin's side. He'd been all wrong about everything to do with his family lately. It should've been him and Inez accompanying Lunurin to welcome the Stormfleet, not Sina and Isko. But maybe stormcaller reunions always spawned lightning?

He was stuck with Jeian waiting to welcome Talaan, who had been steadfast allies since Aynila liberated them from the Codicians. If they could just present a united front, maybe they'd achieve peace and security for Aynila. Alon only needed to get his brother to see that.

"You were right to put a stop to the smuggling operation. We've traced the captain's activities over the last three years. It wasn't all converts and mercy missions. At least two previous visits coincided with assassination attempts on Lunurin and Inay."

It was like pulling teeth to admit it, but some credit was

due. If they had forced the slaver from the harbor, as Jeian had wanted, and been more aggressive in their investigation of the captain from Sugbu, Ortiz wouldn't have escaped. Inez would be perfectly safe—in trouble over the prayer meeting, but safe.

Jeian softened. "And you were right that we need to do more to reduce fears among all our people. Aizza is home resting for the first time all week. She says the infirmary hasn't been this quiet since before the crush. She's happy to have open cots in case of any issues during the Amihan Moon."

Would that Alon could say the same of Inez. What fresh horrors had she stumbled into after the prayer meeting and that endless night in the infirmary?

"I'm glad to hear it. What's more, Inay wants to build on our efforts during the Amihan Moon. We'll need to balance peace and security. With so many diplomats watching, we must be more subtle."

"The trade ship sinking may not have been subtle, but people need to feel safe. If anything, it's what Amihan wanted," Jeian argued.

Alon didn't like that angle. "Let's not lean too much into what Amihan wants if we're trying to keep the infirmary quiet."

"If you're committed to silencing what really happened, we ought to execute Arcilla. He'll only become another focal point for discontent, and he's a witness."

To Inez's crimes went unsaid. Alon glared at his brother. It would continue to be unsaid. By anyone.

"We agreed you'd let me handle it as I see fit."

The cover-up of the quarantined converts and Inez's involvement in the priest's escape, Jeian had agreed to leave to Alon. In exchange, Alon had convinced the Lakan that Jeian had had good reason to pursue the Sugbu smuggler.

"I'm just suggesting the simplest solution." Jeian rubbed

at a blue whirl of ink on his elbow. "But I'll leave the upsets of your house to you. Aizza says I've been… unfair to you in that. Anyway, what is Inay envisioning? We can't have her putting herself at risk, especially now."

Satisfied, Alon presented the rest of his documents. "Here is Inay's plan for the Amihan Moon, and some reports I've compiled on the most likely flashpoints for Aynila, and the visiting diplomats. If we have only this summit to gain allies, let us not divide our efforts. We need a united front."

Jeian made room on his desk and they bent their heads together.

They tweaked with guard rotations, arranged and rearranged allies in their nearness to the steps to best buffer their inay.

A rapid knock and the study door opened. "Gat Jeian! You wanted word at Talaan's first sighting!"

"They've arrived?" Jeian stood, striding toward the window overlooking the port.

"They've entered Aynila Bay with a full contingent of manned karakoa."

Alon joined him, peering toward the mouth of the bay in the distance. His brother put a sight glass in his hand, a huge grin on his face.

Alon looked, not daring to trust the messenger till he saw the decks of warriors, Talaan's pennants streaming in the wind. Not one or two envoys sent for politeness' sake—a fleet of ten warships.

Perhaps there was hope, after all.

~

Captain Tomás, one of the sons of Talaan's Datu, leaped down to the pier, gesturing to his ships, still tying up at their berths. "When my father received word that a Codícian armada had been spotted in Hanay, we outfitted our ships as quickly as we could. Talaan does not forget a debt owed."

Jeian clapped Tomás on the back. "There is no one I'd rather have at my side. You fought well in Talaan with only a few merchant balangays outfitted with lantaka cannons."

"Talaan has not spent the intervening months idle, nor squandered the riches that fell into our hands after your visit with Lady Stormbringer," Tomás promised.

Alon was relieved to hear that, at least among some, Talaan was not viewed wholly as a disaster. If Talaan's support for Aynila could be leveraged against the Stormfleet's reservations, perhaps…

"We can see that." Jeian gestured with his chin at the arrayed fleet, ten ships altogether. In place of the traditional laho prow carving, many had human mastheads—and was that Santo Niño? Alon chose not to draw his brother's attention to it now, when things were going so well.

Tomás's flagship was a fascinating modified construction, not using the traditional lash and lug style Alon was accustomed to. "Tell us about these ships. We have hours yet until the Lakan calls us all to feast, though I can smell the lechon roasting already."

Jeian waved their party into his study as Tomás explained that many of their carpenters and craftsmen in Talaan were now more experienced building a hull in the Codícian style. They had modified their methods to utilize a karakoa's crescent shape and balancing outriggers, to take advantage of the shallower draft and fleeter silhouette of the traditional karakoa style.

Jeian's naval maps were brought out for perusal, and discussion turned to draft depth, inter-tidal currents, and reef ridges.

"The question is, how do we force the armada to meet us on our terms, rather than over deep water and open ocean? They will have the better of our ships there, even with our speed."

"But it is over deep water where our tide-touched are at their best and Lunurin can bring all her strength to bear," Alon countered. "The closer we are to land, the worse our collateral damage will be."

Tomás's lips pursed. "It's best not to pin too much hope on witch magic. We must rely on tactics and numbers."

"Those are not exactly in our favor." Alon didn't like those Codicían words in an ally's mouth.

"I like the odds of our naval superiority better here." Jeian tapped the Sumila Gulf, a shallow coral sea that stretched three or four days' sail beyond Aynila Bay, with only a few deep-draft passages that would allow galleons to pass. "At the very least, their galleons will not be able to chase our ships into shallow water and coral shoals. We have far better knowledge of these waters."

~

His inay presided over the welcome feast, radiant as the full moon over deep water. Lakan Dalisay was swathed in gold and blue silk, crowned in a diadem of pearls. After the fall of the Palisade, Lunurin had spent weeks diving and carefully harvesting hundreds of luminous golden pearls. She'd insisted on harvesting all the artificial pearls she'd grown, so that their sacred oyster beds would have a chance to recover naturally for future divers. Sina had taken them and forged a victory crown of gold tambourine filigree that seemed to cast the moon's light down on whoever the Lakan spoke to.

Dalisay did not often wield her wealth and station so,

being more concerned with the restoration of the healing halls and the training of Aynila's tide-touched. But tonight she was in her element, making a great show of hospitality and a calculated display of Aynila's riches.

The banquet hall was laid with four long tables covered in banana leaves, each with its own roasted lechon. Around each massive roast pig were heaped yet more delicacies on beds of rice. Clams and mussels swimming in red annatto oil. Chicken rubbed in blackened coconut curry. Ginataan crab simmered in coconut milk and lemongrass beside sea urchins stuffed with rice, and mounds of rice noodles topped with quail eggs, sausage, and shrimp.

If there were ever a time to remind their allies of the riches of Aynila's seas, her ports, and peoples, it was tonight. They needed all the sway they could beg, borrow, bargain, or steal.

Tensions were high. There'd not been a gathering of so many for an Amihan Moon for at least a generation. That made it the perfect time to officially meet his in-laws. Over the years since Aynila had been freed, Lunurin had expended a small fortune in indigo ink on letters to her family, and met with many representatives of Calilan's fleet. Alon had written no few of his own letters along with the Lakan extending her welcome and desire for a meeting of their families. But somehow it had been delayed, year after year, the needs of Aynila and Calilan always pulling in different directions.

Now, the Amihan Moon had brought everything together. So he was trying to be grateful as he was cross-examined by her relatives.

Lunurin's mother had pulled her aside, their heads bent together in mirrored posture. Lunurin had her mother's broad shoulders, the fine arch of her brows, and her pride.

With her Tiya Halili she shared the fierce protectiveness and endless willpower Alon had always loved her for. And he saw, too, how Lunurin had learned to hold on to love even when it hurt, long before Catalina.

Still, he would like to say it was going well, that his wife was happy, and his in-laws approved of him. One out of three wasn't bad.

It was almost worse to have her tiyas' undivided attention.

"Your brother is the eldest? Or do you have two?"

"But you are Lakan Dalisay's only gods-blessed heir."

"And none of you have children?"

"Ay nako! Your poor inay. What is she thinking?"

"You are both how old?"

The questions were endless, bouncing conversationally between Halili and Kalaba. Alon answered as best he could.

"No children yet," he managed.

"We've been busy enough with—" Lunurin cut off, her mask of good humor wavering.

Alon hoped only he could see through it. The absence of Inez was palpable, a wound Lunurin's family prodded without realizing.

He redirected. "I've been very involved in rebuilding the halls of healing."

Datu Talim tsked in arch disapproval. "Some efforts are better spent elsewhere. We've seen how effective all these healers are when it comes to an actual battle."

"I hardly think the healing halls and our work there had any bearing on what went wrong in Talaan," he countered.

"Aynila is out of touch. You've forgotten it's at sea where tide-touched are at their strongest." This came from Ragasa. It seemed Talim rarely spoke without his persistent echo amplifying her disapproval. Lunurin's stepfather detested the existence of the healing temple almost as much as her father, an impressive feat.

Lunurin leaped in. "You're right. The healing halls can't train tide-touched for open water as well as we'd like. We'd like to propose a training program to send students to work through the wet season on Stormfleet ships."

Talim's refusal was swift. "No. It would never work."

"But you always say—"

"If you can't see why, we can't explain it to you." Ragasa silenced any further attempts in this direction.

Sina came to the rescue with a redirection even riskier than Alon's. "Speaking of, you never did explain the signs you'd read in Calilan's fires." She issued the challenge like smashing a bottle of lambanog over a burning torch.

Isko threw himself over the conflagration before it exploded in their faces. "But perhaps you could try. With so many wise and experienced katalonan gathered together, what better time to confer than as the Amihan Moon nears? Is that not what we all came together for?"

For a beat, Talim considered whether she'd just been insulted, but then, with a sniff she inclined her head. This expanded the conversation significantly, drawing in Hiraya, the Lakan, as well as katalonan from several parties.

"Power has pooled in Aynila," Datu Talim began.

"As it should, before an Amihan Moon," Sina protested.

"But fewer and fewer gods-blessed are being chosen outside of Aynila. The power should spread and flow over all the archipelago—"

"Fewer gods-blessed will be named in the central islands where Codicían strongholds prevent dives," Hiraya pointed out.

"Along the barrier islands, we've had sightings of the laho making an attempt to swallow every full moon this year. She's grown old and strong, and her hunger is great," Kalaba added.

"She's taken over all the weaves this year." One of the t'nalak master weavers spread the folds of her shawl to display the pattern brought to her in her dreams. It resolved into a massive laho knotted over and under itself across half the tapestry, jaw spread wide around the full moon at its center. The other half of the tapestry was incongruous empty blackness against the busy shining white of the serpent's twisting body.

Freed from the center of attention by Sina's gambit, and the increasingly obscure discussions of omens, Alon pulled Lunurin's attention away from her mother before her fury cracked her mask of civility.

A small, shameful part of him was relieved she wasn't melting seamlessly in with her family. If he was honest, he'd been a little afraid she'd leave him for Calilan if they asked it of her.

But how was he any better? He was hurting her with his secrets too. She just didn't know it yet. The truth was caught, choking in his throat like a fishbone. He'd wanted nothing more than to protect her, to support her and love her, but he was failing. When had he become so selfish?

Alon bent close. Under the auspices of refilling his wife's cup, he shielded Lunurin briefly from the room. She leaned in, tucking her face against his neck. She breathed out a long string of curses, muffled against his skin. Alon tried not to get distracted by the heat of her breath and the brush of her lips.

He pressed a kiss to her temple and a full goblet of rice wine into her hands. "Your mother hates me, but at least she hates Sina more."

Lunurin smothered a laugh, pulling him convulsively close for an instant. She lifted her head. "Goddess mine preserve me, what would I do without you?"

"We've opened lines of communication. For tonight, that is enough."

You are enough, he promised, holding her burning gaze, regretting that she'd had to face them alone earlier.

"*It is fear. They fear me. They fear all we represent*," she murmured, her goddess peering through her eyes. Anitun Tabu's voice was a kiss of lightning crackling behind her words. "*They have grown small with their fleet shattered across the seas. To recognize our strength would be to admit how weak they have become.*"

And then, like it had never happened, Lunurin gulped her wine, the mask sliding back across her face like armor.

She smiled. "Go. I will mind our elders don't get into a fist fight. The Lakan has left Jeian alone. Aizza could probably use your support."

She went to sit beside her Tiya Kalaba, who was locked in deep discussion with the Lakan.

Alon sought out Jeian across the banquet hall. Somehow, the delegates from Ísuga had been seated with Talaan. That could not possibly end well.

Jeian had ties to both groups from his time in exile, having sailed with Captain Nihma of Ísuga who sat beside Aizza now. However, Ísuga was renowned for having spent the last thirty years violently expelling Codicían missionaries... often in pieces. It hadn't escaped Alon's notice that many from Talaan still wore their rosaries proudly.

Alon's hand went to his own mutya in remembrance. He was grateful to Sina for repairing and reshaping it after he'd shattered the false rosary. She could've left the cross-set pearl intact, but he'd been unable to bear the resemblance to his father's treasured crucifix.

Her voice pitched to carry, Captain Nihma declared,

"Talaan has gone soft with its foreign proclivities."

Alon met his brother's eyes meaningfully. He intervened with a hearty backslap and a sharp look at Nihma. "Bold words from dear friends who have been very careful not to pledge ships to Aynila's defense."

Alon winced, but at least it locked her and Jeian in yet more circular talk about manpower, and any insults flung were between themselves, rather than at other delegates. It was the best that could be hoped for. Alon inserted himself among those from Talaan.

"What is the purpose of our great trading hub here in Aynila if not to indulge in foreign proclivities?" Alon observed with good humor, waving over a servant to dish cups of spiced chocolate and glutinous rice. "One of our local farmers has cultivated our volcanic hills with cocoa trees theses last ten years."

Mouths busy with food could not hurl insults. Alon showed off the translucence of his barong's piña cloth sleeve. "Weavers in Akean have been experimenting with pineapple waste. My dyers say it takes color like nothing else. We'd be fools to cast all we've gained away for the sake of tradition."

"We'd not have our current fleet without such innovation," Captain Tomás agreed.

Talaan's feathers smoothed, Alon kept his eyes open for other conflicts. The weight of all that must be accomplished weighed heavily on him. Their traditional allies among the inland rice kingdoms of Pangilog and Lubo had been as evasive as Ísuga when they learned the nearness of the Codicían armada.

They might have the blessings of the old gods behind them, but if they could not bring human allies to Aynila's defense...

All of this would be lost.

25

INEZ DOMINGO

Inez straddled the outrigger, her legs dangling into the streaming current she'd sung up to cradle the *Agawin*. With a twist, she hurled a silver-finned fish over to the largest of the three crocodiles coasting lazily alongside the boat. She hid a wince as her scarred lower back protested the movement.

Inez felt a special kinship for the biggest buwaya, missing a tooth; it had been the one to tear her free of the slaver's anchor. Her mutya and her crocodiles were all she had of Aynila, and their black shadows trailing the *Agawin* were an unexpected comfort.

Leaning into Umali's power and her crocodiles, out over deep water, she could work large and messy, in ways she'd never attempted in the shallow, crowded waters of Aynila Bay. The *Agawin* was designed to sail into typhoons, and easily cut through tide-touched waves. And with no other tide-touched around to tell her she was doing it wrong, it became easier to find what worked. Umali must have said something to the crew, because no one complained at the ship's bucking and twisting, nor said a word about her strangeness as she tested crocodile noises and learned their songs, her tongue struggling to click and pop with the same resonance, to craft currents that cut across the ocean's surface.

Umali peered down at her. "If you keep feeding them, they won't be hungry for the hunt."

Inez held out a hand and Sacay—a tall woman with a bright yellow cloth tied over her hair and a fishing spear strapped across her back—put a red-speckled kulapo into Inez's palm as an offering to the buwaya. Inez tossed the second fish, careful not to twist enough to make her scars protest.

"First catch goes to the buwaya, Captain," Sacay countered. "As thanks for the sea's generosity."

Umali waved her off. "Then make your own offerings. I've need of our tide-touched."

Sacay pouted. "But they like hers better!"

Umali extended a hand, and Inez accepted the help up onto the karakoa. She refused to read into Umali's teasing. *Our* was a perfectly impersonal collective for a captain toward her crew.

Harder to ignore was how much Inez wanted to be needed, to be someone who could be relied on.

"We've sighted a Duutsan trade ship coming down from Taoan. They build fast and light, and come down along deep waters off the coast, where even the Stormfleet rarely patrols. Then they cut through the southern channel round Lusong quickly to outrun any pirates. But with you aboard, they won't have a chance. They'll be carrying sugar and some Tianchaowen fineries to trade for Codician silver in Sugbu or Mamaylan."

Duutsan sailors who frequented this trade route might have actually seen Santa Catalina or evidence of her miracles, rather than rumors heard second or thirdhand. There was a chance, anyway.

They clambered up into the prow, behind the massive carved laho. Inez saw the offering niche, a large copper bowl where the real laho's pearl would sit, filled with rice and salt.

"So that *Agawin*'s likeness will not swamp us during storms, though I suppose I can worry less now we have you." Umali handed her a sight glass.

Inez braced the glass between two carved tendrils of the laho's great flared mane and peered into the blue haze where sky met sea.

"I don't—" she began.

Umali laid her fingertips on her wrist, shifting the glass a degree or two left. "Low in the water. They paint the hull to obscure the shape of it against the horizon. Ships of this type are rarely armed, or only with light cannonry. Without large stores of gunpowder to flash, they have been hard prey for us, but with you..."

Her crocodiles had been showing her how to taste and see through the salt. Inez reached forward with reptile-sharp senses until she found the displacement of another hull in the water. With this guiding sense, she shifted the glass another hair left... *there*.

Three large masts with vast white sails blending into the clouds along the horizon rose over a pear-shaped hull designed for trade over distances Inez could barely imagine. The hull was painted in grey and white stripes, breaking the outline against the haze of the horizon. It shimmered in and out of view, depending how she focused.

"I see it," she breathed. A hunting thrill hit her as she locked the ship in her sights. After all, so many of the Santa Catalina rumors in Masagana had come from sailors along these trade routes. Where better to hear them firsthand?

"Can you slow them?" Umali asked.

Inez tested a drumming thrum she'd learned, gulping air in for more resonance, and reached, but her ability to call up currents thinned at such a great distance. Frustrated, she shook her head. "No, not yet."

"Don't lose them. I'll fill our sails with heat to close the gap." Umali swept off her long ikat jacket of black and copper with beautifully embellished sleeves, and draped it over Inez. "To shield you from the heat. Signal if it becomes too much."

Inez lifted the coat over her head, suddenly understanding why so many of the crew wore their hair covered. She braced herself as the *Agawin*'s sails snapped full with the rising heat Umali fed into them. Up in the prow, the quiver of the karakoa's straining hull was like an earthquake.

Usually, Umali's heat was pleasant. This was another matter. Inez wondered what she had treated the sails and her coat with so that they did not instantly go up in smoke.

The hot air singed the delicate passages of her nose. She turned her face into the collar of the jacket, breathing through the sea spray-dampened material.

Umali's scent coated her tongue: smoky and faintly bitter, like hot bronze, the salt of her sweat, and an unexpected sweetness, which Inez discovered came from a stash of soft carabao milk candies in the jacket's breast pocket.

She burned so brightly, and Inez had not yet seen her call or shape a single flame.

Any forge in the metalworkers' conclave would've welcomed her on sight. Again, Inez wondered what had driven her from her mountain when she felt like nothing so much as the burning magma heart of a volcano.

It felt natural now to let Umali buoy her, just as she filled the sails. Inez reached across the shining blue waters toward the Duutsan ship. Like a basking crocodile on a beach, claws slipping against fine shifting sands, it moved with a ponderous slow roll. It had been at full sail, running before the wind—until it began to rock and founder, fighting the spinning counter currents Inez commanded.

The wet season winds were in its favor with its many large sails, but Inez was stubborn, and the gap between the two ships was closing.

The *Agawin*'s crew arrayed themselves on the upper deck, weapons readied, their three lantaka cannons primed toward their prey.

Umali called Inez down before the powder was packed, her laho-hilted kampilan sword drawn, its angled edge molten hot. "Keep close."

Inez nodded and held their prey fast in the jaws of the sea.

The boom of the three bronze cannons was loud. Well-aimed shots, one of which sent the top mast of their prey crashing down. Umali burned, magnificent, and frightening.

After a brief panic, and one last mighty attempt to break free from Inez's counter current, the Duutsan vessel ran up a white flag.

A cheer went up from the *Agawin* as they boarded. Inez was swept along in Umali's fiery wake. It was as easy as catching and riding the surf to shore.

A part of her worried once she had her prey before her, she'd lose her head, the way she had on the slave ship. She'd been so angry, the black bottomless depths of her soul so hungry, she'd lost the most important prize: Ortiz. As easy as it was to get swept along in Umali's battle fervor, she couldn't let herself forget her own objectives.

Before she knew it, she was on the wide, tall deck of the Duutsan ship.

It shocked her how small a crew such a huge ship required—only fifteen men, including the captain. The *Agawin* was crewed by forty-five, and Inez had seen karakoa of similar size in Aynila carry a hundred.

They were subdued quickly, only the captain protesting his manhandling. The boarding crew did not even bother tying anyone save their leader, keeping the men kneeling side by side along the far rail at the point of Sacay's fishing spear. Soon enough, the deck hatch was opened, releasing a caramelized sweet smell stronger than anything Inez had ever encountered.

Umali set the boarding party to carrying boxes of the sugar loaves onto the *Agawin*.

Inez studied the Duutsan crew. She'd often heard the sisters of the convent complain that the Duutsan traders who came into port in Aynila were godless heathens, who'd abandoned His Holiness the Pope, and could not be considered true believers at all. But this crew did not all look Duutsan. Some were Taoan sailors, brown as Jeian. And one…

She zeroed in on their pilot, with his bright green eyes, and a worn circlet of prayer beads around his wrist. "You. You're Codicían, aren't you?"

Perhaps she'd have more luck learning the truth of Santa Catalina from someone who'd been to the Codicíans' central archipelago strongholds than she'd had on Masagana.

The man straightened, glancing around at his fellows before he answered. "I am." He spoke with a thick accent, unfamiliar to her.

"I'm looking for Santa Catalina. Have you heard of her?"

"Are you seeking a miracle?" The pilot tried to lean around Sacay and her fishing spear. His eyes raked over Inez in a way that made her skin crawl.

Inez narrowed her eyes. "It is my business what I seek."

The man tipped his chin. "Tell me of it anyway, that I might aid you. In exchange, do not let me meet whatever fate you have in store for the others."

Inez raised her brows. "You'd turn on your own crew so easily?"

She knew that the crew would likely be released, hulled just above the waterline and left to limp into the nearest port for repairs.

"A pilot who wishes to see old age upon the south seas does not question which way the tides are running."

"How poetic." Inez nodded to Sacay, who allowed the pilot to stand. "But unless you've actually seen Santa Catalina, you are of no use to me."

"Six months ago, when we last made port in Sugbu, I heard she was newly returned to the archipelago after a vision of Aynila's—"

"Return to God's holy light," Inez parroted. She'd already heard this one. She turned away. His information was too old to be useful. The yawning maw of her disappointment put an edge to her desperation—the same that had driven her into that convert meeting, into freeing Ortiz. She struggled against the black pit of it in her belly.

That was when he lunged. Inez felt a jar of—was that holy water?—smash against the side of her head. The pilot grabbed for her mutya necklace, trying to rip it off her, but with Umali's repair it only yanked breathlessly tight. Did he think her a drowned ghost, or some demonic apparition to be banished by the holy relics of his religion?

The ringing in her ears and choking grip disoriented her enough that she was dragged back against the rail, behind the line of his crewmates. Umali's shout of fury rang across the deck.

All signs of peaceful surrender and a civilized exchange of goods were gone. Long knives came quickly into empty hands. The rising battle fervor of her captain swept Inez up, dragging her free from the reef edges of panic, like she'd been lifted free by the rising tide.

"Witch! Do you really think such a paltry band of riff-raff as this could take our ship without a fight? Do you think us cowards as well as fools?" the pilot hissed.

A less foolish man would've killed her when he had the opening. Inez twisted, struggling for air as the Duutsan crew, outnumbered three to one, lunged for the pirates, who now had their hands quite full with cargo. The surprise of breaking the white-flag surrender gave them a momentary advantage.

Sacay cut down one, then two, but was quickly forced back beside Umali, who cried out to the *Agawin*'s crew. Inez tried to plant her feet, tried to gain enough air to sing her need to the sea.

Her captor tightened his grip. "You don't need a saint's miracle. You need a priest to put you to the pyre. Don't you dare summon so much as a ripple, or I'll break your neck."

The fury in her belly crested up, powerful as a tsunami. She might not be able to sing up waves, but she could drag him down to them. She seized his choking hands and threw herself backward, hoping that crocodile armor would insulate her from the cacophony of the sea.

The far rail hit the small of her back. The next pitch of the deck was perfectly timed. Tottering precariously on the edge, Inez caught Umali's eye across the chaos of the deck. Inez smiled and crashed her head backward into her attacker's nose.

They went over. He tried to free his hands from her mutya to grasp for the rail, but Inez didn't allow it, holding tightly to him as they tumbled down toward the sea. If he wanted to attack a sea witch, let him see what that meant.

The waves reached up to catch her. Crocodile instinct took her then, and she rolled, tearing free. In that moment she was not a tide-touched, adrift among the waves, fighting to keep herself separate and intact. She was just another dark, sleek body who tasted blood.

Her crocodiles rumbled in agreement. They circled, tails lashing with eagerness.

The pilot came up gasping for air, cursing her and her water witch devilry. The Codicíans had invented no new damnations for Aynilans in thirty years. Blood streamed down from his crushed nose. The water ran red.

"First catch." An offering, as easy as the fish had been. After all, Aman Sinaya had many children of teeth and claw. Inez couldn't afford to falter now. She had to race as far as she could on borrowed power and crocodile songs before the power of the Amihan Moon faded, if she really meant to find her sister.

Her buwaya accepted. The circle closed, and the pilot was dragged down, leaving only reddish foam upon the surface of the waves. Inez treaded water, trying to determine how best to scale the side of the ship to aid her crew.

The sound of the fight overhead changed. There was a crack of rigging and sail as a burst of hot air filled the remaining sails. Screams rose.

Several sailors flung themselves overboard, clothes and hair aflame. Their screams cut off suddenly as they hit the water. Inez ensured they did not come back up.

None of the Duutsan crew were still alive when Inez was hauled, dripping, from the sea. Umali had torn down their white flag of surrender and dragged it across the bloodied deck before casting it into the waves. It hung there, a ghostly shape against the blue of the sea.

They cleared the deck, and Umali split off a portion of the crew to deliver the merchant ship to a port for salvage. Inez helped Sacay toss the bodies of the captain and crew down to the crocodiles below. Her back ached, old scars pulling as she strained, especially tender where she'd hit the rail.

Umali tried to pull her away from her gory task, but Inez shook her head, keen to avoid the dressing down she was sure to get. She'd put the *Agawin*'s crew in danger. She was souring things here as quickly as she had in Aynila.

Too soon, it was done. Umali pulled her into the captain's quarters. "Your balisong knife is a sharp tooth, but for boardings, you need more range."

She pulled down a smallsword, highly decorated with a silver and blue enamel hilt, and a thin three-foot blade, light enough for Inez to balance easily in her grip. "Here. It's a good make, though foreign."

Inez accepted, her cheeks still hot with shame. "Why are you giving me this? I ruined what could've been a bloodless prize."

Umali tipped her chin up with warm fingertips. "It wasn't your fault."

The knots of shame Inez had worked up since she'd been pulled from the company of her crocodiles and reminded that she was only a woman chasing after an impossible rumor, loosened.

"The Codicían recognized you were gods-blessed. They planned to target you from the moment you turned the tides against them. They sullied a white-flag surrender."

"But I—" *Was stupid and put everyone in danger chasing rumors that gained me nothing.* She couldn't bring herself to say it. Even if it was true.

"It is yours. Look how well it fits in your hand. Pretty and sharp." Umali grinned. "Like you."

Inez sputtered.

"Now come, you've turned my few crates of sugar and silks into the prize of a full Duutsan fluyte. That deserves celebration," Umali decreed, captain again and seeing profit to be made.

Aboard the Agawin, the rowers found their posts on the outriggers, clearing the ship's belly for cargo. The sails were rigged so that Inez could focus on drawing a tailing current to ease the damaged Duutsan vessel into port.

She twirled the hilt of the smallsword between her hands, studying the fine silverwork and gleaming enamel. It was more art than weapon, though the edge was wickedly sharp. Her cheeks warmed, remembering Umali's comment.

She listened with half an ear to the debate about where best to offload the ship they'd unexpectedly acquired.

"What of Masbad? Large enough for the salvage, and I heard they drove out the Codicíans. It's a safe port now," Sacay suggested.

"And they'll pay in bronze ingots, or even gold. But the straits around the southern tip of Lusong and Masbad are the Codicíans' access to their colonies on the central archipelago. We don't need another holy water incident, or a run in with a proper galleon," Umali mused, with a teasing smile at Inez.

"It's a risk. Especially with tensions rising between the Codicíans and Aynila." This came from the helmsman, Lim.

Dangerous news for Aynila. And yet, for the rumors Inez was still determined to chase, all the way back inside a Codicían nunnery if need be... hadn't she been told her sister had blessed a relic in Masbad?

26

❖—❖

LUNURIN CALILAN NG DAKILA

Lunurin was being punished for losing her temper with the Stormfleet over the bay.

She had been not-so-subtly disinvited from accompanying her inay. "A stormcaller on the volcano's slopes is the last thing we need," were her exact words before she'd gone to meet Sina and Hiraya to make the final preparations for the Amihan Moon.

Lunurin tried to tell herself it was just firetender business that she'd have nothing to add to. But it stung that her inay would choose to spend time with Sina, who she now personally disliked as much as she already disdained most of the Lakan's family, over Lunurin when time was so short.

"Your tiyas will be with you." Talim pressed her cheek to Lunurin's and left the breakfast table, having at least accepted Lunurin's invitation to stay with her and Alon. But Lunurin knew this was an admonishment as much as anything else. She was being minded, like an unruly child.

Ostensibly, her tiyas were graciously making introductions

to the Stormfleet captains Lunurin had not had time to meet at last night's feast. But the introductions rapidly became more contentious than gracious.

"My niece, Lunurin, was in Talaan when we lost Captain Batao. She was your cousin, isn't that right?" Halili might as well have announced that Lunurin had killed Batao by her own hand and sunk her ship, abandoning the survivors to the waves.

"Many more may have been lost if she had not been there at all," Kalaba interjected.

Lunurin tried to defend herself. "It was Stormfleet captains and Aynila's navy who made the joint decision to attack while negotiations were underway."

"Stormfleet ships should never have been so close to Lusong to begin with. We can't spare them from the barrier islands." Batao's cousin was already in agreement with Halili, it seemed.

"It was the dry season," Kalaba demurred.

"And yet her storm still sent allied ships under. Getting dragged into conflicts with the Codicians only puts our people at greater risk."

"Losses I also grieve, but let's not forget those ships also faced Codician bombardment. And with so few ports left where Codician galleons can expect safe harbor, aren't Stormfleet ships safer than they've been in years? This gathering would not have been possible five years ago," Lunurin argued. "Look how Aynila has prospered without the yolk of Codician control."

Tiya Halili only shook her head. "This is only a brief lull, just as some years send no great typhoons hurtling towards our islands. A seasoned captain knows better than to imagine they will come no more. The Stormfleet has greater concerns than this disaster, which Aynila insisted on dragging down on your own heads."

Kalaba frowned at her wife, but said no more.

And so it went. From ship to ship, from meeting to meeting.

"Let us help each other," Lunurin offered, desperate to find some common ground. "You say your supply ships are raided by pirates. With Aynila as your ally, your stormchasers would not need to send supply ships alone for fear of Codicían reprisal."

She was scoffed at for believing Stormfleet ships regularly visiting a port so central to the archipelago would not add to the problem she herself presented.

One captain was particularly blunt. "In the fifteen years you've been in Aynila, you've made life upon every Stormfleet ship more difficult and dangerous. You act as a lodestone for the worst storms the Great South Sea can spin, and it is our ships and our lives on the line as we try to do our duty."

Lunurin bit her tongue. *Do you think I did not try to leave?* she wanted to shout. *It was Calilan that sent me away, and Anitun Tabu herself who ensured I landed in Aynila.* Now, years later, they wished to complain of the result. As if Anitun Tabu had not been demanding she walk a typhoon across the water into Aynila since she was twelve years old.

Lunurin did not say these things. She kept trying. "If so many of your young gods-blessed are leaving for easier lives and less grueling work, why not engage with the healing school? Not all who come to our halls wish to stay in Aynila. Not all are meant to heal. A great many would welcome a berth with the Stormfleet if it meant seeing distant ports and half a year's leave at the dry season."

"And think of all the advanced healing techniques they could teach our tide-touched," Kalaba counseled.

"The Stormfleet does not accept those who aren't prepared to dedicate their lives to guarding the archipelago from Anitun Tabu's rages. I'll not waste time and energy on students who will leave after a season."

Lunurin was rebuffed for suggesting storms came only during the wet season—and that the Stormfleet might be forced to change its traditions to keep their ships crewed.

The fact the Stormfleet wanted nothing to do with Aynila's efforts with the healing school made Lunurin suspect they viewed the entire effort as a fool's errand, doomed either because it had rebuilt upon the place where so many of the sea's chosen had died, or because they were spitting in the eye of the Codicians who would no doubt return to wipe them out again. Kalaba alone did not seem dead set against it.

She didn't even try to broach Halili taking on Rosa's training while her tiya was being so obstinate. She was glad she'd not brought Rosa along today. There was enough consternation just over Lunurin. She didn't want to remind anyone of the newest Aynilan stormcaller.

She could feel herself nearing a breaking point. She wanted to shake the Stormfleet captains and Halili, and demand to know how anything would improve if they refused to engage with even the smallest steps to address their difficulties.

No wonder Kalaba looked so tired. Did she deal with such stubbornness all the time?

They had all come to Aynila eager to see her power for themselves—and yet every time they faced the reality of it, they wanted her to conform to what they expected of a storm-caller instead: never causing storms, only unspooling them or leading them off course. She should always be positioning herself to ease the work of the Stormfleet, which would mean a ship's berth patrolling the barrier islands or returning to

Calilan. As if the natural state of their goddess were clear skies and not the typhoon.

Lunurin thought bitterly of Talaan. Could she blame them for their stubbornness? So many of these captains had already decided she and Aynila saw them as expendable. Why should they lend their ear now for a fight they were even less likely to survive?

This was repeated to her face so many times she lost count. But couldn't they see that she, too, had lost much to the power she wielded? They said she was not a proper stormcaller. Had they forgotten what it was to serve Anitun Tabu, Goddess of Vengeance? Did they not feel her fury in the storm, her grief in the rains, her laughter on the rising winds?

"Will you let them bury their heads in the sand till the storm surge comes in to drown them?" Anitun Tabu asked in a caress of the warm sea breeze across her cheeks.

If they could not stand together now, it would only be a matter of time till the Codicians succeeded in eradicating every gods-blessed from the archipelago. Did the Stormfleet think they would consider it enough to wipe Aynila from the map? Lunurin and Sina had taught them the archipelago contained so much more to fear than water witches.

Lunurin knew that if they failed, it would not end with Aynila.

~

Lunurin's painful entreaties to the Stormfleet were finally cut short by a gout of smoke and steam from the peak of Hilaga.

Even as she flung herself back aboard the little balangay she'd taken to meet her tiyas, shouting breezes to fill the sail, she saw the plume breaking up in the wind, with no signs of lava or a larger eruption.

It's a year for fire, she reminded herself. It could be a positive sign. They needed more fire.

She met Talim and Ragasa, her loyal shadow, at the waterline just as Sina and Hiraya all but threw them off Hilaga and into the Saliwain, backed by what seemed like half the conclave. So many furious firetenders: the black sand shivered under their feet.

"Come here and try that again, and I'll throw you into the caldera myself!" Sina beckoned like Talim was a dog. This did not bode well for Lunurin being able to talk everyone down.

Hiraya was feeling no more diplomatic, heat waves simmering off her skin. "If this is the kind of help you bring, you and the Stormfleet are banned from stepping foot on Hilaga before the Amihan Moon."

"If you aren't prepared to do what a year of fire requires, then your failure will be on your own heads." Talim was equally furious.

Lunurin didn't want to intervene, but was duty bound. "Is everyone alright? Do we need to take anyone to the healing halls?"

All four swung to face her.

"She tried to set fire to Hilaga's rainforest!" Sina pointed at Talim.

"Even you must see your volcano is far too placid, smothered by the energies of storm and sea. A forest fire now will give us a fighting chance to properly welcome the Amihan Moon," Talim protested hotly.

"Or it might burn the entire conclave to the ground and deprive us of charcoal for our forges for years." Hiraya's words crackled. "You have no respect for our traditions."

"Your own spark-striker birds should've set the blaze long ago. This mountain needs a burn." Ragasa backed his wife.

"You're lucky we stopped you and Hilaga only let off some steam," said Sina.

Lunurin ushered Talim and Ragasa aboard her little skiff before Hiraya or Sina lit them on fire as Isko arrived.

Lunurin pulled a tactical retreat. She let her winds carry them into the center of the Saliwain and out toward the bay, confident Alon would see to any injuries, and Isko could help Sina and Hiraya set Hilaga to rights.

The little boat was silent but for the slap of waves on the hull, and Lunurin's breeze filling the tripod sail. Talim and Ragasa sat side by side, mouths in matching grim lines, avoiding her gaze.

Fed up with talking in endless circles and constant apology, Lunurin let out a frustrated sigh. "I guess I wasn't the only one who needed minding. Dare I ask what happened?"

Her inay kept her face turned away from Lunurin and stared out over the water. "A stormcaller wouldn't understand."

"I could try!" Lunurin cried. "I could try, if you would explain it to me."

Her inay didn't react, only looked to Ragasa, who shook his head. They'd never believed in "feeding into" Lunurin when her emotions were high. They'd believed it would help Lunurin learn better control of her dangerous passions. Then, as now, Lunurin wished her inay would not hold her spirit banked and away from her, would for once try to meet her halfway.

Lunurin took a deep breath. She becalmed the wind in their sail, letting them drift aimlessly. "I'm not some foolish outsider. I am your daughter. I want all the same things

Calilan does. We should be each other's most dependable allies. Tell me why—"

"The only way Calilan will support Aynila is if you agree to rejoin the fleet permanently," her inay answered, cold and calm, her gaze fixed far beyond Lunurin.

"What?" Lunurin's shock was a crackling knot of lightning in her chest. She was glad she'd released the breeze from their sail. She didn't need it mimicking her turmoil.

"All the captains who ally with Calilan agree. You are a danger to every ship in the Stormfleet if you remain on Lusong. You are shifting the entire weather pattern of the archipelago. Calilan used to be every typhoon's natural passage north and safely away. The placement of our fleet and our stormcallers ensured it," Ragasa added, his tone a perfect match to Talim's. Lunurin hated him for it.

"He's right. You break the pattern remaining in Aynila. You are far too strong to not be the final lodestone guiding storms north from Calilan, like Halili. Your tiya needs someone to take her place," Talim declared.

Finally, Lunurin understood. Ever since she had broken her dugong bone talisman and embraced her power, the Stormfleet couldn't compensate for her. It must be worsening as Stormfleet ships grew fewer and their stormcallers older. Every year, more holes opened in the network of ships and stormcallers that guided storms around the archipelago. As they splintered and their numbers dwindled, they were less and less able to fight the effect of Lunurin's presence in Aynila.

Every fiber of her being wanted to hurl her rejection of the proposal back at them, harsh as a slap. After all she had suffered and lost, she would never leave Alon and Aynila. Not even to gain a place in the Stormfleet, although the girl she'd been at fifteen had always wanted it. Not if doing so would leave this city that she'd sacrificed so much for exposed and vulnerable to the Codicíans' wrath. Not for her mother, who even now looked to Ragasa first, not her own daughter of whom she was asking the impossible.

Lunurin forced herself to try to find a middle ground. "I have married the Lakan's son. I cannot simply abandon my duties to Aynila. But I could dedicate my time during the wet season and go out with the fleets, if you need additional support."

"It is not enough," her inay responded. "You are of Calilan. You should never have been sent away."

Lunurin almost laughed. She doubted Ragasa agreed with that.

"But I was. The past cannot be undone. And surely you will not deny that my coming to Aynila was what Anitun Tabu intended all along?"

At last, Talim turned to look at her. "Even so. You come from too long a line of katalonan to remain as you have, especially not after the incident in Talaan. You clearly cannot keep your power in check alone. Worse yet, your use of it endangers the fleet. You have walked your terrible storm into Aynila; it is long since time for you to come home. Return to your family."

Lunurin held her inay's proud, dark gaze, and wished Talim could actually see her. The Lunurin who had been forced to flee Calilan fifteen years ago might have been moved by this, still wracked with guilt over the Inquisition's sinking of the Stormfleet. Sister María, who had grown hard and desperate within convent walls, might have been grateful to be shown even this amount of recognition by her family.

But now?

"Alon is my family." And Inez, Sina, Isko, Dalisay, and

Hiraya. She had been welcomed with open arms into her Aynilan family from the moment of her marriage. "Aynila is my home. I am a katalonan here." It had become so much truer over these last five years, rebuilding her city, recognized by her community and her Lakan.

In confirmation, the winds over the water circled close, listening for her slightest direction.

She would not turn herself inside out in the name of a family that refused to see what she was. Who did not even respect her. She would not repeat the mistakes she'd made for Catalina—not for love, and never for guilt.

Her inay brushed all this off. "There are no children to think of. You could leave."

"You owe the Stormfleet this much, at least, for all the years we've spent trying and failing to redirect your storms," Ragasa added.

"Why do you let them sail into ship-killers?" Lunurin demanded. "Storms I call with Anitun Tabu singing in the gale winds? You know they cannot be turned. Why lose good ships to folly?"

"Because they are Stormfleet-sworn, and it is their duty to protect our archipelago. No self-respecting Stormfleet captain would give up on turning a storm," Talim retorted, all stubborn pride.

Lunurin wanted to tear her hair out. Would they accuse Sina of killing Stormfleet gods-blessed if they scaled Hilaga's sides and cast themselves into the volcano's lava chambers?

"What you're asking of me is impossible." The words tasted like failure, of both Aynila and her goddess.

"Then Calilan cannot stand with Aynila in what comes," Talim said. "If you treasure this city so much and do not wish to be its ruin, you will see reason."

Rather than come to their aid, her "family" intended to use their desperation against her. Lunurin's fury was a moon-maddened laho she was failing to ride. The winds began to whip and tug at their sail. There were deaths she was responsible for, like the ships lost as the Inquisition hunted for her after she'd sunk the *San Pedro*. But every Stormfleet ship that misjudged their capabilities? Every crew lost at sea? She would not be saddled with those lives too. Not when their captains and her family knew exactly what she was.

Lunurin rose and slapped her hand down, collapsing the snarl of her fury and impressionable winds. The surface of the sea lay still and smooth as a mirror. She wished she could so simply calm her own heart.

She spoke very softly into the perfect stillness. *"Have you forgotten I am ruin?"*

27

◆

ALON DAKILA

The Amihan Moon was rising tonight and the healing halls were already in chaos.

There had been a fight; that much was clear. A dozen sailors with injuries ranging from black eyes to missing teeth, one horribly dislocated jaw, a few fractured knuckles, and Alon and Aizza were at wit's end.

Aizza took the most serious injuries to the healing pools, while he took over the infirmary. He sent for Jeian when he saw Aynilan sailors in the mix: missing incisor, broken nose, and a set of busted ribs.

He advised Bernila to dump that last one straight into the bay—he might be able to row again within the week. Alon took on teeth, which were tricky, trying to preserve the nerves and blood vessels.

When the sailors' furious captains arrived reigniting the brawl, he gave a shout of frustration and overturned the healing basin he was working over.

Saltwater rushed across the floor, seizing the feet of

everyone who'd stood from their cot, and each of the captains up to their knees.

"Have you no respect?" Alon's voice cut through the ruckus, hard and clear as a bell. "I'll not beg the Sea Lady's mercy on your behalf a second time if you spill blood in these halls." He gave a short, hard shove, which forced all but the captains to sit down or fall, invisible hands of saltwater holding them fast.

He now had a clear view of Jeian in the middle of the secondary altercation, another patient slung over his shoulders. Alon released his brother and helped get the unconscious sailor onto a stretcher. Dread gripped him as soon as he made contact. It was another drowning on dry land, just like what Inez had done to the converts.

He locked eyes with Jeian, who subtly shook his head.

Alon had infirmary aids move the patient into a private room, and herded the rest—Tomás, Nihma, and a captain he didn't recognize by name, but who looked Stormfleet—along behind. "Let us continue this very civilized discussion in private where we will not risk the wrath of the Lakan and my brother's wife for sullying these halls with violence."

These were exactly the kind of flashpoints they needed to prevent during the Lakan's ceremony at sunset tonight. It did not bode well that instead, they'd kicked them off early.

Looking to his brother for some explanation, Alon examined the patient, noting a crushed tibia in addition to the deep healer's sleep.

"There was a fight," Jeian said.

"I surmised that much." Alon gestured to the other captains, urging someone to fill in what had happened. "Whose is he?"

Tomás spoke up. "One of mine. An Aynilan sailor attacked him."

"And I told you, my man did nothing wrong. We were trying to keep the peace between your three crews who'd decided to take each other's heads off," Jeian retorted.

"He's barely breathing!" Tomás protested.

"We needed to stabilize the worst injury. He was hurting himself more awake," Jeian said to Alon, making it clear he should not draw attention to how that "stabilization" had been botched.

Alon would have to wait to learn what had gone wrong when there were fewer witnesses. "It'll make the healing go easier." He backed his brother, keeping to their agreement of a united front, though Jeian being in the middle of today's brawl wasn't a promising start.

"It's not—" Tomás began.

"You don't want him awake for a break like this," Alon insisted. "We might keep him from needing a cane for the rest of his life."

He had the aids take the patient to Aizza at the healing pools. She had the most experience.

And just in time as Tomás, the Stormfleet captain, and Captain Nihma started hurling accusations and insults at each other, which only served to muddy the waters further. But Alon was able to pick out a few key details.

The altercation had started between Talaan and a Stormfleet crew that had lost people during Talaan's liberation. No one knew how the sailors from Ísuga became involved. But at some point, the waters of the port had turned choppy. The sailor from Talaan had his leg caught as the closely moored ships rocked.

Understandably, Captain Tomás wanted every tide-touched in the brawl called to account for injuries. The Stormfleet wanted reparations for their dead. Nihma was furious over the damaged ships and picking a fight with every convert she'd ever met. Jeian was right in the middle of it, not improving the situation despite his best efforts.

So it would fall to Alon once again to be peacemaker.

Once he had a read of the situation, he spoke over them. "The Stormfleet has no due cause to expect reparations over a battle they chose to initiate. It wasn't Tomás's men we fought in Talaan."

The Stormfleet captain sputtered, but Talaan was appeased. Alon speared Nihma with a look. "Today's injuries and damage will be seen to by Aynila's healers and ship-builders shortly. As your hosts, we will take responsibility. Does that satisfy you?"

Nihma nodded begrudgingly, still glaring at Tomás.

"I need to deal with the most serious injuries. Can I depend on you to keep your crews in check, or will you put my healers at risk?" Alon challenged.

This finally sent the other captains on their way to see to their battered crews.

"What was all that? Why is Tomás so aggravated? What did your tide-touched do?" Alon demanded when he was alone with Jeian.

"He's aggravated on account of the rumors. He showed up at my office with a whole entourage to determine the truth." Jeian gestured for them to head toward the main infirmary.

"Rumors?" Alon prodded.

Jeian listed them off. "Apparently, several Aynilan converts petitioned Tomás to request the release of Brother Arcilla to exile in Talaan, on account of converts being snatched off the streets, tales of torture, men having their fingers fed to crocodiles in the bay..."

Alon closed his eyes briefly, damning Pedro, and hoping

fervently his spy had stuffed Inez into a bag and was bringing her home right now. It was the only possible way Alon could redeem himself from the mess he'd made.

But he'd received no updates on Inez yet. He instead had confirmation that the Codícian armada had set sail from their resupply stop in Hanay upon a strong northeastern wind. Should that count as an ill-omen too?

"Here, ask Gani yourself." Jeian signaled to one of the lightly bruised sailors waiting to be seen.

Gani was older, streaks of grey in his long black braid. Not a young, inexperienced tide-touched like Inez. That was even more worrisome.

He sketched a bow. "Captain, Gat Alon, was he revived?"

"Tell us everything that happened," Alon instructed as they went to the healing pools where Aizza was treating the sailor from Talaan. Did it mean anything that it was now gods-blessed among the navy struggling the most with the Amihan Moon's power? He'd have brought it up if he didn't think it would raise Jeian's hackles.

"Something has felt… off this week. I thought it was a head-cold from wet season damp, but now…" Gani told him.

"You tried to heal one of the men injured in the fight," Alon prompted Gani.

Gani stayed back from the water. "Well, yes, at the end. At first, I was just pushing the really stubborn ones off the dock. But the waves had a mind of their own. I've a steady hand for ships, never even clipped an oar, but suddenly three moored karakoa from Ísuga near smashed the dock to kindling. His leg was crushed. I'm not a great healer, but someone had to stop the bleeding… except it wasn't just difficult. It was wrong. I could feel it."

It was like Inez's struggles over the last months all over

again. Dreading what he knew came next, Alon exchanged a look with Aizza.

Gani shrugged helplessly. "The healing was going bad, he kept screaming and—"

"So, you tried healer's sleep, but somehow pulled deeper. He drowned on dry land," Aizza filled in, her expression grim.

Gani nodded. "And I thought I heard—and mind you, Dayang Aizza, I'm no katalonan, nothing like you—but I thought I heard a voice, an actual voice, from the depths. But it wasn't the Sea Lady I know. I yanked myself out of the water entirely, and I'm not touching salt until this summit is passed, and Aynilan waters feel right again."

What was going so wrong with the power of the Amihan Moon? And what did it portend for tonight?

28

◆

INEZ DOMINGO

They'd pulled the karakoa ashore for the night. Inez's trailing crocodiles rested their bellies upon the white sands under the *Agawin*'s beached outriggers.

The crew had left her the last scraps of their provisions, sheets of dried squid, before heading into a small fishing village nearby to barter sugar for fresh food and lambanog spirits.

Umali trailed after them shouting, "Food! Don't forget we need food! At least in equal measure to spirits, or we'll be living on pusit for weeks."

Inez had elected to remain behind and guard the ship. With her reptilian companions, no one would be foolish enough to challenge her, so there was no need for anyone else to miss out on a night of carousing and celebrating their prize.

She tossed the dried squid down to her crocodiles. Would they leave her behind tomorrow, as her ability to grasp at and feed them the moon's power waned? She would miss them. She'd already caught herself assigning them nicknames, like they had for her. Himig, the biggest, who'd spoken to her first and loudest, teaching her crocodile songs, her missing tooth just starting to grow back in. There was Payat, skinny, with three bent tail ridges. Sariwa had a greenness like new rice seedlings to her eyes, rather than the bright gold of the others. And so on.

Would she be able to listen in on their simple basking pleasures tomorrow morning? Or would this strange connection be severed, rendering her useless to the *Agawin*'s crew. And worse, to her captain. No matter what Umali had said, Inez did not think she'd have much interest at all in a useless tide-touched.

And Inez wouldn't be pitied again, especially not by Umali. She couldn't bear it.

She'd find another ship in Masbad. Surely her share of two prizes would pay her passage onward?

"How far will you go?" Himig, toasting her belly on the sun-warmed sands, inquired in a lazy rumble. *"How deep will you reach? How much blood do you require to soothe your belly?"*

"My belly needs no blood," Inez retorted to the rumble of well-fed reptilian laughter.

"Your hunger betrays you, little crocodile. Worry less and feast more," the great she-beast advised.

She flopped down on the deck, staring over the water at the black shadow of the anchored Duutsan vessel. How far she had drifted from a version of herself her family in Aynila would recognize. What would Alon say if he knew she'd fed fifteen men to the sea today? What would he think of how much more at ease she was in waters churned bloody than over the pearl beds of Aynila?

And if she lost all this tomorrow, could she bear her own

tender skin, with no crocodile armor, no reptilian songs to the deep?

So she was in no mood to join her new crew's revelries. Or rather, she was… But she didn't want to feast and drink beside Umali, laughing and radiant in her victory, knowing she'd have to leave all this behind when her stolen power waned.

As the full moon rose out of the sea, gleaming like mother-of-pearl and shining over the waves, Inez was struck by longing for home. She should be there now, preparing to welcome the Amihan Moon with all Aynila's gods-blessed. It was a blessing that touched each volcano in the archipelago just once in a lifetime. If she missed this one, it was unlikely she'd see another.

She wondered if a laho would really swim up out of the deep to devour the moon tonight. Sina and the other fire-tender katalonan spoke of it as a surety, but Inez knew no one who'd seen a laho in fifteen years, not since one had tried to capsize Jeian's ship with Lunurin and Alon aboard.

Again, Inez wondered if Aman Sinaya was so very merciful to balance out the ravenous hunger of all the anito who called her vast blue breast home.

Umali folded down to sit beside her. Inez tore her gaze from the silvery glow shimmering across the water, trying not to be equally dazzled by the way the moonlight caressed Umali's sea-dark features. The captain had unbound her kerchief and let down her topknot. Her ink-dark hair spilled down her back like a river of indigo silk.

"I thought you'd gone with the crew?"

Umali shook her head. "No drinking for me tonight. Can you feel it too? The energy of the sea, sky, and earth at its peak? I think the laho will make a try tonight. It makes me wish to have celebrated an Amihan Moon over Mount Tumubo."

"Could you ever go back?" Inez kept her gaze on the moon, trying to remember how many finger-widths above the horizon the perfect bowl of Mount Hilaga sat.

Umali extended her burned arm between them. In the silvery-blue light of the moon, her scars looked black against her skin, like they'd been rubbed with soot. "Do you recall when Mount Tumubo erupted?"

Inez fought off a shiver in remembrance. They'd felt the earth shake before the sound of the eruption reached them. Mount Tumubo was north and east of Aynila, part of a chain of mountains down the eastern edge of Lusong. Tumubo had roared for days like a wounded beast. The skies over Aynila had turned an eerie orange, then, as fine ash rained down, black as midnight at midmorning. The strange ash clouds spawned terrific crashes of lightning and thunder without a drop of rain. Inez had tied wet cloths over the faces of the church school's younger children. The black cloud had hung over the city for days, the ground quivering underfoot like a plate of flan with every roar from the distant volcano.

It had been worse in Pangilog—there were tales of flowing rivers of ash swallowing whole towns. Lakes made, then unmade, sending tons of water, ash, and debris galloping down toward the sea, catching people as they tried to escape.

Inez lifted her gaze from Umali's burns to her profile, her wide cheekbones and full lips.

"But you can't be more than a few years older than me. What were you, ten?"

"I was twelve, and named to Amihan only months before."

"How…" Inez reached toward Umali's hand. She wanted to ask for the hows and whys. But she wasn't ready to answer such questions about why she'd fled Aynila and what she thought she'd find. She had no right to pry. She pulled back, just before her fingertips grazed the thickest band of scarring around Umali's wrist. "Forgive me. You don't owe me that story. Some don't need to be shared."

Umali closed the gap, placing her hand in Inez's. "That tale is not one for a night when Amihan's power is at its peak and old scars remember their ache. But I would not otherwise begrudge you the telling. Let's just say that firetenders are meant to keep our charges peacefully sleeping, not wake them to ruin and destruction. Just as I imagine tide-touched are expected to heal, not feed crocodiles and sing their songs."

Inez's own scars panged in sympathy. She clutched Umali's hand, grateful for the utter lack of recrimination in her words. As if their mutual failings held no more power than this: expectations they'd shrugged off. Inez only wished she were so confident in what she was doing now.

Inez's fingertips traced across the ripples of dense scar tissue, palpitating where nodules had adhered to the delicate ligaments and bones of her wrist. She wished she could soothe away the ache Umali spoke of. But that odd fluttering in her throat was back, and she didn't know if she wanted to lean into it or crush it.

She did want to bask, languid as her crocodiles, in the easy warmth of Umali's presence, even if she couldn't bring herself to speak her own secrets into the magically charged night air. She might be a terrible healer, but half of healing scars was stretching, manipulation, and time.

After a while, Umali flexed her fingers in Inez's grip. "What are you up to? I recall you were very insistent that you are a tide-touched who can't heal."

"I can't. Scars don't need healing. They need breaking up." Inez lifted her shoulder, tipping the scars exposed by the wrap of her sarong to the light. "I should've asked Sacay to get me coconut oil. Sorry, I know it's uncomfortable. I'll stop." She released Umali's hand.

Umali rotated her wrist, testing the range of motion. "You say that, but I like the feel of your hand on mine."

"Oil would be better." Inez hoped the darkness hid her blush.

Umali laid a hand on her shoulder. "May I offer the same to you?"

Inez hesitated. She shouldn't. She might not be nearly so welcome tomorrow as she was tonight. Leaning into Umali's power in the heat of battle, that was no different than how Lunurin could pull on those around her like wind filling all sails in a storm. This offer seemed... much more intimate.

Worse, what if she didn't like it? Sometimes, even letting the Lakan help her with her back was... awful. But Umali's heat was magnetic, as welcoming as slipping into a hot bath. She wanted to test those waters. She loosened her sarong at her nape, letting the cloth across her back slip down toward her waist.

"Don't dig too deeply, but the heat might do me good."

"Yell if it hurts too much. You don't like to twist. Is it here—oh, and where you hit the rail too." Umali scooted behind her, examining the full scope of Inez's scars. She lightly touched the silver clasp she'd welded into place on Inez's mutya. "This almost got you killed. Should I add a weak point, so it can't be used against you?"

Inez stroked her fingers over the scales of her mutya necklace. She'd returned her balisong to the center, no longer needing to hide part of her mutya away for security.

"No. I couldn't bear to have it snatched away from me."

Umali hummed in understanding and laid her hands over the curve of Inez's back, where the scarring layered and a wide band of bruising had bloomed, a souvenir from her first sea battle. She rubbed smooth circles over her skin. Inez stopped breathing for fear of what pitiful sound would escape her. Umali's heat sank deep, far more deeply than she'd expected.

She braced for the prickling tearing pain, for the way her scars would ache, the muscles seizing into knots, ready to yell *Stop!*

But the discomfort never came. Her skin tingled pleasantly as the pulsing tension in her muscles eased away. Her own breath fell into sync with Umali's, even and slow, feeding the forge fire heat flowing ever so gently through her hands.

"Would you tell me how you came to the sea?" Inez asked, trying to understand how the terror and devastation of Mount Tumubo's choking ash clouds over Umali's childhood had not prevented her from being who she was today, burning bright as the sun with her furies and her joys.

"I was sent to train with the Stormfleet. The surviving katalonan of Mount Tumubo believed distance and saltwater would insulate me from the heart of the volcano so that they could send her back to sleep." Umali swept her hands up and down Inez's back, folding her gently forward over her knees.

Inez hoped her words covered the way her breathing hitched, as she smothered a moan of pure deep satisfaction. "If you were sailing with the Stormfleet, why are you now raiding foreign merchants and sinking slavers?" She wanted to keep Umali talking—and stroking her skin.

"I have the worst luck in the world," Umali joked. "The splinter fleet I trained with clashed with an Inquisition galleon coming out of Aynila. They sunk us under a volley of cannon fire. After the battle, the *Agawin* and I washed up on a nearby shoal with a few other survivors. Sacay was one. I was the only gods-blessed who lived. We floated the ship, repaired her, but without a stormcaller or tide-touched, what use were we to another Stormfleet fragment already struggling to keep afloat and out of the Inquisition's line of fire? We were just extra mouths to feed. They might have taken me, but not my crewmates. And I wouldn't leave them behind. As no Stormfleet captain would have us, and no port in the archipelago with a Codicían presence would welcome a Stormfleet ship…" Umali shrugged out of her coat and draped it over Inez to keep in the warmth of her ministrations.

Inez drew the coat around her shoulders. She breathed in as Umali's scent engulfed her, and the flutter in her throat escalated.

"So you had no choice but piracy?" Umali did not seem reluctant to her profession.

"There were probably other choices. But I craved freedom. I could not see myself hiding from Codicían discovery as a nameless sailor toiling on a trade ship, hiding my mutya and keeping my head down. I can never set foot on another volcano, so joining a metalworking enclave like Aynila's was an impossibility. The sea suits me, and piracy is a better life than serving the Stormfleet. At least if I am killed for my crimes as a pirate and a thief, I'll have enjoyed the spoils."

Umali leaned close and reached into her coat pocket, retrieving two of the pastiyema candies. Inez accepted one, unwrapping the rice paper and letting the milky sweet dissolve on her tongue. The caramel sweetness drifting from the cargo added a new but delightful element to the treat.

Her crocodiles would approve of Umali's philosophy.

"I meant to ask about your jacket, about the crew too. Why did only the Duutsan's sailors' clothes catch fire? I've never seen you cast a flame, only heat."

Umali chuckled. "Oh, you're sharp-eyed. The silk's

been treated with metal-salts. It's a secret the katalonan of Tumubo have handed down for a long time. The story goes that a firetender katalonan and a tide-touched healer fell in love. The tide-touched wife was so upset to see her lover return from her duties to the volcano scorched and burned that they worked together to create a cloth that would not catch fire even when sparks rained down upon it or the forge fire crept too near. It's the same with the sails, and much of the *Agawin*. She's as fire-proof as wood can be. So I can be who I am without fear."

Inez studied Umali's bearing, her exquisite confidence, the clear burning purpose and invitation in her gaze. She was struck through with a longing, not for home, but for the kind of surety Umali had carved out for herself despite the tragedy and destruction that was an indelible part of her past.

Was Inez strong enough to do the same for herself? She did not feel it. She still felt tangled in a past that tried at every turn to ruin her, like a net dragging her under. A past that haunted her like the scars she could not reach to soften and stretch on her back, always tender, threatening to tear open if ever she moved without fear.

Her thoughts must have shown on her face, because Umali tucked a fingertip under her chin, capturing her gaze. "Whatever it is you're running from, or towards, I see how much… happier you are at sea. I've stolen my freedom aboard the *Agawin*, but I would share it with you, if you wished."

Inez's heart lodged in her throat. Was her desperation so obvious? "Why? Why me?"

Umali tilted her head. "Because I see a hunger in you I recognize. Gods-blessed like you and I are not made for healing or making, for caretaking or lulling volcanoes to sleep."

Inez wanted to believe she could be made of the same stuff as burning bright Umali.

And maybe it was just the Amihan Moon's magic singing through the air, or the way Umali's hands on her bare skin made her heart race, but Inez leaned in and pressed their lips together. She wanted a taste of the joy curling her full lips, and the hot sweetness of her mouth. She wanted to seize something for no other reason than she was hungry for it.

Even if she woke tomorrow and everything was changed. She would be truly, deeply, indulgently selfish now.

Umali grasped the front lapels of her jacket, pulling Inez in closer. The heat of her washed over Inez from head to toe. Inez let herself be swept away by the sweet, molten yearning between them, just like she'd ridden the updraft of Umali's blazing power into bloodlust and battle. She'd done things she'd never dreamed of, following in Umali's wake. Why not this too?

The press of Umali's body against hers was a shock. Soft breasts and lean belly, and the way it made her breath seize in her throat. She froze.

Umali's grip loosened. She pressed her brow to Inez, her hot, panting breaths sweet on her cheeks. "Have you never?"

Something ugly in Inez convulsed on the question. But she refused to let go of the burning desire Umali had kindled between them. She didn't care if it burned.

"Never. Not like this," Inez answered.

She pulled Umali's mouth back to hers, determined to steal just a bit of Umali's fire for herself to see if it filled the black pit in her belly better than blood.

29

LUNURIN CALILAN NG DAKILA

Lunurin mounted the steps to the Lakan's palace. She pushed aside comparisons to other times standing here, borrowing a saint's regalia. After all, she was not alone. Sina and Aizza were at her side, singing in the ambon to bless the sharing of wine with Aynila's allies.

Sina was resplendent in red and yellow, wearing a head-dress of heat-blued brass feathers mimicking a spark-striker bird's fan-tailed mating dance.

Aizza herself was swathed in rippling waves of translucent indigo silk, a huge golden laho torque chasing the moon about her neck.

For Lunurin, Casama's teams of tailors had crafted a flowing "rain" of white and gold and the palest sky blue, like an ambon woven into cloth. A cropped blouse with sleeves like bells gave way to layers of tapis skirts in translucent piña fiber, embroidered in gold and indigo droplets that cascaded in a long train down the steps behind her.

They each of them paled in comparison to the full moon

glory of the Lakan at the top of the steps, prepared to share blood and wine with their allies and welcome the blessing of all the gods and saints of Aynila.

The plaza below was packed. Tension sang in the air as Alon cut a shallow slice into the back of the Lakan's forearm, blending blood into a huge gold-and-pearl-studded goblet of rice wine.

The Lakan thanked their guests and allies, and Alon lifted his voice, interpreting for those who might not be able to read her signing. "May the bounty of this Amihan Moon be shared with all who would share my cup and stand with Aynila against our shared enemy."

The Lakan's well-wish was a pointed offering to the diplomats who held places of honor on the steps. Lunurin did not dare turn her head to see how her family had taken it.

One by one, those who had sworn themselves already to Aynila's defense—allies from among the inland rice kingdoms and Talaan—mounted the steps to add their blood and share a cup with the Lakan. Last came Ísuga. Lunurin wondered if they had been waiting for this moment to pledge themselves, or if their katalonan had calculated the distance between Aynila and the far southern island and feared they would miss out on their share of Amihan's bounty if they did not act.

It was an unkind thought. Jeian's ties with Captain Nihma must have turned the tide in their favor.

The Lakan beckoned Lunurin. "Does Anitun Tabu bless our alliance?"

Alon passed her a small brass knife, sharpened to a razor's edge.

The cut was so swift and sharp, the beading of scarlet was a surprise. The blood ran down the back of her arm and dripped into the last mouthfuls of wine.

Before the pain registered, Alon closed his palm over her arm, sealing the wound as if it had never been. Blood, salt, and deep brown skin, mingled. How fitting.

Alon lifted the goblet first to the Lakan, then Sina and Aizza. Lunurin met his gaze as he pressed the cup to her lips. The rice wine was sharp and sweet, but could not completely cover the metallic tang of blood. She drank last and deeply, draining the goblet.

She, too, was promising to stand with Aynila, after all.

She bowed to the Lakan and turned to face the crowd, letting down her hair to summon fireflies of lightning overhead, adding to the gilded glitter of the ambon at sunset. Thunder rolled across the plaza, and her goddess's voice boomed, *"Aynila, a storm came and your Lakan stood for you. Aynila, a storm is coming and your katalonan stand for you. Aynila, will you greet the storm?"*

The answer rose from the courtyard like the patter of rain across tile roofing, rising to a crescendo.

This part was harder. Jeian and Alon hadn't wanted them to do it. Inez would have hated it. But Lunurin crossed herself and offered up Aynila's special prayer for Santa María, Our Lady of Sorrows. The many calling the metered responses from across the plaza carried prayers to her too.

The Lakan was right. If they could walk this balance for Aynila, they'd be able to share a future worth fighting for. They could not leave space for men like Ortiz and Arcilla, who hated and feared the gods-blessed, to lead these prayers and turn hearts against them, as Catalina had once been turned.

Aizza went next, offering the blessing of Aman Sinaya, followed by a hymn Lunurin had helped her learn to Santo Niño for miraculous healing in the midst of calamity. Her voice rose and fell in pleading entreaty. Where Lunurin's voice training had been to carry thunder in her throat, Aizza had trained hers to drag at heartstrings as easily as she could draw the tides. A number of delegates from Talaan wept.

Before the sun dipped below the horizon, the Lakan signed, "Finally I offer my thanks for the blessings of Amihan and Mount Hilaga on this most special of nights."

Sina lifted her hands, fingertips twisting together, sending streamers of fire into the air, turning the ambon to steam. Then, she punched the flat of her palm upward, flinging the tendrils of flame high over the square, outlining Hilaga's peak in blazing light as sunset bathed the mountain gold.

Even Lunurin, expecting it, gasped with awe at the display.

~

As Alon lifted her onto the Stormfleet ship, Lunurin tried to hope that this last-minute invitation from her inay meant that her family's stance had softened. Perhaps they'd even been influenced by the Lakan's entreaties at the sunset summit. They must at least be willing to speak of compromise. She hoped. Alon had refused to let her come alone after Lunurin had shared her inay's ultimatum.

Lunurin had brought Rosa too, fearing this was their last chance to find a suitable teacher for her. With her family so against Lunurin remaining in Aynila, she was even more convinced training Rosa herself would be a mistake. Kalaba had promised to make some introductions. Rosa was quickly swept off with some younger Stormfleet members hunting for food and more wine.

Lunurin eyed the distance from the moon to the caldera. The air had a shimmer like high noon over the lava flats, magic, not heat, distorting the perfect cone of Hilaga.

Alon stepped lightly onto the deck beside her with his liquid tide-touched grace. She was grateful to have him beside her tonight.

Hilaga was dark against a halo of silvery moonlight, just a sliver of its full face visible over the caldera. Aynila's port was blanketed in a bamboo forest of ships rising and falling like the breaths of a sleeping carabao on tide-touch-gentled waves. They'd kept the waters leading to Hilaga's slopes clear.

"How close?" Alon asked.

Lunurin cast her senses outward. Beyond the still night air, a brewing storm drew nearer. The laho-riled waves and wind of long ago rose in her mind's eye, as today it raced across the sea to meet the moon. This storm seemed bigger. Frighteningly so.

"Not long now. You'll be able to feel the waves soon," Lunurin said, and clutched Alon's hand tightly, determined not to be separated from him.

Alon squeezed back, sure and solid as always.

Gazing about, Lunurin realized she was the only one afraid. No one in Calilan's Stormfleet had faced the terrible storm that'd forced Jeian's ship to make port in Aynila. And still the churning deep-water strength of the storm roaring toward them was like nothing Lunurin had ever felt.

Lunurin looked to her Tiya Halili and her inay. "Is it always like this?"

"Yes, of course!" Halili assured her, offering her the cup of lambanog being passed around the deck.

Her inay said nothing, looking grim—but that was because she'd been banned from the firetender rituals for the Amihan Moon on Hilaga's slopes.

It must just be remembered fear. Lunurin had been so young then. She took a bracing gulp and tried to join the festival atmosphere, even as the laho-drawn storm rolled inexorably over the sea, nearer and nearer. Lanterns had been hung from bow to stern. Outriggers of many ships had been lashed together so that their occupants could totter, more or less gracefully, between them to mingle, sharing food and drink. Jars of palm wine and stronger coconut spirits had been pouring generously since the Lakan's blessings on the steps. No few sea-hardy sailors had already had to be fished from the bay. Lunurin had tried to keep an eye on Rosa, but she'd lost her among the crowd. Katalonan and musicians of every creed gathered upon decks, awaiting the all-important moment.

Lunurin was, despite herself, as excited to see this as she once had been as a very small child when the moon had rested atop Calilan's volcano. She wished keenly she could be sharing it now with Inez, as well as Alon and her family.

She'd not yet been named to Anitun Tabu last time, and hadn't been able to feel the dizzying rise of the world's magic. But she remembered how the laho had eeled overhead, trailing blazing copper-fire, sea mist falling like rain. Most of all, she remembered the tremendous crash of music as every soul attending the Amihan Moon sang out at once. Drums sounded, gongs rang, and voices rose.

That night, as at all the Amihan Moons before, the laho had been so frightened by the cacophony, it spat out the moon and dove into the sea, sending all the gathered magic of the Amihan Moon rippling outward, replenishing the seas and islands for another generation. It was a sacred duty that all the people of the archipelago owed the moon, lest they be left in darkness, the bountiful tides of their islands stilled. It was for this sacred duty so many had gathered at Aynila's invitation.

Lunurin crossed the crowded deck, drawing Alon in her wake to join her inay and tiyas before the vast rowing drum. Talim raised large bamboo drumsticks.

Slowly, the moon rose. They waited. Lunurin leaned into Alon, anchoring herself in the deep calm well of his soul as the air thrummed at a fever pitch, her head spinning from that single sip of lambanog.

Alon wrapped his arms around her waist and squeezed. He rested his head on her shoulder, whispering, "If we go into the water, we go together this time."

Despite her unease, Lunurin let out a startled laugh. With Alon beside her, even if everything fell to disaster, they'd find their way through. If the last years had taught her nothing else, it was that.

A strange, wild wind rose. Hundreds of lamps across the bay winked out, till the only light was the moon's, which now sat in the wide bowl of the caldera like an egg in a nest. The wind smelled of salt, magic, and hot copper. Lunurin had forgotten the smell of that long ago laho-riled storm.

She stared into the darkness of the bay toward the open water. Had that been a flicker of molten copper flashing bright through the dark water, or only a gleam of moonlight on the waves?

The laho leaped from the sea with a joyous roar, horned snout slicing through the water like a blade. It had grown large with the magic of the Amihan Moon, large enough to dwarf even Hilaga's great height. Seawater rained down as it rose from the sea, higher and higher over all the assembled watchers. The laho stretched its great fanged jaws wide, the glowing pearl of its brow pulsing bright as a second full moon. It was magnificent and terrifying.

And then that hungry maw closed, the full moon

vanishing into the belly of the great sea dragon as it coiled on the peak of Hilaga to digest its meal. Amihan's sacred flames dimmed, kept alight only by the will of Aynila's firetenders fighting against the dark. Their faint light lay a coppery glow along the edges of the laho's scales, the dragon-pearl pulsing a deep, sated red.

As one, the people cried out. The crescendo of sound that rose over the bay made the air in Lunurin's lungs vibrate. She squeezed Alon tightly, and opened her mouth, singing out the old words with her inay and tiyas, feeling more than hearing Alon's own full-throated response vibrate through his chest at her back. Her inay's bamboo sticks burst into flame, trailing sparks as she beat the huge drum. Stone lithophones and brass bells rang out from the Ísuga contingent, while the whistle of bamboo flutes and resounding beat of brass gangsa rose from Pangilog river boats.

The darkness remained unbroken but for the faint, satisfied glow of the laho atop Hilaga, its trailing tail fins draping down into the bay, dripping seawater and foam. The moon did not reappear.

A single cry, lonely and loud on the open water, gave voice to the fear in all their hearts.

Young turned to the old, asking in hushed whispers, "How long until the moon returns?"

Katalonan from across the archipelago conferred in low, frightened tones. On Hilaga's flanks, Amihan's nest, the sacred fires tended by Aynila's firetenders, flared bright, smoke spiraling up—and then guttered to barely burning coals. Terror rippled through the assembled watchers.

Lunurin stared upward and willed the laho to release its prize. It had supped far more than its share of the Amihan Moon's power. Now. It must release it now.

A voice in the darkness hissed, "It's her fault. She's infected us all with her ill-luck. She should've been drowned at birth."

Alon could not contain himself. He put himself between the speaker and Lunurin, his voice loud in the dark. "How dare you—who are you to say such—"

Lunurin closed her eyes, praying to her goddess, pleading for all she was worth. *High lady of the heavens, return to us your moon. Grant us its light and your blessing. Please, if you have ever listened for my voice, let it be now.*

She already knew that angry voice in the dark. It was her inay's husband, Ragasa. It was always his voice, leading the mob. Denouncing her, her mixed blood and her power that he hated and feared and wished desperately was his own.

And her inay, who wouldn't or couldn't protect her. How could she, when she'd always chosen what was best for Calilan? And that meant Ragasa, never Lunurin.

The sky was dark. The moon was gone. All the wild magic of their islands was muted and distant as the laho glutted itself. Even the tides ebbed without the moon's pull.

"Everything she touches ends in death and darkness!" Ragasa declared.

"Aynila is free thanks to Lunurin. She gave everything to serve as Anitun Tabu willed, to claim vengeance for Aynila's lost tide-touched."

It was Talim who spoke then, not to defend her daughter, but to rebuke Alon. "All the better to drag you and your fool mother to greater ruin. You've invited the Codicians to come back and destroy Aman Sinaya's temple a second time. Why should we follow you to the death you chose?"

Her inay's bitter words washed over her in the dark. She remembered Kawit's face. Black blood and blacker sand.

"You never should've rebuilt on ground where so many

tide-touched died. You've cursed yourselves. Aynila never should have upset the balance. We might some of us have survived, albeit in hiding, but now that the Codicíans have seen what she can do, they will not rest until every gods-blessed in the entire archipelago is dead, until there is nothing but scarred earth and sand for them to claim as their own." Halili's fear pelted Lunurin, sharp as hail.

Kawit's dark gaze, so clear and bright. His ancient plea. "Will you grant me vengeance? For the true Lakan and her kin, for all the tide-touched of Aynila, will you cry our deaths to your goddess and see us mourned as we deserve?"

His tirade granted their blessing, Ragasa railed, his voice loud and high in the darkness. "She will be the end of us all, and you are blind not to see it. She never should've been allowed to leave Calilan."

Lunurin was quiet and still no longer. The fury of her goddess rose in her like a thunderhead, towering and dark. Anitun Tabu was vengeance. She was the storm. And Lunurin would not be shamed for the stuff of her soul, for the fated duty writ into her bones. Not by anyone.

The words boiled out of her. "*You sent me away!*" She turned and stepped around Alon to face her family directly. "You cannot fear me, decry me as an ill-omen, and still demand I return to the Stormfleet."

She was angry. So angry for all the tide-touched lives lost to Codicían pyres. "You call our slow death, our brokenness, *balance*. You say Aynila should never have fought back. You have no idea how much Aynila lost to Codicían greed. And yet, Alon and the Lakan have never wavered, not once. They have been steadfast and sure. They are healers. They have never let fear hold them back from what is right. They have never let fear hurt those under their protection."

The power within her coiled like a cyclone, a hunger for destruction that no longer frightened her. She and her goddess were of one heart, a bright, singular truth that no amount of fear or shame or disbelief could shift.

"That cowards should cry shame in the face of fortitude. Walang hiya ka! You've let yourselves grow small and weak. Your blood is thin. Fear drives you before it like the wind drives flotsam on the waves. A Stormfleet that can no longer hear when the islands cry out for rain is undeserving of my blessing."

Anitun Tabu cursed her family and the fleet in one terrible howling breath and stepped fully into Lunurin's skin. Or perhaps Lunurin grew outside of herself. Like a wisp of a cloud sucking up wind and water over warm seas, together they became something greater, a typhoon made flesh. They weighted the world with their presence. All the power of the skies was theirs.

Hilaga's internal flame was too low, Amihan's nest barely embers, her firetenders struggling to prevent the sparks from dying. Lunurin and her goddess blew, and the whipping winds obeyed them, breathing life into the coals of sacred flames, until they roared into the night sky, blazing and bright.

In the belly of the beast, the moon began to pulse in time with the bellows of their lungs. The laho began to squirm in discomfort, its meal too rich.

As one, Lunurin and Anitun Tabu let down their hair with a shake of their head, freeing their mutya with a twist. They raised one arm to the moonless sky above and drew down a rope of storm. Wind and cloud twined together, sure and strong as abaca fibers. The cyclonic rope skipped over the surface of the bay, picking up seawater with a roar.

They flicked their wrist, catching the sea dragon by the tail where it curled like an overfed python about the peak of Hilaga. Their hands curled around the writhing end of their cyclone and gave a mighty heave, dragging the laho down into the waters of the bay with a tremendous splash. Their cyclone dissolved in a spray of mist.

The laho lay in the sea, too stunned to move. Lunurin stepped forward, balancing upon the quivering outrigger.

"*Lintik ka!*" her goddess cried, lightning crackling around them in a dazzling robe of light.

They dashed forward, from boat to outrigger—and where there were no ships, they walked lightly upon the wind itself. Just as the laho began to thrash, realizing that someone had come to deprive it of its prize, Lunurin's foot landed on one gleaming copper scale.

They curled their toes for grip against the rough surface and launched themselves toward the lashing head. They wrapped their arms around the great frilled mane, seizing its horn and fanged jaw with hands gloved in lightning. The strength of the raging gale flowed through them, just as it did the laho, but Anitun Tabu's power was primordial. She and her goddess pulled. They prized the laho's sword-lined maw apart until the silvery gleam of the moon shone once more. The laho reared high into the air, trying to win free, but they would not be dislodged.

They reached in and seized Amihan's moon before the laho could snap its jaws shut once more. Raw magic pulsed against their fingertips, the gathered power of the archipelago resting in the palm of their hand. At once, they felt the imbalance. The laho was a creature born of deep sea and endless storm. For a whole generation, the Codicians had held dominion, forcing the magic of the archipelago smaller and smaller. It was recovering, but its resurgence was unequal. While Hilaga slept, Amihan slumbered too. But Anitun Tabu's keen attention had been focused on Lunurin, this city, her people. Paired with Aman Sinaya's temple and the return of so many tide-touched, it had given the laho the edge it needed.

But they were here now, and scales could be rebalanced.

They dragged the moon free, hurling it back into the sky, flicking it high with a bolt of lightning that split the air bright as the golden hammer of noon. A great crack of thunder followed as the moon returned to its proper place and Lunurin was flung back into her mortal body.

With a twist, the laho tossed her free from its neck.

The sea dragon that had seemed no greater a moment ago than a particularly troublesome and greedy crocodile, now coiled in vast and endless turns around her as she fell, down and down toward a sea thrashed to whitecaps. The waves were so far away.

Lunurin held her breath, pulling her arms in tight, and tried to hit the water feet first. The height seemed incomprehensible, the wind rushing upward not slowing her descent at all. She shut her eyes and braced—

The water reached up and caught her in hands sure and strong as Alon's own, dragging her clear of the laho's thwarted rage as it boiled out toward open water.

Alon met her partway, having abandoned the Stormfleet and the forest of ships in the shelter of the port for the open water of the bay and her fight for the moon.

He hauled her from the sea, and they both fell back into the bottom of the small bangka. The little ship's outriggers were near to snapping off in the waves, despite all Alon was doing to calm the waters.

Lunurin lay in the bottom of the boat as the little craft pitched and heaved, clutching Alon's arms, dripping saltwater and shaking with exhaustion. Alon held her tightly, his words a low torrent of gratitude to the sea and all his ghosts for catching her and returning her to his arms.

"I'm alright, I promise," Lunurin assured him.

Alon pulled back, checking her all over for confirmation. Satisfied she bore no mortal wounds from her battle, he let out a shaking breath. "I should've tied us together from the start. Weren't we going into the water together this time?"

Lunurin reached for his face, smiling—and paused, staring at her fingertips.

Alon took her right hand, turning it palm up for closer inspection. The pads of each of her fingertips gleamed silver like living mother-of-pearl inlay. Lunurin tapped her fingers to her thumb, testing the sensation. The iridescence felt like skin, but it did not come off.

Alon ran a finger lightly over the pad of her thumb. "It has your fingerprint."

They both stared upward at five new dark spots upon the face of the full moon.

"Is that… a good omen?" Lunurin asked.

"We need one. You are a katalonan of Aynila. If you say it is good, we will celebrate it," Alon declared as he helped her up from the bottom of the boat and tried to orient them back toward the protection of the port.

Lunurin twisted up her hair, securing it with her mutya and easing the howling wind that was whipping the surface of the bay, making Hilaga's sacred flames billow and roar. "How many of our guests did I just capsize?"

And how many potential allies had she alienated, calling down Anitun Tabu's curse on their heads?

Lunurin did not ask the latter half of the question. Instead, she stared over the water, the scene stark in the silvery light of the full moon, restored at last and rising over the bay.

The contingent of Stormfleet ships that had been anchored in the port were sailing toward Alon and Lunurin. Lunurin did not imagine her family had been moved to come to her aid, like Alon.

She did not let her gaze seek out her inay's and tiyas' forms. She did not wish to see them. This was not the parting she wanted sealed in her mind's eye.

Fifteen years ago, they had been right to hide her from the sight of her goddess. They had been right to send her away as a girl. She'd been too young to bear Anitun Tabu's terrible gift then.

But did she not deserve their defense and trust now, as a woman grown? And they dared to demand her return. Knowing she would be hated and feared, a pariah and an imposition to whatever Stormfleet captain they saddled with her presence.

Lunurin bolted to her feet, the little bangka pitching dangerously. "Rosa! We can't let them take her, not after I just cursed them all for cowards and fools."

She twisted down a lock of hair, splitting a breeze into a dozen tendrils to seek out her student. There was an answering tug on the other end of the wind's questing whiskers.

Before she could beg Alon to send them chasing after Rosa, there was a schism among the Stormfleet ships. There were raised voices and a rush of wind and wave before a handful of ships broke off from the others.

To her shock, Lunurin saw that her Tiya Kalaba had commandeered the helmsman's oars on the lead ship defecting from the Stormfleet—and to her relief, Rosa was with her.

Could it be possible that, for once, Lunurin's power and fury hadn't driven away all of those she loved?

Alon brought them alongside Kalaba's ship. This time, Lunurin did not wait for aid, stepping lightly with the wind across to the deck.

She went to her tiya and bowed, offering a deep mano po. "Forgive me, Tiya. I ought not have laid such an accusation against you."

Her tiya raised her up and pulled her close. Lunurin saw tear tracks running down her face and drying on her cheeks. She pressed her damp cheek to Lunurin's. "We have to change. If we don't, it will not matter if the Stormfleet survives Aynila's destruction. Inquisition galleons will finish the sinking of our weak and scattered fleets in short order."

"*I won't let that happen*," Lunurin swore, and heard her goddess's voice echo her in the thunder. Her majesty and power were still so near. She was buoyed and supported by Anitun Tabu's presence instead of feeling like a cracked clay jar with all the vitality wrung out of her now that she had released her grip on divinity. It was so much easier to bear her goddess within her skin when she wasn't fighting against her nature.

Kalaba stilled. She lifted Lunurin's gleaming right hand and pressed it to her brow, mirroring Lunurin's earlier mano po. "We've spent so long fighting our better instincts. For years, I have tried and tried to make Halili and Talim see it, but they refuse. I hardly know if Calilan recognizes what it is that burns within you."

Lunurin wanted to soften the lines of grief on her tiya's face. "How can they, when my very existence endangers them? My being in Aynila will only mean more stormcallers are named here, and more storms are drawn here. My goddess's eyes are always upon me." She looked significantly toward Rosa.

"Do not take our failures upon yourself. You have so much on your shoulders already. We believed, when we sent you away after the attack on Calilan, that allowing the fleet to splinter would save lives, but it has created easy prey not only for the Inquisition, but for pirates, and any number of other calamities. We have lost more ships to storms in the last ten years than the rest of my lifetime combined. To lay the blame at your feet is just Calilan's way of avoiding our own culpability." Kalaba shook her head. "And yet here I am, splintering our fleet again. Halili may never forgive me this. But I had to, for you. For too long I have said and done too little for fear of what would be broken."

Lunurin's throat went tight. "You mean, you don't think I must leave Aynila? You don't think I would be wrong to train Rosa here?"

"I remember when there were many stormcallers on the central islands. Simsiman was known for them in my childhood. They had great power and could end droughts by letting down a single lock of hair. They did not join the Stormfleet, far more attuned to agricultural matters. It was only as the Codicians built their forts that stormcallers were forced out to the outlying islands and settlements, and finally into the Stormfleet to avoid detection."

Lunurin clutched her tiya tight, overwhelmed beyond words to not be condemned for doing what her goddess had asked, that not everyone agreed with Calilan's accusations that she bore the whole blame for the Stormfleet's troubles.

30

INEZ DOMINGO

Inez woke warm, shielded from the morning dew, still tucked under Umali's coat. She burrowed her face deeper into the smoky sweet folds, hiding from the dawn. Inez pressed her fingertips to her lips, a bit shocked at how far there had been to take kissing. Just kissing.

After the terrifying disappearance of the moon and the ebbing tide had sent Inez dashing to the water's edge, its return had illuminated the night in a whole new light. They'd settled in the sand alongside the beached outrigger, to bask in it, warm and comfortable in each other's arms.

A resonant satisfied rumble agreed that the *not-sun-very-warm* was a delight worth wallowing in. It came from very close, accompanied by the slithering of smooth belly scales on soft sand, forcing Inez to abandon the cocoon of last night and the memory of Umali's kisses.

Where Umali had been, there was a divot, still radiating the banked-coal heat of her presence, but notably empty. Inez glanced over her shoulder. Piled in the sand, drawn by the heat, lay her crocodiles, gold and black scales and tangled bodies all but nestled at her back.

Well, this would be a thrilling way to discover whether they were *her* crocodiles still, wouldn't it? Was she about to suffer—very briefly and brutally—for the folly of making blood sacrifices to hungry anito? Inez moved slowly, stilling when golden eyes opened to regard her.

"So much worry, little crocodile. How long will you fear the depths of your own salt soul? The sea has darkness too. Do you think you will not float in deep water?" Himig challenged her.

Only one way to find out. Inez rolled to her feet, bare toes feeling for sandy footing around scaled bodies. She left Umali's coat folded above the waterline and waded into the surf.

The too loud, too much, overwhelming sensation of the Amihan Moon's magic had ebbed, a faint sparkle that tingled on her skin like salt drying. No longer wearing her skin raw. The water rose higher, over her hips, then to her ribs.

She opened her mouth, tongue and throat, working for the low reptilian warble she'd been learning. She hadn't forgotten the sounds overnight, either. Inez roared a crocodile song to the waves, and the deep rose in answer, a swell rolling in toward the sheltered beach. It rose as the water grew shallow, rearing up over Inez's head and crashing down. Inez tumbled along with the sea. The churning wave was still cold from the deep, electrifying on her sleep-warm skin. Just before she began to panic, doubting her own ability, she floated, salt buoying her up.

She might be a strange tide-touched, but not strange enough that Aman Sinaya had stopped listening. She let herself rise and fall, drifting with the movement of the sea.

When she at last began to swim back for the shore, she saw

Umali on the beach, watching her antics with an indulgent smile. Inez blushed to the roots of her hair, debating whether she should sink to the bottom instead.

Umali waved, calling out, "Don't go disappearing into the sea now. Come, I got you something. Better protection for a sea-boarding, like your smallsword."

Inez returned to the beach, wringing seawater from her sarong with a flick of her wrists.

"I went into the village this morning." Umali presented Inez with a bundle before pulling her aboard the Agawin, heading to her sea chest.

Inez followed, examining her gift.

There was a salwal waist wrap woven in bright oranges and yellows, and a gauze-fine cream blouse. At the center of the bundle were rolls of wide ribbon, undyed, the jute fibers still gleaming naturally golden and warm. She looked up, realizing these were Umali's own colors, matched to the family weaving patterns of her Pangilog salampé sash.

It must just be old habit. Firetenders liked warm colors, the way tide-touched wore indigo.

"To wrap your calves and forearms," Umali explained when Inez held up the ribbon in inquiry. "Is the shirt soft enough? I don't want it to bother your back."

"Yes, thank you," Inez managed.

She was surprised when Umali paused her rummaging to drop a kiss on the corner of her mouth. "You'll be glad of the fire-proofing, you'll see. I can't always be giving you my coat."

Inez bit down on still kiss-tender lips. Umali was downplaying it, yet this gift felt important—protective, but not patronizing. Umali was clothing Inez like all else she treasured: her Agawin, her crew.

It felt like too much. It had only been days. It had only

been a few kisses. How could Umali be sure she was worth it, or sure she was staying?

Luckily, Umali was too busy digging in her sea chest to notice that Inez was overcome by the gift of a shirt. She lifted a wax-sealed clay jar of pale green salt crystals. "They grow from the sulfur seeps high up on Mount Tumubo. It doesn't take much dissolved in seawater to treat the full yardage of a new sail."

Her new clothes dried quickly in the sun and wind of their passage toward Masbad. Inez rubbed the fabric between her fingertips, trying to discern a visible effect of the strange green metal salt. But there was none she could see. And she couldn't deny the new attire was soft against the scars of her back, a welcome shield from the sun yet light and airy, taking in every breeze.

The change in the air might only be the whole world breathing a sigh of relief after the fevered pitch of the Amihan Moon, but for the first time, Inez felt hope seeing a port filling in the horizon, rather than desperation.

~

The cathedral in Masbad was impressive, two tall belltowers lending it height. The brass bells themselves hung silent as the morning rains swept in over the isthmus and enclosed bay, the air thick with humidity.

It looked so imposing, she almost feared she would enter and discover the Codicíans had not been driven from the port after all, but Inez was determined to see the purported relic of Santa Catalina for herself. She needed to find some proof Santa Catalina wasn't just a Codicían lie, like Santa María turning to wood and salt upon the shore. That she was chasing something real, and not only her own ghosts.

Inside the church, she could see the outlines where hammered gold ornamentation had been stripped from the altar and doors—no doubt by the local metalworkers as soon as they'd driven the Codicíans out. Perhaps the façade was not so intact as she'd thought.

She found the reliquary housed in the only metalwork inside the church that remained intact, a gold and brass box through the lattice of which she could see a small, water-logged prayer book.

Hope and excitement lanced through her, bright as the dawn. Inez bent closer, trying to see the entire book through the filigree. Her sister had been here! It wasn't all rumors and Codicían lies, here was something physical and real and...

Catalina's prized prayer book had been bound in black calfskin, hadn't it? Not red.

Inez could see where local indigo inks had run, staining the pages shades of blue. Catalina's book of psalms and prayers to the saints had been an import from Codicía, its tissue-thin pages printed in dense, inky-black lettering.

A mother with a toddler on her hip joined her before the reliquary. Once again, Inez had the jarring experience of listening to prayers to Santa Catalina, guardian of martyrs, begging her to intercede to lift the penitent from the rising floodwaters of tribulation, to lay hands of blessing upon the prayerful.

"Did she really survive with only this?" Inez asked.

"Look, you can see the mark of her hand where she gripped as it lifted her from the rising flood. Can you imagine?"

"When was the relic brought to Masbad, do you know? Was it after the fall of the Palisade in Aynila, or when Santa Catalina returned from Canazco?" Inez asked.

The woman clasped her hands together. "I was here when

she came. In the middle of Mass, she went into holy ecstasy, speaking in tongues—and my son, who never speaks, spoke back to her like he understood her perfectly. It was just a few months before the priests were driven out. The power of her miracle is still here. I like to bring him when I can, it helps loosen his tongue."

"What was she like? Tell me everything," Inez pressed. Finally, someone who had seen Santa Catalina in person.

"She had a golden glow, as if the Holy Spirit illuminated her face. She was beautiful, and so pious. I never saw her stop clutching her rosary. She must have been so hot wearing that long dark veil and her habit. It wasn't the fine light stuff like we weave here. Heavy woolens from Canazco."

"Was she mestiza like they say? And her rosary, what did it look like?" Inez needed details. She might be describing any Augustinian nun.

The woman hesitated. "She could be. It's hard to say. Sainthood made her look unlike any woman I've ever seen. Her rosary was gold, a gift from the metalworkers of Masbad, tambourine beads and the most beautiful crucifix."

A sinking sense of doubt grew in Inez's belly, frustration leaking through her lies. "And have you heard where she is now? I followed word of her relic here, but my petition needs the blessing of the saint herself, and there are so many rumors, it's hard to know what to take for truth."

"Well, I've heard…" The woman leaned close. "If you need more than hearsay, you'll have to find one of the holy fathers. They know the most."

"How can I find one when even Masbad has driven them out?" Inez lamented.

"There is one. My husband refills ships' water barrels upriver and ferries them down to the port. Yesterday he brought home a jar of holy water from a father he met aboard the Lusitan ship that recently left harbor, headed north for Amagang."

"I hope it will be a great help to your son," Inez offered, her mind already scrambling ahead, eager to rush back to Umali with the news.

The Lusitan ship would be going north toward the Tianchaowen coast, and it must pass Aynila. This priest might be expecting to be slipped into the city just as Ortiz had been—which could make him part of whatever conspiracy of prayers and relics the Codicíans were spreading about her sister.

The northeasterly winds would aid the Lusitans' progress. But she and Umali working together might catch them before they could clear the narrow straits and enter the Sumila Gulf. With Umali and the crew of the *Agawin* at her side, she'd at last catch up to a source of the rumors about her sister.

All she needed was a priest.

~

She found Umali aboard the *Agawin*, overseeing the loading of bartered bronze into her hold.

Inez told her of the Lusitan ship, though she held back the details about Santa Catalina and the priest, almost afraid that if she shared the truth of the rumor she'd chased so far, her chances of catching it would evaporate. Killing Ortiz had severed the thread that hauled her out of Aynila like a fish on an invisible hook; she was desperate to lay hands on another line that would lead back to Catalina.

"It's true, they've been coming down and across the archipelago to avoid Tianchaowen waters, then back north after they sell their captives in Moklayu. It's why we sail this area. I can guess the route they'll take in this season, with the northeastern wind. There are only a few options with the draft of their ship," Umali mused.

"Can we catch them?" Inez asked.

Umali smiled. "We only know if we try."

Soon, the port was falling away in the distance. Inez sat in the helmsman's seat, guiding the *Agawin* out over deep water and leaning into Umali's power, both of them urging sea and sail to push the ship as fast as she could go.

Umali sat in front of Inez on the deck, honing the edge of her kampilan blade. "This will be different from the Duutsan trade ship. We cannot expect that they will surrender, even in the face of two gods-blessed. Remember, the Lusitans raid to fill their holds and are prepared to fight their way free. They often carry silver and gold from the slave markets back to their masters in Amagang. And the bounties on them have made them fat prizes for the Tianchaowen navy and priva-teers like us."

Inez refused to let doubt enter her mind, focusing on her eagerness for the fight, gnawing like hunger in her belly. This time she would not flinch. The black depths of her own desperation had overwhelmed her aboard the slave ship, and ultimately lost her the one thing she was pursuing. She'd been so raw and new then, without a captain and crew to lean on. Perhaps now she could dive deep and not lose her purpose.

Umali chuckled. "Here I am, warning you about blood-shed, and you look ready to pry the ship open with your teeth. No wonder you don't heal."

A week ago, Inez would've hated anyone who made light of her failures. But with the Amihan Moon waning, and her tie to her crocodiles and their songs still with her, Inez dared to hope that she'd find her way in her power, even if it wasn't the one Alon and Lunurin had wanted for her.

31

LUNURIN CALILAN NG DAKILA

Lunurin refused to ask, but she was sure Isko had run the numbers on the allies lost versus gained by her wrestling the moon back into the sky. Aizza crowing about the new ballad of the laho she would write was not helping with her feeling like a walking omen. So she left Alon and the Lakan to handle assuring their now blood-sworn allies that Anitun Tabu had no further curses in store.

Lunurin took all her maps and notes on the fleets to her tiya, cross-referencing them with Kalaba's knowledge and Calilan's records. Kalaba had already identified the Stormfleet captains Calilan had not invited to the Amihan Moon, as well as a number of new splinter groups Lunurin hadn't known of. There were now over twenty localized groups no longer paying heed to Calilan. It also meant it was more difficult and dangerous to engage with storms, the smaller fleets lacking the support, training, and coordinated network of stormcallers all pulling at once that Calilan had provided.

"They wouldn't have stood behind Calilan's decision, and so they couldn't be allowed to hear Aynila's petition. My wife likes to put forth the impression that she still commands the fleet of twenty years ago. Half the reason the fleets remain so splintered is because Halili will not admit there is a problem for long enough to work towards solutions." Kalaba grimaced.

Lunurin laid a hand on her tiya's. "Is that why you left?"

Kalaba shook her head. "Yes and no. I have been the water of our relationship so long, mending and tending what breaks in her wake. Cleaving to her and flowing along the path of her decisions. Curving our path by patient wearing away at her stubbornness, like a river through stone canyons. But the crisis at hand demands I act now. And it is my relationship with my wife that I will work to mend, should we survive."

"I am sorry that I forced you to the decision," Lunurin said softly. "I'm sure she will come to understand."

Kalaba nodded. "I hope she will, but I also know how stubborn Halili can be. What we need now are allies."

Lunurin turned back to the task at hand, circling a number of captains Kalaba said often patrolled the Sumila Gulf. "Time is short, these will be our best bet. I cannot leave Aynila exposed by going much farther afield. Will we be ready to sail tonight?"

"We must be. I will help introduce you to those who will listen," Kalaba promised. "At the very least, it will let the gods-blessed of my ships scout the waters and winds of the Sumila Gulf. Reef maps are all well and good, but the tides through the bay are powerful. Sandbars and shoals shift rapidly."

Sina hurried into the room. Lunurin had sent word of the debacle with the Stormfleet last night, but she'd been engaged in the firetenders' rites on Hilaga until now. Fine black ash still coated her hands, detailed baybayin letters in black ink running under her eyes and down her cheeks. "You aren't going alone. I've been granted Hilaga's blessing. My mother and sister can hold her while I go."

Lunurin had been expecting that Sina would be unable to leave Hilaga after her stunt with the laho. She'd been unsure how so many upsets would affect their sleeping volcano. Relief rushed over her like a cool breeze as she embraced Sina. "I'm so glad. I know how you hate open water, but I could not do this without you."

Sina pressed her cheek to Lunurin's, smearing the baybayin lettering of firetender prayers to Amihan into one vast black smudge.

"I know you. And now I know the Stormfleet. You let them off more easily than I would have. How could anyone turn their back on you after last night?" Sina clicked her tongue. "Fools, one and all. Can't they see?"

Lunurin waved off Sina's words. "How can they? They only see the child I was. Why should Aynila's plight be their responsibility? What need do they have of us?"

Kalaba barked out a bitter laugh. "They may say so. But they need what Aynila has more than they are willing to admit."

Lunurin frowned. "What do we have?"

Kalaba smiled wistfully. "You can't see it, can you? You've become Aynilan. You're used to the way power pools here."

"What do you mean? Because of the Amihan Moon?"

"Not that alone. It is you, Lunurin, the favored daughter of your goddess. You weight the world with your presence. Those around you are changed. You pour your strength into these people and this city, and it thrives. I see how all the old gods favor Aynila now. So much has changed on Calilan since we sent you away. Every year, fewer and fewer are named gods-blessed."

Lunurin pursed her lips. "I still should not have laid such a curse upon them. How can I ask them to stand for Aynila when the Stormfleet is already in danger?"

"Anitun Tabu spoke not a curse but the truth. Calilan has grown weak. Our hands are no longer open to receive blessings. I fear in running from the coming battle, we have sealed our fate. For years now, we have labored to ensure Mount Calilan sleeps deep, so deep she no longer murmurs her will to our firetenders. Our stormcallers grow so weak they would not dare to face a typhoon. They perish in wet season storms they should be able to control. Even our tide-touched struggle to heal alone. We told ourselves that survival demanded we make ourselves small, and so small we became."

Lunurin had preserved in her memories the Calilan of fifteen years ago. She had hoped and believed then that leaving Calilan would save it from the ravages of the Codicíans, their fear and greed. But it hadn't, just as hiding in a convent had not prevented Anitun Tabu's revenge. As the Lakan had reminded her, they could never return to the Aynila of the past, or the Calilan that Kalaba now mourned.

Her tiya's grief brought tears to Lunurin's eyes. She offered the only comfort she could. "I too hid. I spent a decade making myself small. But when I held out my hands and asked for the vengeance Aynila deserved, my goddess did not turn her face from me. Calilan, too, can choose to stop being small."

Kalaba shook her head. "I cannot see how. At every turn, we've chosen hiding and survival. We've lost ourselves."

"It begins here, by building a future for the archipelago

beyond tomorrow's survival. When we aren't chasing a past lost to us but growing into the future and teaching that balance to our students and children. That is the future I am fighting for, not just for Aynila, but for all our islands. I will make a future in which Anitun Tabu has more than grief and vengeance to offer her daughters," Lunurin promised. *"A future where gods-blessed walk in the sun without fearing to be known for their strength."*

~

With Kalaba's admissions about her marriage buzzing in her head, Lunurin knew she had to take proper leave of Alon.

The Codicían armada might only be weeks away. For all he might wish it otherwise, Lunurin knew that without Alon's mediation, there would be no Aynilan alliance to face the Codicían armada.

Lunurin could not wait until the ships here in Aynila were supplied and readied to sail. They needed whatever Stormfleet allies she could gain with her tiya's aid in the Sumila Gulf. So she went to her husband, dragging him away from a fractious council meeting in the Lakan's palace.

"Lunurin, can this wait till tonight?" Alon asked.

Lunurin tugged him into a recently emptied guestroom. The servants had not yet been able to turn it over with all the diplomats and visitors who'd been leaving Aynila since last night. But at least it was private.

"It can't. I'm leaving tonight."

Alon's expression pinched. "Don't tell me you mean to go after your family. If they could see what you did last night and still turn their backs on you, I don't think anything you do or say will convince them."

"Not Calilan. My tiya says there are factions of the Stormfleet in the Sumila Gulf that were never invited to the summit for fear they wouldn't stand by Calilan's decisions. I will petition them myself. I know that Aynila's allied ships are not yet resupplied and cannot set sail, but my tiya's handful of Stormfleet ships are used to moving quickly. We can leave tonight. By the time you join us in a week or two, I will have found us allies, or at least a place to make our stand for Aynila."

"Lunurin—"

He didn't want her to go. She could hear it in his voice, in the way his arms curled around her, desperation in his eyes.

"I'm not abandoning Aynila. You will join me in the Sumila Gulf in weeks, if not days. I can do this. It was a mistake to think I could change my family's mind about me. But it will be different this time, with Kalaba aiding my introductions instead of Halili sabotaging them. I will have Sina. I won't be alone. Now kiss me, so I can take the taste of you with me. I want your touch imprinted on my skin, whatever tomorrow brings." Lunurin curled her arms around his neck, dragging her nails down the back the way he liked.

Instead of melting into her the way she wanted, Alon stepped away. Lunurin whined in protest, low in her throat, trying to draw him back to her. "Alon, please—"

Alon covered his eyes with a hand, dropping to the edge of the bed. "There's more. More I've not told you. I know you must go ahead, and I know I cannot go with you. I know you are doing this for Aynila, as you must. But there's more I've kept from you, and if you plan to go alone, you must know. It's about Catalina."

Lunurin's heart crumbled like hail, icy sparks of fear and dread falling into her gut. "What about Catalina?"

What do you know? What have you not told me? She wanted to scream it, but Alon looked so worn and frightened, just as he had when she'd almost severed her spirit from her body, or when she'd tried to run after Inez. He had been on his knees then, his need a naked wound.

"The Codicían missionaries have been spreading rumors that she's returned to the archipelago." Alon's words were slow. Lunurin wanted to shake him. But she also wanted to run away. She did not want to hear this. She did not want to know.

"Where?"

"I don't know!" A thread of frustration leaked through Alon's agonized expression. "I've tried. My spies have turned the archipelago upside down for her, and for Inez gone after her. They've visited hundreds of ports, chased down so many rumors. I do not know if it is true, but I'm sure it is a trap set just for you. Your aunt, Abbess Magdalena, has returned to Simsiman. She is the only one who would know to use Catalina against you like this. I was so afraid if you knew…"

"You thought I'd leave. You thought I'd rush to find her. That's what you've been so afraid of?" Lunurin said the words slowly, tasting the bitterness of them on her tongue. Her terror for Inez was a distant roar suddenly renewed and far too close with the understanding of what had sent her aboard that slave ship.

"Yes. At first, I just wanted to protect you. Until I learned the truth, how could I hurt you with such a useless, dangerous rumor?" Alon pleaded, his hands lifted toward her, supplication in every line of his body.

Lunurin's internal turmoil dragged at the northeastern winds of the season, the weather echoing her emotions as it always did. She struggled to keep her upset from riling it any further. At this stage in the crossing, stronger winds would only draw their enemies to them more quickly.

She wanted to leave him, hands open and pleading and empty. But Aynila would not be served by her fury. She took his hands in hers, gripping so tight she feared she might harm his bad hand, but she needed something to ground herself, and she'd always found that anchor in him. "Why? Why didn't you tell me?"

"I intended to, as soon as there was anything real I could confirm, not just rumors and misdirection. You should have seen how badly Ortiz *wanted* me to tell you. I know he meant nothing good with the information. I just didn't want to hurt you."

It was not the parting she'd imagined. She'd wanted to wrap herself in the security and love she only felt in Alon's arms. Soak it up like a cloud growing heavy over open water. Saving it up to face more Stormfleet captains, whose distrust and suspicion of her made her doubt all she'd done for Aynila and her goddess.

"And the lies, the deceptions? They aren't hurting me? When Inez snuck into that convert prayer meeting—why didn't you tell me then? Why keep hiding it? If I'd known—" Angry tears welled up, hot and aching.

Alon crushed her to his chest as the wind moaned over the eaves of the Lakan's palace. "Forgive me. I was so afraid—"

Lunurin seized Alon's face in her hands, staring into his eyes. "Of what?" she cried. "What could be so terrible it was worth losing my sister?"

Alon bowed his head into her hands, miserable with regret, his voice hoarse. "I was afraid you'd leave me. With Inez in danger, if you'd learned Catalina had returned... It was too much of that past life come back to haunt us. You have always put your family first. And I thought I could bear always coming last in your consideration. But now, when our doom is on the horizon... I couldn't bear it. I couldn't bear, after all these years, after everything she did, still being your second love. It was selfish and stupid, but I was too afraid to find out what you'd choose. And then it was too late, Inez was gone, and I knew you'd never forgive me if she came to harm. I can't lose you."

The admission stunned her into silence.

"How could you ever think that? I let Catalina go years ago!" The silver buttons of his barong scattered across the floor as she tore it open.

The moon-gilded pads of her fingers found the lightning scar that stretched over his abdomen, the depression of the wound she'd closed. A wound Catalina had made. Alon's warm skin, smooth, then rippled like water over the scar, jumped under her touch. "I chose you then, when I pulled down the church on her head. And I chose you again when we sent her away."

"I—" Alon's voice shook.

Lunurin pressed her lips to his, angry, so angry. Her heart ached at how he doubted her. When she loved him too well, even now, to hate him for what he'd done. In him, she could sink the terrible tangle of emotions that threatened to strangle her without fear of how it would affect anyone beyond the two of them.

Alon kissed her back with a desperation she could taste, sharp and bitter as fear. He clutched her as if she'd be lost from him like mist before the dawn.

"I chose you over my inay and my tiya. I have chosen you and my duty to Aynila over every other tie in my life! And still, you don't trust me?" She twisted her fingers in his hair, dragging it loose the way she couldn't afford to tear at her own tightly coiled locks, her tightly held control.

He let her, groaning into her skin, a hot, aching sound that did nothing to appease the anger and desire melting into each other.

"I never wanted to hurt you like this. I swear, I just didn't know how—"

"What have I ever done to make you doubt me so?" She shoved him back and down onto the bed. She was straddling him before he could recover from the surprise, pinning his hips beneath her.

"Nothing, nothing—but with the armada bearing down on us and everything with the Amihan Moon and your family... I chose wrong. You are so much more than I can ever deserve, and I couldn't bear to admit I'd failed you. Forgive me. All I've ever wanted is to protect you and stand at your side, for as long as you'll let me. I never thought I'd hurt you like this."

He'd lied because he loved her. She depended on him alone to be her safe harbor, a shelter from the storm and all the expectations upon her.

"You have always been enough for me." Lunurin pressed the words into his skin, tempted to write them there in lightning the way her vows were stitched on her heart. "And we have always been enough to face what comes, if we face it together!"

"*I love you, I'm sorry.*" A mantra he muttered into her hair, panted into her skin, and traced up and down her back with his touch as she fed her storming fury to the unbearable heat between them so it wouldn't tear the Lakan's palace down around their ears and rush their enemies to their doorstep.

"How could you let Codicían lies twist you up trying to shield me?" she whispered, as their bodies fit together, in familiar sweet agony. "You say I'm the one liable to go chasing the past for old guilt and lost love, but you let your fears tear our family apart."

All the air pushed out of Alon like she'd gutted him with the accusation.

Lunurin ground down, needing him as close and deep as possible. Would that she could fit the shattered trust between them back into wholeness as easily. At least she might force out the terrible fear that had driven him to such lengths.

Release struck her like lightning. Like wrath. And Alon curled around her shaking, first with release, then with sobs.

She held him tight, knowing she must leave him with the tide.

32

INEZ DOMINGO

After what seemed like endless hours with the Lusitan ship growing no closer at all, they suddenly caught a break. The larger ship was forced to take in their sails to navigate through the narrow passages of lush reefs and barrier islands where the Ibalong Straits met the southern edge of the Sumila Gulf.

The *Agawin* with its shallow draft skimmed right over at full sail, with all the tail-lashing speed Inez could gather rushing them onward.

Umali's attack began without a warning shot, her presence no longer comforting as a cook fire, but a blazing ray of sunlight, near impossible to look at directly.

Heat struck the ship, bubbling the pine tar-coated hull and making the canvas sails smoke. Like an offering to Amihan.

Here, there were no sacred flames or brass lamps, their wings spread and burning, only Umali, a woman ablaze. And Inez was determined to ride the waves of her battle fury as far as they'd take them both. She would not let Umali regret taking her up on this bounty. She'd prove to her captain she wasn't a liability—and to herself that she hadn't been a fool to chase this rumor of Catalina.

If anyone could catch a ghost lost at sea, wouldn't it be a tide-touched?

"Now!" Umali cried.

Inez extended a clawed grip, seized the rush of the incoming tide spilling into the shallower gulf, and turned it. Where before it had run the deep, safe gap between the jagged reefs, it now cut crosswise across a shatter-sharp ridge of coral and oyster bed. Inez drove the *Agawin* and their prey alike toward the ridge.

The Lusitan ship struggled against her. Sails were rigged, the great three-masted ship struggling to catch the wind and stave off the sudden drive of her currents. They could only slow the inevitable.

Umali's heat caught them in a shimmering wave. Despite her captain's warning words, Inez thought surely the Lusitans would surrender as soon as they ran aground and their sails went up in flame. They'd have no choice. And she needed the priest alive.

But the moist wet season wind was just enough to coun-teract Umali's attack. It not only prevented the slaver's sails from flashing, it protected their gunpowder stores. Before Inez's tricks with the tide succeeded in running them aground, the slaver managed to fire off a volley.

Inez threw herself flat just as the heat surrounding Umali exploded, hot as a fireball, without a single lick of flame. Inez smelled hair burning. But the loaded scattershot and shrapnel was molten before it reached the *Agawin*, splattering harmlessly off the hull and dripping, sizzling, down into the waves. Still, cries rose anywhere hot metal landed on bare skin. The Lusitans were clearly familiar with fighting off the smaller, quicker karakoa. They'd loaded shorter range, wider spray shrapnel instead of the solid cannonballs they'd turn against larger, easier targets like Tianchaowen junks.

Umali stalked up and down the center of the *Agawin*'s fighting deck, flicking her fingertips and yanking the globules of hot metal off her crew. She swept her arms out, then back in a complicated gesture, and every speck of glowing metal aboard the *Agawin* went black and cold.

She pulled Inez to her feet. "They'll get off another round before you run them aground like this. Bring them broadside. We'll see how they like scooping molten metal off their crew."

Inez released her energy from redirecting the flow of the tide. She turned her full attention on the cradle of salt surrounding the great black hull, to the waves lapping at her sides. The slave ship was large, its momentum through the water set by the wind, over which she had no control. She gave a low roar, made to vibrate through the water, traveling great distances and even greater depths.

The waves rose at her call. Slowly, slowly, the slave ship turned and caught a combined volley of the *Agawin*'s three lantaka cannons and the full burning hammer blow of heat that was Umali. Inez heard screams. She saw black cannon maws turn cherry red, then white. Metal ran down the side of the ship, some falling in their entirety below decks. Smoke billowed as the hold filled with smoke and burning molten metal.

Inez curled her tongue for a sharp piercing whistle, dragging up a great wave that crashed across the center of the ship, dousing the spreading flames as the slave ship rolled—and then the *Agawin* was alongside. Inez chased Umali's singed footsteps up the sloping hull. But as the ship began to right itself, Inez lost her balance, dangling from the grappling line.

Worse, the back-roll of the slave ship displaced a wave of water, threatening to capsize the *Agawin*.

Inez tried to counter the swell, but the volume of water was too great. It forced the *Agawin* out and away, the rest of the crew's boarding lines falling short.

Inez pulled herself up hand over hand, frightened to leave Umali alone on an enemy ship. At last, she managed to clear the railing. Umali was a whirling dervish of heat and steam, her kampilan blade a searing, smoking edge. With waves of heat and the cut of her sword, she pushed the slavers back from the rail, clearing enough room for Inez to join her on the deck.

"Bring the *Agawin* back around!" Umali ordered. "I'll keep them off you."

Secure in her footing, Inez reached again for the *Agawin*, which had deployed oars and was attempting to get close enough for a second boarding. From the choppy sea and disoriented currents, Inez's song pleaded for glassy seas and still waters.

She'd nearly brought the *Agawin* close enough when Umali swept out her blade, just a hair clear of Inez's cheek. The gunshot was eardrum-shatteringly close. Hot lead melted down the blade.

Ears ringing, Inez tore her attention away from the flat of Umali's sword, which had just prevented her head from being blown apart. A priest in a black cassock stood equally rattled as Umali's fury roared outward like a forest fire. She'd cut down three slavers between her and the priest before he even registered his weapon was melting in his hand.

Umali broke through the line of slavers keeping her and

Inez pinned to the rail and leaped for the priest, the arc of her blade blazing bright as the sun in a sure, clear line that would cleave his head from his shoulders.

"I need him alive!!" Inez cried out.

Umali twisted, her blade shearing down. The melted gun and a severed hand fell to the deck instead. The priest screamed, falling back as slavers closed in on Umali from all sides.

Inez yanked the seeping water of her initial wave back up, sending a rolling surge across the surface of the deck. She caught men at the knees, hurling them down. A bubble of space opened around Umali, who lashed out with ripples of heat that set the overhead rigging alight, and the edge of her blade, as hungry as the laho at its hilt, its long edge red with blood. But the priest was dragged clear, disappearing into the black maw of below decks.

No! Her prey, escaping!

Before Inez could fling herself into the belly of the ship, Umali caught her chin in a burning hand. "The *Agawin*, Inez!"

With a shout of thwarted rage, shaking herself free of her crocodile intent, Inez spun, put her back to Umali's and sent her wave higher, seizing men near the far rail and pitching them over, down to the circling crocodiles in the waters below.

Screams of terror suddenly cut short.

The brine of wave calling on Inez's tongue was replaced with a warm, metallic rush of blood and the jolt, roll, and tear of the buwaya. Satiation broke through the inhuman urge to chase the priest down into the blackness below. Had the Amihan Moon still been high, dragging at her, she might've let the predatory instinct sweep her away. But Umali had reminded her she was not a crocodile, for all the bloodlust singing through her. She wouldn't give in to her desperation; she would find her balance. She and Umali couldn't take the ship alone.

She cried out to the waves below, bringing the *Agawin* firmly alongside. The boarding crew made a second attempt.

This time, ten of the *Agawin*'s crew managed the jump. They made quick, brutal work of the men felled by the sweep of Inez's wave across the deck.

"Now, Inez!" Her captain's order cut through clash.

Umali and Inez fell back to the rail and their crew. Inez leaned into the heat and power of her captain. She planted her feet, let the weight and shape of sea-calling pool on her tongue, heavy in her jaw, and cried out to Aman Sinaya.

She saw the moment of realization. The Lusitan captain cursed her water witch devilry. His crew broke, terror bright in their eyes, but there was no escape.

The surface of the sea tipped, the *Agawin* rushing down and away, deploying its oars to turn and ride the face of the wave. The slave ship was too bulky, its keel too deep to turn into the wave. Sliding sideways down the swell, it crashed aground. The jolt and scrape of timber on reef was like teeth on bone. The pirates were prepared, braced to the rail. The slavers were not. Umali's hot arm curled around Inez's waist, keeping her pinned close as the ship yawned and their feet lifted off the deck. Bodies spilled down into the water. Her crocodiles feasted, churning the sea foam red.

The sea returned to its natural paths and the slave ship leveled, though the deck still listed, hung up on the reef. The ship was theirs.

Umali released her. "Now we hunt your prey, little crocodile. And I need not fear losing you to a slaver with a death wish."

The forward compartment was crew quarters and cargo. She and the *Agawin*'s crew tore through, carrying away gold and valuables. But still Inez could not find the priest. Had he been dumped into the slave hold in the chaos?

She went down into the rear holds. With Umali's presence steady as the sun on her back, she plunged into the belly of the slaver in search of her missing priest.

The darkness closed around her like murky water, shot through with light only where the fight on the deck had punched holes. Inez hesitated at the foot of the ladder, letting her eyes adjust, the drawn blade of her smallsword catching the light and casting it into the darkness around her. She'd thought she'd be ready to face the memory of her time below decks, the shackles and the stench of suffering that could never be scrubbed from the timbers.

The hold should be empty, right? They were only carrying gold and perhaps some trade goods back to their masters in Amagang. There would be little human cargo below.

But the ship carried Black children. Stolen not from Tianchaowen, but from the opposite side of the world, a Lusitan colony in Mosangbike. They huddled below decks, sickly and terrified. Children as young as five or six, bellies bloated—malnutrition? More likely flux from contaminated water. Some were as old as twelve or thirteen, though they were just as weak and wasted. How long had they been locked below decks? How incomprehensibly far were they from home?

Inez might have barreled onward. She had been a child as terrified as these, once. She had no comfort in her to offer, and no healing would be done by her hands—only the blood of those who'd stolen them away. She knew, too, how little that would fix.

Umali descended the ladder, and the noise she let out was so soft, so wounded, Inez forced herself to pause the hunt for her priest. Where would he go? Even if he managed to leap free into the water, her crocodiles would find him. And, wounded as he was, he'd be a fool to try to swim for shore.

She sheathed her blade and held out her hands, palm up and empty, to one of the bigger girls who'd put herself between the littlest ones and them.

She asked a question. The only word Inez could pick out was "Lusitan."

"Dead," Inez said and mimed the words. "All dead. Everyone who hurt you. We've come to take you out of this stinking hole. Will you let me help?"

She wasn't sure if there was any understanding in the girl's face, but she took Inez's hand and let herself be lifted onto the deck, too weak to climb out on her own. At last, Umali found her voice and called down the crew. They began carrying children up into the light and aboard the *Agawin*.

They cleared the first layer of the hold of ten children, still alive. Not all had been. It was hard to tell if they had perished in the battle or from the conditions below decks.

Inez lied to Umali. "They were gone long before we came upon them."

And still, they did not find the priest. Inez began to get anxious imagining ways he might've escaped her. Then, finally, she found a third hold compartment down in the bilge, the hatch smeared with blood.

The renewed trail dragged Inez onward, sure as a crocodile hunting a wounded fish through muddy water. At last, down in the deepest bowels of the ship, she found him with the bilge and ballast and part of the reef. He'd collapsed, and the rising water or blood loss had caught him.

Umali helped her drag him into the upper hold, near the shattered deck, where the holes that cannons had fallen through sent sunlight streaming into the darkness. He wasn't breathing. Desperation lanced through Inez like lionfish spines. She grasped for the saltwater in his lungs—it slipped away from her awareness like live shrimp through her grasping fingertips. Healing had no part in the hunting crocodile prayers she'd been learning. She screamed in fury as she felt his heart shudder and stop.

Her ragged nails caught on the black of his cassock. The sight of those shredded black threads dragged awake the dark and terrible ugliness that lived deep down inside her. It came roaring up from the depths of her spirit, a maw of endless black that wanted to gnash and kill everything, silence everyone. Grown used to buwaya whispers, Inez did not flinch. She dove in.

"You don't deserve to die yet!" She growled a crocodile demand, yanking with such brutality, she didn't care if his lungs came out of his chest along with the water drowning him.

The priest came to with a garbled scream, bloody foam and water gushing between his lips. Not a good sign, but she didn't need him to live long. She just needed to know.

She dragged him upright. "Tell me where I can find Santa Catalina. I know you know where she is!"

The priest only vomited more blood and foam, and died in retching agony.

Inez cursed loud and long, flinging the body away in disgust. The hold pitched as her fury dragged at the sea. She'd needed him alive. Whatever she'd learned and gained from the Amihan Moon and crocodile prayers, in healing she was as lost and broken as she'd always been. More harm than help, a poisoned well. She'd only killed him faster. Her fury was a howling beast within her, denied the answers she'd promised it. She did not know if there was enough blood in the world to sate it.

She'd been wrong, thinking she could learn to balance the ravenous pit inside her, thinking it was a depth she could learn to navigate like she'd learned to sail the *Agawin*. What was in her was too broken to be fixed, too unpredictable to be trusted.

Umali waited till she'd worn out her teeth-gnashing fury. When she came back to herself, the priest's body had cooled and stiffened, and the slave ship had slid deeper into the sea, water beginning to lap at their feet. Inez stared at Umali. Half her face lay in darkness, half stark sunlight, impossible to read. Inez waited for the questions. Questions she'd avoided so long, even in her own mind.

Instead, Umali said, "Do you know why I hunt slavers? The Tianchaowen bounty is good, but the Lusitans make dangerous prey. Their ships are heavily armed, and their sailors are experienced fighters. There are plenty of fat trade ships that would make better bounties at far less risk. I'm sure you've thought it."

"Why?" Inez croaked. Her voice was hoarse with screaming. She wanted to bolt out of this terrible black hold. She could feel the nearness of the sea, and her crocodiles. She could just swim away to where she would not have to face the terrible illumination of Umali's searching gaze.

"Lusitan slavers stole my half-brother. He was ill, and my mother decided to seek out a tide-touched healer. Mount Tumubo is an inland mountain. Not many on her slopes are named to Aman Sinaya. We journeyed in a small river bangka to the coast. We arrived near dawn. My mother left us aboard while she sought the healer. My brother was so sick. Crying and crying. I couldn't soothe him. That's what drew the attention of the slavers. They shoved torches in our faces, asking questions I couldn't understand."

Inez's heart hurt. She did not like to think of burning bright Umali, a terrified child in a stinking hold like this.

"My brother was Ita and dark-featured, like those children. The Codicíans and Lusitans prefer Black slaves in their great houses. They must be brought so far at great cost and suffering. They assumed he'd escaped one of their ships. The Ita are inland mountain peoples, rarely coming down to lowland ports. A man snatched him from my arms. I screamed and screamed. But another started dragging me towards their ship. I fought like a feral cat. But I was not their focus, so they cast me aside. Someone in the port held me back. They were protecting me, but it might've been better if they'd let me be taken out over saltwater. As it was... Mount Tumubo's old lahars, mud, and ash flows stretch all the way to the coast. I turned fire into lava and woke the volcano."

Inez pressed a hand over her mouth, afraid a gasp would interrupt Umali's terrible tale. Her words painted a picture she could practically smell. A port town, the river pouring into the sea, and a wide brackish delta. The black pine-pitch that slaver hulls and Palisade walls shared.

"The torch the slaver carried flared, tall as a man, hot as a bonfire. They still don't know how I did it, the other katalonan of Mount Tumubo, but where there was flame, I created molten lava, and the weight of it collapsed over the men stealing my brother. It is a rare firetender who can control true lava. I panicked. Lifetimes, Tumubo had slept. She is not a restive sleeper like Hilaga. But my mountain heard my distress, as if I were crying my plea to Amihan's messenger birds from her peak instead of far downriver. I was the only one who could get close. I had to pull the lava and cooking bodies off him with my bare hands. If he had not been so small and so young, he never would've been shielded. I have to thank Amihan for that. Neither of us would've survived my disaster, except that I was so far from the peak when I did it."

"Did... he live?" Inez asked at last.

Umali took a deep breath. "Yes. But so many more than I intended perished. Now you know why I can't ever go back."

"I'm sorry." Such a paltry thing to say in this black pit, over the body of the man they'd killed.

"I've made my peace with my loss. Will you tell me what you are running from or towards, and what Codicían churches and priests have to do with it?" Umali asked.

Inez wavered, but Umali had bared her scars. She owed her captain the truth.

"Until I was thirteen, I was raised in a Codicían convent. I was to become a nun, like my sister. But I caught the eye of a priest. Soon enough, I was pregnant. It became impossible to conceal." Inez lunged through the words, as if by speed and lack of detail, she would not have to dwell upon him a moment longer than needed. She could not bear to paint her past in the detail with which Umali had shared her own tragedy. The wounds were too fresh. To acknowledge how she'd hurt, the fear, and the hiding, it would be too much. "Do you know what they do to pregnant postulants?"

Umali must have heard it in her voice. She strode across the hold toward Inez. "You're right, some stories are better not told. Stop. You can stop."

Inez held up a hand, holding her off. "You should know. Someone needs to know. I am not reliable, and you should not lean on me. I'm not like you. What is broken in me is something far worse than a power I cannot control, or sleeping gods who listen too well. I was still a child, one raised in a Codicían nunnery. I did not dive till I was much older."

"I shouldn't have asked. Inez, please."

"I was pregnant and I was afraid. They would have had me caned or put in the starvation cages. I wouldn't have survived. I had to make the pregnancy go away, though I knew my sister would never approve. It was Aynila's tide-touched who granted me the sea's mercy."

"You were a child. You needed help," Umali said.

Inez nodded. "Yes, but that's where it all went wrong. My sister was terrified of water witch devilry—a devout nun, a better nun than I ever would've been. She betrayed the healer who helped me to the Inquisition so we could keep our place in the convent. They only demanded that I confess and make proper penance for consorting with witchcraft and seducing a priest. My sister agreed in my stead to save my immortal soul, and so I was caned. And the tide-touched of Aynila died."

"That's not your fault."

Inez released a long slow breath. "Almost no one in Aynila would ever say it was. But the help they gave me doomed them, and my sister betrayed them. Now, Codicían priests insist my sister has returned. Santa Catalina, come at last to return Aynila to God's holy light. There are relics, miracles, sightings of her all across the archipelago, and I've no idea if any of it is true or not. I fear she's being used against Aynila all over again, and I can't let it happen. I'm afraid... I'm afraid if anyone else finds her first... I know she'd deserve to face the Lakan's judgment, but I could not bear it. I've been hunting rumors of Santa Catalina so I can find her and send her far away from Aynila and the Codicíans. I chased them straight on board a slave ship. Twice."

The rush of the telling should've been a relief. Instead, Inez felt her insides knotting even tighter, fighting against being dredged to the surface and into the light.

Umali's brow furrowed. "Why should you be responsible for what she did? Are you her keeper?"

Inez bared her shoulder, the scars dark and aching. "I won't ever be free of her. She made sure of that. She is a ghost, a haunting I carry with me. Even after I was named to Aman Sinaya, even after I've come so far. How am I not just as responsible for her, as she was for me and my scars?"

"Even so, why hide what you hunted?"

The hungry pit inside her was still so near. She'd thought she was prepared to face it, able to swim those depths in borrowed crocodile armor. She'd been wrong. "I cannot bear to see the parts of her in me. She broke and brought ruin to everyone she loved. I can see the same fault lines in myself. Why else do I call to the sea with crocodile prayers? What else twists my hands to hurt and never heal? There is something wrong in me. You shouldn't trust it."

"Nothing about you is wrong. Don't compare yourself to her memory. If you would see your true reflection, look into the sea—or my eyes," Umali declared, seizing her hands and drawing her close, a furnace of light and life, everything Inez wasn't. She wanted to grasp for it and steal it for herself, but she clenched her fists, holding herself stiff and away.

The truth dragged out of her in the face of all Umali's faith, shining bright and deeply misplaced. "I can feel it. There is a dark, deep pit in me that won't be sated. Not by death, not even by desire. I've tried everything to fill it. I've gorged greedy and desperate. I used the Amihan Moon's glut of power, snatched crocodile prayers, fed lives to the sea like water. Even you. I used you too, stealing your warmth and drawing on your battle rages. Lying to make you chase my ghosts. I thought maybe a drop of your fire would warm my belly. But look. Look what I am." She swept out a hand, taking in the mangled priest and the great mess she'd made of him. "Nothing will be enough. Nothing can fill a broken cup."

Umali kissed her, pouring her fire into Inez like molten gold into a crucible. Inez drank deep, till even the terrible need in her belly sank down once more to a low ebb.

"Why would I begrudge one starved to eat their fill?" Umali whispered, before urging her too, back up into the light.

33

ALON DAKILA

His spies' reports and all the best wind readers among their allies put the Codicían armada just over a week out from the Sumila Gulf, and Alon at last had word of Inez. The Lusitan slave ship, the *São Martinho*, had been sunk. Pedro was searching for survivors.

Alon received the news only hours too late to warn Lunurin. He almost wished he'd been left in the dark, rather than being trapped in Aynila, helpless to do anything. It was as if the sea had swallowed both Inez and Lunurin at once, just as their enemies closed in.

To make matters worse, Aynila's alliances, sworn in blood and wine before the old gods and saints, were growing uneasy at the very moment they could not afford any delay joining Lunurin in the Sumila Gulf.

But Jeian and the captains from Ísuga and Talaan were unable to establish a clear line of command. The confusion botched efforts to supply their ships with provisions, ammunition, and gunpowder. Supplies went missing. Aynilan

319

merchants—as well as their allies among the inland rice kingdoms—balked. Everything came to a head when two crews again came to blows over a delivery of ammunition from the metalworkers' conclave. Hiraya kindly solved this by lighting the men's hair on fire.

As Isko recounted the debacle to Alon, he concluded, "Sina will be sorry to have missed it. To prevent further burnings, strife, and the dissolution of our merchant class, Aynila Indigo's warehouses are now acting as intermediary and quartermaster."

"Were the burns at least seen to in the healing halls?" Alon asked as they hurried to meet Jeian for planned training exercises on the bay.

"You underestimate Hiraya's restraint. At worst, they've mild smoke inhalation and a proper sense of shame," Isko assured him.

"At least someone has restraint." Alon rubbed his face.

He'd spent the morning making the difficult decision about which of their healing students could be assigned berths among the allied fleet. After Jeian's astute suggestion of pairings, Alon and the Lakan had set to pairing their best, most experienced healers with students who could be trusted aboard a bangka. Amid the unpredictable tides and currents of the Sumila Gulf, even a weak or inexperienced tide-touched could be of aid, especially in outmaneuvering a galleon's guns.

But the hardest thing was having to tell a distraught Rosa he was standing by Lunurin's decision to leave her behind in Aynila.

"How can I take Aynila's last stormcaller away?" Alon asked, rather than pointing out that every tide-touched he was allowing to volunteer had at least a year of training and Rosa had none. There'd been no time.

He'd brought a number of those students with him now as a peace offering to Talaan. There was no way their ships would be able to remain in formation or effectively navigate the dangerous shoals of the Sumila Gulf without a few tide-touched among their ships.

Alon tried not to dwell on the fact that none of these volunteers were originally from Talaan. Bernila, who'd been rescued from the Codicían fort there, had insisted on remaining in Aynila, saying only, "Aynila appreciates gods-blessed. I'll not die where I'm not wanted."

Talaan hadn't had many gods-blessed in a long time; most had been driven out or killed by the Codicíans. Those who'd remained in hiding had accepted Aynila's invitation after the fall of the shipyard, leaving Talaan behind.

He lifted a hand, waving down Tomás. "Captain Tomás, I've found volunteers from the healing school. Tide-touched who are willing to join your crews and help guide your ships. With the aid of a good helmsman, and some time to familiarize themselves, they will be a great advantage."

Tomás's expression flickered as he surveyed the handful of tide-touched accompanying Alon and Isko. "You want me to take on new crewmembers right before a battle? Accustom my helmsmen to their effect? No, it's too great a risk."

"Then take them on as healers and lookouts," Alon argued. "With the way the tides in Sumila re-carve the ocean floor, you can hardly trust to depth maps. Even my most inexperienced students will keep you from running aground."

Tomás shook his head again, a hand straying to the crucifix around his neck. "Forgive me, Lord Alon, but I must decline your generosity. I fear my men would not appreciate such advantages. We've been unfamiliar with them too long."

Alon read between the lines, and did not insist again. Talaan had only been free of Codicían control six months. Aynila hadn't rebuilt trust between her people and her gods-blessed overnight, either—their recent convert troubles were proof it was still a work in progress five years later.

He redistributed his volunteers among Aynila's and Ísuga's ships. They were doubling the number of tide-touched assigned to each berth, but it would mean a better division of labor between current crafting, wave singing, and healing.

From the deck of Jeian's guilalo flagship, they watched the first attempt at joint maneuvers in Aynila Bay. The calm waters here bore no similarity to the unpredictable cross currents and violent tides of the Sumila Gulf, but at least they could learn to work with each other.

Jeian's men had their largest karakoa on the water, with one outrigger flagged in blue. Each was controlled by an experienced tide-touched and a half-crew of rowers to represent the galleon's slower speed and maneuverability. The goal was to treat the flagged side as a cannon's broadside and ease their ships out of the line of fire, while getting close enough to hull the "galleon" below the waterline or steer them onto a reef or shoal.

Alon watched mixed groups of ships from Ísuga, Aynila, and Talaan make the first attempt. It was utter chaos.

"We're not even shooting at them, and they're about to sink themselves," Jeian cried.

"I think you should. They seem to think this is some kind of game," Isko observed, clinging white-knuckled to a tie-line. He liked open water no more than Sina, but would not leave them all to face the coming calamity alone. He'd hated to send Sina ahead as much as Alon had dreaded parting with Lunurin.

"Did Nihma just shove a Talaan ship between themselves and the 'broadside'?" Alon asked with a grimace.

Jeian lifted his spyglass and signaled his discontent to the captain. "Does she think a single karakoa will stop a cannon-ball? Now we've two ships sunk."

The ships from Talaan had no idea how to work with or around the tide-touched-crafted currents of their neighbors. And all three groups seemed to view the others as expendable.

When sails were rigged for the second exercise... it got worse. At one point, Alon flung himself astride the outrigger to reach the bay to physically grab and pull two ships apart before the impending wind and current-accelerated collision could ram and sink them both.

Isko muttered, "We might as well wait for the Codicíans to send conquistadors into Aynila and try our luck hand to hand."

"We can only get better from here?" Alon suggested.

That was when they received word of the assassination attempt on the Lakan.

34

LUNURIN CALILAN NG DAKILA

When they arrived in Masagana, Lunurin and Sina met with the local magistrate to learn when the Sumila Stormfleet had made its last supply run. Kalaba, meanwhile, met with several merchant contacts who sometimes supplied Calilan, to learn what they knew of the local fleet.

The magistrate frowned in thought, consulting his ledgers. "Forgive me, Lady Dakila, but the Stormfleet has not visited Masagana since the end of last year's wet season six months ago. Here are the records of their last requisition of supplies."

Lunurin frowned. "It's early in the season yet. Maybe they've shifted their patrols farther out, or south? Have any gods-blessed visited Masagana for supplies?"

"None that I know of belonging to Sumila Bay's Stormfleet... but there was a firetender captain in port last week. She collected the bounty for the sinking of a Lusitan slaver."

The cloud of worry Lunurin had been trying to force to

the back of her mind so that Inez being missing didn't drive her mad rushed forward, engulfing her like a stormfront.

"Not the one that left Aynila a week ago?" Lunurin choked out the question. "Black-hulled and tri-sailed... the *São Martinho*..."

"Yes, I believe so. I never saw the ship myself but..." The magistrate pulled open a drawer and produced the *São Martinho*'s manifests and registration papers.

"When?" Lunurin asked, as Sina pushed forward to study the manifest. She couldn't breathe. She wanted to drop everything and go after Inez. It would be an abandonment of her duty to Aynila and Anitun Tabu, but Inez needed her.

"Just days ago. I paid out the bounty and reward for the Tianchaowen captives who survived myself, to a captain... Umali."

"Was there a tide-touched Aynilan woman among the captives?" Sina asked, holding out a hand at about chin height.

"Long dark hair, mestiza, with scars on her back," Lunurin added.

The magistrate shook his head slowly. "You may ask the other survivors. A few have already been put aboard ships returning to their home provinces, but a number remain in Masagana."

Lunurin had already spun around, determined to learn all she could. "Thank you, we will ask," Sina told the magistrate with a bow, and rushed after her.

Lunurin was busy running the math. The slaver would've been sunk one, maybe two days out from Aynila. Alon's spies would just now be reaching Aynila with the news.

"Lunurin, I'm sure she's alive. Alon would know if she'd been lost at sea," Sina called out.

"Would he? The tide-touched village on Hilaga was so

much closer. With all the tangled energies of the Amihan Moon, I could hardly tell up from down! How could anyone pick one lost tide-touched from the vastness of the sea?" Lunurin's desperation was nearing a hysterical pitch; she struggled to rein it in. The afternoon shower over the water roiled suddenly, spawning lightning.

If Inez wasn't lost at sea, and she wasn't among the other survivors here in Masagana, where was she? How far had she gone to chase the rumor of Catalina's return?

Lunurin's questions found no answers among the newly rescued Tianchaowen captives, most of whom had no idea what being tide-touched meant and had been trapped in the darkness of the hold throughout the attack. But their description of the attack solidified in Sina and Lunurin's opinion that a tide-touched had been involved in the sinking of the slaver. It couldn't have been Inez, but a firetender couldn't have so riled the sea without aid.

Lunurin's heart ached to imagine Inez in such a terrifying battle.

Thunder rumbled louder out over the water. Lunurin flinched, closing her ears to any portents of the storm. She did not want to be a katalonan or Aynila's Lady Stormbringer right now. She wanted to be Inez's sister, and her little sister had fallen into a trap meant for her.

All the justifications she'd made to herself before the Amihan Moon, and even after Alon's terrible revelation, shattered like pine trunks in a gale. Inez was just bycatch, entangled once again in a larger struggle for power that Lunurin had failed to see before it was too late to wrest her free without scars.

She pressed her hands over her ears, trying to block out her goddess in the thunder. Without Alon's steady depths to anchor herself and drown her turmoil, it felt like she would spin away into the storm at any moment.

Lunurin turned to Sina. "What have I done? How can I turn aside now, knowing how she's suffered? Knowing the danger she's in? I've failed her again."

Sina grasped her shoulders. "I will not judge you. I have made ash and char of many well-laid plans in the name of my family's safety."

"How can I choose?"

"Don't choose now. We don't know enough. With what's coming for Aynila, would you truly want to have left her there? If the slaver was sunk, let us hope it took the priest down with it. Inez has avoided whatever the Codicians intended in dragging her aboard a Lusitan slaver. I can think of many reasons a pirate might wish to keep a tide-touched aboard."

Lunurin had to believe Sina was right. She must. She must, to convince herself that Alon's spies with their head start were far more likely to catch up with Inez than she was.

35

ALON DAKILA

The Lakan's study was in shambles.

Two bodies were already stiffening, one crumpled on the floor and one folded over Dalisay's desk, a sharp bamboo stylus stabbed into his throat.

"What happened?" Alon asked.

"Captain Tomás convinced me I needed to listen to a petition regarding those converts who are still being held on suspicion of being Codicían spies," his inay signed slowly, one-handed, while Aizza tended to a slash down her opposite forearm. She'd killed the first attacker herself.

"It's deep, I fear you'll need stitches," Aizza murmured.

Alon went to help her.

Isko bent, studying the first body. "I would not have expected it to go in so cleanly."

"Bodies are very fragile," Dalisay signed, grim-faced.

"The second man?" Alon asked, helping press his inay's wound back together as Aizza stitched, swift and sure.

Juan, the tall Black freeman who'd once worked in the

Palisade abbey, and who now oversaw the servants of the healing halls and infirmary, answered. "He had a gun. I did not mean to kill him. It would have been helpful to have someone to question."

Alon traced the arc of the unseen blow. A decorative Tianchaowen jade vase, gifted by diplomats from the mainland, had crushed the base of the man's skull. He might have been dead before he hit the floor, before the Lakan's guards even entered the room.

"I thank you for acting quickly," Alon assured him.

"I asked him to observe, because I wanted to know how many of the converts who have been causing... difficulties used to frequent the Palisade church. I'm not convinced our convert problem is local." The Lakan pointed with her lips at the man on the floor. "The way he spoke, Mamaylan, I know that accent."

The other two converts who'd led the petition had been arrested, but swore they had no knowledge of their companions' intentions. Alon was for the first time glad Lunurin was far away aboard a Stormfleet ship. There at least she was safe from Codicían assassins. He hoped she and Inez both were.

Jeian paced between the two bodies, the tattoos on his arms flickering like fireflies. "And two of them turned out to be Codicían assassins? We end this foolishness now. We ought to put Arcilla and every other convert still being held to death. Especially those two!"

"Jeian, hold on—" Alon needed to know how long these two had been in Aynila. If assassins were still being smuggled in...

"If Tomás takes issue with Aynila executing assassins, he's no ally of ours," Jeian spat.

"We need Talaan. We can still—"

"If you suggest we cover this up, when Inay could have been killed!" Jeian shook his head. "I'm firing your personal guards. What were they doing? How was anyone able to bring weapons into your study?" Jeian stormed out, ignoring Alon completely.

Alon considered the man whose brains were leaking out across the polished wooden floor. He looked almost peaceful. Death would be easier than dealing with his brother right now.

"Go after him," his inay ordered. "We need all the witnesses alive."

Alon pressed his cheek to hers. "I'm glad you are safe. Will you keep Litao with you for my peace of mind?"

Then he rose and went after Jeian.

36

❦

INEZ DOMINGO

Once the chaotic business of finding a port with a proper tide-touched healer who'd be able to help the slaver's sickly survivors had been settled, they remained in Lusubin a few days more.

A good portion of the crew was in favor of sailing back north to collect the bounty in Masagana before finding a nice quiet barrier island port to wait out the biggest and most dangerous storms of the wet season. They'd be able to live well for months on their spoils. Inez was still trying to figure out how to tell Umali she had no desire to return north. She couldn't. Not without laying the truth of the rumors to rest. Not after she'd come so far.

Umali had not brought up what had happened down in the hold of the slaver, and Inez did not want to raise it, too shocked by all she'd admitted out loud. Yet, when it came to a vote to where they would wait out the storms, Umali convinced the crew that they ought to capture one more prize along the rich central archipelago trade routes first.

She laid the decision at Inez's feet like an apology. "Let's work together, little crocodile. I can hunt gold as well as ghosts."

And so, they lay in wait on one of the main routes through the central straights.

They did not have to wait long before they sighted a Codicían-registered ship carrying goods and passengers northwest from Sugbu. It seemed Aman Sinaya still smiled on Inez's quest, despite how bloody it had become.

The registered ships were merchant vessels in service to the Codicían crown, who took the risk of solo voyages without the protection of a galleon convoy. It was a recent decision made by the Spanish crown since they'd lost Aynila and Talaan, shipyards capable of building, repairing, and servicing galleons.

The deeper waters of this wide channel were in Inez's favor. The weather was overcast, and growing steadily worse, a light rain falling that would conceal their intent from their prey.

Umali set the *Agawin* on an intercepting course.

She held out her hands to Inez in open invitation. "Be as greedy as you like. I've told you I'll gladly share."

After three sea battles, meshing her power with Umali's was as easy as timing her breath while diving the oyster beds. They eased silently through the murk of clouds and mist coming up on their prey slowly, then all at once as both Umali and Inez gave the *Agawin* a push. The moisture around Umali vaporized in a gust of steam. For an instant, Inez lost sight of the enemy ship entirely, tracing it only by the deep draft and cut of its keel in the water.

With two gods-blessed and the weather on their side, it should've been an easy plunder. But for all that the Codicíans sent their registered ships without the protection of a true galleon, this boat wasn't nearly as vulnerable as the Duutsan trader had been. Its powder stores were protected against sparks and lightning. The sails were reefed in preparation for the storm to worsen, with a unique series of vents designed into the fabric so that a stormcaller, or Umali's unique heat waves, couldn't use a crosswind to send them belly up.

As the *Agawin* swept upon them, the ship dropped six balanced anchors, preventing Inez from effectively turning the ship. Her waves crashing harmlessly along its sides, her currents pulling without the ability to capsize or turn it.

And though Umali's heat caught them up, causing an early discharge of their four main guns, the sailors didn't panic, and the fires weren't spreading to their interior powder stores.

Umali quickly switched tactics, ordering the remaining rowers to their places, and Inez to turn them. The great bulk of the Codicían ship was like a wall before them. Where was there to go?

"Now!" Umali cried, her sure hand on the helmsman's oars. Neither Inez nor the rowers hesitated. They heaved, and the *Agawin* shot forward, guided by their captain's hand. The heat-hardened prow bit through the rear rudder of the Codicían ship with a tremendous crunch, their multiple anchors working against them, allowing the *Agawin* to shear off the rudder completely.

They boarded before their prey could pull up their anchors and make a run for it on the rising storm winds.

The battle for the deck was chaos. Rain came down thick and fast as they fought hand to hand. Inez kept behind the line of fighting, at Umali's back. With the anchors preventing her from rocking the ship, even the crash of her biggest waves barely reached the deck. She tried to do as much damage as she could before the rain diluted the salt on the deck too much.

From the corner of her eye, Inez caught the sparks of a

lit fuse. An unprimed rear gun rolled forward on the upper decks, black maw poised to take out the *Agawin*'s boarding crew and half the Codicían ship's own sailors.

"Cannon!!" Inez clawed for all the water she could reach. Like the sweeping lash of a crocodile's tail, it swept the line of fighting across the deck. Some were quick and caught the far rail. A handful of both crews went over, down into the choppy waters.

"No!" Inez lunged to the rail, not trusting her battle-riled crocodiles to differentiate friend from foe in the foul weather.

Umali pivoted with her. She grabbed Inez in her arms, pressing her against the rail, covering her with her body. There was a thunderous boom, as if the heavens themselves were splitting open.

Umali burned, true flame sweeping up and out of her like a shattered oil lamp. It flickered harmlessly over Inez's treated clothing, quick as a kiss. The sails above burned, raining down sparks and ash. And Umali crumpled to one side, the blazing battle rage of her presence guttering out.

Blood spread around her, staining the deck black. In a flash, Inez saw the molten lead cooling on her skin, eating holes into her jacket, a splatter of thwarted death across the decks. One jagged shard of blackened iron protruded from the back of her shoulder.

A guttural roar ripped out of Inez. She lunged forward, planting herself in front of Umali's prone form, protective as a crocodile over its nest. Her waves weren't high enough, the heavy rain thwarting her, dripping from her grip rather than lashing out sharp and cutting. Enemies closed in. Crocodile songs were not enough. Inez was not enough, cold without Umali's fire to lean into.

That familiar choking desperation rose up in her. Inez seized it, not caring if it ate up and spat out everything and everyone before her, or if she never came up again. She dove deeper, reached further. Down and down, to find she was not alone in the depths. There was hunger, and a darkness that knew her. A hunger that could only be filled by the moon. The laho. Though thwarted and angry, she was resplendent with the power she had supped from the Amihan Moon as she came rising from the deep.

"I need more," Inez demanded, bloody and breaking. The words came with a visceral tearing sensation, a yawning and sharp-toothed agony Inez had spent so many years fearing would be her destruction. She rode the copper-edged darkness up from the deep.

The sea boiled. Something massive sheared off the anchor chains, first one side, then the other, the ship swinging out wildly, pitching and rolling, at the mercy of the sea at last.

Inez no longer had to work with only the pittance of sea spray and rainwater. The depths came roaring over the decks.

She held the silver of her short sword in one hand, her balisong in the other, and their keen edges cut her waves to slicing whips that tore flesh like crocodile teeth.

She pushed their enemies back, giving the *Agawin*'s boarding party breathing room to recover from her wave, protectively circling their captain. With a rallying cry, Inez leaped for the stairs of the upper deck, where the Codicían gun crew was trying to get off another shot.

The sea rose with her, a tidal wave she could never have moved alone, not even with crocodile songs—but an old and powerful behemoth of the depths was with her. She rode like a flood through a city: ruin and churning bodies in her wake. Terrified men broke and fled. Some even tried to surrender. But she'd received no mercy from Codicían hands. She would show none now.

The depths she had called knew no mercy.

Inez would've killed them all, snuffed them out like candle flames before a flood. Nothing else mattered but that they had extinguished Umali's burning presence and left Inez alone—until she heard the captain's prayer. He clutched at his rosary falling back from her. "Oh, Santa Catalina, lift us up by your hand from the witch-cursed waves!"

The water gloving her arm seemed to glow faintly with copper threads. Inez used its weight and momentum to drive the man back into the mast.

She heard bones crack, but couldn't bring herself to care. "Where is she? What do you know about Santa Catalina? Tell me before I feed every one of your crew to the sea."

The man only whimpered. Inez hissed her fury, granting her crocodiles permission. *The fair ones, they reek of gunpowder, tobacco, and pine tar. Make it slow.*

Screams rose from the waves. Inez dragged the captain to the rail, where he could see his foundering crew. Long dark shadows in the water. The struggling swimmers looked so small. Her crocodiles were well-fed—it looked like sport as they tore free an arm, a leg. The sailors clawed at the sides of the ship, trying to escape the water's tearing teeth. But there was no escape. Not from Inez's crocodiles or the black maw of her own desperation, drawing on something deep and terrible. The laho, emblazoned on the *Agawin*'s prow, seemed near a friend now, at home in the hollowness inside her with its deep, vast hunger. That's what the laho was: a bottomless hunger from the depths that nothing of the sea could satisfy. Just like Inez.

But Inez would not lose the trail of her ghost. Not now, not when she was so close.

"Tell me!" Inez demanded, shaking the captain.

"Simsiman! Our Lady of the Rosary is in Simsiman. She

has been visiting every fort, gathering ships and captains. She will grant her blessing to any who take up the fight to reclaim Aynila!" the captain cried.

"And she's in Simsiman now? You've seen her with your own eyes?" Inez pressed.

Sacay dragged a survivor across the deck, preparing to cast him to the crocodiles.

"Yes, yes, I swear it! She blessed this rosary herself on my last crossing, just weeks ago."

Finally, a firsthand account, not months or years old. And she could do nothing about it. Simsiman might as well be Canazco across the Great South Sea for how impenetrable the Codicían fort was. Inez cursed.

In disgust, she pitched the captain overboard and rushed back to Umali's side. She pressed her hands around the jagged black shrapnel, trying to will herself into the salt of Umali's blood to hold back its tide. If she could stop the bleeding, maybe Umali would be able to recover. It was there. She knew it was there! She could still taste it on her tongue from her buwaya's blood sport.

She grappled for a finger-hold, not daring to make a sound, for fear of how crocodile prayers shredded even what they loved.

Sacay organized the crew. They filled one of the Codicían ship's shoreboats with seawater and dragged it to Inez's side. Inez pulled a deluge of saltwater over Umali, trying to find the calm and focus Alon had coached her toward so often.

"Aman Sinaya, please!" she prayed but the vast spread of the sea was not moved. The tides of Umali's blood would not heed crocodile prayers. She was no healer; she was hunger and a belly that would never be sated.

She might have been granted the sea's mercy, but it was not a blessing she could share. She had broken too early and lost too much.

37

LUNURIN CALILAN NG DAKILA

The sky was clear and blue in the way it only was after a storm swept through. They wouldn't get a better window than this. Lunurin awaited Kalaba's signal, confirming the other four ships of their small fleet were prepared. Sails were taken in and stowed. Helmsmen and tide-touched were at the ready to keep them turned into the wind and waves. Sina—already struggling with the distance from Hilaga and sea sickness—had been preemptively tethered to a tie-line.

Lunurin let down her hair. A single thunderhead boiled up overhead, blotting out the sun. It grew and grew, a billowing white tower taller and wider than any smoke signal. She let it suck up water from the sea like a sponge, twisting winds through her fingers to keep their cloud from spreading out, only up. The weight of it in the air above was palpable. Sina sat behind her, plaiting and unplaiting sections of Lunurin's hair, letting the rain down from the cloud in unnatural staccato bursts, while Lunurin focused on keeping her billowing storm as focused and contained as possible.

She tilted her head back, focusing on her storm overhead, letting it start the spin that would make any stormcaller in its range pay attention. Sina's fingers raked through her loosened waves and the rain came down in sheets, making it impossible to see even the other ships of their little fleet.

They waited.

Distantly, she felt another stormcaller trying to draw her storm southeast, farther into open water. Sina helped her twist her hair back up, giving over control of the storm's path. The storm set off, and by its direction, Kalaba set their sails for the other Stormfleet cluster.

Three stormrunners of the Sumila Stormfleet met them over the deepest part of the gulf, where they'd have the most ease and distance to disperse a storm.

Kalaba's ships ran up their flagging, identifying themselves as Stormfleet out of Calilan. Lunurin quickly dispersed her storm, letting it spread, no longer a thunderhead but bands of high-altitude mare's tails. With the prevailing wet season winds, there was little danger of them swirling back together again.

The Sumila Stormfleet's hesitation was obvious. Their ships kept tight formation, offering no invitation to approach.

Lunurin sent Kalaba's greeting across the water on a friendly breeze. "Kalaba of Calilan greets you, Sumila fleet. Is that Captain Galang's ship I see? You were missed at the Amihan Moon over Mount Hilaga. I had hoped to see you at the gathering."

A stormcaller aboard sent back Sumila's answer as the two groups slid slowly closer on careful tide-touched currents. "Kalaba? You're too old to be out storm-chasing. Is Calilan so short of tide-touched you're back on wet season duty?"

For the first time since reuniting with her family, Lunurin

dared to feel a spark of hope. It was the warmest reception she'd gotten from any Stormfleet captain so far. She and Kalaba sent their ship skimming forward to meet Galang's, which broke formation to join them.

"Diplomatic duties this year," Kalaba countered, once the ships were close enough to speak easily.

Galang was easily as old as Kalaba, but had striking black hair worn loose around a mother-of-pearl-beaded collar, the round pearl of her mutya centered between her collarbones. Another tide-touched. Had they trained together in their youth?

Kalaba gestured to her. "This is my niece, Dayang Lunurin Calilan ng Dakila. She is the stormcaller who sundered the Palisade in Aynila."

Galang's response was measured as she studied their party. "Ah, this is about the Codicíans, isn't it? There's been so much increased traffic towards their central sea-lanes through the southern edge of the Sumila Gulf. They must be preparing for something."

"The retaking of Aynila," Lunurin answered.

"A shame, to be sure—but you'll forgive me if I cut this meeting short, since there's no brewing typhoon about to destroy Masagana. We have a calamity of our own we must return to and cannot spare ships or gods-blessed to Aynila, imminent Codicían attack or no."

"Calamity?" Kalaba inquired. "Do not tell me it was misfortune which kept you from the Amihan Moon gathering?"

"I'm afraid so. Three of our supply ships were captured by pirates and are being held for ransom. We can aid no others while our fleet-mates are in peril. The rabid dogs have nested themselves in Inalikan, and we've no way to pay the bounty or root them out without endangering our captured crews. The rest of our fleet is there negotiating the ransom."

"Then let Aynila be of aid to you now," Lunurin cut in. "Aynila Indigo can easily supply the ransom of three ships."

Lunurin needed any gratitude or debt she could claim from the Sumila Stormfleet. She could only hope that the pirates who'd sunk the slaver planned to request a similar ransom for Inez. Aynila's healing school was well known for their generosity when it came to acquiring tide-touched students.

Galang's expression shifted, the hardened mask cracking. "My pride would have me turn you down. But come, let me introduce you to our fleet's leader. He may be willing to hear you out. His husband is one of those held ransom."

38

❦

INEZ DOMINGO

Umali was fading. Inez had transferred her to the *Agawin*, leaving the crew to finish sacking their prize. They were making their way back to Lusubin as fast as Inez and the rowers could push them.

Inez had discovered a long wound, partly hidden under the red cloth Umali wore tied around her forehead. The impact had probably knocked her unconscious, and the shock from her injuries explained the rest. Inez cleaned the head wound, trying to determine how deep the injury went. A year of working in the healing halls hadn't prepared her for this.

How had Alon ever healed Lunurin or his own mother? Seeing Umali so still, all the great heat of her fiery presence fading like coals without air, her lungs crackling as blood leaked in…

Inez had never felt so helpless. Her skin burned hot and cold, her head buzzed with panic, her belly a black pit of desperation. After what she'd done to the priest just days ago, she was more useless even than the rest of the crew. At least they wouldn't kill Umali faster.

When the packing around the shrapnel bled through, Inez decided to cut Umali's jacket open to better dress the wound. With the edge of her balisong knife, she sliced the fine black fabric, exposing the jagged shrapnel still lodged in Umali's back, torn skin gaping to reveal severed muscles. The shard had slid in behind her shoulder blade, punching a hole in her lung. Inez could hear the building fluid in her labored breaths. Inez cut further, carefully peeling the jacket off her skin. She tried to remove the worst of the molten metal with the material of the jacket, exposing weeping red burns that splattered across Umali's back. The pattern reminded her so much of her own scars that her skin ached, her breath coming short and hard through her nose.

Catalina's prayers for forgiveness and the whistling crack of the abbot's flaying bamboo cane replaced the roaring panic in her ears. Her stomach turned, and she had to sprint up from the sheltered hold to be sick over the side of the ship.

She spat and rinsed her mouth, then scrubbed at her tears and running nose with seawater and hoped the rest of the crew would think it was just nausea. She couldn't do this! But someone had to finish the dressings.

Before she could convince herself to go back and face the blood and ruin she'd made of her captain, Sacay pulled her aside. She pointed over the opposite side of the *Agawin*, where the crew had cut down the rigging from the Codicían ship and created a sling between the *Agawin* and its outrigger. "You could try…"

She didn't have to finish. The hope shining in her expression stabbed Inez through like a dozen shrapnel spikes. They'd tried to make a space where she could safely lower Umali into the sea and heal her without delaying their mad rush for land and help. After all, she was tide-touched. "You saw me try. I can't even stop the bleeding, much less heal her—"

The sun made a brief, bloody appearance between the low-hanging clouds and the horizon, painting the water in shades of red.

Sacay held her gaze. "You could try," she repeated. "You protected us, and the captain protected you. Please. Try."

"I'm no healer, and you don't want me to try. I killed the last man I tried to heal. He died choking on his own lungs," Inez spat, angry and vicious in her helplessness.

Umali began to cough, a wet, wretched sound. Inez broke away from Sacay, rushing back to Umali's side. She rolled her, mindful not to disturb the shrapnel still protruding from her back, helping to drain the blood from Umali's airways, keeping her from choking on the fluid or her own tongue.

Umali's face was cool to touch, no longer flushed with her own internal fires, her nail beds and gums gone a ghastly grey. She was dying. Even at this speed, they would not make port in Lusubin for hours.

Sacay crept down into the lower deck, past the curtain that demarcated the captain's quarters from the space for the cargo and crew. The *Agawin* was not like foreign ships, designed for months-long habitation. It was rare not to pull their ship ashore overnight on some strip of beach or make port.

"Could you really make it worse?"

"She could die screaming instead of slowly from blood loss." Inez scrubbed the back of her arm across her face, ashamed of her own weakness.

Sacay took her by the arm. "You need air. Come." She pulled Inez back out onto the upper deck.

Inez made her way up into the cool rush of night air. They were racing toward help—but not fast enough. Inez cried out her incipient grief to the sea, a crocodile lament of wounded mates and punctured bellies, giving an additional burst of speed to their passage. The deck under their feet vibrated, the *Agawin* protesting such velocity. The helmsman, Lim, offered her the salt stores kept for drying fish, and Inez poured several handfuls into the sea, sending up buwaya prayers, and begging to be granted a healer's touch, just for tonight. Beyond the irregular rush of the currents Inez had crafted for the *Agawin*, the sea lay becalmed, still as a lake after the passage of the laho and the vengeful waves Inez had used to flood the Codícian ship. She raised a prayer of anguish, of ships lost at sea, of empty nets, of rising storm surge and too few tide-touched to protect Aman Sinaya's people.

She begged the sea to grant her mercy. *"Aman Sinaya, gentle lady, please, grant me a healer's touch tonight and I'll never ask it again."*

But the Sea Lady could not speak to her. Inez had too much hunger for vengeance and not enough room in her heart for mercy. Her fault lines were not her sister's, but she would never heal as the tide-touched of Aynila taught. She could shape the sea but could not grasp its mercy, only the hunger of its darkest depths and its angry, sharp-toothed anito.

Inez slumped, defeated, empty but for the blackness of her grief and the ache of her old wounds.

"We saw how you called out and the laho lashed the sea to froth. We should thank her too," Sacay suggested.

The prow of the *Agawin* was aglow. A dozen oil lamps had been lit and seated in each of the footholds of the prow, so that the laho's spine gleamed with copper firelight. The flames flickered and flared wildly in the wind of their passage.

Inez offered up her gleaming silver smallsword alongside myriad other prizes the crew had placed in the offering dish. There was Codicían silver, rice and salt, handfuls of spices, and ivory dice. Her smallsword did not fit in the dish, but she unwrapped the jute ribbon from her right arm and tied a loop to hang it from the laho's carved jaw.

Out toward open water, the laho surfaced, arches of scale and fin, her great copper mane and sharp horn limed in light by the waning moon. Even at this distance, Inez felt unspeakably small and grateful for the *Agawin*'s years of offerings to her likeness, begging her not to capsize a ship that sailed in her honor. What had she been thinking to call on something so great, no matter how desperate she'd been?

The laho's eyes shone like lamps, a reflection of stolen moonlight. Her maw was lined by curving batangas blades, her copper scales big as kalasag shields. Hers was the oldest hunger, never sated. *"Little crocodile, why beg and plead for the power you could steal? We of deep water do not wait for the bounty of the surface. We drag it down. You know how to snatch the vengeance you deserve. Will you not grasp for the life you crave as well? Or will your hollow belly go unfed?"*

And then she was gone, with hardly a ripple to show where she'd been, her molten copper glow fading slowly into the depths.

Inez turned to Sacay, who knelt frozen, staring after the laho.

"I'll try. It may be for the worse, and she'll never thank me for it, even if I succeed. But I'll try."

Inez needed every drop of focus and power she could steal or borrow. The crocodile-sung current she'd crafted fell away, and the *Agawin* slowed.

Inez dropped into the swirling water, hooking her arms through the netting to keep herself braced. Sacay lowered Umali down to her. Inez propped Umali's chin up on her shoulder, clear of the lapping waves. Her captain's body pressed to hers, far too cool, far too still. Inez curled her arms around her, wrapping one hand around the jagged chunk of black iron lodged in Umali's back, the other braced on her shoulder blade, pinning her.

She reached deep, not for the salt flow of blood, and not for a healer's calm, the salt well of mercy that should be in every tide-touched's soul. Inez reached deep and found the furious desperation she'd spent years trying to ignore; that she was just learning to fathom and use out on the open water, rather than being used by it.

Inez pressed her feet into the netting, and she pulled.

Umali groaned, her voice choked with pain as the water ran red.

Red as the bath in which Inez had been delivered of the terrible, pitiable thing DeSoto had put in her. Red as the decks of a pirate prize. Red as the priest coughing up his own lungs instead of prayers to deaf gods and blind saints.

Red as the sea foam when her crocodiles feasted, now drawn near by scent.

Inez knew intimately the red that death ran, how the taste of it in the water soothed her fury as nothing else could. But it was also the red of life. Red as surviving as her back was rent to tatters; red as the yards and yards of stained bandages as her body knit itself together under healer's hands. Red as rising from the Lakan's healing bath, herself alone for the first time in months. Red as fighting back-to-back with Umali. Red as the heat of Umali's magnificent burning fury.

Saltwater and blood mingled. Inez dove down and down

into cold blackness without end. Years she'd spent afraid she would move wrong and that terrible desperation would cut through her tender skin to ruin everything. Tonight, she would make it do the opposite. She would undo the ruin her hunt for answers and Catalina had wrought. She would not fear the merciless deep or anything in it.

Pressing her hands over and into the gaping wound, Inez did not let herself falter. It was too large; even Alon and Aizza together would not have been able to knit a wound like this into wholeness. But Inez did not care if she broke, or if the crushing depths living in her belly were not what she needed. She would take what she'd never been given.

Inez seized Umali's fading heart. The crush of deep salt, a pressure nothing could deny. She pressed down, hard, and demanded that it beat. The sea's cradling depths pulsed with all the renewed magic of the Amihan Moon. Inez snatched it for herself and forced it into Umali's cooling, failing frame through the hole gouged in her back. She fed herself and her fury and her grasping, selfish hunger into the working, locking her legs around Umali as she came to, screaming.

"You. Don't. Heal." The words rasped out of Umali between belly-wrenching screams as she writhed, her entire being instinctually trying to escape Inez's terrible touch.

"I never have," Inez whispered, pressing her cheek to Umali's.

She demanded that deep water replace the blood she couldn't grasp. In her arms, Umali shivered and shook, her body rebelling against the freezing wrongness of it. Inez dragged muscle, tendon, and skin back together. She had torn through enough sinew to know how bodies sundered. She would make this one whole.

She did not stop. Not when Umali closed her teeth on the

meat of Inez's shoulder and bit down. Not when she broke skin, and their blood mingled in the salty water, their pain entwined like mangrove roots.

Umali's body twisted at unnatural angles as her muscles pulled taut like rigging in a storm. Her teeth, lockjaw tight, fed her pain back into Inez. She responded in kind, filling Umali up with all the magic she could bear, till the salt grew thin and Inez's vision blurry. Until Umali burned against her like metal overheated in the forge, threatening to lose all shape and memory of itself. Until she was hoarse with screaming, her teeth red-stained with blood, her breath rasping and ragged in Inez's ear.

Healing should not be like this. But life could be stolen in many ways. When Inez grasped for more from the sea and her hands came up with nothing but flakes of blood-tinged salt, she caught Umali's face in her hands and pressed their mouths together, tasting the rust of their mingled blood, the pain she'd caused sharp and acrid, a clash of teeth and heat.

Healing was as red as that kiss.

39

LUNURIN CALILAN NG DAKILA

The pirate stronghold on Inalikan was built atop a tall, jagged outcropping of black volcanic stone that jutted out in a fist-shaped peninsula, surrounded by white sand beaches and waving palms. Even with the efforts of the Stormfleet's tide-touched, a direct assault would be dangerous and costly.

The Sumila Stormfleet—made up of ten stormrunners and four sailed guilalo supply ships—had set themselves in a wide semi-circle around the jagged fist of rock and the crowded beach cove, blockading it, forcing the pirates to acquire all their supplies from the small island. The pirate force was a motley assortment of red-sailed Tianchaowen junks, double-outrigger karakoa, and square-sailed lanong galleys. They were keeping the pirates hemmed in, but were unable to negotiate the narrow, rocky approach to the beach without risk of being reefed or cut down by the pirates' artillery.

Lunurin guided Kalaba's ship alongside the fleet's seventy-five-foot flagship. They were welcomed aboard by Captain

Lihat, who wore his grey hair in a braided knot, fixed in place by several mother-of-pearl hair sticks with his lightning-shaped pearl as a pendant.

He studied her. "When we heard songs of Lady Stormbringer, I assumed you'd be twelve foot tall and crowned in lightning."

Lunurin rubbed together her mother-of-pearl-tipped fingers self-consciously, but smiled. "I can be that too. But among friends, I am only Lunurin. I save the terror-crowned-in-lightning bit for my enemies."

"Galang tells me you're offering aid with our stalemate."

"I am. We may share a pirate problem. Your supply ships are held ransom, and I'm looking for a pirate captain, Umali, who collected the Tianchaowen bounty for a sunk slave ship a week ago. Aynila is willing to pay your crews' ransoms to gain information about the pirate Umali."

"I fear the situation has become more complicated than simply lacking the funds for a ransom. We managed to pay the agreed-upon sum; now, the pirates are demanding we give them two tide-touched in a hostage exchange."

"As what? Insurance?" Sina exploded.

"Indentured crewmen. They want tide-touched to guide their ships so they can match Stormfleet speed and maneuverability. But obviously, I cannot consign any more of my crew to pirates, even if they are holding my husband hostage."

Lunurin studied the formation of the Stormfleet ships. "I take it you are attempting to regain your crews by starving them out?"

"It's risky, and slow, but I cannot hand over any of my tide-touched even temporarily and expect our fleet will survive this wet season's storms."

"If you're already willing to accept some risk, I can propose a solution that will bring this stalemate to an end much more quickly." Lunurin found herself unexpectedly eager to be facing a problem that was past the point of diplomacy.

~

Captain Lihat's counteroffer of a stormcaller and a firetender, as the fleet could not spare their few tide-touched, was accepted—with the provision that they pay a higher ransom, as a firetender couldn't guide a ship. The Sumila Stormfleet retreated, abandoning their blockade of the pirate stronghold.

Lunurin was ready to pay the difference in gold, but Sina proposed a different solution. Gold was too quick to change hands. Why not pay the difference in silk and dye? She pointed to their shipboard supplies, all crated and sacked in Aynila Indigo's branding. Isko's handiwork, his hope for their safety and success. "Think how much longer it will take to unload and hand off. Much better than coin."

Lunurin grinned. "Oh, that is clever. Thank Isko for me once we've seen this through."

They consulted Captain Lihat's knowledge of the cove, its prevailing winds, and his tide-touched's knowledge of the best approach to the beach. Lunurin wrote up the proposed value of their ransom offer, and a demand for an in-person hostage exchange on the beach, where no side had the advantage of the other.

40

⏺—◆—⏺

INEZ DOMINGO

They made port in Lusubin near midnight. Calling what Inez had done *healing* would be a lie. But Umali was alive, if barely moving, curled around the agony Inez had wrought, her voice long since gone from screaming. Inez and Sacay rushed her to a local tide-touched healer. Terrified what Inez had done would not stick—or worse, would not improve.

The healer had barely touched Umali, before she turned on Inez. "By all the mercy in the sea, what did you do? What are you?"

She pressed three damp fingers to Umali's brow, putting her to sleep. Her body finally unknotted from her pained contortion, and relief washed over Inez too.

Inez did not send people to sleep. She drowned them. She had no good answers for the healer.

"She's our tide-touched, that's our captain. She was wounded by cannon shrapnel," Sacay explained.

"A tide-touched didn't do that. Couldn't!" the healer exclaimed.

353

"I had to stop the bleeding," Inez stammered. "I know it was dangerous."

"So you hold the tide of her blood until a properly trained healer could come! Not *this*! Dangerous? What you've done is worse. It's wrong! I hope you never touch the sea again, if you're going to use it like this," the healer snapped as she bent over Umali, trying to fix all Inez had done.

Inez flinched. Would Alon say the same if he saw what Inez had become?

She slunk back to the *Agawin*, unable to bear Sacay's pity while the healer worked on, filtering seawater and poisons from Umali's blood before infection set in.

Aboard the ship, the waiting crew was rowdy with relief of having made their desperate run. Inez was in no mood to celebrate. Claiming fatigue, she declined to drink to their captain's good health.

Lim tried to ply her with freshly steamed siopao dumplings stuffed with pork and eggs. Inez snatched the food, belatedly ravenous, and clambered up into the prow. She balanced behind the laho's carved mane, where she'd be out of the way of the celebrations on the deck below. Otherwise, she'd just bite someone's head off.

The dressing down she'd been given by the healer was still ringing in her ears. Her bitten shoulder was one big dull ache. She'd forgotten to get the healer to look at it. Maybe she should climb back down for the lambanog, if only to give the bite a good clean.

When Sacay and Umali at last returned from the healers, a rousing cheer went up from the crew, and in short order they'd swept Umali off for a proper feeding up, which she needed after so much healing magic.

Her crew would look after her. They'd been there long

before Inez had come along. Inez didn't begrudge them that. Besides, they had a lot to celebrate. They'd made it rich off a dangerous prize, winning twice the amount of Codicían silver as they'd been paid in slaver bounties, and their captain was whole once more.

Inez still couldn't bring herself to join in.

Finally, she'd parsed something true from all the rumors and hearsay of Santa Catalina. All it had taken was the sinking of three ships, and untold slaughter. She'd tortured and lied, and now her hunt for miracles had mired itself in the cold, sucking mud of reality.

If she went to Simsiman, the Codicíans would kill her as a water witch or a pirate, they could take their pick. She was equally unable to go back to Aynila. She was a traitor—and worse, a tide-touched who harmed and killed. An aberration. Would Umali even let her stay aboard the *Agawin* after what she'd done to her?

She'd let her desperation drive her so far, only to become hopelessly entangled, without a path forward in any direction. No matter how hard she struggled, no matter how much blood she spilled, she was only one tide-touched, and the Codicíans had killed so many more experienced and powerful than her. Katalonan who had served Aman Sinaya for their entire lives had lost them to Codicían pyres.

She wasn't fool enough to think her year of failed training in the healing halls and crocodile hunger was enough to crack a stronghold that even Lunurin had never suggested attacking directly.

Her back aching from her cramped position and her belly sour with regret, Inez dove from the prow into the cove, needing to escape the trap of her own head. The dark waters closed around her. She let herself sink down to the sandy bottom. It wasn't as deep as she might have liked. But she wasn't alone. Dark and still against the pale sand were her resting crocodiles.

She stayed down with them a long time before she finally let buoyancy lift her to the surface. A stream of bubbles broke beside her, and slowly Himig rose up from the depths, a black shadow swallowing all the light of the *Agawin*'s lamps glowing on the water. Sometimes she swore her crocodiles went hours before coming up for air. She wished she could do the same.

"Little sister, where is your back-sunning-well-fed-hot-sand-nap satisfaction? You dove well."

"Not you too," Inez complained. *"Umali deserves some space after what I just did."*

"Have you tried singing to your mate so she will come back to guard the nest with you?" Himig suggested.

"The Agawin is not a nest." Inez didn't even try to address the other part of that statement.

"Cradles what is precious. Keeps egg-eaters away. It is a nest. And we are helping you guard it," Himig refuted her simply.

Before Inez could come up with an argument against a crocodile's reconciliation plan, the shadows shifted. Umali gazed down over the edge of the *Agawin*, haloed in lamplight.

"Oh good, I worried you'd gone chasing your Santa Catalina on your own."

"I'm stupid and a failure as a tide-touched, but I don't have a death wish," Inez muttered and swam back toward the ship, pulling herself up onto the outrigger.

Umali extended a hand. "A fat prize. Sacay tells me you uncovered a firsthand sighting of your Santa Catalina, and I'm not even dead. I would hardly call that failure."

Inez disregarded Umali's hand, making the leap unaided. With a twisting, wringing motion she pulled the saltwater from the old sarong, drying off before she retreated below decks to get some space. It wasn't Umali's fault that she couldn't do anything right.

Umali followed gingerly. Inez could see how she was favoring her left shoulder—a reminder of how badly she'd botched the healing. She'd locked up Umali's good side with a tangle of scar tissue no amount of proper healing would ever be able to undo. Not after the sheer desperation Inez had poured into her through that open channel.

"It's not stupid to want to put old ghosts to rest," Umali tried.

Inez exploded. "I never should've gone chasing one in the first place! You were dying. What if we hadn't found a proper tide-touched healer in time? And all I have is the proof that my sister is perfectly unreachable and gathering a fleet of faithful murderers to destroy Aynila."

Umali caught Inez's face in her hands and kissed her, cutting off her spiraling fears.

The heat of her rushed over Inez's head and deep into her chest, teasing apart all the knotted tangles of fear and regret, melting them away as crocodile counsel hadn't achieved. They stumbled back over coiled ropes onto the folded sail where it had been stowed out of the way during their push for the port.

A whiff of dust and sweat mixed with the feeling of weight on her in the enclosed space, a muddled terror of long ago. Inez didn't freeze; freezing never helped. She gave a twist, slithering free, like a crocodile escaping a bask for cool water.

Umali's warm hands let her go. She watched Inez quietly,

with no questions, no expectation either. The invitation of a lamp burning in the window, whether Inez chose to come in or not.

With a gentle push, Inez tipped Umali over onto her back and buried her face in her clothing, nuzzling down into her so soft breasts and breathing deep of the smoky metallic sweetness that was only Umali. Inez caught the old fright awakening in her chest and crushed it down into the depths— no light, no air, as dead as drowned priests. She reminded herself that the salt of Umali's skin was healing sea salt, the sweetness of her kisses like licks of flame. She breathed her in, like a diver preparing her lungs. If blood could sate her belly, why shouldn't she grasp for Umali's fire and use it to burn out every lingering memory of the Palisade?

Umali's arms cradled her closer, her warm fingertips petting down her nape. "So may I be grateful for my rescue from the jaws of death, little crocodile?"

"Hardly a rescue," Inez huffed, her earlier ire still not fully appeased. But she straddled Umali, sinking down closer, intoxicated by her heat, how it sang her body awake in ways she'd never dared to go hunting for.

Inez wanted to be as comfortable with greed as Umali.

Umali chuckled, her breath hot as she nuzzled into Inez's neck, kissing the hollow beneath her ear. "Aren't you happy I'm alive?"

"Happy you almost got yourself killed protecting me?" Inez retorted, turning Umali's head to inspect the long scar bisecting her hairline just above her ear. She parted Umali's hair and traced the scar, strange and raised, with a scale-like pattern demarked by faintly gleaming copper edges. Inez hoped it was the lamplight playing tricks with her eyes.

Umali hummed in appreciation, leaning into Inez's

fingertips. Inez threaded her fingers deeper into her hair. She admired how the lamplight caught the reddish undertone in its blackness, like blowing over a dark coal to reveal the internal glow.

"Happy I convinced you to take an unnecessary risk?" Inez chided softly. All the sharpness had leaked out of her tone, replaced by a hushed awe at Umali's beauty.

"I'm happy you protected my crew. I couldn't have shielded them all," Umali countered. She pressed a soft kiss to the corner of Inez's mouth. "What I was trying to say before you stormed off and I got distracted by how prettily you sulk is that I've thought of a way to help you put this ghost of yours to rest."

"Mmhhn?" Inez inquired, far more interested in catching Umali's lips for a proper kiss.

"The Codicíans have put out a call for privateers to aid them in retaking Aynila. On such an invitation, we might be able to slip into Simsiman long enough for you to discover if your sister truly has become a Codicían saint."

Inez blinked down at her in shock. "You'd really take that risk for me?"

Umali carded Inez's hair back from her face and smiled toothily. "Let's finish this hunt together."

"But first..." Inez needed to taste and steal just a bit of Umali's easy confidence. She leaned in, catching those smiling lips with hers.

Umali wriggled beneath her. She ran heated palms down to the small of her back, lower, hitching Inez close, squeezing, until Inez felt like hot wax in danger of combusting under her hands. Inez entwined their legs, gripping with her thighs, just like they'd been entangled in the water. Only now, the desperation between them was as bright and gilded with promise as the dawn. Inez was determined to catch it, in her teeth if need be.

Umali nuzzled her face into Inez's neck, her chin knocking the dull ache in Inez's shoulder into sparks of pain, and Inez yelped.

Umali pulled back this time, shifting the ties of Inez's sarong, revealing teeth marks sunk into the big scar that curled over her shoulder. She turned Inez toward the light. The bruising had taken on strange colors over her dark scars, the paired red crescents scabbed and swollen.

Umali hissed. "Now that doesn't look like gratitude at all."

She pressed her lips apologetically to Inez's shoulder.

"Wouldn't be a crocodile healing if no one was bitten," Inez joked. She lifted a hand to the tie of the sarong and let the cloth fall away, the muggy night air as close on her skin as Umali's warm breath. "Now come back here. I'll give you a matching one, if you want to be even."

"I'd like that."

Inez gasped, all cleverness obliterated as Umali feathered kisses light and hot as the lick of candle flames down her front, into the valley between her breasts, before kissing her way to each summit.

Inez let her own hands roam, sliding Umali free of borrowed clothes, marveling at the lean brown body she exposed. So wonderfully like her own, all the weathering and scars a part of the greater whole. So interesting in the ways she differed—her muscled arms, and if she'd ever had half the body hair Inez sported, it'd burned off her arms and porpoise-sleek legs in firetender antics, save for the soft patch between her muscled thighs. And the way their legs tangled back together, fitting so well, a pressure and heat just where

Inez needed as she latched her mouth onto the tender salty skin of Umali's throat and left a mark of her own.

Umali was busy conducting her own exploration, the heat of her hands and then her mouth bringing sparks of pleasure to places Inez hadn't known could feel so good. And between them, that slick, easy friction stoked the fires in Inez's belly to roaring flame. Inez stepped into the inferno, trusting as she had every time before that Umali wouldn't allow her to be burned.

In the bed-of-embers aftermath, Inez drew languid circles with the tips of her nails across the small of Umali's back, liking the way her toes curled and pointed. The muscles of Umali's leg bunched and pressed to the apex of Inez's trembling thighs, where she was hot and so perfectly melted.

41

LUNURIN CALILAN NG DAKILA

The next morning, they alighted on the beach in a small guilalo temporarily borrowed from the Sumila fleet. Lunurin eyed the shining bronze lantaka cannons that were set into the rocky black outcroppings, hemming the white beach in on both sides. As promised, for the exchange the Sumila fleet had abandoned their blockade. Lunurin and Sina were alone. *Good.* There would be less collateral damage that way.

"Close enough?" she asked Sina.

Sina wiggled her fingertips experimentally. "Oh yes, perfect."

Lunurin surveyed the well-armed party that had gathered to meet them on the sand. The pirates were a motley mix of sailors and warriors from across the archipelago and farther afield, Tianchao and even Moklayu.

There'd been a time when even unarmed Stormfleet supply ships would have been utterly off-limits even to those so far on the edges of society as these. After all, wind and waves sank all ships in a storm.

But since the Stormfleet had splintered, all that had changed. Now, apparently even pirates felt bold enough to hold gods-blessed against their will—not just for ransom, but for indentured servitude. Fury at such audacity crackled over her skin.

The overcast skies darkened, thunder rumbling in the distance. *"We should teach them caution."*

Lunurin took a deep, calming breath. She would not ruin this hostage exchange as she had the last one. The static kiss of electricity on her skin faded; she and her goddess were of one heart and mind. This was not about diplomacy or winning allies. The clear, shining solution to this problem stretched before her, bright lightning drawing the shortest path between sky and land.

The sand shifted underfoot as they crossed halfway toward the pirate captain leading the negotiation.

"Stop there! Are you the stormcaller and the firetender? I want proof I'm not being tricked!" the captain called.

Lunurin gathered up a coil of wind and sent her words across. "I can control a breeze enough to fill three ships' sails."

Sina spread her hands, sparks of fire hovering over her fingertips. She clenched her fist and they went out. They must appear to be ordinary gods-blessed, not the pair who had washed the Palisade into the sea. Just two Stormfleet gods-blessed who were weak enough to be offered up by their captains in exchange for more lives.

The captain nodded, satisfied, and sent men to the guilalo to unload boxes of "dye" and "silk" onto the sand.

Lunurin counted the Stormfleet hostages: twenty men and women. She picked out Captain Lihat's husband, Bati, a tall dark man whose mutya was in a dozen mother-of-pearl inlayed bangles worn on both arms.

"Satisfied?" Lunurin asked, eager to move this along and get the hostages clear before the pirates discovered "dye" and "silk" were only water and provisions.

The pirate double-checked the promised numbers of crates and sacks and nodded, cutting loose his hostages.

"Is that everyone?" Lunurin went to Bati, as if she were an old friend, bidding her farewells.

"Those that are still alive," Bati confirmed, with a baleful glare at his captors. He struggled across the sand with a noticeable limp. Many of the hostages were wounded.

Lunurin embraced him, her orders quick and low. "Push off from the beach and brace yourselves. The sails are lashed tight. Stay clear."

Lunurin stepped back from the line of captives, returning her attention to the pirates, who watched her sharply for any sign that she and Sina meant to make a break for the guilalo. But with their injured, and on the open beach, before so many drawn weapons, an attempt to run would be foolish.

Sina counted with a subtle thrumming of her internal fires: *one, two, three.*

The guilalo had just pushed off from the beach when Lunurin brought down a wailing wind.

"*We will let them know what it is to hunt Stormfleet as prey.*" Anitun Tabu's words came howling between the tall black cliffs.

The sails cracked like a whip and the guilalo was flung out beyond the rocky outcropping into open water like a cannon shot. Her wind tore through the pirates' ships where they sheltered in the cove, capsizing a number and crashing them into the rocky cliffs.

The pirates who'd been unloading the ransom were closest and rushed them, weapons drawn.

"They're clear!" Sina cried, confirming that the little guilalo was beyond cannon range.

Lunurin let down her braided bun. The howling winds she'd called began to whip and coil, driving sand into eyes like needles and burrowing into the skin. Sina threaded her hands together and sent a wave of flame outward. Metal heated, buttons and buckles soaked in heat, scalding skin. Necklaces and arm cuffs became a dangerous agony. Swords and stolen rifles dropped to the sand, too hot to touch. They threw themselves to the ground, trying to put out their burning clothes.

Lunurin swung around to meet the pirate captain and his motley army as they rushed to the aid of their miserable fellows.

"Surrender!" Lunurin demanded. "Surrender now and I might let you flee. I am Lady Stormbringer. I've destroyed far greater fortresses than this mound of rock."

But the pirates were smarter or more desperate than she'd given them credit for. The captain had seen what became of his other men. He ordered his remaining crew to throw down metal weapons and jewelry outside of Sina's range before rallying them for the rush.

"You can take two unarmed women!" he cried.

Men had thought so before. Men had been wrong.

They rushed across the beach with a ragged cry, wielding bamboo spears, wooden clubs, a few odd whips and weighted flails. The twisting dervish of Lunurin's winds caught spears as they were thrown, hurling them harmlessly into the sand.

From the armaments on the cliffs, crews manning the cannons scrambled to take aim. Lunurin would leave those to Sina; cannons were her specialty.

Sina reached deep. Every island had a sleeping heart of

fire that was never far from waking. The ground shivered. Fissures opened at the base of the volcanic cliffs, fractures traveling upward through brittle stone. Cannon shots went wild, driving a bloody furrow through the line of men trying to fight past the wall of Lunurin's wind.

Lunurin grasped a spear. Drawing static along the tip, she swung it through the air, casting fireflies of lightning out in a wide arc.

"*Run, if you wish to live*," Lunurin commanded, her goddess burning in her eyes, the storm gracing her skin lightly as a kiss.

The pirates flinched back. Their captain goaded them on. "It's a bluff! She's exhausted herself! If we attack at once, we can overwhelm them!"

The specks of lightning she'd cast hovered just over the sand, guides for the fury of the goddess in the gathering clouds overhead. Lunurin waited a beat, two, letting the pirates get close.

"*Lintik ka!*" she cried, and drove the base of her spear into the sand.

The simultaneous lightning strikes shook the beach, leaving glassy scars. Men collapsed mid-step, burned alive from within.

The survivors screamed and broke, some up toward the cliffs, some toward the water and the ships that Lunurin's winds had made kindling of. Lunurin gathered her storm of tangling winds, twirling it tighter and tighter, a fine cyclone sucking up sand and water in a frothing turbulent rope. She swung it out, catching the pirate captain by the leg and dragging him back.

"Let's try again. I'm Lady Stormbringer. I have questions about a certain firetender pirate captain sinking slave ships in the Sumila Gulf. If you can answer my questions, I won't kill you all like the rats you are."

The man shook his head, wordless. Sina swept out wide arcs of flame that caught in the thin beach vegetation, forcing men who'd been fleeing up toward the high ground of the cliffs back onto the beach. The fires caught on the rack and ruin of the cove, the few ships that were still seaworthy trying to avoid burning flotsam.

"We could smoke them out!" Sina sang helpfully.

"I'm told her name is Umali. She sank a Lusitan slaver leaving Aynila last week," Lunurin said, tightening the lasso of wind till it began to scourge the man's flesh.

"She's not here! We don't run with her kind. The *Agawin*'s captain is crazy! She's a demon who sinks foreign ships for fun. She'll take prizes no one sane would attempt."

"Did you think a few tide-touched captives would let you attempt such prizes?" Sina shook her head. "You fool. They'd have sunk your ships before you made it over deep water."

"Where can I find her?" Lunurin pressed.

"She hunts the main trade routes farther south. She rarely comes so far north as this. The prizes aren't rich enough."

Lunurin had a ship name and a direction. It would give Alon's spies something to run down if they lost Inez's trail. For now, she had to focus on ending the threat of pirates in the Sumila Gulf to Stormfleet ships. She nodded to Sina, who let the cliffs and the ships burn.

Anitun Tabu's voice carried across the ruined cove. "*Let it be known that the Stormfleet is under my protection. Those who think fleet ships are easy prey will have to contend with my fury.*"

Lunurin dragged down a stiff prevailing wind that drove the fires up into the pirates' nest, and pushed the burning wreckage across the cove to the leeward side where it burned hot and green with salt. The survivors fled inland, desperate to escape the smoke.

Finally, Lunurin and Sina swam out beyond the ruin they'd made of Inalikan cove to be hauled aboard by the rescued Stormfleet captives. Lunurin set their little craft skimming out toward the agreed meeting point with the rest of the Sumila Stormfleet.

They were welcomed aboard Captain Lihat's ship as heroes. Tales of their exploits and rout of the pirates were eagerly shared by the grateful hostages. Lunurin listened to the retelling, watching warm reunions across the fleet. She was hopeful that gratitude would prevent the tale from souring the way so many had toward her and her power after Talaan.

She was rewarded when Captain Lihat and his husband Bati approached her, having seen to the worst injuries among their rescued crewmates. Lihat bowed to her. "The Sumila fleet is in your debt."

"The service your fleet provides Aynila and all the ports in the gulf is invaluable." Lunurin hesitated—but she would find no more favorable ears than these. "In usual times, I would leave you both to care for your wounded and reorganize your fleet, but I must ask if you will grant us your expertise and ships one more time."

"Our expertise in these waters is at your disposal. I owe you the lives of my crews and my husband." Lihat was effusive, but Bati seemed more reserved.

"What need has Aynila of Stormfleet ships when they have a stormcaller with as much power as you?" he asked.

"The calamity we face cannot be solved by my power alone. The old gods smile on Aynila, but that has not saved us in the past. A Codician armada was sighted in Hanay a week and a half ago. If the seasonal winds hold, they could reach Aynila in as little as a week. We're seeking allies among the Stormfleet to aid Aynila's allied fleet in sinking the armada before they can blockade our city."

Lihat hesitated. "In the midst of the wet season, I would feel in dereliction of my vows to the Stormfleet if we abandoned the Sumila Gulf to make a stand for Aynila."

"And I would not ask you to leave. The Sumila Gulf is ideally located, a confluence of waters where the armada will meet with their reinforcements from forts in the central archipelago, before they move on Aynila. Your knowledge of the gulf would be invaluable to Aynila's allied fleet, as it was to Sina and myself today," Lunurin insisted.

"You think we stand a chance against a Codícian armada? I have lost hundreds of lives and dozens of ships over the years to Inquisition galleons."

"Because you faced them alone. Because as an archipelago we have always been many peoples divided by our islands, our rivalries. Unity has never been our strength. But if we could stand together, we would be hunted in our own waters no longer. Aynila needs allies today, but we will not forget who aided us. Together, we could end the threat of Inquisition witch hunts and pirate attacks for all of us. I want a future in which the Stormfleets are strong and welcomed in every port."

Captain Lihat considered her. "I fear that if a handful of pirates can deprive me of three ships and crews, we will not be the allies you hope for in the battle to come. But I am no fool to ignore the direction of the prevailing winds. I have not seen a stormcaller with such power in a long time. The Sumila Stormfleet will join Aynila. Let us lay a trap the Codícians will remember for generations."

42

◆━━◆

ALON DAKILA

Alon wanted to tear his hair out. He'd convinced his
brother not to murder their best leads on the assassins—
but his luck had ended there.

Word of the assassination attempt spread along with
Jeian's enthusiastic efforts to ensure the Lakan's security.
Relations between their allies had grown especially tense just
when they most needed to trust one another.

Jeian hadn't reacted well to learning the assassins had
petitioned Captain Tomás first, asking him to bring them
before the Lakan. It had taken Alon and Aizza combined to
keep him from outright accusing Talaan of colluding in the
attack. Alon's best efforts to convince Captain Tomás that
the issue wasn't his religion were getting somewhat lost in
Jeian's zeal.

After a particularly difficult round of meetings regarding
chain of command among the allied captains, Tomás had
come to meet privately with him.

"Gat Alon, I get the feeling that me and my captains are

no longer as trusted as Aynila's other allies. Did we not swear over the same cup as everyone else? In fact, we promised ships and men to Aynila's aid long before any of the inland rice kingdoms or Ísuga."

Alon winced. "Of course we have not forgotten this. I pray you will forgive the stress we have all been under since the attack."

"I do regret any role I might have had in putting Lakan Dalisay in danger. I hope you will convey this to the Lakan and Gat Jeian for me."

"We would never hold you to blame. Aynila's difficulties with converts are not new." Alon rubbed absently at his bad hand. The long hours of meetings had kept him in the brace too long.

"I do not believe you make them easier by your actions. If you drive men into darkness and secrecy, they will meet dark allies," Tomás observed.

"I see the wisdom of your words, and the Lakan does as well. She has done her best to unite Aynila, both converts and traditionalists. It has been a delicate time."

"Precisely because it has been so delicate, I make my offer. Rather than arrest so many, Talaan would be willing to accept converts into exile. I can hardly believe all of them are spies and assassins. Most are perfectly innocent of any wrongdoing."

"As were *most* of the petitioners my mother met with," Alon countered. "But I will take your offer to the Lakan. If you would let me make one in return?"

Tomás waved him on.

"Consider again my offer of tide-touched to guide your ships. Half the difficulty of these endless discussions over formation and chain of command is that the others are so unsure of how to work alongside your ships."

"I assure you that in an actual battle, the technological advances of our ships and weaponry will be more than enough to even any advantage your untried volunteers might offer."

It was true that Talaan had leveraged Codicían building techniques. Their hybrid karakoa were twice the length and width of Ísuga's greatest warships, large enough to be outfitted with stolen cannonry that rivaled the firepower of Sina's and Hiraya's best work.

"Just think on it, as I will think on your offer," Alon repeated.

43

❦

INEZ DOMINGO

Fort San Pedro in Simsiman was a four-sided stone fortress that squatted overlooking the port and mouth of the river. Barrier islands further sheltered the port from the strait that ran between Simsiman and Mamaylan.

Behind the fort, the church of La Punta rose starkly red and white toward the summer thunderheads hanging heavily over the city. Vast fishponds lined both edges of the winding riverbanks, like pools of captured sky.

Simsiman had been an early Codícian stronghold in the archipelago, built upon a joining of sea-going channels where the three central islands came together. There had been a gold-rich Moklayu vassal state here before the Codícians arrived, and the region retained their strong ties to the distant archipelago in the south.

As they'd made the journey from Lusubin, the crew had slowly stripped away and hidden all the *Agawin*'s identifying elements. The flame-like pennants decorating the laho's crested mane were stowed, a white flag of parley run up in its place. They'd shrouded the laho-carved prow itself with sailcloth. The entire crew had to hide their mutya, tucking medallions, bracelets, earrings, and anklets out of sight. Inez hesitantly removed her necklace, looping it around her upper arm under her sleeve and hiding her balisong knife separately in the wrappings around her calf. Finally, she wheedled with their crocodile entourage till only Himig remained, swimming after them as the rowers took the oars and they let the northeastern wind fill their sail to enter the port.

As they crossed under the shadow of the great gun towers on the southern corners of the fort, Inez reached out and clutched Umali's hand in hers, letting her lover's heat banish the chill of old fear. They'd be in and out long before anyone thought to test a band of pirates for witchcraft.

They laid anchor a little way out from the protected port, not wanting to make a sudden approach that might be taken as an attack. They were met by the harbormaster. Inez hung back, unsure if she feared more being recognized by any survivors from Aynila, or as a water witch. She let herself melt back, lost among the crew while Umali negotiated their entry.

Umali waved her white flag in a friendly manner, Lim translating for her in rough Codicían. Inez had declined to act as translator, not wanting to stand out in any way.

"Hello! We've heard Simsiman is paying good money to hire privateers to help retake Aynila. Aynila is rich. We'd like a share of the plunder."

"Big talk, but we've got all kinds of riff raff showing up looking for easy money."

Umali unfurled the Lusitan slave ship banners, two, side by side. "No easy money. We're professional privateers, hunting Lusitan slavers for Tianchaowen bounty."

The harbormaster seemed interested, but shook his head. "Aynila is overrun with water witches. If you'll turn tail and run at the first sighting of one, you're no good to me."

Umali smiled widely and unveiled the laho-carved prow. "This was a Stormfleet ship, till we killed her crew and took her for our own. There's nothing faster or more maneuverable. We'll be valuable against the Aynilan fleet."

The Codicían finally cracked a smile. "Now that is impressive. Tie up on the leftmost pier. You'll hear from the port authority soon."

~

Inquiries around the port revealed they were in luck. Santa Catalina had just ended a period of seclusion in honor of the solemnity of the Most Holy Body and Blood of Christ. She would be in attendance at today's Sunday Mass. A rare and precious opportunity, as she rarely made public appearances. They were warned to arrive early if they hoped to gain a blessing from the saint herself.

Inez had told Umali a dozen times she needed to do this alone. But Umali insisted that none of the crew were going ashore on their own, and Inez was no different.

They slipped deeper into the crush filling La Punta church—standing room only—hours before the Mass was set to begin.

After all the churches she'd visited since leaving Aynila, Inez hadn't expected this one to affect her. Unlike the others, abandoned by their holy orders, the church in Simsiman felt like stepping back through time into the Palisade. The rituals and prayers, even the overwhelming scent of the incense censers, it was like nothing had changed. Inez hated it. She did not ever want to be back in this moment, back in this place, back in the time when she'd been so vulnerable and afraid and no one had seen what was happening to her.

Inez half expected to look up and see Lunurin in her Santa María, Our Lady of Sorrows vestments, dutifully doling out blessings to the parishioners for the Saint's Day Festival. Inez remembered suddenly how Catalina had envied Lunurin the role she'd been allowed in the Church ritual. Had she at last found the sainthood she so craved here in Simsiman?

Fleetingly, forgetting the army Santa Catalina was supposedly raising, Inez hoped she had. Catalina's happiness did not have to look like her own. She wanted to believe that the sanctity and purpose the Church had promised weren't all lies and empty words. Once upon a time, she'd believed them too. The rituals and rigors of convent life had seemed a wonderfully steady thing to rely on in comparison to the desperate poverty that had forced their mother into a miserable, violent marriage. Until it hadn't been able to protect her or keep any of its vaunted promises.

Inez processed through the motions of the Mass, Umali mimicking her a half-beat behind. Luckily in this crowd, any missteps would be impossible to see.

Inez wanted to leave. She wanted out from under this roof, away from the prayers. She didn't want any part of this empty pageantry. But she'd come this far. She had to know. She had to know what had become of her sister.

As they entered the concluding rites after communion, Inez's attention sharpened. The greeting and blessing would be soon. The father leading the service bid all those who had gathered for Santa Catalina's blessing to come to the front.

Inez froze, terrified suddenly that the veil and distance might be enough to disguise her from the casual observer, but not her own sister. The crowd around them made the decision for her, eager petitioners pressing forward toward the altar.

As Santa Catalina was at last led out from the vestry, a hush of reverence fell over the crowd.

And for one terrible moment, Inez thought it was all a trick. Some other woman masquerading as a saint, just as Lunurin had done in Aynila. This was not Catalina at all. It couldn't be.

The poor woman was bent, almost hobbled with age. She required the aid of two altar boys to walk. All that was visible of her were gnarled and skeletal hands pressed prayerfully before her.

Hemmed in by the eager crowd, there was no choice but to shuffle forward, getting closer and closer to the bent old crone. She had been brought forward to the communion rail, where she knelt and held out a silver rosary, the glittering beads hanging down from her grip like a spill of pearls. The congregation knelt before her one by one, pressing her hand to their brows in mano po, heads bowed to receive her blessing.

At this distance and over the push and mutter of the crowd, Inez could not make out her words. Instead, she listened to the congregation.

"My brother heard her speak in tongues!"

"They say the spear wound of Christ manifested in her side!"

"My mother said it weeps holy water."

"They say she had a vision of the reconquest of Aynila!"

"My father is a captain. She granted him a blessed rosary that will protect him from drowning at the hands of water witches when they retake Aynila."

These last words were a shock of cold water, reminding Inez why she'd come: she mustn't let Catalina bring Aynila to ruin again.

Grown men wept, kissing the glinting rosary beads. Women ushered their children forward, hissing and prodding until they had gotten the saint's blessing. And then it was Inez's and Umali's turn. Inez knelt, dipping her head down to press her brow to the saint's fingers.

Finally, she caught a glimpse of the silver crucifix clutched between those skeletal fingers.

It was Lunurin's. Inez recognized the delicate detailing of the tambourine beads, the rust still evident in the deep hollow recesses where worshipful fingers could not polish it away.

The saint murmured a blessing and finally she recognized something of her sister in this strange, sunken shell of a woman. She'd have known Cat's voice anywhere: whispering in the dark; harsh with crying; murmuring low in prayer; crying out in fear. Inez had never heard it like this. She looked up.

The saint was no bent crone. Catalina stared down at her, face hollowed and skeletally drawn. Her eyes were half-lidded and unfocused, with none of the blade-like sharpness they'd always had. Her lips were cracked and bloody, a strange white ring about them as she continued her ceaseless, unintelligible mutter.

Inez strained her ears and picked up on scraps of disjointed psalms.

"The floods engulf me.
I am worn out crying for help—
When the waves of death surrounded me,
The floods of ungodliness made me afraid—"

The sing-song cadence of the psalms were all wrong, interspersed with bouts of unintelligible "speaking in tongues" that the petitioners had spoken of.

Not Codicían, not even Aynilan. A mishmash of sounds partly belonging to both languages.

Catalina was shrunken, her white habit hanging from bony shoulders. Her once full, soft body had collapsed in on itself, as if she'd spent her weeks of seclusion ravaged by fever, or the intervening years in famine.

"Catalina?" Inez's voice was too loud, her horror a living, breathing thing inside her. She seized her sister's hand, trying to snap her out of whatever strange reverie possessed her.

Cat did not respond. She did not even seem to register Inez's words or presence. This was nothing at all like the festival pageantry Lunurin had once participated in. Catalina's sainthood had ravaged her body and mind, leaving behind a frail shell muttering liturgy to be trotted out by the Church as an object lesson in piety and penance.

Inez wanted to be sick.

Umali intervened before she could draw the attention of the priest overseeing the farcical ritual. "Do not monopolize the saint's time, there are others who would like to petition her," she chided, dragging Inez away from her sister and out of the sea of people desperate to receive Santa Catalina's blessing.

Inez wanted to scream. She wanted to beg Catalina to see her, to wake up, to tell her what had happened in Canazco. But in this terrible place, it was like the Inez who'd sunk ships and killed men to find the truth had never existed. She was just a frightened little girl, terrified the priests might notice what was wrong, and even more terrified that no one would.

Inez shut down. She did not fight Umali, who pulled her back into the transept. She knew how to pretend everything was alright. She knew not to rush. She didn't push, following the flow toward the doors at the shuffling pace of the crowd. She stopped at the holy water font, performing the sign of the cross properly. She even thanked the ushers.

She did not run until they were halfway across the church plaza.

She wanted to cast herself into the waves and wash away the shadow of herself that had possessed her inside that church. Could it also wash away the memory of what had become of Catalina? She wanted to run, and not stop. She wanted to point the *Agawin*'s prow toward deep water and leave everything she'd discovered behind.

Umali caught up to her before she made it to the port. "Inez, slow down!" Her voice carried, a battle command Inez's body had learned to obey.

She stopped. All the flight drained out of her, replaced with a bone-deep exhaustion. Umali caught her at last and after one look at her, steered her under the overhang of one of the roadside food stalls, ordering something wrapped in a banana leaf to secure them a spot at the low table that had been dragged out into the street.

"What happened in there? Was that your sister or not?" Umali asked, trying to pull Inez around to face her.

Inez closed her eyes to block out Umali's warm, searching gaze. "It was." Saying the words aloud made it worse. So much worse.

"What happened to her? She didn't seem... well."

Inez shuddered all over. "I've never seen her like that. She was devout, a true believer. But she was never... I thought it was someone else, some frail, senile old woman, but—it's her, horribly, terribly changed. I don't think she even knew I was there. She didn't know any of us were there!"

Inez suddenly remembered all those pitiable, tortured

female saints Catalina had always talked of with such zeal. Santa Lucía, who had gouged out her own eyes rather than have a man remark on their beauty. Santa Margarita, whose indulgences and discretions of youth were atoned for in her later years of penitence and fasting. Santa Catalina, and her visions of devils and angels. She'd spent the past years in religious ecstasy.

What had the Church done to her sister?

44

LUNURIN CALILAN NG DAKILA

Captain Lihat made good on his word. He gathered the three other stormcallers of his fleet, and they were joined by two who had broken off with Kalaba from the Calilan contingent, women who seemed leery of Lunurin, but remained at her tiya's side out of longtime loyalty.

"Let me show you how the Sumila fleet has stayed ahead of Inquisition witch hunts all these years."

The others sat shoulder to shoulder in a circle at the center of the deck, each stormcaller leaning over and braiding half their hair together with the person to their right. A light misting rain fell, the skies overhead darkening slowly. Lunurin held herself back, afraid to interfere in the ritual.

But then Captain Lihat opened a space in the circle and extended a hand, inviting Lunurin to take her place among them.

"Wait!" This was Tiya Kalaba, her face creased with worry. "Lunurin is different, not just powerful. Anitun Tabu burns within her. I have seen it, and I've seen gods-blessed driven mad by less."

Captain Lihat did not close the circle. "If you are fearful, step back now. I, too, have seen how our goddess moves through her. There are some things I would risk to brush so close to Anitun Tabu, if only for a moment."

One of the stormcallers from Calilan stepped back. None of the others moved. Lihat extended his hand once more to Lunurin.

Lunurin had to blink back a sudden rush of unexpected emotion. For so many years she had been alone, the only stormcaller in Aynila. Before that, she had been a disappointment and a danger to the stormcallers of Calilan. She had never dreamed of being invited into a ritual working such as this.

She stepped forward, taking a seat between Lihat and the young woman beside him. She reached up and loosed her hair. It uncoiled heavily down her back, piling up behind her on the deck. With her pearl-topped hair prong, she divided her curling mane, handing the left half to Captain Lihat, and hesitantly extending her hand to the young woman beside her. She was not much older than Rosa, handing over a silken fall of hair that had just reached the small of her back. Like Rosa, she had not been growing it out for the many years Lunurin and Lihat had been.

Lunurin followed Lihat's lead, twining their hair together like abaca fiber ropes, twist and counter twist, tethering herself to the younger stormcaller. As she finished her work, pinning the base of the twist together by weaving her mutya hair prong through the joined strands, the intimacy and sanctity of the moment overwhelmed her.

Unbidden tears ran down her cheeks, the rain coming down harder. *"How long has it been, my children, since so many gathered in my name?"*

Lunurin felt her goddess rise up within her, reaching out

to the other hearts joined to hers in the circle, a conduit by which Anitun Tabu's voice could reach them without driving them mad. Lunurin turned her face up to the rain and sang out in thanksgiving to her goddess for her blessing. She waited, breathing deep, gifting the others the moment in communion with their shared goddess.

"Will you rise with me? They are coming, killers and thieves, holy men with empty words and killing pyres."

Lihat's hand closed around hers spasmodically, his own tears mixing with the rain. "High Lady of the Heavens, Anitun Tabu, Goddess of Storms and Vengeance, we are honored to serve."

Together they were cast up on the northeastern winds. The distance stretched, farther than Lunurin had ever traveled, even with all her goddess's power at her disposal, even with Alon as her steady anchor.

Bound securely together with so many others, her sense of herself did not thin. Her power did not dissipate upon the endless winds. Sparks of seed lightning spun, coiling tightly, twisting the clouds, just as the stormcallers had twisted their hair.

Together they gazed down through the great eye of the goddess's storm. Lunurin beheld the Codicían armada, like a herd of great black wild boar huddled together against the worsening storm.

The Codicíans were wise to the weather tricks of the tropics. Teams of rowers labored at the oars, fighting the storm winds. Men sweated over the bilge pumps, keeping the great fortresses afloat. Their sails were stowed, timbers treated, and bellies of gunpowder netted in iron chains against lightning. Each galleon sported sixty guns or more. Lunurin had never in her life seen more than three such ships in one place; now, there were twenty coming to destroy Aynila.

But she was not alone. Anitun Tabu's power was anchored and amplified by the weaving together of all her children.

"They have scattered our people, divided and conquered. Let us show them what it is to fear the storm."

Lunurin reached out to the others and together they spun their storm stronger, the winds faster, sowing lightning and hail. A hungry waterspout chewed off the oars of one ship, leaving it unbalanced, spinning helplessly. On and on they worked, as the tenuous connections to their bodies pulled them slowly and inexorably back toward the Sumila Gulf. As they went, they sowed the seeds of a dozen new storms, unfavorable crosswinds and pockets of hot dead air. It was a working of such scale and distance, Lunurin could never have accomplished it alone. But she knew, having seen the armada's size, that their storm had bought them time, not triumph.

She sank back into her body, back into a woven circle of stormcallers, now slumped upon the deck in various states of utter exhaustion. She shared a bloody-minded smile with Lihat.

"Let them enjoy our warm welcome."

"I hope they choke on it," Lunurin agreed.

The others laughed with her, vicious and pure in their shared fury and the nearness of their goddess. Lunurin desperately hoped that Aynila and her allies would survive the coming clash. She wanted to be able to share this feeling of communion with Rosa. She'd never dreamed she would have the chance to share such community and connection with others like her. She'd been too long isolated and alone. She'd forgotten what it was the Stormfleet did so well. Binding together gods-blessed, making mere humans strong enough to face the typhoon.

Once they had unraveled their circle, Lunurin turned to Kalaba, who had tears running down her cheeks.

"Oh, Lunurin. What if we were wrong about everything?" her tiya cried.

Lunurin rushed to her, taking her hands. "Wrong? Nothing is wrong. No one was hurt. See!"

"We trained you to always hold yourself separate and away from others, for fear of the damage you could do. We kept you away from working with other stormcallers. It was because of what it did to Halili when she pulled you from the arms of Anitun Tabu when you were twelve. But I see you now. How you have grown into your power and your balance with your goddess and somehow... I have to convince her that all our fears were unfounded."

Lunurin folded Kalaba into her arms. "You will. *We* will get that chance. And to make sure, we must send your fastest ship. They must take word of the armada's location back to Aynila."

She needed Alon at her side for what was coming.

45

ALON DAKILA

Alon made eye contact with Isko, seeking assistance to steer the gathered captains into safer waters. Jeian would be no help—since he'd recently learned of Talaan's private meetings with the Lakan and Alon. He wasn't taking it well.

Isko only signed, "No help for it," barely suppressing the chagrin that pinched his expression.

They'd gotten their teeth into the topic of what must be done if they reached the Sumila Gulf and Lunurin had gained no new Stormfleet allies. The fact this would be a death sentence was, unfortunately, apparent to everyone in the room, and tensions were running high. Various proposals turned some allies into sacrifices while others would fallback to make a final stand in Aynila.

After Tomás put forward a particularly cutthroat plan, Nihma declared, "It should be Talaan that takes the greatest share of the risk. Ísuga has already sacrificed too much for Talaan's freedom."

The fight was breaking out along the same lines as it always did: hardliner traditionalists versus Christian converts.

"Ah yes, of course—you've never had to live crushed in a Codicían fist. Ísuga could pull out of this alliance tomorrow. Where do you think the Codicíans' will turn their sights after burning Aynila, except the second shipyard they lost?" Tomás shot back.

"At least I trust Nihma won't waste energy bending over backwards on behalf of spies and assassins," Jeian said.

The ideological rift was growing difficult even for Alon to bridge.

Still, he wearily waded into the middle before things came to blows. "Can we focus on the problem at hand—"

Jeian turned on him. "You stay out of this. It's no mystery where your sympathies lie."

Alon took a long, deep breath. "I don't know what you could possibly mean by that."

Jeian sneered. The long days arguing in circles were taking their toll on his brother, who far preferred action to talk. They were all growing short and tired as the date of their departure got closer and the dangers more apparent. "We all know that if it weren't for your wife's Codicían ties, Calilan's Stormfleet might have stood by us."

Alon kept his voice very steady. "I hardly think you are implying my wife is anything but dedicated to Aynila's defense. She has gone ahead, with only five ships, to delay the Codicíans in any way she can. It is more than any of us can say for our efforts."

"Then explain why you're still covering for her traitor of a sister. We all know what Inez did. You are as soft on spies as Talaan," Jeian spat.

Alon stared at his brother for a beat, two. They were all under so much stress. But Jeian had promised not to scapegoat Inez. Some things were simply off-limits.

Alon hauled back, and punched Jeian directly in the face. The raised mother-of-pearl inlays of his brace cut his brother's cheek open.

The meeting devolved from there.

46

◆

INEZ DOMINGO

Inez might have given in to her initial revulsion at what had become of her sister—might have fled headlong from Simsiman and all she'd learned—but by the time they reached the *Agawin*, an armed squad of conquistadors were waiting to escort Umali to a meeting with the port authority.

Inez should have melted into the background as a crew-member of no significance. But the idea of leaving Umali alone, surrounded by enemies, went against every instinct of the battles they'd fought together. She couldn't do it. And so, Inez found herself escorted beside her captain into the fort. The vast stone curtain walls closed around them like a tomb.

"So, you're the captain sinking Lusitan's ships?" a terribly familiar voice inquired. And Inez realized none of this was about faith or fate at all. It was a trap whose teeth had just sprung closed.

Abbess Magdalena looked up from her desk, her eyes raking over them sharply. She was entirely recovered, it seemed, from the lingering illness that had forced her to leave Aynila to seek treatment in Canazco. It angered Inez to see her so hale, when Catalina seemed to be teetering between death's door and madness.

"It's a trap," she whispered in Aynilan, desperate to warn Umali.

Umali's spirit burned suddenly bright. Her gaze roved over the guards, the towering stone walls, the guns on the parapet. Calculating the odds and improvising a plan. But they were alone, far from the sea, separated from the *Agawin*, her crew, and even Inez's crocodiles.

Inez hoped that the years would disguise her. She sank back behind her captain, who strode forward, all glittering distraction.

"Yes. We're a crew of privateers, and the Tianchaowen bounty for slavers has been generous. We've come to Simsiman to see if your offer might be as enticing."

"We're offering first run at the sacking of Aynila once the city is retaken," was Magdalena's opening offer.

Umali frowned. "We get paid in silver for Lusitan prizes now. I hardly see why I should join a months-long siege in hopes of rewards that might not materialize."

Magdalena scoffed. "With the might of Canazco and all of New Codicía behind us, I hardly think the siege will last longer than a week—"

She locked eyes with Inez. Hers, so bright and green, widened in recognition. She smiled beatifically and pointed at Inez, as if she were lower than a dog. "Seize her."

Inez did the only thing she could. Instead of spinning back-to-back with her captain and fighting—dying here at her side—she flung herself across the room, putting her back to the wall.

"You tricked me!" she cried, her voice high, brittle, accusatory.

Umali held her gaze for a beat, two. Her hand was on her kampilan sword, half drawn. She sheathed the blade and smiled at Magdalena. "You've a sharp eye. I thought you might be interested in our Aynilan stowaway."

The words cut deep. Even Inez almost believed them.

The guards at the door lunged for her. Even knowing it was hopeless, that she was entombed in stone walls, too far from the sea, Inez fought back, her balisong knife clenched in her fist like a claw. But her opponents were armored. She surprised the first man, who fell clutching at the gushing wound under his arm, but the others were careful, keeping her back with drawn sabers. She fought hard, but without the advantage of her tide-touched balance upon a pitching deck she was quickly subdued, her mutya stolen from her.

Through it all, Umali stood aside, all the great heat of her constrained so tightly, Inez could not feel the flicker of her heart nor the fire of her spirit. Could not even draw on her strength to try to break free. Inez was alone. And it hurt. It hurt, even knowing it was better this way. She had no right to bring Umali down with her.

"For her weight in silver, we will fight for you," Umali countered Magdalena's offer.

Magdalena accepted gladly. "I can pay you a finder's fee now, the rest to be delivered before we sail."

Inez began to laugh bitterly.

She wanted to weep. In all her time in the convent, she'd never been worth so much to anyone. Now, betrayed, abandoned to her enemies, she was worth more than a Lusitan slaver. At least Umali would be paid for the trouble of ferrying her so far. Inez hoped she and the *Agawin* ran as fast and as far as the winds would take them.

Umali accepted the bag of silver and walked free without a single glance back. Inez wished she'd never laid eyes on her. Had she really kissed the lips that had just leveraged her downfall for silver?

She was dragged to kneel before Magdalena's desk, her mutya thrown down on the table before her.

"If it isn't little Inez Domingo. Catalina will be so happy you've come."

47

ALON DAKILA

His inay hissed in displeasure as she tended to the vivid bruising purpling on Alon's bad hand. Jeian's face had been harder than he'd expected.

Across the same small healing room, Aizza muttered recriminations over Jeian's busted lip and cut cheek.

Alon refused to be the one to make peace this time. He was tired of being the one who was constantly expected to do the right thing.

As if sensing his thoughts, his inay swatted his shoulder, signing, "I expect better of you!"

Alon grunted, but managed not to ask why she didn't expect better of Jeian. He knew he was being childish. He knew there were bigger, more immediate problems than the fact his brother distrusted his wife and her family. But he felt so helpless stuck here in Aynila, plying at reluctant allies with Inez lost at sea, and Lunurin headed directly into the teeth of danger. She'd nearly killed herself trying to delay the armada; without his anchor, who was to say she wouldn't again?

Jeian spoke first. "I shouldn't have said that, but knowing Aynila's survival is in your wife and her goddess's hands is a terribly helpless feeling. For all her power, Anitun Tabu is a fickle goddess."

"Lunurin is not fickle. You were not here. You have not seen how long and hard she fought for Aynila, for our people, when winning even one life back from Codicían cruelty was a triumph. She stayed and kept the fist from closing."

Isko pushed open the sliding door. "Forgive me, Lakan. As happy as I am to see we're back on speaking terms, I regret to inform you the Talaan contingent has set sail without orders."

Alon and Jeian leaped up and ran for the entrance of the temple complex. They stared out over the wide stretch of the bay, where the hybrid ships from Talaan were indeed setting sail.

"Let us hope they are tucking tail and running home, and not about to tell all our plans to the enemy. We should've known better than to trust converts," Jeian spat bitterly.

Alon watched the departing contingent split, making way for a Stormfleet ship flying Calilan's colors and skimming into the bay at such speed it actually pulled several Talaan ships in its wake, rowers laboring at their places as they were dragged backward toward the port.

Alon and Jeian rushed to meet the ship and learn what news from Lunurin had required such speed.

With fresh news of the armada's progress—mere days' sail in good weather, perhaps a week given all the storms the Sumila fleet and Lunurin had laid in their path—Alon made a decision.

"We take whoever will come and whatever supplies we can lay our hands on, and we meet Lunurin in the Sumila Gulf. We sail tonight."

48

INEZ DOMINGO

The cell was so bare and dim, it took Inez a long moment to realize she shared it with Catalina. It seemed a more fitting place for a prisoner than a saint. Even the simple utilitarian convent of Aynila had been the lap of luxury and indulgence compared to their current quarters. The room had only a woven rattan mat on the stone floor for a resting place. A slit window let in a sliver of grey, overcast daylight. Beside her sister's waterlogged prayer book, there was a simple wooden bowl, and in the corner a bucket for necessities.

Inez could hold her arms out and touch each wall, so long and narrow was the cell. All she could see from the window were the church towers.

The distance from the sea and her mutya knife was a spiritual flaying, layers of protection ripped away and shredded. But she'd hoped she might be able to see the port. She didn't know if she'd wanted to see the *Agawin*'s berth empty and know they were safe. Or confirm she'd been truly abandoned.

Inez tore herself away from the sliver of light.

Her sister lay under a threadbare blanket on the mat, barely seeming to breathe. Inez crept to her side, half afraid of what she would discover.

Catalina lay on her side, not sleeping, but not aware either, her half-lidded eyes flickering restlessly back and forth, her lips moving in ceaseless prayer. Her hands were clasped together before her, knotted around Lunurin's silver rosary.

"Catalina, Ate, it's me, Inez, your sister Inez, I'm here." Her voice came out strained and fearful. Inez hated herself for it. "Catalina! Wake up!"

She shook her sister gently, trying to rouse her as if from sleep. But Catalina reacted no more to her presence now than she had in the sanctuary. Inez frowned at the material of her sister's habit. As the woman in Masbad had described, the cloth was heavy, thick and rough. It might be wool, but seemed coarser. Alon would not have used such stuff as sacking to pad dye bottles, much less as clothing.

Bending closer, she nearly gagged at the terrible stench of decay. Peeling back Cat's lips, Inez's fingers touched the rime of salt clinging to them. She rubbed her fingertips together in confusion. She bent again to examine Cat more closely. Her teeth had grown brittle, broken and translucent in places. There were open bloody sores on her tongue and inside her cheeks.

Inez had heard of ascetic orders of nuns who took vows of poverty and penance, but this ruination went beyond Inez's worst imaginings. Captives from the bellies of slave ships, suffering months of malnutrition, contaminated water, and lack of sun had been in better health.

She reached for the bowl of water, wanting to help her sister rinse her mouth. But when her fingertips dipped into the bowl, she realized it was saltwater. She scooped with her fingers, trying to gather it into a globule in her palm, blinking in confusion when it drained away from her until she remembered they'd stolen her mutya.

So why had they left her with saltwater? It couldn't have been as a temptation to Inez. It had already been here when they'd shoved her in. And why were Catalina's lips lined with salt?

Inez did not like to think on the possibilities, deciding instead to keep trying to make her sister comfortable. With only the mother-of-pearl necklace still hidden in the folds of her salwal waist wrap, the pearl of her balisong knife far from her, she couldn't pull the saltwater, but she should at least try to flush her sister's mouth sores. She'd have to lift her up to keep from drowning her.

Cat was so frail, Inez was terrified she'd hurt her. As she lifted, Catalina cried out in pain. But at last, she roused, her gaze focused, not on Inez, but on the bowl. She grasped for it, pulling it toward herself with a sudden frenzied energy.

"Easy, easy." Inez tried to stop her. "Let me help you rinse your mouth."

But Catalina had already dragged the bowl to her lips, swallowing a large gulp before Inez tore it away from her.

Catalina paid her no mind. Instead, she grabbed for the bucket in the corner and began to hurl, purging the Holy Communion she'd taken during Mass in a terrible, wrenching, gasping gurgle.

Was she purging her meals so regularly that they now provided her with the saltwater to achieve it?

Inez stared at her sister in frozen horror as she at last slumped back to her mat, her back to Inez. She returned to her muttered psalms. She might not have noticed Inez at all.

Half in terror of what she would find, Inez gently rolled her sister flat on her back and tore open the shirt. It split in her hands easily; dry rot had long ago set in, weakening the fibers.

Inez gasped. Layers of overlapping gouges had merged into a vast network of scabs and abscesses etched across Catalina's breasts and torso in the shape of the cross. Her side was one massive bedsore, gone black and necrotic where her hip pressed to the thin mat and stone. Her skin hung loose from her body; dehydration and starvation had melted the flesh from beneath it. Drinking saltwater rather than fresh would have sped up the process. Her sister moved bent and hobbled like an old woman because of the pain of her body rotting before she was in the ground.

Was it starvation? Infection? Or saltwater poisoning that had so addled her as to induce hallucinations and delirium? A proper healer might have been able to tell, might have been able to help, but Inez was neither. In her state, Catalina was not strong enough to endure what she'd done to Umali, even if Inez could recover her mutya and get her sister to the sea in time.

There was the scrape of a key in the door. Inez scrambled to cover Cat with the rough-spun blanket. An animal should not be kept in such conditions, much less her sister.

The desperate fury she'd spent the last weeks learning to wield broke through her horror. She lunged to her feet and grabbed up the wooden bowl, determined to kill whoever came through that door with her bare hands.

The door opened and Pedro de Isla stepped through. Inez pulled her savage downward swing with the edge of the wooden bowl a few bare inches from his eye. They blinked at each other. Alon's spy was dressed as a father of the abbey in a black cassock.

Pedro flinched back, belatedly, his hand with its two missing fingers rising to shield his face. "Good God! You would deprive a man of his eye when he's already a cripple!"

Inez growled at him. "Serves you right for surprising me."

"You're a hell-cat, just like your sister." He reached into a pouch and handed over her balisong knife.

Inez did not ask if he meant Catalina or Lunurin. She wasn't sure she wanted to know. Instead, she clutched her mutya tight, hiding it away.

"Good, let's get you out, so I can get paid." Pedro urged her toward the door.

Inez did not move. "My sister."

Pedro shook his head. "I never found out if she's actually here. I've never made it this far into Simsiman before. Be glad I made it to retrieve you. Do you know how hard it was to gain access to the cloister?"

"She's right here." Inez pointed behind her to the frail body on the floor.

"Good God." He crossed himself.

"Your god had everything to do with it," Inez spat.

"Can you revive her? I did not plan on an escape with an invalid."

"We have to try. What's the point of springing me from this trap and leaving the bait?"

Pedro grimaced, but went to help her try to rouse her sister. As they lifted her, Catalina cried out again. Inez winced. How had they gotten her into the church for Mass?

"Santa Catalina, time to go, you need to get up. You are late for Mass," Inez tried.

Somehow, this did get through to her. Cat's eyes flashed open, wheeling and bloodshot. She moaned. Her protest was a meaningless jumble of sounds and broken words. She held out the rosary as if to ward off the devil, and Inez seized upon it. "Catalina, I'm taking you to Lunurin, the one who gave you this rosary. I'm bringing you back to her, back to Aynila. Just stay quiet and come with us."

Catalina's crazed eyes focused on her for one brief, terrible moment.

"Aynila," she mouthed, then her eyes rolled back in her head. "Burning, endless burning. Pyres from hell, the rising waters of the flood will not extinguish them. They burn and burn. I hear their screams! I smell their roasting flesh!"

With each word she grew louder and louder. Pedro backed away from her in terror. Inez slumped down, her poor mad saint of a sister thrashing in her arms. Cat used the pointed end of the cross in her hand to gouge at her own chest. Blood ran anew as Inez struggled to wrest it away from her. But Cat's grip on the rosary was the only strength she had left.

"We have to go!" Pedro urged. "Leave her. We run, or I'll never get you out."

Each bony ridge of Cat's spine dug into Inez's chest, harsh as the wounds she'd re-opened down her front. They'd never get her out, not like this. But how could Inez leave her tearing at her own flesh, her teeth crumbling in her mouth, her body slowly rotting around her? Her mind lost to holy deliriums… and her guilt.

She was dying.

She was dying, and Inez knew no healer skilled enough to fix this ruin. If they left her, the Codicíans would only drag out this suffering long enough to use her against Aynila and Lunurin all over again. And Cat so clearly did not want that, plagued as she was by her visions of tide-touched pyres. She was already so weak—did she have weeks, or only days?

What mercy was there in leaving her to die alone in this

stone cell to be used by their enemies? Inez would put down a dog rather than see it suffer so.

For the first time since she'd been named to the old gods, Inez knew why she had been chosen by Aman Sinaya, Merciful. For so long she had thought it was a mistake, some cruel cosmic joke, proof that her personal spiritual failings could transcend any religion. What else was a ruined nun and a tide-touched who couldn't heal?

Inez dragged the spilled saltwater back to her hands.

It was a mercy Catalina would never have thanked her for. A mercy she wouldn't have believed in. But Catalina had once placed the salvation of Inez's immortal soul above her survival of the abbot's cane. Now it was Inez's turn to decide. For all Catalina had done, all the lives lost to her betrayal, all the pain and agony she'd caused, and all she now suffered.

Inez asked the yawning black desperation in her belly. She asked the deep and distant sea, and all the blood she'd spilled to get here.

There was no salvation in suffering, no glory in penitence. Death should come quickly.

She pressed her hands to her sister's temple and kissed her brow.

Inez sent her down with one hard push, quick as an undertow. Catalina was so weak, her mind maddened and scattered, she had none of the usual resistance of consciousness to a healer's persuasion. She sank with one final strangled whimper down into the still and silent depths.

She went slack and still in Inez's arms just as the door burst open. Several sisters and priests rushed into the room. Pedro melted back into the sudden crowd, one brother among many.

"Get away from the saint!" someone cried.

Her sister's skull felt thin and fragile as an eggshell in her hands. Inez stared down into her face, lax and restful at last, no broken psalms or visions of doom. With one hard twist, Inez snapped her neck. All Inez's breath hissed out of her, long and harsh, aching in her throat with a crocodile's resonant song of grief and shattered nests and too many enemies to count.

"Demon! Devil! She's murdered Santa Catalina!" a priest screamed, trying to drag her away from Cat. Her balisong blade came to her hand, flicking open smoothly.

She silenced that one with a roar. Blood red on the hungry edge of her blade, spraying hot across her face. But she was only one tide-touched with a small knife and a handful of saltwater.

As she was disarmed and dragged at last from her sister's broken body, Inez let go of crocodile prayers, wailing high and loud to no one at all. The sea was too far, her love had left her behind, her sister—Catalina was beyond all their treatments and torments now.

49

❖

LUNURIN CALILAN NG DAKILA

When the ships from Talaan were sighted coming up from Aynila, Lunurin was relieved. She'd feared Aynila's allies would be unready to join them despite her message of urgency and the nearness of the approaching armada. Though it surprised her to see none of Aynila's, Ísuga's, or the inland rice kingdoms' pennants mixed in among the approaching ships. It seemed odd that they would've outpaced the rest of Aynila's allies without any tide-touched or stormcallers to speed their progress against the wet season winds.

Nonetheless, Lunurin organized a ship with a greeting party to guide the Talaan fleet out from the original agreed-upon meeting place where Aynila Bay met the gulf to where the Sumila fleet waited.

She called out a greeting to Talaan as their scout ship approached. "Captain Tomás, we are pleased to have you join us, may I guide your ships in to join our allies in the Sumila Gulf?"

There was no flagging raised to signal their answer.

Sina scanned the fleet again with a spyglass. "Maybe they didn't hear? They're not slowing."

Captain Galang, who had elected to join her to guide the new ships into the Sumila fleet's, shook her head. "Your allies do not look very friendly right now. They've put all hands to deck—to ram, or pull a runner."

Lunurin sent her voice again across the waves. "I am Dayang Lunurin Calilan de Dakila—"

The breeze carrying her words was blasted apart by the tailwinds of a warning shot that landed just short of the Stormfleet ship. Lunurin eyed the trajectory. Codicían cannons had far greater range and accuracy than most native lantaka ship-mounted guns. They'd missed on purpose.

Galang signaled her crew, and quickly reversed the currents guiding their ship closer to the Talaan fleet, getting clear of the larger fleet's intended heading. "I'm no strategist, but that seems downright hostile, even if they've decided to pull their support and hide out in Talaan to wait out the results of the battle."

Lunurin was suddenly incandescently furious. She'd shattered years of work at alliance building for Talaan's freedom. *And this was how they would repay her generosity? Did they think her a gentle goddess? She was the storm.*

The sky overhead darkened and thunder cracked like shattered vows. Talaan had shared blood and wine with the Lakan. They had taken a vow before all the old gods, and Lunurin had sealed it with her own blood. The fury of her goddess coiled within her to strike, a cyclone budding in the clouds over the Talaan fleet.

But Lunurin hesitated. She had shattered the Codicían shipyard in Talaan. Had Talaan ever had a choice but to throw their lot in with Aynila? There had already been so much death and destruction, and there would be more yet. Did she want it to begin by killing the very people she had put everything on the line to save?

Sina sensed it and seized her arm, pressing heat and all a firetender's certainty into her. "They will join our enemies. How else will they bargain for their survival after the destruction of the Talaan shipyard, except by turning traitor and bearing word of Aynila's defenses? We will have to fight them either way. Better to end it now, before we must contend with galleons as well. Together, we could stop them now."

Galang nodded grimly. "We are only a single ship, but I and my crew will stand with you."

"No. We don't know for certain. Like Calilan, they might simply be unwilling to die for Aynila, and I'll not force them to. I won't turn on our own before we've even seen our enemies with our own eyes." Lunurin pulled back her winds, guiding their ship farther out of the path of the Talaan fleet, clear of cannon range.

Galang frowned after the Talaan ships as they headed toward the eastern horizon, but said nothing.

"This is war. Ask the tide-touched what came of never striking first," Sina said.

Lunurin shook her head. "This is not how our fight begins. Not here, against the very people I shattered our alliances to free."

50

INEZ

In Magdalena's turbulent fury, Inez recognized so much of Lunurin it was eerie. Like a terrible, twisted reflection in polluted waters of a future Lunurin could have had if they'd remained in the Church. If she had grown old grasping for power within convent walls.

But no. Inez shook herself. For all that Lunurin shared her aunt's knack for power, and the particular line of her jaw that throbbed and knotted as she ground her teeth, she would never have let anyone come to such harm under her care. Especially not Catalina.

Inez's hands had been shackled before her. She held them turned outward, not touching. The salt of her sister's drowning had dried in a fine grit across the lines of her palms. The crystals prickled her skin when she closed her fingers, making her lungs quiver dangerously. She wanted to wail and gnash her teeth and make more of them bleed, but she was among enemies and alone. She must not show Magdalena any vulnerability. Crocodile armor was good for more than swimming rough waters.

"Have you any idea how much effort you've undone?" Magdalena cried.

Inez cocked her head. She borrowed Himig's tone of lazy curiosity. "Did you mean to kill my sister more slowly?"

Magdalena glared. "Do you know how hard it is to make a saint? I've done it twice—though Lunurin was rather a failure in the end. Leaving Aynila was my mistake. But I learned, and your sister—your sister was a masterpiece. We've only been in Simsiman a few months and Santa Catalina had them all groveling at her feet, desperate for a brush of her holiness, willing to kill and die for her blessing."

"She would've been dead either way in a few weeks, maybe less." Inez said the words so calmly. Her heart twisting in her chest, her palms prickling. She needed it to be true.

Magdalena blinked, brought back from her vision of saintliness and the power she gained by propping it up. "If she'd cooperated like Lunurin, I wouldn't have had to be so drastic. She was already having the visions in Canazco. But she refused to return with me."

It hurt to realize her sister had tried not to be used against them all a second time. Inez did not want to imagine the myriad little agonies nuns were so good at inflicting, and how quickly penance-driven Catalina would've succumbed to them. She'd always been so given to extremes, so guilty even of life's loves and pleasures. And that was before she'd betrayed them all.

"So you tortured her until she went well and truly mad."

Magdalena sniffed. "I can hardly expect you to under-stand the deeper mysteries of faith when you fell over yourself to offer your soul up to devilry, murder, and witchcraft. No wonder your sister left you behind."

Such words had lost the power to sting Inez. The reality of the reward Catalina had won for her faith was simply too terrible. She'd been such a fool for chasing ghosts.

Inez needled back, "You're just upset your trap caught me and not Lunurin. How many priests did you lose spreading your rumors of my dying sister? Would you like to know how many I killed? How they prayed? Your Santa Catalina couldn't save them from drowning."

"Animals. God only knows why my brother insists you can be brought into the arms of civilization." Magdalena glowered. "I never should've taken you off the hands of your whore mother."

"I wish you hadn't." If she'd been abandoned, unwanted from the beginning, it would've hurt less than losing everything like this. "Better for us all if I'd never become a Church foundling, never been baptized Inez Domingo."

Inez had severed whatever tie remained to that old self when she'd snapped her own sister's neck, rechristening herself in saltwater and Codicían blood.

"Perhaps, but all things are according to His purpose." A concerning thoughtfulness came over Magdalena. "It's true I never expected to catch you, and I had plans for your saint of a sister before you decided to undo all my hard work. But you will be a fine replacement for her as my bait. I made Lunurin. Do you think I don't know how she can be unmade?"

Inez scoffed and tried not to believe the terrible zeal in Magdalena's gaze.

"You'll see for yourself. We set sail to join the armada's attack on Aynila tonight."

51

LUNURIN CALILAN NG DAKILA

To Lunurin's incalculable relief, Alon and the allied fleet of Aynila arrived in the Sumila Gulf only a day later.

They only had time for a quick embrace. Lunurin pressed Alon's cheek to hers, breathing in deeply the salt of his skin, the sea breeze, and the bitterness of clinging indigo dye that followed him wherever he went. "You're here."

She had no words now for all that had passed since their furious parting, but Alon's strong arms clasping her close were enough.

"Would that I had as much luck wrangling our allies as you clearly have."

Lunurin smothered a grimace at the reminder of her complicity in the failure with Talaan from beginning to end. After the aborted altercation with their fleet, she'd storm-gazed again with Captain Lihat. The Talaan deserters were on course to join the Codician armada and showed no indication of turning south toward their home port, just as Sina had warned.

She pulled away from Alon reluctantly to perform all the proper introductions between the Sumila fleet captains and the allied leaders who had come from Aynila.

The plans laid with Talaan were summarily discarded when Lunurin confirmed their duplicity. Worse, Alon had had word before they'd left Aynila that Simsiman had raised a fleet of privateers and registered ships, sighted in the southern waters of the Sumila Gulf—no doubt to join and aid in the resupply of the Codicían armada after their difficult crossing.

Taking the various headings of each fleet into account, it soon became apparent that there was only one logical place to make their stand.

The Tumaga islands were a cluster that defined the eastern edge of the Sumila Gulf. They would be an ideal place for the Codicían armada to refresh their reserves of water and food before circling around the treacherous reefs of the complicated island network and making the final leg of the journey to Aynila.

For the same reason, the Tumaga islands would provide the ideal terrain for the allied fleet. Their extreme tides, unpredictable currents, and shallow channels edged by razor reefs made it a difficult crossing for those without gods-blessed to guide their ships. At this time of year, the islands saw four tidal changes in a single day, with as much as seven feet of rise and fall. The tricky coastline of the dozen uncharted internal isles and reefs would make it hard for galleons to pursue fleet ships without risking a reefing. If the galleons could be lured into an engagement during the false lull of high tide and tricked into giving chase into the dangerous waters between the islands before the sudden two-hour fall to low tide, the allied fleet would have a fighting chance.

"Of course, it's not the full advantage we'd have had when the Codician fleet didn't have local allies perfectly capable of chasing down our ships among the islands," Jeian observed.

"Without tide-touched among them to craft their currents, we will still have an edge on Talaan. I was not going to sink allies for a change of heart, just as I did not prevent Calilan's Stormfleet from going their own way," Lunurin said.

Jeian shook his head angrily. "Your hesitation is what made Talaan go so wrong in the first place. Are you a stormcaller or not?"

Lunurin did not flinch. "So I am. I am a stormcaller, and you should be ever so grateful that I hesitate. Look at me! A goddess of vengeance weighs my hand and whispers in my ear, ever urging death, destruction, and retribution. Hers is a fury that knows no hesitation. You do not wish for me to abandon every human mercy and uncertainty. You do not wish to face the storm without my mediation. Why do you think we have gods-blessed and katalonan to ease the way between our gods and our people? We could so easily be annihilated by the ferocity of their elemental nature. Ask your wife what feats of healing and perseverance it takes her to prevent you from breaking your own bones and tearing your muscles to shreds when you move with all the strength of the sea flowing through you."

This, at last, seemed to make Jeian rethink any further rebuttal.

Lunurin shook her head. "If you would turn the fury of my vengeful goddess on all who hesitate, all who flee rather than face the coming calamity, how then would we be any better than the Codicians? What kind of ally would that make us?"

"We could've fired on them as they fled Aynila, and we

did not," Alon interceded, re-grounding the argument. "And if Simsiman has raised privateer and pirate allies, we were just as likely to face native ships before Talaan's defection. Lunurin made the right decision. Now, together we must forge the best path forward that remains to us."

This, thankfully, pivoted the conversation back to the logistics of reaching the Tumaga islands before the Codicían armada or support ships from Simsiman.

52

INEZ

The entourage they dedicated to transporting her to the port was almost funny. With her feet chained together, her head and arms clasped in a wooden stock, she could barely wriggle. Magdalena did not trust that stealing the pearl of her mutya would have declawed her entirely.

Despite the odds, Inez scanned the port for any chance at escape. She saw so little to turn to her advantage. The *Agawin* was gone, and the sea was painfully dull and distant with only her mother-of-pearl necklace. She strained to listen for crocodile whispers, but heard nothing over the surf.

Even without the pearl of her mutya and bound, if she could cast herself into the water, the sea might not let her drown. Or it might, but at least Magdalena's trap would be empty. It was a risk worth taking.

She waited till they had gotten her aboard a shoreboat and were rowing out toward a massive fifty-gun galleon, before she lunged to her feet and toppled herself into the waves.

She struck the water, and the relief at the contact, at

not being alone and far from the sea, sang in her veins. She began to sink, the depths welcoming her in. But then the buoyancy of the wood stocks lifted her back to the surface. Her chains pulled tight, dragging her toward her captors, a fish on a line.

Shouted orders sent sailors into the water after her. They struggled against the clasp of the sea to drag her aboard, and Inez heard a faint whisper, *"Little sister!"*

A scream, as one of the sailors in the water was dragged down. Himig surfaced, her golden banding like sunlight through palm fronds, as she cut through the water, silent and hungry. Her jaws opened wide, her sharp teeth already red.

There was a crunch of wood as she tore oars free, and more cries as men fell into the water, conquistadors sinking fast. Amid the chaos, Inez heard the sharp blasts of gunfire. Himig roared in pain. Even her thick armored hide was not impenetrable.

"Run!" Inez tried to croak a crocodile warning. *"Run! They have guns and harpoons and—"*

But her buwaya couldn't understand her without the pearl of her mutya, her power stolen from her hands.

Himig snapped down on the chain tying Inez to the shoreboat and rolled. Blood poured from so many wounds down her side. The strength of her roll tipped the shoreboat, spilling more Codicíans into the sea, but it wasn't enough to capsize. The waters were red, salted with so much blood, so much of Himig's blood.

She rolled again, dragging Inez briefly under, weaker this time, weakening. A harpoon lanced down, sinking deeply into the softness of her belly.

"Please, please," Inez begged. *"You have to leave me. Swim far away and never come back."*

Himig rolled once more. Another shoreboat pulled along-side, guns raised, harpoons at the ready.

"*I enjoyed our hunts, little sister.*" Himig let go.

With the last of her strength, she launched herself half aboard the second craft, snapping and tearing until finally, struck through with six harpoons, bleeding from uncounted bullet wounds, she stilled. Her clawed forelegs went limp, and she slid down into the water where she floated still and quiet beside Inez, her crocodile songs and whispers silent.

Inez wept and screamed as she was ripped from the arms of the sea and dragged down into the belly of the flagship galleon. There was a painful kind of symmetry to it. She'd killed their saint, and they'd killed her anito.

It was such a small tragedy among all the horrors, but somehow the grief of her sister and her buwaya piled on top of each other magnified. Inez felt herself breaking. There was not enough armor in the world to insulate her from Umali leaving her behind so easily and the *Agawin*'s absence. Her sister's last breaths against her neck. Himig's blood now drying on her skin. The black desperation in her belly writhed, cutting Inez deep.

She was alone. And from this trap there would be no miraculous escape. She would be used against her family in Aynila, just as they'd planned for Catalina. Would that she had her mutya. If only she could make herself heard, surely the laho might help her drag this galleon and all aboard to the bottom of the sea.

Better she die now and let Lunurin and Alon think her a traitor and a coward who'd run after ghosts and never returned.

53

ALON DAKILA

He discovered Rosa first.

While redistributing Aynilan healers to new berths to ensure all their ships would have enough tide-touched to navigate the difficult waters of the island chain, he found she'd somehow traded places with one of his tide-touched students and gotten herself taken along with the allied fleet. In a healer's robe borrowed from the infirmary, to the untrained eye she did look a great deal like the other trainees he'd brought aboard.

"How?" Alon deadpanned.

"Bernila helped," Rosa admitted, her hands twisting together.

"Who'd you trade with?"

"One of the other healers from Talaan. She had family among the defectors. She didn't want to fight them."

Alon winced. He'd not thought of that risk in the rush to gather their remaining allies and join Lunurin.

"Please don't tell Lunurin! The fleet is so large, she never even has to know I'm here," Rosa begged.

"If you are going to be Lunurin's student, then this is an important early lesson. She *will* find out. It's best to come clean as soon as possible."

And if Lunurin decided to leave them both stranded on a deserted island instead of getting Rosa killed, so be it. Alon had made so many mistakes these last weeks; he'd not repeat this one. He ordered the captain to run up the flagging to signal to Lunurin aboard Kalaba's ship.

~

Static crackled over his skin with the promise of lightning, but Lunurin didn't shout. The distant rumble of thunder conveyed enough.

Rosa's rivers of explanations flowed over her. Lunurin released a long slow breath, the sweetly metallic scent of lightning breaking apart before a cool sea breeze. "Go, you will remain with Kalaba. She has experience reining in willful young fools."

Rosa went without another word of protest.

Alon pulled Lunurin away into the cargo hold of the Aynilan Indigo merchant ship, sensing she needed a moment of privacy. Time had grown perilously short now till they would face the Codicían armada. Who knew when or if they would find a moment alone in the crush of the fleet?

"What more can go wrong?" Lunurin's frustration sank claws into his skin.

"I'm sorry, I've failed you again."

"I just wish there was time or some way to get her clear of this. She's only been a stormcaller for a few weeks!" Lunurin lamented.

"Sending her to Kalaba was a good idea. She won't do

harm to anyone and will be as safe as she can be," Alon assured her.

Lunurin flung herself into his arms. Alon seized her close with a desperation he had not dared show before all their allies. Lunurin returned his grip, strong and solid and here with him. He hadn't lost her yet.

"I've made so many mistakes. They just keep piling up. Are you sure I made the right decision?"

Alon pulled back to meet her gaze, trying to understand the uncertainty in her voice.

"I know you will always defend me, especially to your brother. But truly. Have I doomed us all by letting Talaan go, by letting the Calilan Stormfleet fracture?" Lunurin asked.

Alon cradled her face in his hands. "It should never have been solely upon you. Not the Stormfleet, not Talaan. You have not doomed us. No matter what, I trust you. Always. Always."

Even in the dimness of the hold, he read the doubt on her face and it buried daggers in his heart. Because so very recently, he hadn't trusted her. Not enough to tell her the truth. Alon's chest ached. How had he hurt her so trying to protect her? "I'm sorry that I ever made you doubt that. Forgive me. I should have told you about the rumors of Catalina much sooner. I was so afraid to lose you that I may have destroyed our family. But it was my fear talking. It has nothing to do with you or anything you've done. Do not doubt yourself because of my failings."

Lunurin kissed him. It was a different kiss than their parting one had been, the fury and hurt a distant memory.

"I love you. I will always love you. And today I love you because you don't think I'm some invulnerable instrument of vengeance or a disaster waiting to happen, but a woman whose heart might crave protection."

Alon held her in his arms and prayed to all their gods that he'd be allowed to protect her through what now came.

~

The sails of the armada were visible on the horizon before the full scope of their doom became apparent, like white-winged seabirds hovering over the floating carcass of a whale. And for all that Lunurin had described to him their enemy from storm-gazing with the others, Alon was wholly unprepared.

Their decoy ships were strung across the mouth of the deepest channel access to the Sumila Gulf; the proverbial needle the deep-drafted galleons must thread through the Tumaga islands, to reach Aynila. Hidden all along the channel, the rest of the allied ships lay in wait. They would divide and reef the incoming galleons who took the bait of hunting the decoy ships retreating toward Aynila. But rather than continuing to close in on their decoys, the galleons laid anchor in the deeper waters beyond the gulf, ignoring the easy prey of Aynila's allied fleet.

To add to the problem, they'd missed the window for the quick drop of the turning tide. The channel was now nearing its lowest point. It would be hours before the tide rose and their ploy had a chance of working. Their decoy force would be easily wiped out before then.

Alon shared a tense look with Lunurin. They waited—and finally saw a ship under a white flag bridging the gap.

Alon narrowed his eyes and saw that it was one of the hybrid shipbuilds from Talaan. *Traitors.*

Jeian's flagship fired a single shot, which landed just short of the ship, a stark, cold message. *Near enough. Relay your message from there or be sunk.* It was only fair.

The voice that called across the water spoke Codicían, but even with a spyglass Alon could not pick out the speaker among the many gathered on the deck of the Talaan vessel. "Abbess Magdalena requests a parley with María Lunurin de Palma under the blessing of Santa Catalina of the Rosary. She proposes a meeting on the beach to discuss how this standoff may be resolved peacefully."

The past loomed large. Alon was back on the bridge facing the Palisade. His inay was burning and his wife was going over to the enemy with nothing but a fishing spear and her goddess in her eyes.

Lunurin took his hand in hers, anchoring him. "No matter what they try with Catalina, we go together. Not alone. Never again. Together, we are strongest. Together, we can stand against anything."

"How will you respond?" he asked.

Lunurin shook her head. "My aunt wants to lure me out. Why else spend so many lives spreading the rumor of Santa Catalina? You were right to fear it. Somehow, she has laid a trap for me. How do you think we should respond?"

Alon wanted to say, *Let's sink the messenger. We don't have to listen to any more lies. We can force them to retaliate and chase us into the narrows.*

But the huge floating fortresses across the water were so large, and so many. In comparison, their "fleet" was but a handful of fishing boats. How had they imagined they would sink just one galleon, much less twenty?

They weren't in any position to be hasty.

"Let's let them talk," Alon decided. "If only to delay till the tides are in our favor."

He called their reply across the water. "We will not parley on land. But if the abbess would like to meet with Dayang

Lunurin Calilan ng Dakila, we will meet her over the open water between our two fleets. No onboard cannons."

Alon refused to revisit this nightmare without every advantage that open water would grant him and Lunurin both.

54

LUNURIN CALILAN NG DAKILA

She'd be happy if she never again faced a family reunion over deep water, under stormy skies. Lunurin let the rowers close the distance with the Talaan vessel that had finally returned from the enemy lines bearing her aunt. They were both now flying a white flag, but Lunurin did not rush them along, unwilling to tip her hand, or hurry into a trap. She and Alon had boarded a Stormfleet supply ship, one of the few among the allied fleet without cannonry. The Talaan ship had had to be refitted, cannons unmounted and hauled away.

They needed time for the tide to rise. Right now, the smartest thing for the armada to do would be to send their privateer army to hunt down Aynila's allied fleet among the islands while the galleons sailed safely around to raze Aynila to the ground.

Like her family from Calilan, Abbess Magdalena had long ago formed an opinion of Lunurin: useful, malleable, an element she fully understood and knew how to control. Years had hardened the idea into place. There was a chance that no matter what she'd heard, Magdalena's logic would easily dismiss all the rumors of the Palisade's destruction as the freak weather of the tropics. The rest could be explained as the doings of the Lakan, a known and dangerous water witch, intent on utilizing the reputation of Santa María, Our Lady of the Drowned, for her own ends. After all, that was exactly what Abbess Magdalena herself would have done.

Lunurin squeezed Alon's hand, reminding herself that she had him at her side. She was not alone.

"I'm with you," Alon assured her. Lunurin half wished she'd kept Sina at her side too, but it was bad enough that she was walking herself and Alon into a trap to buy a few hours. Adding Sina to the mix of potential losses was too high a risk. Jeian and Isko, in rare agreement, had been against it from the start.

Lunurin studied the privateer fleet. "With the water this low, they've even more reason to send the privateer ships to wipe us out, without a single galleon weighing anchor."

The two ships pulled alongside each other, close enough that Lunurin could have leaped across to the other deck to embrace her aunt—or hurl her into the sea.

The abbess looked well, healthier and stronger than when she'd set sail for Canazco. Lunurin wished she'd perished on the south sea crossing like so many before her.

Lunurin did not speak. She would have been happy to send Magdalena to the bottom of the sea without engaging in this foolish parley at all. But. Alon was right. Every moment they delayed the clash with the armada till this evening's second low tide drop meant a greater advantage for the Aynilan fleet. At least she was walking into the trap with her eyes wide open.

"No greeting for me after all these years apart? I'm wounded, María. Are we not family?" Magdalena called out.

"Are we?" Lunurin inquired. "As I recall, my father never acknowledged my claim. I'm surprised you have not also sworn me off after all that has passed."

Abbess Magdalena waved this off. "Your father's disregard for the waters of the womb is all well and good for an archbishop. His is the public arena of God, guns, and gold. But women understand where blood truly lies thickest."

"You know him so well. Is that why you always do his dirty work?" Lunurin asked.

Magdalena smiled beatifically. "I know you too. You've always been happy to make yourself useful to the winning side. Surely you can see you've made a mistake. Why die here? Look at your so-called allies. Do you think a handful of canoes can stand against the might of the Codician Empire? You've already lost more than half your forces. How many broke and ran when Talaan abandoned you?"

"How many missionaries did you sacrifice in your machinations and schemes?" Lunurin countered.

"So they did find you. I hoped they would. Don't you want to ask me about dear, faithful Catalina? You sent her into my hands so very trustingly."

Lunurin had already hardened her heart to this. She wouldn't take the bait. She leaned into the deep calm of Alon's spirit, and let it buoy her up.

Magdalena cocked her head and smiled, studying Lunurin's expression. "Oh, I've made you angry. You always did have such a soft spot for that woman."

Alon spoke now, easily taking up the slack. "What are your terms? Why bother with this parley at all, if you're so sure you can retake Aynila?"

Lunurin took a deep breath. She'd let go of Catalina long ago. Magdalena could not hurt her with such barbs.

"The husband. I'd wondered if you were rendered as mute as your witch mother. Fine then. Our terms: retreat now. Leave Aynila undefended. I'll even let your little family of heretics sail off if you never bother us again. We'll be able to take care of the Lakan and her temple to false gods as easily as we did the first time."

Alon bared his teeth. He'd lost too many to Codicían pyres. And Lunurin would die before she let such horrors be revisited upon Aynila.

She stepped up to shield him from her aunt's barbs. She had so much more experience hardening herself to them. "And if we won't?"

The trickling of time had never felt so slow. She and Alon had hoped they might, with the back and forth of negotiation, fritter away the long hours till the turning of the tide returned the channels to a depth the Codicían galleons would chase them into. With the shallower water, the dangerous shoals of the Tumaga islands were much more apparent. Any sane captain would call off the chase far too quickly, before the crews with tide-touched and stormcallers had a chance to run them aground. But looking into her aunt's suddenly eager expression, she knew they'd made a mistake.

"I'll make your family of heretics smaller now," Magdalena promised, with the same cold, vicious smile Lunurin had turned on her own enemies.

A flag was run up, signaling to the other galleons.

Lunurin pivoted quickly, trusting Alon to guard her back against Magdalena, prepared to defend against whatever trap was about to spring closed. Would the galleons really open fire on them with Magdalena so close?

On the flagship, Lunurin finally saw her father, Archbishop de Palma. So like him to hang back in comfort and safety, letting others do the legwork. Then they hauled a small woman up out of the hold, chaining her up on the foredeck before a firing squad.

It was Inez.

"No!" Lunurin cried out before she could curb her reaction. Every ounce of power she could bring to bear coiled within her, lightning in her blood, a storm on her lips. *"So many of the sea's children have been lost. We will not let another slip through our hands."* Her goddess's lament was so much power at her back, a maelstrom of fury to be unleashed upon her enemies.

But Magdalena had woven a spell of her own, one of fear, of repression, of the woman Lunurin had been in hiding in the convent. Sister María, the woman she'd been for ten years, who'd loved Catalina, and feared her own power. Lunurin was turned back in time, frozen by it. Her magic and the truth of her goddess burning in her eyes had doomed Catalina. If she gave in to the wild, unbridled instincts of her goddess now, she'd only repeat all the mistakes of her past.

Fear cast the scene in stark strokes. At this distance, she'd never be able to fell each rifleman before one got off a shot. She wasn't enough. Her power wasn't enough. If she moved or breathed or dared to fight, she would doom Inez, a pawn once more caught between the Church and Lunurin.

Lunurin had let Catalina go. She could've done it again. Cat had made her choices, until not even Lunurin could save her.

"You see? I am being quite generous. Just stand aside now and I'll return Inez to you. I'm sure your mother-in-law is very proud of what a terrifying witchling you've raised. I'll tell her so before we execute her for insurrection."

Lunurin had thought she was ready to stand aside and

let Inez seek her own fate too. But now, looking into Abbess Magdalena's cruel green eyes, she knew it had been a trap from the beginning. One crafted especially to tear out her heart and all the vast singing power of her goddess in her skin. She'd once shattered her family and her world for Inez. To lose her now, like this!

"You want to ask, don't you?" Magdalena needled.

"Ask what?" Lunurin mouthed the words, gutted and gasping, unable to see any way out of this trap. She and Alon were alone; they'd broken up their Stormfleet allies among the rest of the fleet, and scattered half of them through the narrows of the Tumaga islands. With just the meager decoy force at their back, there was no way to save Inez.

"What became of your Catalina? Inez went so far to find out. Aren't you curious?" Magdalena's mocking voice was too much. Lunurin wanted to close her eyes. She'd never felt so horribly helpless. "She always did so want to be a martyr. And then her own sister came and killed her. What better end for Santa Catalina, Our Lady of the Rosary?" Magdalena dangled the silver cross, the one Lunurin had sent with Catalina so that her aunt might be reminded what Cat had been to her.

It was too much to bear. That she herself had sent Cat off to bait the trap of Aynila's doom, thinking it a mercy. They had killed her. They'd taken Inez. Somehow, every fear she'd ever entertained had come horribly to pass, and once again nothing could prevent the fallout.

Guilt and old regrets choked her. She was hamstrung by her fears, exactly as Magdalena had intended. Stormcallers did not save, and no amount of vengeance would fill this hole in her heart.

55

INEZ

Inez had been chained to one of the great iron rings used to anchor cannons on deck. The weight of the rifles being aimed at point-blank range was only mildly alleviated by one of those rifles being in the hands of Pedro de Isla.

She had no idea how, but that man could insinuate himself into any group. For someone with only eight fingers, he was spectacularly unremarkable. She hadn't recognized him the second time until he'd dropped her stolen mutya back into her hands, while he was loosely chaining her to the ring.

Pedro had given her bonds a theatrical rattling test, whispering, "Wait for my signal to jump overboard."

She'd not tried the shackles for fear of drawing attention. There were already so many eyes and weapons leveled on her. It would not take much for one person to slip up. The archbishop himself was mere feet away, peering across at the ongoing negotiations with Aynila's allied fleet through a spyglass. Inez could make out nothing beyond the two white flags, streaming in the wet season winds.

Inez scanned her surroundings for anything that might be the distraction she needed to make it across the twenty feet of bare deck to the rail. She was lucky that her whole purpose was to act as bait, so they'd not opted for an executioner's hood. Bad enough to have to manage her escape hobbled and shackled.

Inez was so, so angry that she'd fallen into this trap, that she would be used like a bludgeon against Aynila and her family all over again.

"*Hello, little crocodile. Quite a trap you've found yourself in.*" The deep-water hunger of the laho whispered into her mind.

"*I need a distraction, not to be distracted,*" Inez hissed back. She was alone, alone and terrified. Cat was dead. Himig too. Umali had sold her for silver.

Inez turned all her hardened edges outward like crocodile teeth to stave off the grief trying to break her. Vicious in her desperation to make all the world bleed with her.

Suddenly, there was a large swell in the ocean. Inez felt the kick of it even under the vast bulk of the galleon, cold water carried up from the deep. Was the laho still listening? She cast her senses wider.

That was when she finally saw the *Agawin*. The ship had begun to drift ever so slowly out of formation with the other privateers in front of the galleons.

Umali hadn't left her behind. Relief and terror crashed over her like a wave, a tumbling disorientation. She wasn't alone, hadn't been abandoned. But would she now watch Umali die and the *Agawin* sink trying to spring her from this trap, just like Himig?

To all outside eyes, the *Agawin*'s anchor had broken loose. Her crew was rushing about to keep from fouling the other ships in formation. Rowers strained in their places, fighting the "drag" of the slipping anchor.

But around that effort, Inez could see the *Agawin* was preparing for boarding. Her sails were positioned just so for Umali to punch heat into them and send them flying. Boarding hooks and ladders were at the ready. The panicked crew "struggling" with the anchor ropes were ready to cut loose when the rowers and Umali had aligned them for the final push.

Shouts rose as the *Agawin*'s prow scraped a neighboring red-sailed junk. In conjunction with the next large swell, Inez focused on the tides, delicately plucking so that the nudge sent the entire junk listing and dragging at its anchor rope, a cascade of panic and disarray sending several more crews scrambling. The bigger the distraction, the better; the fewer eyes on the *Agawin* and Inez, the safer they'd all be. In response, the rowers and helmsman of the *Agawin* overcorrected, sending the boat swinging back toward the flagship galleon.

Inez was braced and ready when the *Agawin* closed. Heat hit the deck like a hammer of pure sunlight, like the whole ship had been shoved inside a furnace. Umali's power flowed over her, warm as an embrace. Inez threw herself down, screwing her eyes shut and holding her breath. She prayed the firing squad had been aiming high.

The simultaneous gunfire shattered her eardrums, her head ringing. But she did not hesitate. Pulling on her captain's battle fury, she rolled and wrenched herself out of the loosened shackles with one smart scrape of skin.

In a flash she was up—but the archbishop's men were well trained, already drawing other weapons and closing in. They were wary of a tide-touched at sea, as they should be.

Pedro created the next opening she needed, taking a wild swing at her head with the bayoneted tip of his gun that caught the soldier beside him in the eye. That man fell screaming, clutching at his face. Inez lunged for the gap.

Not quick enough. It closed as the archbishop himself stepped into her path. He thought he could prevent her escape? The battle fury in her belly was a feral beast, the sea all around them listening for crocodile prayers.

Did he think she was still the helpless postulant he'd left behind in Aynila? The fool. She'd teach these Codicians that she was so much more than easy prey, than bait. A helpless hostage to be used against everyone she loved.

With a scream, Inez drew her balisong knife and seized the archbishop by the throat.

She was sick and tired of being chained and tied, pushed and threatened. Let them taste threat. Let them taste her mercy. She was not like Catalina, and she would prove it. Even if it killed her.

Surprise was on her side as she dragged the older man in front of her like a shield to the rail. Somehow in the confusion, she'd picked the opposite side from the *Agawin*, headed toward deeper water rather than the allied fleet or the cluster of islands before them.

Even tide-touched, with so many ships and guns, she'd be vulnerable in the water. She reached deep, desperate for something, anything. She was strong, but she would be pressed to lift the archbishop over the rail with her without some advantage. And her crocodile hunting instincts were too loud. She was not about to release her prey, not even to make her own escape.

There was no more time to think as she reached the rail. It was the greatest ship she'd ever shifted, but the fury in her belly was the blackness of deep water. With the single-minded determination of a predator, she roared a crocodile prayer. The great galleon yawned, tipping in Inez's favor. With a mighty heave Inez flung herself over the rail, her weight and the shifting deck dragging the archbishop with her.

As they fell toward the deep blue waves, Inez saw a flash of copper scales breaking the surface, dragging up another deep-water swell.

"I bring an offering. I need more than a distraction. I need the sea to turn upon my enemies."

"You wish to turn the sea?"

All she saw rising from the waves were curving teeth, a jaw wide enough to slip down whole. Swimming in a croco-dile feeding frenzy had taught her many things. Inez kicked away from the archbishop and tucked in her limbs, missing the razor-edged teeth by inches.

Inez found herself safely caught among the strange sea-kelp tendrils of the laho's dripping mane, not unlike the way she'd once nestled into the *Agawin*'s carved prow with a spyglass in hand. The archbishop was not so lucky.

The laho's vast head gave a little upward toss, Inez clutching tight to not be thrown free. But the laho was only flinging the archbishop up briefly to get a better angle, like a long-necked heron flipping a large fish to swallow it down whole.

"Then we must go deep, little crocodile."

The laho dove. The sea closed over them, the grey light that shone through the clouds overhead fading fast. The pressure was unlike anything she'd ever experienced. Her ears popped, and her lungs ached. But she held tight. Down and down and down, the water pressed in on all sides. They fell through the water like a stone, like iron chains.

They arrived at a depth the sun had never reached, where the sea had no mercy, only a crushing black weight and deep hunger. Time stood still.

Inez's lungs were pressed so tightly, they did not even cry out for air.

Inez felt… cradled, in the way every other tide-touched in her life had described but she'd never truly felt, not since that long ago night in the Lakan's healing bath when blood and lightning had relieved her of the evidence of DeSoto's sins.

Now the sea was all around, and it was everything she needed. Everything she'd ever lacked, a welcome pressure on the raw wounds of her past torn open anew, keeping the blood from rising. But more than that, in this place Aman Sinaya was not the gentle lady Alon served. The salt here was a brutal blackness, waiting to snatch away life and breath and never give it back.

Inez had never felt more at home.

"Sing with me, little crocodile, and we will raise the deep."

56

❧ ❧

ALON DAKILA

This had been a mistake. What had he been thinking, putting Lunurin at risk for the sake of a few hours? It would be hours before they reached their second high tide of the day. They'd gained nothing for wounding Lunurin so deeply.

The way she folded upon seeing Inez in danger, and their own helplessness to save her, so quietly and terribly broken, reminded him of nothing so much as when she'd returned to his home years ago, Inez bleeding out in her arms. And here they were again. Betrayed, with Inez's life on the line. An impossible choice, and Lunurin caught terribly between her vows and her love for her family.

This time, it was his choices that had put her in this position.

Before Abbess Magdalena could twist the knife any further, Alon broke the diplomatic ship away with an inelegant shove of water that got them out of range, and rocked Talaan's ship, throwing Magdalena and others off their feet.

435

They'd pull back to their lines, regroup and decide what to do.

Safely out of range, Alon bent to Lunurin, trying to reassure himself that the silence of her spirit and her wounded crouch was not physical. Like mounds of frozen hail upon the waves, she was icy and inconsolable. "Lunurin, talk to me, please."

As their craft fell back between Jeian's and Kalaba's ships, Alon heard his brother shouting across to him. But he couldn't bring himself to tear away from Lunurin and her pain.

Jeian swung across on the outriggers and shook him. "Alon. We have to move. Something is happening. Aizza says it's some kind of storm surge. Their privateer fleet is in disarray. This is our best chance to draw them into the narrows."

"Not with Inez—I can't ask Lunurin to—" They depended on her so heavily, and it had been too much.

Sina swung over from Kalaba's ship, spitting mad at having been forced to stay back. Isko was at her heels, a position he maintained not even bullet wounds would keep him from. Sina bent at Lunurin's other side, trying to rouse her to action.

Jeian dragged him up and away from his wife's wounded huddle. "If we do our part, our allies will uphold theirs."

Jeian slapped a spyglass into his hand just in time to see a small explosion, a wavering cloud of heat briefly engulfing the Codicíans' flagship galleon. It rippled across the water, snapping their sails with hot dry air. Making their tide-touched work to hold their ships steady.

Had their munitions caught fire?

"That wasn't one of ours, right? That's well outside your range," Isko observed.

Alon looked to Sina for confirmation. "Can't be. I'd recognize the heat signature if it was one of our firetenders," Sina agreed. "But I can feel their strength from here, like Hilaga erupting."

"Then we move now, with the ships we have. If we can put a dent into their privateer forces, their galleons will be forced to give chase themselves," Jeian declared. His crew ran up the planned flagging for the attack, their quickest ships closing the gap on crafted currents.

They opened fire on the privateer frontline, their tide-touched adding to the chaos as they tangled anchor chains and churned the seas rough.

Alon couldn't tear his eyes away from the chaos on the deck of the flagship galleon.

Inez went over the rail, and vanished down behind the vast fifty-gun flagship. Heart in his throat, Alon counted the seconds, trying to judge the height from such a distance, but he never felt her hit the waves. Dread and desperation crested over him. He tried to reach across the water to snatch her back to them, as he had when Lunurin had wrestled with the laho, but at this distance, with so many ships on the water, even picking another tide-touched spirit from the salt was near impossible.

Alon forced himself to believe that the sea would not be what snatched Inez away, after everything else she had survived. They would find her. He just had to get closer.

"Lunurin—" What could he say? *Inez has fallen overboard amid a sea battle. Don't worry.* And Jeian was right, the sea was rising. It couldn't be the tide, and no storm surge riding under Lunurin's storms had ever felt this way to Alon, but he couldn't deny what he sensed.

He turned to Jeian. "We change the plan. Use the storm

surge and turn the tides ourselves. You take Aizza left, I will go right. We send Kalaba running down the center. Like a funnel, together with the rest of the tide-touched we can drag them into the trap ourselves. They don't have to chase us."

Jeian embraced him. "Aman Sinaya guide you."

He stepped back and made the leap back aboard his own ship. Alon called the plan across to Kalaba, who dragged a protesting Rosa away, sending their ship falling back.

The advantage of surprise and the disarray among the privateer fleet was short-lived. The Codicíans soon primed the big guns of the galleons, unleashing the devastating broadsides for which their floating fortresses were known. But their feint had succeeded in its primary goal: their enemy had engaged, and not in the calculated manner they should have, sending the privateer ships to do their dirty work. Five of the armada's vast black galleons lumbered forward, straining ponderously to turn their guns upon the tiny allied fleet, even trapping a number of the privateer ships within the deadly sweep of their broadside.

Alon cried a prayer to the sea and began to pull. The tide had just begun its rise. It was on their side as he and the thirty other tide-touched spread throughout the island chain fed their power into the tide. They pulled together and the sea turned, dragging the first line of galleons like harpooned whales in from the deep open waters and into the gulf's treacherous grasp.

The survivors of their decoy force slipped out of the drag of the riptide, darting back at the massive main body of the armada.

It was a start. Alon stared at the remaining fifteen galleons, including the flagship, still anchored securely beyond the gulf, and tried to imagine succeeding in this ploy twice more, once the armada had clearly seen how they could be drawn in. He bent to where Sina still crouched beside Lunurin, trying to snap her out of her stupor.

They needed her. They needed her, and the immense fury of her goddess.

Tactics alone would not save them.

57

LUNURIN CALILAN NG DAKILA

What finally reached her was not Alon's desperate pleas, nor Sina's urging. It was not the cannon fire or the screams of their allies as ships sank.

It was the roar of the laho. A sound that had pervaded her nightmares for years after the fateful storm at sea when she'd accidentally named Alon to the old gods. A legend made real she'd wrestled with in the waters of Aynila Bay. The laho was the magic of their islands made flesh, a being of sea and storm fed on all the vast power of the Amihan Moon. And all three of their goddesses were angry.

The dragon rose from the sea, dragging with it a vast surge of churning waves, cutting a path of destruction through the main body of the armada that hadn't been drawn into the allied fleet's trap.

Inez was perched on the laho's streaming mane. Roaring too, a strange and powerful prayer to the sea that carried across the water as she and the laho coiled in on their enemies, entangling the fleet, tearing anchor chains free, circling closer and closer toward the conflagration still burning at the heart of the fleet.

And for the first time in years, Lunurin saw *Inez*.

Somehow, she'd fallen into the same trap as her family— from Calilan *and* Codicia. Just as her family would never understand how she'd grown and changed since she was a girl, she'd refused to see Inez. She'd spent so long seeing only what had been done to Inez that the years of growth, and the power she now wielded, had gone not just unnoticed, but denied.

What else had Lunurin failed to see?

"That you've allowed human fears and expectations to shape who you let yourself be. Fly with me, Daughter, and we will be the storm."

"Forgive me. I have let old ghosts make me forget who I am." Lunurin reached out and seized for Alon's strength like the running tide, for the deep magma chamber-churn of Sina's spirit. They reached back, hauling her to her feet.

"Inez has given us an opening we shouldn't waste."

Alon sent them skimming into the heart of the unfolding battle, and Lunurin began to spin up a great storm over the sea.

It was time. Time at last. Lunurin let down her hair. The dense grey thunderheads overhead thickened. Her goddess was the storm, her tears in the rain, her laughter in the wind, the curve of her cheek, the silver lining of the rising thunderheads readying to release their deluge.

"Be one with me. Untethered. Free. Fury upon the waves. Let the Codicians see what true divinity is, the storm upon the sea."

58

❧

INEZ

Somewhere in the mayhem of this vast sea battle was the *Agawin*. Umali had put her ship and her crew at terrible risk to give Inez a chance to escape the trap she'd fallen into. Inez had to find her!

As she and the laho churned the sea to froth, capsizing smaller ships and harrying the vast galleons, Inez searched for the burning battle fury she'd grown so used to fighting alongside.

At last, over the bursts of cannon fire and roaring waves, she saw a shimmering column of pure heat punch through the low-hanging clouds overhead. *There.*

The *Agawin* was encircled on all sides by enemies. One of the helmsman's oars had been shattered in the fighting, and despite the rowers' and Umali's best efforts, as embedded as they were deep behind enemy lines, it was impossible to break free.

Inez had to help. If not for her, they'd never have been mired in this fight to begin with. The laho barreled toward the galleon flagship, intent on shearing through its vast rudder—bringing the ship's broadside around and lining up the *Agawin* with their major guns.

Inez let herself fall free of the laho's mane with murmured thanks. She hit the water, coiling together a twist of currents to propel her toward where the *Agawin* spun helplessly in the water, besieged by smaller privateer ships.

She hadn't thought through how the laho-lashed waves and ongoing sea battle would churn the sea into a deadly crush of ships, debris, and towering waves. From the back of the laho, the *Agawin* had seemed very close, the water not nearly so chaotic. From the sea, her vantage point was quite different. The only thing she could see was the nearest deep trough sucking her down, and the pummeling of the vast white caps forcing her under. The incredible churn of the water paired with the darkness of the gathering storm clouds made it almost impossible to orient herself, much less reach the *Agawin*.

Before she could panic, she heard a familiar underwater rumble of greeting as a pair of crocodiles rose from the depths. Inez threw out her arms, catching a bent tail ridge and the scaly bend of a foreleg as she was born up through the churning water back into the air.

"*Little sister, you cannot hold your breath well enough for rough waters such as this,*" Payat chided, just as the prow of the *Agawin* appeared.

The ship was drifting dangerously crossways before an oncoming surge. Inez turned the *Agawin* into the wave, pushing herself as high as she could out of the water on her crocodiles' backs, waving wildly. She let her power spill around her, trying to calm the waves enough that she might be able to swim toward the *Agawin*.

Somehow, Umali saw or sensed her. The crew cast her a line and, at last, Inez was hauled from the dangerous churn of the sea into Umali's arms, like swimming up from the crushing depths toward sunlight on the surface of the water.

"Take the helmseat!" Umali cried.

Inez raced to do so. With a tide-touched aboard, the sea no longer spun the *Agawin* helplessly. Inez kept them turned into the worst of the waves, steadying the deck so the crew could properly aim their lantaka cannons. At her side, Umali lashed out, able to direct her heat properly.

"Try to break us out towards the islands!" Umali directed.

Inez guided the laho's wild waves into a front, determined to open a path for the *Agawin* to slip free of the chaos at the center of the armada.

The *Agawin* went screaming down the faces of her waves, ramming less fortunate ships, shattering rudders, shearing through outriggers and crushing hulls.

Umali lashed out like the bronze hammer of the sun, catching up the ships Inez left foundering. The square sails and rigging of a lanong galley burst into riotous flame.

"On our left! A broadside readying to fire. Take us in along their belly!" Umali cried.

Inez sent the *Agawin* skimming just under the blast. The air overhead shivered with the force of the explosion. Her ears rang, eyes stinging with sulfurous smoke.

"Can you blow their powder stores?" Inez asked. There was no way they could keep this up.

Umali shook her head. "There's too much powder, too many ships. The chain reaction will blow us all to smithereens."

Inez swung them around the prominent beak of the galleon, just barely missing being rammed as they slid around the far side into a breath of open water.

"Up ahead, foreguns, take us right!" Umali ordered. Inez obeyed.

They dodged and ran, their crew firing at the waterline of the great galleons until they ran out of munitions, struggling to break through the reinforced beams and planking.

Even damaged, with Inez at the helm and Umali filling their sails, her keen sense for lit priming enabled them to outmaneuver the larger, slower galleons, but there were so many. The waves and wind, and the coiling arch of the laho's serpentine body twisting through the waters added additional dangers. In the thick of battle, it was only a matter of time before Umali misjudged the range and aim of enemy armaments and the *Agawin* became so much more flotsam, especially as the galleons around them took aim at every unnatural twist of water and peak of wave in an attempt to kill the laho.

As once more they missed being turned into kindling by finger-widths, the *Agawin*'s outrigger caught on half-submerged wreckage, fouling them. Sacay and Lim leaped to the outrigger, trying to hack through the downed rigging lines.

Even with her senses spread across the sea, Inez couldn't see a way to slip free of their enemies. Distantly, she could make out a line of Stormfleet ships engaging with the front-line of the armada. But they were too far away.

"Umali! I can't get us clear!!"

Umali threw up her arms. "Get down!"

The crew and Inez all sought cover as a wave of heat boiled outward. Grapeshot melted into a burning rain of molten metal. Umali pressed close and hot alongside Inez, her heaving breaths on the back of her neck. Inez strained to free the *Agawin*, throat raw with crocodile prayers to shape deep-water currents, pulling with waves like claws, but the *Agawin* only fouled more firmly in the sinking, knotted wreckage that would be their doom.

There was nothing more she could do. They were surrounded.

Inez pulled Umali's mouth to hers and kissed her hard.

"Stuck fast?" Umali asked.

Inez nodded. "I'm sorry, I can't get us free."

Umali kissed her back and said, "Then let us burn brightly, one last time. We'll see how many we can take with us."

Inez nodded. Instead of trying to clear a path to break free, she sang wave and current in toward them. The more ships she could catch up in Umali's reach, the better.

Umali's heat doubled. The *Agawin*'s sail began to blacken overhead. It grew hotter yet, the tar of the nearest ships beginning to bubble, run, and catch fire, flames licking up the sides. When Umali desired that a thing should burn... nothing could stand in her way.

Inez wrapped her arms around Umali tightly, not caring how it burned. When the blast hit, she did not want to be alone.

Thunder split the sky, louder even than the ongoing barrages of cannon fire. The eye of the storm opened in the roiling grey mass of clouds overhead. The wind roared, a howling force that whipped the waves so high they crashed over galleon decks and drove the vast black behemoths before it like leaves in a gale.

Lunurin was here. She and her goddess had joined the battle. A wave of relief washed over Inez. Magdalena's ploy with Cat, with her, to hamstring Lunurin had failed. Inez and her folly would not be the reason Aynila fell.

A flickering lash of the laho's tail sheared off the *Agawin*'s entangled outrigger just as around them, the sea turned to a raging torrent, and the whole tangled, burning armada was dragged into the shallow shoals and reefs of the Sumila Gulf. As the current pulled the armada out of formation, Inez seized the opening, slipping the *Agawin* free into the cliff-pocketed coastline, narrowly avoiding a collision with attacking Stormfleet ships, who—taking them for one of their own—let them slip behind the battle lines.

59

LUNURIN CALILAN NG DAKILA

Lunurin had raised a howling gale that stripped coconut palms bare and strained sails and rigging to breaking. Inez and the laho had turned the sea; now, the tide-touched spread across the allied fleet kept drawing it up so it rushed to fill the low bowl of the gulf, dragging the armada into the narrows between the islands. None of them could have done it alone, but together, by flood and fury, they drove the enemy into a trap of their own. The sea was a roaring river, pouring through the narrow wending channels and passages into the Sumila Gulf.

Alon sent their ship skimming after the armada into the narrows. Lunurin twisted most of her hair back up, easing the gusting winds and blinding rain before they lost visual on their enemies, or hindered their own ships rushing from their sheltered coves to join the battle.

"We have to find her," Lunurin shouted.

Alon gazed across the battlefield now strung out between a dozen islands and reefs. "Inez?"

DAUGHTERS OF FLOOD AND FURY

Lunurin shook her head. "Magdalena. I will waste no more years fighting an endless shadow war with her and her missionary spies and blighted saints."

Sina pointed to where several of the galleons had already begun to re-form their protective formation around the flagship. They were joined by the privateer ships that hadn't fled at the first sighting of the laho.

"Seems as good a place to start as any. Who else could rally their captains in the face of the laho and such blatant witchcraft?"

"If we can't break them out of formation, even the shallows will not give our ships the advantage we need to run them aground. We'll never get our gods-blessed close enough," Alon said.

They joined the rest of the allied fleet, slipping out of pocket coves and shallow channels to harry the galleons that had become isolated as they'd been pulled into the narrows, Stormfleet ships re-forming around them.

The Talaan flagship, with its strange hybrid construction, was a part of the armada formation, which meant Magdalena must have made it back to a galleon and not been lost to the mayhem after the laho's appearance. *Lintik!*

By wind and wave, Lunurin and Alon joined the other gods-blessed of the fleet in trying to drive the galleons out of formation. Her winds roared, hail the size of cannonballs pounding down. She lashed the armada with all the power of the storm.

The galleons that could redeployed their anchors and a complicated series of lash-lines, linking together ships that'd had their anchors sheared off by the laho. They battened down, prepared to wait out her fury.

"It's not working! They're somehow more dug in here

than over the deeper waters," Alon cried as Talaan, with their greater maneuverability and Codicían cannons, managed to swing around and sink three allied ships who'd been trying to pierce the hull of a galleon.

Lunurin sent a gust of wind, forcing Talaan to turn aside or be driven onto the cliffs, while Alon lunged to touch the sea. He yanked still-beating hearts out of range, casting survivors up on the beaches and sandbar shoals.

"If they won't be moved, let's attack them where they are." Sina pointed toward the two galleons that had somehow caught fire earlier in the battle, now smoldering fitfully where they'd drifted aground without any living crew left to guide them. "It'd be a shame to let them go to waste. They're usually too fire-resistant to catch, but clearly, I've just not wanted them to burn hard enough."

"Yes. Let's get closer to make sure we're in range when the powder stores blow," Isko complained.

"Better we send them drifting down the channel and into the armada when the powder stores go," Sina countered.

Lunurin signaled to Kalaba's and Jeian's ships. They'd need to work together with their strongest tide-touched to hope to move them. If they hadn't started to take on water already.

Lunurin took over, guiding their ship by wind into the shallow cove where the wrecks burned, freeing Alon's focus. Together with Aizza and Kalaba, he strained to free the galleons.

While they worked the galleons free, Lunurin guided a low and steady wind over the smoldering wrecks. She guided the heated winds up, worsening her storm. Beside her, Sina fed her power into the fires, until with one loud *whump* of displaced air, they relit, flames licking anew up blackened masts.

It took all three of their tide-touched shepherding the wrecks along, one ship on each side and one in front, to drag the galleons free from the sand and pull them back out into the main channel.

"Oh, that's burning fast. We have to move. We're burning through the hull quickly," Sina warned.

Lunurin cried out a warning as one of the masts wavered and began to fall. She sent up a twist of air, trying to slow its descent, and sent Kalaba's ship skimming clear. Now, the mast was coming down directly over Jeian's vessel.

Aizza tried to push the guilalo out of the way, but she wasn't fast enough. Jeian shoved his wife clear, catching the burning mast across his shoulders before it could shear through the midline of his much smaller ship. His tattoos shifted from black to the blue of sea fire in the crest of a wave.

Aizza screamed.

Somehow, Jeian held, preventing the burning mast from sundering his ship in two.

Alon and Sina leaped into action, Sina dousing the flames before they caught the guilalo's sails. Alon dove into the water, lifting the foremast from where it dipped into the waterline. With the strength of the sea running through him and Jeian both, they lifted, casting the smoldering mast over into the water.

Jeian collapsed. Aizza rushed to his side to see to the massive burn across his back.

"The galleons, we have to move them!" Sina screamed, reminding them all of the firestorm they'd created.

Lunurin bent, pulling Alon from the water. "He has Aizza. We can't stop now."

"We can't do it without Aizza." Alon wiped the water from his eyes, staring up at the billowing black smoke.

Lunurin took his hands and breathed all the strength of the storm into him. They worked together, her strong winds upon the surface, Alon and Kalaba seizing the hulls below the waterline in the sure grip of the sea. Side by side, they sent the two towering infernos on a collision course with the defensive crescent the armada had formed. This time, they kept clear of falling debris.

The allied fleet harrying the armada saw them coming, pillars of flame and inky smoke merging with the clouds. The galleons shifted their attention to sinking the twin fire ships bearing down on them. But forced onward by Lunurin's howling winds, and Alon's steady currents, no amount of cannon fire could force them from their path.

The armada's flagship got off one more devastating blast before the burning ships crashed into each side of the defensive formation. Sina and the other firetenders among the allied fleet concentrated their focus on the towering pillars of smoke and flame.

"DOWN, NOW!" Sina screamed as the powder stores caught. Burning debris exploded outward, and the galleons nearest were shredded in the shockwave rippling across the water.

Lunurin didn't move. Didn't hesitate or doubt.

Before the shockwave could turn their own smaller boats to kindling and hurl them into reef and rock to shatter, Lunurin and her goddess commanded the explosion-roiled winds in one voice, *"Split and gather in, spindle tight. You shall be oar eaters and ship breakers."*

Lunurin carded her fingers through a hank of her hair, splitting the strands. It took all her vast power and focus to capture the violent shockwave and mold it to her implacable will.

DAUGHTERS OF FLOOD AND FURY

The shockwave obeyed, breaking apart along five lines of her dividing fingertips and twisting in. Cyclones rose out of the water, wind and wave making a ravenous hot roar.

Her every instinct said to let the cyclones rent their fury where they willed, but Lunurin held. They drew at her, pulling all her attention and focus, like ropes looped at each wrist and ankle, pulling tighter and tighter.

She didn't dare set her creations free upon the narrows. Far too many of their own allied ships had rushed in from the protected coves and shallow shoals to target the remaining galleons, which were trying to break free of their anchors and burning lash-lines. Loose upon the water, able to grow between sea and sky, her cyclones would do more damage than the explosion.

The cyclones pulled. Gathering strength from the winds of the storm overhead and water from below, they grew, dragging her to her breaking point. Just as she was sure they'd escape her and wreak untold havoc upon their allies, Lunurin felt Rosa's power reach out, tangling into hers and seizing the line. They held together as other pairs of stormcallers among the Stormfleet carefully gathered in each cyclone, lifting the burden of guidance and control from her shoulders.

One by one, the massive cyclones were tied into the control of others, until she and Rosa held only one. It was still so much. Lunurin struggled to split her attention between the short leash holding her spiraling behemoth and the lashing storm overhead. They wanted to feed into each other and tear everything upon the water apart.

Better to crush it out now, before it got too big for her to control.

Kalaba's ship pulled alongside, and Rosa leaped across to her. "Let me help!"

Remembering how she'd been able to guide the others of the Sumila fleet as they'd flung themselves far across the sea on high-altitude winds, Lunurin held out her hands. "Yes, stay close. Tell me if it's too much."

She pulled down a lock of Rosa's hair and twisted it together with the strands she'd split to form the cyclones.

Their tangled power straightened like threads before the spindle, twisting tighter, stronger, just like her cyclone. They leashed it to their beck and call. The center of the spiraling behemoth was stained with the sulfurous black powder smoke that had spawned it, the vortex too strong for it to dissipate.

Together with the rest of the stormcallers, they scattered the galleons, not letting them re-form any kind of defensive line. Like a pack of dogs driving wounded carabao to ground, they harried the galleons with wind and wave, the treacherous tide dashing them on the reefs and rocky volcanic cliffs.

Jeian's captains focused on the smaller privateer ships who'd not broken and run at the first sighting of the laho, preventing the more maneuverable ships from driving the Stormfleet's gods-blessed off the galleons.

Lunurin and Alon hunted along the scattered battle line. They lent their strength to turning the tide against the bigger and better-armed galleons. Sina coaxed any patch of flame hotter and higher, spreading the fires of the initial explosion far and wide. The surface of the sea burned in her path. Smoke rose to meet the low clouds of Lunurin's storm, a burnt offering to old gods.

Then, they spotted them—a single galleon and the Talaan flagship that had somehow survived the firestorm, attempting to escape back into open water where the floating fortress would regain its advantage.

"She'll be there," Lunurin said simply.

She studied Rosa. She was quiet, too quiet, her attention riveted to the massive cyclone before them. Had Rosa ever had to push this long or this hard? Battles were an endurance that had to be learned.

"I'm fine. I can hold," she promised, white-knuckled with concentration.

Over Rosa's protest, Lunurin unspun their hair.

"I could've—" Rosa dropped mid-speech, eyes rolling back, as the tether of their hair loosened and she lost contact with Lunurin's internal storm. Isko caught her and pulled her out of the line of fire.

Satisfied she wouldn't run so far and so fast she dragged Rosa to her death, Lunurin cried out to her goddess, asking once more for all the vast power of the storm spread over the sea.

"*It is yours.*" A promise kept. She was the Stormbringer, after all.

Lunurin fed it all into her cyclone. She'd once spawned a typhoon from nothing over dry land. She took that force, twisting it smaller and more precise, till all the raging fury of a miles-wide typhoon gyrated on a point no larger than the palm of her hand. It was a fury that rent the sea floor, that dragged everything into its vortex.

It dragged at her control—but she would not have to hold it long.

Nothing could escape the inward pull, not water, not wind, and not the strange hybrid construction from Talaan. Lunurin's cyclone ate through it like it was made of banana leaf. But even her behemoth rebounded off the storm-battened and gale-reinforced galleon. Lunurin and her goddess howled in twin rage. "*Nothing shall stand before me. Nothing should dare live where I will there shall be death!*"

Alon joined her in the prow, having handed off the helms-man's oars at last to their stalwart captain. His voice was low and steady in her ear. "Let me help too."

He reached across the debris-strewn waters of the bay. He'd never lost the ability to grasp and hold with all the strength of Aynila's drowned ghosts, and now he used it, feeding wreckage into the cyclone. Reinforced planking was hurled back out at the fleeing galleon with forces far greater than typhoon winds. Storm shutters failed. The deck was rent with holes and the rudder sheared off. Together, sea and storm clawed furious fingers into the galleon, tearing away at it, bit by bit.

With a crack like thunder, the galleon's mainmast fell. Alon scooped it toward them in a large wave, and Lunurin launched it through the hull of the fleeing galleon, pinning it to the sea floor. Harpooned as surely as she'd once speared the governor of the Palisade through the neck.

She freed her cyclone on the open waters beyond the narrows, letting it untwist at last in a spray of saltwater and smoke. She raised her hands to the heavens, prepared to call down lightning to spark the exposed powder within the shattered hull, but Alon laid a hand on her wrist.

"Not yet. You deserve the truth. Let's find the abbess."

~

They found Abbess Magdalena trying to escape in the galleon's single intact shoreboat. No longer sneering and superior, Lunurin nearly pitied the old woman—until she remembered how masterfully Magdalena had played on the religious divisions among their allies and Aynila's converts, sowing treachery and distrust with her spies and assassins before she'd lured Inez into a trap.

As Alon dragged the shoreboat backward against the rowing of the surviving crew, Sina cast her heat out. Sailors and soldiers panicked and threw themselves overboard to avoid the burning of their armor, belts, guns, and swords, till it was only Magdalena alone.

"After all the trouble the Palisade survivors have caused Aynila... did you think I would be so merciful a second time?" Lunurin asked.

"If you think this is anything but a setback—! You'll never take Simsiman."

"When the rest of the archipelago sees how we've repelled your armada, I doubt we shall be in want of allies for the siege," Alon observed.

"Witch-spawn!" Magdalena sneered.

Lunurin clicked her tongue and twisted lightning out of the air, coiling it around her wrist like a costly bangle of white jade. "None of that. Tell me, what became of Catalina?"

Magdalena shook her head. "You always were such a damned fool for that woman. Shall I tell you how desperately she contorted herself into the perfect penitent nun? How she fasted days at a time, living only on the holy sustenance of communion? How she tore the wounds of Christ's Passion into her own flesh to overwrite the unworthiness of her past? I've built up a few saints before her, but it's rare to see such devotion to martyrdom in one of my creatures."

Lunurin did not waver. She too had been one of Magdalena's creatures, once. "You couldn't have asked for a more faithful daughter. And you ruined her to fit your own ends."

"Ruined her? I made her!" Magdalena spat. "She was nothing! A hired soldier's and whore's daughter. I made of that unworthy mud something holy. They will be worshiping her bones in Simsiman for generations."

Lunurin turned away, content to leave Magdalena to make her own way upon the ocean, alone in a tiny shoreboat. No one cared for the fate of lost mestiza girls. Lunurin had been a fool to believe Catalina might be different. She'd only found a different end.

But as she signaled Alon to release Magdalena, the little shoreboat wobbled and capsized, pitching Magdalena—still ranting about her saintly creation—into the sea. Lunurin saw the snap and gnash of crocodilian snouts and scaly gold-and-black-patterned backs, before an unfamiliar Stormfleet karakoa missing one outrigger came around a pocked volcanic cliff. Inez perched in the prow behind the battered carving of a proud, roaring laho.

"Don't listen to a word she said!" she cried. "Codicíans always lie."

Lunurin moved. With the wind-walking step she'd learned while wrestling the laho, she crossed the gap of water between the two ships and caught Inez up in her arms.

Inez yelped in surprise, the damaged karakoa listing toward its broken outrigger, but Alon caught them both, stabilizing the ship.

"It wasn't Cat! Just someone who looked like her. Some poor mad woman. They knew better than to bring her before you, you'd never have fallen for the trick like I did. I was stupid—so, so, stupid—" The lies tumbled over one another out of Inez's mouth. Lunurin would know. She was the one who'd taught her to lie.

Inez, like Alon, was so desperate to shield Lunurin from all she'd learned. Lunurin couldn't hold the love at the heart of the impulse against them. Had she not once offered such lies to soothe Catalina?

Lunurin hugged Inez tightly, till the panicked stream

of words trailed off at last. Inez returned her embrace with trembling arms.

"I love you. You have not been stupid. You have been strong and brave, and I'm sorry I couldn't see it earlier. I love you, but I do not want my love to blind me to who you are." Lunurin breathed the strength of her un-spooled cyclone into Inez, till the shaking eased from her fingers. Lunurin recognized the terrible battle-drawn exhaustion she was fighting all too well.

"Even if I hurt people?"

"Even then."

"Even if I hurt Cat?"

"Cat..." Lunurin breathed deep. The wound of her old love was still there. But it was time to let them both heal from what Cat had done. "Catalina made her choices. Again and again, she chose her faith over you and me and even her own well-being. You made yours. And if they have brought you back to me, then they were the right choices. Whatever you saw, and whatever you did, I love you and will welcome you home with open arms."

Inez squeezed Lunurin so tightly her ribs ached. "Magdalena didn't lie. I couldn't let them keep using and hurting her like that. It was going to be horrible and slow, and I couldn't save her, so I made it fast. Don't hate me."

Lunurin squeezed back, her heart breaking for Inez. "Oh, Inez. I could never."

By some cruel twist of fate, Inez had been far wiser and stronger than she and Alon had ever been when it came to Catalina. What had their mercy ever granted her but suffering?

The setting sun dropped below the dense grey storm clouds overhead, bathing the waves in a warm golden glow.

It lay across her cheeks and Inez's back, warm as an embrace. She stared out over the rack and ruin they'd made of their enemies. How fitting that the Codicians should meet their defeat at the hands of the daughters they'd least wanted to acknowledge.

60

ALON DAKILA

They had won. His brother was miserable, battered, but alive, and well enough that he and Aizza were gathering up survivors. Getting every remaining allied ship seaworthy was the highest priority as they hunted across the smoldering waves for survivors.

Lunurin, Sina, and Umali had stepped away to the opposite side of the *Agawin*, trying to figure out how to lash together a temporary outrigger so that the ship could sail into port under her own power.

Inez hung back from this effort, working beside Alon to sift beating hearts from saltwater. She hummed a rumbling, sometimes hissing, song to the sea, the likes of which Alon had never heard.

They both blinked in surprise when Pedro de Isla drifted in on the next wave they pulled in, half-drowned, but still breathing.

"I almost want to know what gods he prays to," Inez muttered.

Alon shook his head. "Gold, he says. But survival is not always kind."

He regretted the observation as soon as it was out of his mouth.

Inez finally turned to him. "What sainthood did to her... She was in so much pain... I couldn't let it go on. But if I could've—if a proper healer..."

He'd put so much doubt into Inez when he'd only ever wanted to help her. Yet somehow, crocodiles and a young firetender who burned sharp-edged and piercing as the sun off saltwater had done more in a few weeks than Alon and Lunurin had managed in years.

Inez was never going to find a calling within Aynila's healing school. And he'd been a stubborn fool for failing to see it.

Alon thought back to the night long ago, fighting with Lunurin for Inez's life over that bloody tub. His inay had calmly observed how tangled up inside Catalina was, even then.

"To heal the body of battle wounds is different than slow killers like starvation and stubborn illness. The spirit must be open to aid for even the most well-trained and powerful healer to have a chance. Your sister was tangled and wounded in spirit for a long time before the Palisade fell. I think we both know she would never have trusted a tide-touched healer to help her, not even you."

"So I wasn't wrong to..."

When Inez had been named tide-touched, he'd taken it as a sign she would not take after Lunurin or Sina, that she would find a more peaceful path. He'd been wrong.

But there was one thing that he could offer her. Alon shared the lesson that was often the last and hardest in a healer's training. "Sometimes, drowning by a healer's hand is the most merciful thing we can offer. It's not something I would have wished for you to learn this way. It should not have been you making such a terrible decision. But you were not wrong. I was wrong to try to make your focus healing when your gifts so clearly lead to other paths."

Inez nodded solemnly. "Then thank you for teaching me enough that I could offer her that, at least."

61

INEZ

Inez hadn't imagined returning to Masagana like this, with fifty or so survivors from the Stormfleet and Ísuga packed aboard the *Agawin* alongside their own wounded, and of course the unkillable Pedro de Isla. She'd helped Alon and Aizza with triage, sending their most grievously wounded off on ships with healers.

The allied fleet spent a few days in Masagana, stabilizing the injured, scouting the battlefield for any remaining survivors and getting their ships repaired enough to make the return journey to Aynila.

Inez was relieved that Jeian and Aizza had quickly gone on ahead to inform the Lakan of their victory. How Jeian had still been walking with so many shattered bones was a mystery Inez did not want answers to. He needed the halls of healing, quickly.

It also meant she was able to avoid any—perfectly true—accusations.

When the *Agawin*'s broken outrigger was properly repaired,

and her crew well enough to leave the makeshift infirmary Alon had set up, Inez knew it was time. Which was why she'd dragged Umali to tonight's family dinner aboard Kalaba's ship.

"This is a bad idea. Your sister's tiya accused me of being a pirate and a thief," Umali whispered.

"Well, was she wrong?" Inez asked with a wry grin. Tiya Kalaba had been none too pleased when she'd recognized the *Agawin* as a Stormfleet vessel.

"No, but—"

"Then hush," Inez insisted, heaving their offering of fried lumpia they'd bought off a street vendor up over the rail.

Lunurin waved them over, stealing a crisp roll while they were still warm. Her mother-of-pearl fingertips gleamed, reminding Inez of Alon's brace of rings. "You're early. Kalaba's still out with a few other captains seeing to a tough repair. But I think in a day or two, we'll be able to set sail for Aynila. The Sumila Stormfleet has agreed to join us for a short time to see to the biggest repairs and resupply. The Lakan will be glad to be able to properly thank all who contributed to the armada's defeat."

"Most of the seriously injured are stable enough to make the journey and will get better care in the healing halls," Alon agreed, joining them. "It will be good to go home."

Inez chewed her cheek nervously. They were both so clearly under the assumption that Inez intended to return to Aynila with them.

"The *Agawin*'s repairs are already complete," she blurted.

"And where do you intend to sail next?" Lunurin asked, turning to Umali.

Umali smiled. "I expect word of the armada's defeat will bring a great deal more Duutsan vessels down from Taoan, eager to fill the gap left by the Codicians."

"I'm told you've a preference for bounties. Aynila would also be willing to offer a standing bounty for the capture of any pirates preying on Stormfleet ships. I intend to keep my promise to the Sumila Stormfleet, ensuring their ships will be safe in these waters. And we will expand from here."

"I'm going with her," Inez cut in without any grace or sense of timing, bracing for Lunurin's reaction.

The beat of silence was too long. Inez rubbed nervously at her shoulder and wished there were a better way to do this. But if she tried to disappear without an armada to distract Lunurin, they'd never make it out of the harbor.

"Are you sure?" Alon asked.

Inez nodded, keeping her gaze anywhere but on the two of them. "Alon, didn't you tell me if I ever wanted something different for myself, you'd support my decision? Aynila has too many memories for me. On the *Agawin*, I am free of them."

Lunurin laid a hand on her cheek, making Inez lift her gaze from her toes. "Of course, we will support you. If this is what you want, then go with our blessing, but there's no need to flee in the night with nothing but the clothes on your back. I hope you and Umali might come home, pack your bags, and say your goodbyes properly. It would be a terrible shame for you to miss the Lakan's victory feast. I've already heard snatches of Aizza's ballad recounting your riding of the laho."

Inez blinked back sudden tears. The way she'd left, all the people she'd hurt, she'd half expected to be told if she didn't intend to come home and atone, she ought never return.

"Well, I wouldn't want to miss that—but only if she's including your laho-related exploits I keep hearing of," Inez managed.

62

LUNURIN CALILAN NG DAKILA

Finally. A feast among allies where their fate was not balanced on the head of a pin, the tone of a whispered word, and—of course—her family and a dozen strangers' opinions of her. The breath-held tension of every moment of planning, negotiation, and strategy like bands of iron around her lungs had finally shattered.

Of course, there was still much to be done. The Lakan had sent messengers to all the archipelago with word of the armada's defeat. Lunurin and Kalaba had written to Calilan, inviting her inay and tiya to reap the benefits of the victory they'd not contributed to.

Captain Galang laughed heartily with Kalaba. "Would that I could see Halili's face when she reads it. Have you ever been this angry at her? She must be beside herself, but she'll come around. They all will when they see how we've triumphed."

"And what of Talaan? Their datus have owed loyalty to the Lakan of Aynila since long before the Codicians arrived,"

Captain Nihma asked. Her arm was still in a sling from a nasty dislocation. "Surely you will not let such treachery stand."

"Though most involved have already died for it?" Alon cautioned. A few Talaan survivors had been fished from the turbulent seas, but not Captain Tomás. They were being held until the Lakan had come to a decision.

"I do see the need for leadership in Talaan who can be depended on and will better find balance between their gods-blessed and their converts. In light of their betrayal, I am prepared to extend my control more forcefully, if need be," Dalisay added.

"We took Talaan once. We can do it again." Jeian bumped shoulders with Nihma, and they both hissed in pain.

Alon went to check on them.

Isko teased Jeian, "What was it you were telling us about obeying healer's orders?"

"Aizza cannot build a brace big enough for all of you, if you call on the power of your tattoos before your bones are completely healed," Alon added, waggling his bad hand for emphasis.

"And all these are discussions for the future," Lunurin added. "Today is for celebration, for recognition of our heroes and our fallen."

What they lacked in the wild, euphoric energy of the rising Amihan Moon, they more than made up for in the head-spinning relief of having survived. The Lakan had welcomed all Aynila to come and celebrate the return of her brave defenders.

Foodstuffs that had been gathered and stockpiled in expectation of a siege now laid a victory feast. Rolls of dried taro leaves had been stewed in coconut milk spiced with ginger, lemongrass, garlic, and fermented shrimp paste, dotted through with whole shrimp to make steaming spiced platters of laing.

Daing, salted and sundried fish of all kinds, had been prepared. From squid and small smelt tossed in garlic and fried crisp to daing na bangus cooked down with vinegar and chilies till rehydrated and shredded into rice, accompanied by steaming heaps of rice served on banana leaves and big pots of ginataang with saba plantain, ube, and taro root cooked in coconut milk. For dessert, slabs of ube biko, sticky rice with purple yam topped in caramelized coconut milk. The mingling smell of spices, fresh rice, and the myriad stewpots made Lunurin's mouth water.

Earlier, Lunurin, Sina, and Aizza had sung the names of the fallen to the sea, sky, and up to Amihan's messengers, the spark-striker birds circling Mount Hilaga. The Lakan and her sons had made offerings of rice and betel nut to the waves to ensure the kaluluwa, the souls of the dead, made quick passage into Maca.

Now Lunurin sat beside Alon, leaning into his side, half listening as Aizza began to sing the battle's ballad, recounting the bravery and great deeds done.

"You could've asked her to leave you out of it this time," Alon whispered.

"And rob Anitun Tabu of her due, when she so loves to hear voices lifted to her in song? No. Anyway, I think Sina's fire ships will steal the spotlight."

"I've heard her working on one to commemorate you wrestling the moon free of the laho... You know she loves laho ballads the best."

Lunurin grinned, thinking back to the lovingly shared song of Alon's own naming.

She scanned over the attentive crowd, searching for Inez. She'd politely declined a place of honor beside the Lakan, sitting instead with Umali and the *Agawin*'s crew. Bernila and some of Aynila's younger tide-touched shared their table; Lunurin was glad to see that that rift too was healing.

Inez was leading the group in a less-than-surreptitious drinking game regarding the contents of Aizza's ballad. Another mention of "laho-riled waves" caused an eruption of elbowing, smothered laughter, and a round of lambanog.

Lunurin privately suspected that Inez's insistence that they would sail with the dawn would become more of a noon parting.

"I'm half expecting you to tell me you'll be spending the wet season hunting pirates yourself," Alon murmured in jest, but Lunurin could hear the thread of worry in his tone.

"Do not tell me you doubt me, after all this?" Lunurin took his face in her hands and looked deeply into his dark eyes. "After all we have been through? I am not doing anything that will take me from your side for at least six months. We might finally have the breathing room to try for that heir your mother is being very kind not to say anything about needing."

Alon's cheeks colored under her fingertips, warming to her touch. "Not you, never you. But will you be able to part with her?" he asked gently.

Lunurin let her hands fall back to her lap, tapping the silvered ends of her fingers together in thought. "If Inez feels she needs to go and grow free of our expectations—if she needs more distance yet to escape the shadow of the Palisade... After everything with Catalina... How can I stop her? All I can do is make sure she knows Aynila will always welcome her home."

Alon squeezed her against him. "If she doesn't, at least the bounty you offered will keep Umali visiting. Clever, by the way. Two... no three problems, one neat solution."

Lunurin smiled. "I'm glad you think so. Calilan may never thank me, but if they will not make the changes needed to reunite the Stormfleet and see it supplied and restored, then with Kalaba's and Lihat's support, I will make Aynila the hub Calilan once was. With Kalaba's help, and time, Calilan will see reason when we succeed. I want to build a better future for all the archipelago, not just Aynila. And that begins with a united Stormfleet."

"Shall we together be the safe harbor the Stormfleet needs?" Alon asked.

Lunurin pressed her brow to his, overwhelmed with a surge of gratitude for his ever-ready support. "Yes, together."

63

INEZ BUWAYA

They decided to wait out the worst of the wet season storms in Pehlewan. Much of the crew dispersed to families and home isles until the next season's raiding. With Inez and Umali working together, they could easily sail the *Agawin* with only a skeleton crew.

Inez reveled in white sand beaches and cerulean coves made for a tide-touched at play. She wandered vivid and lively ports filled with regional delicacies she'd never seen or tasted. Umali showed her all her favorites, and they discovered new ones together. Lim regularly had to be dragged away after sinking far too much money into the local cockfighting arena.

Inez had never visited the southern reaches of the archipelago that hadn't fallen to Codicían control. But after two months in Pehlewan, she began to understand why Jeian had formed such kinship with Ísuga, even taking up their tattoos.

They lived simply and richly, with a freedom to enjoy magnificent bouts of laziness during the warm afternoon rains that Inez gave herself to with crocodilian dedication, moving only when absolutely necessary. The crew took up projects of fancy that the raiding season left no time for. Sacay had begun an ambitious carving, turning their new outrigger into a buwaya to swim alongside their laho-shaped prow.

When the tailwinds of the season's final typhoon left Pehlewan behind, the sky was the brilliant blue that only came after torrential rains. The sea was calm as glass, as if all the rile of the storm surge had exhausted even the waves.

Inez hefted a bag stuffed with ripe tabo aboard the *Agawin*. Possibly too many to eat before they started to turn, but the fist-sized brown fruit hid succulent white flesh that was better than mangosteen, floral and tangy, so she'd decided to eat herself sick trying. She'd already hidden a stash of pandan-infused milk candies in her sea chest to ply Umali with later.

Umali joined her, sliding onto the padded mat Inez had installed on her bamboo sleeping ledge, as both their backs needed the extra softness now. "I made you something."

Inez turned from her packing. "I admit I've been terribly curious about what you've been slipping off to work on every rainy afternoon."

"But not curious enough to move," Umali observed.

"You can't interrupt a good nap in the rain," Inez protested. "It defeats the purpose. Sariwa and Payat agree with me."

Umali smiled. "I bow to their wisdom."

She held out a beautiful wooden box, inlayed with silver and local red coral. "It's a bit heavy."

Inez accepted, feeling the weight shift within like liquid.

"Why? This isn't a courting gift, is it? You should've at least waited to give it to me next time we're in Aynila," she teased, only half joking, somewhat intimidated by the fine workmanship of just the box.

"Open it. Open it," Umali chanted.

Inez lifted the lid to reveal what looked like a pool of silver, shining like moonlight where the sunbeams hit it. She reached in, spreading a chain-link belt. A writhing laho cast in silver made up the buckle; the rest was hundreds upon hundreds of small silver hoops in a wide band, supporting a skirt of chain from which dangled silver bells shaped like crocodile teeth. She gave it a shake, listening to the sweetness of the sound and marveling at how the silver rippled like silk.

"This is fit for the Lakan. Where would I wear it?"

"It's bronze dipped in silver, so it will be good protection," Umali said. "I made it with your silver."

Inez's brow furrowed. "My silver? I recall spending most of *my* silver on those imported Tianchaowen lenses for seeing underwater. The reefs here are amazing. And I don't have a third eyelid like my crocodiles."

"The silver I sold you out for," Umali clarified.

Inez froze. After all that had passed with her capture in Simsiman, the terrible decision she'd made, and the desperate battle to escape the Codicían armada, she'd been enjoying what she thought was their joint decision to *never* speak of it again. She'd been happy to revel in new places and discoveries and Umali's easy rapturous joy. This was a softer side to Umali, carefree without the keen edge that command in battle required. And there'd been so many discoveries to be made, tangled together on secluded white sand, Umali's hot skin turning drizzling rain to steam.

Umali reached out and lifted one of the bells. It didn't ring. It was white, not silver. "From your big buwaya. Sacay stole it to make offerings to appease her spirit, because we didn't have time to properly offer her back to the sea. We'd have given it to you sooner, but the welding was much more time consuming than I imagined."

Inez wrapped her hand around Himig's tooth, the still-sharp point pressing into her palm. "You didn't have to—" Her voice was starting to shake. She willed it even. Himig would be proud.

Umali took the belt, and clasped it around Inez's waist. The metal took up the heat of her hands easily, hugging Inez tight. Inez swished her hips despite herself, feeling the now-balanced weight move and ripple with her body, making the bells ring. There was a music to it, each one tuned to a harmonious note in the whole. She saw a few larger rings on the belt Umali had included where she could attach her smallsword.

"I'll show you how to still the clappers when we go raiding, but for now…"

Inez put her hands over Umali's where her fingertips still traced the curve of her hips and waist, checking the fit. "Why are you doing this now?"

"Because I've never left one of my crew behind like that. Much less someone I love." Umali frowned, chewing on her words. "They might have just killed you. I had no way of knowing they wouldn't. My crew was furious, you know. Sacay almost staged a mutiny."

"She'd stage a great mutiny," Inez agreed, trying to keep her voice light despite the knot in her throat.

Umali nodded solemnly. "Before we're back on open water, before we take another prize. I needed more than words to prove it to you. I will never leave you behind like that again."

Inez fingered the teeth Umali had made, listening to the crocodile song she'd forged. At last, she met Umali's burning bright gaze. Umali who had seen all of her, followed her down to the black bloodthirsty depths and loved her for them.

"If we are closed again into the teeth of a trap, we will fight our way out together, or not at all," Inez promised.

The End

ACKNOWLEDGMENTS

I have to thank my husband, Robert Johnson, for tirelessly believing in me and keeping me alive and mostly sane during the month-long binge-writing sessions required to bring this story into the world. I'm so grateful for his collaboration on the Stormbringer Saga Map, which I wouldn't have been able to illustrate without his 3D modeling skills to create and morph a topographical map of the Philippines into the Stormbringer Archipelago.

To my agent, Ramona Pina, thank you for your advocacy and advice. I wasn't sure I had a second book in me, but you were.

A thousand thanks to my editor at Titan Books, Katie Dent: we finally got more dragons! Working with you has been a delight and a privilege. Thank you for loving my terrible toxic ladies as much as I do. Thanks to Louise Pearce for her sharp eye. Also to the rest of the Titan team who answered my many questions and supported this story: Bahar Kutluk, Katharine Carroll, Kabriya Coghlan, Claire Schultz, Charlotte Kelly, Isabelle Sinnott, and Katie Greally.

And to Nat MacKenzie, my cover designer, who completely outdid herself. I didn't know I could love a book cover more than *Saints*, until I saw her art for *Daughters*. I can't say how much it means to see these books side by side with two bold brown Filipinas front and center.

Thank you to my family, especially my Tita Rosie for being my on-call Tagalog language expert and to the whole Penaloza clan, your support for me and my stories means so much.

Finally, my thanks to the amazing community of writers, friends, and critique partners who helped make *Daughters* the rich and wonderful story it is. Thank you to Mia Tsai and Faye Delacour for always being available to talk sense into me. To my alpha reader, Ben, I wouldn't have finished the first draft without your keeping me accountable. To my critique partners and brainstorming buddies Carla Garcia, Vanessa Le, Molli Jackson Ehlert, Raven Traylor, and Mary Tosin. To the whole Gsquad for listening to my rants and helping keep me on track: Keir Alekseii, Logan Graham, Gwen Vines, Erin Fulmer, Kyla Zhao, Mel Grebing, Cheyanne Monkman, Adria Bailton, Jenny Kiefer, and Meredith Mooring. And the PitchWars Waffle Squad: especially Abigail Barenblitt and Lillian Barry. Thank you also to The FilAm Writer's Kubo, FilTheShelves, the Inclusive Romance Project, and the Ramoniacs. Writing can be a lonely effort but you've provided so much community.

ABOUT THE AUTHOR

Gabriella Buba is a mixed Filipina-Czech author and chemical engineer based in Texas who likes to keep explosive pyrophoric materials safely contained in pressure vessels or between the covers of her books. She writes adult romantic fantasy for bold, bi, brown women who deserve to see their stories centered. Find her online @gabriellabuba and at gabriellabuba.com.

For more fantastic fiction, author events,
exclusive excerpts, competitions, limited editions and more

VISIT OUR WEBSITE
titanbooks.com

LIKE US ON FACEBOOK
facebook.com/titanbooks

FOLLOW US ON TWITTER AND INSTAGRAM
@TitanBooks

EMAIL US
readerfeedback@titanemail.com